Sam reached for her h

MW01688905

It felt so cool and small in his giant one. Using his thumb, he gently stroked the back of her hand. He raised it to his mouth and kissed the palm.

Prudence gasped sharply from the surprise of it. Immediately, Sam let go of her hand, stood and walked a few steps away from the sofa.

"I'm sorry," he croaked. "It was very forward of me."

Forward of *him*? Prudence couldn't believe how forward *she* was being. How forward she was feeling. She rose and walked over to him. Tenderly, she raised a hand to his thickly bearded cheek and felt the surprisingly soft, silky bristles of his beard. Her thumb lightly brushed over his lips in invitation.

Sam's eyes darkened and rounded beneath his spectacles. Looking into her brown eyes, he could see desire matching his own. Could he trust his impressions of what he saw reflected in her eyes? He had been miserably wrong before and it had nearly destroyed him.

"I don't take kindly to being teased," he said cautiously, fighting the urge to kiss the thumb that was making him crazy.

"I'm not a tease, Sam Blake. I don't understand why I'm feeling what I'm feeling, but I know I want to."

He grasped her hand in his and pulled it away from his cheek while his other hand slipped beneath her chin and pulled her face up as he lowered his head to meet hers.

When he kissed her it was as if lightning shot through both of them. His mouth was hungry for the taste of her, his body hungry for the feel of her soft body against his harder one.

As Sam wrapped his arms around her and drew her against him, Pru could feel his strength and heat. Instinctively, she moved closer into his warmth. Her hands laced through his thick, curly hair. Although the softness of his beard should have given her a hint, she was surprised to discover that his hair was baby fine and silky beneath her fingers. Her lips parted of their own accord and she felt the teasing of his tongue as he tentatively sought to see if she would admit him.

Pru pulled away slightly and took a deep gulping breath. Sam was concerned that he might be overwhelming her. He was becoming harder by the minute and feared that his trousers would no longer conceal his ardor.

"Are you all right?" he whispered.

"You take my breath away, Sam Blake. I've never felt this way before."

The Hero's Best Friend

By Elise Dee Beraru

ISBN: 1-58749-113-3

Copyright 2001

Earthling Press • USA

The Hero's Best Friend Copyright 2001 by Elise Dee Beraru
Isbn: 1-58749-113-3

All trade paperback and electronic rights reserved.

Printed in the United States of America. No part of this book may be used or reproduced without written permission, except in the case of brief quotations embodied in reviews or articles. For more information address the publisher.

This is a work of fiction. People and locations, even those with real names, have been fictionalized for the purpose of the story. Likewise, the medical and technological advances described were historically accurate, but may not have existed in precisely the manner and in the institutions as they were described.

Published by Earthling Press
A subsidiary of Awe-Struck E-Books, Inc.
Printed in the United States of America

Available in electronic and print formats
<www.awe-struck.net>

Cover art © 2001 by Kate Moore Photo

Editors Kathryn Struck and Dick Claassen

Dedication

This book is dedicated to the memory of John Matuszak and Dan Blocker, my inspirations for Sam Blake, both of whom left too soon and deserved a happy ending.

It is also dedicated to a pair of friends on either end of the country who have pushed me as a writer when I needed to be pushed: Linda Campbell and Lois Smith.

Author's Note

This is a work of fiction. People and locations, even those with real names, have been fictionalized for the purpose of the story. Likewise, the medical and technological advances described were historically accurate, but may not have existed in precisely the manner and in the institutions as they were described.

Chapter 1

The Texas Panhandle—1885

The mayor of El Molino stood by the hitching post next to the jail and held out his hand to the duster-clad man who had just finished putting a sizable sum of money in his saddlebag and lacing it closed.

"Mr. Randolph," said the mayor, "I don't know what we would have done without you, clearing out the Black Hole Gang."

Clint Randolph shrugged and turned to perfunctorily shake the mayor's hand. "It was a job and we did it."

"I've been authorized by the town council to offer you the position of sheriff of El Molino."

"Thank you, but no, Your Honor. I think it's time Sam and I were moving on."

"Sam who?"

Clint sighed. "Never mind. We'll be off, I reckon."

Swiftly, the range detective swung himself into the saddle of his black stallion and, touching the brim of his hat with his fingers, nudged his mount into movement. A moment later, a huge dun gelding followed, its equally large rider in rhythm.

About an hour later, far outside town, Clint pulled his horse to a halt and dismounted. The other rider also stopped and dismounted. Clint unlaced his saddlebag and pulled out the money. Leafing through the greenbacks, he divided them and handed a portion to the other man.

"Here you go, Sam. Fifty-fifty, as always."

Sam Blake smiled bitterly, though the turn of his lips was barely visible behind the soup strainer mustache and bushy beard. He yanked off his camel-colored Stetson and ran splayed fingers through his thick, black, unruly curls before clamping the hat back down on his head. "Yeah, fifty-fifty. Did you hear the bastard? 'Sam who?' Why do I put up with it year in, year out?"

Clint shrugged and looked up into his friend's face. If Clint Randolph was six feet two, Sam Blake was more like six feet five. Four years older than Clint, Sam was built like a bear contrasted with his broad-shouldered, slim-hipped partner. Clint was as smooth-skinned and bronzed as the Indian grandfather whose blood he carried, while Sam was bearded and hair-matted.

Friends since boyhood, they became partners when both were in the Texas Rangers, but even then folks never quite noticed Sam's contribution. Those who noticed him often failed to see the intelligence in the dark brown eyes behind the round, wire-framed spectacles, never suspected the college education behind the taciturn façade. Also unnoticed when compared to Clint Randolph's lightning draw were Sam Blake's far more accurate skills. Sam might not be as fast out of the holster, but he almost never missed what he was aiming at.

"We really should have wired the money to our accounts," Sam said. "I don't like traveling with this much cash."

"I don't exactly have an account," Clint responded.

Sam rolled his eyes toward heaven. "Where the hell do you put your money, then?"

Clint looked indignant. "Reckon I put about 95% of it into whiskey, women and good times. The rest I just waste."

Sam sighed again. "You plan on riding the range forever?"

Clint shrugged. "Reckon one of these days I'll get myself a small spread and run some horses."

"With what down payment? You can only get 160 acres free if you homestead. That's not enough for running livestock. Clint, you're what—coming onto thirty? I've seen those old saddle tramps, fifty, sixty years old, owning nothing but their tack and a change of union suits..."

"Thank you, Mother." Clint swung back into the saddle as Sam wrapped his share of the bounties on the rustlers in a clean bandanna and shoved the packet to the bottom of his saddlebag. He could wire the money, save perhaps $500.00, in the next town they passed through. He would feel a lot better once the remaining $4,500.00 was safely earning interest in the Bank of Santa Fe.

"We'll be in Rincon in a few days. Ought to be able to find a ready woman or two there," Clint mused.

"I can hardly wait," groaned the bearlike man as he remounted.

"Just because that whore in Santa Rosa got scared when she saw that big cock of yours is no reason to swear off women."

Sam flushed to the roots of his unruly hair. Until that moment he was unaware that his best friend knew his shame.

"Jeez, Sam, you been keeping it buttoned up since then? That's got to be a couple years ago already."

Two years, five months and fourteen days, Sam thought to himself, *but who's counting?*

"Can we talk about something else?"

"Sure." Clint began to slap at his pockets, then reached inside his duster and felt around. "Sam, you got any tobacco? I could sure handle a smoke right now."

Almost inaudibly, Sam replied, "I stopped smoking nearly a year ago."

"Oh...yeah," Clint responded awkwardly.

"Why Rincon?" Sam asked. "Is there a job?"

"Yeah, got a wire forwarded while we were in El Molino. Seems there's some rustling going on. Ranchers are offering a nice sum to clean them out."

"Did you agree?"

"Yeah."

"I'm your partner, Clint. Do you think it might be appropriate to discuss a job with me before taking it?"

Clint's brow rose. "God Almighty, Sam, the telegram was addressed to me. You always get your share."

"I just wish that you'd remember that I'm your partner, not your sidekick. Just because idiot mayors in dirtwater towns think you're the brains of this outfit doesn't mean you should start going around thinking you are, too."

"If it wasn't for me there wouldn't be any jobs. I may not be the brains, but I am the one they hire. What would you be without me?"

The two men rode along for a long time before either spoke again.

"Sam, do you ever think about settling down?"

"Define settling down."

"You know, buying a place, marrying, having kids?"

"Yes, no and no. Why, do you?"

"Yeah." Gesturing to his shoulder, Clint said, "I'd like to find a pretty little girl who comes up to about here and raise a whole passel of kids."

"That's a nice dream. Takes money, though."

"Yeah, but you've got money. I've never seen a man so stingy with a buck as you. Why bother if you don't want to get married?"

Through gritted teeth, Sam said, "I never said I didn't want to get married."

Clint turned to look at Sam. "But you won't?"

"No."

"Why the hell not?"

"Because I've looked in the mirror lately."

"Shit, *amigo*, don't let one little whore put you off women."

"I'm not, but at least she got as far as seeing my cock because I tossed two bucks on the table. No good woman ever got past my face and form. Hell, even my name is dull as ditch water. Samuel Blake, nothing to recommend that. Some of us were just never meant to be married, I suppose."

Rincon, Texas

Prudence Hofheinz leaned over the frame and tried to concentrate on the block she was quilting. Her eyes always welled up when the mothers of Rincon talked about their infants. At thirty years old, she was the same age as so many of them, but she had no experience with babies.

Prudence was the schoolteacher in Rincon. She taught all grades from first through eighth, but she didn't have the same relationship with her students that their parents did. She had learned that the last nine years.

But then, why should she? Prudence had grown up in Chicago as the Girl Most Likely to Die an Old Maid. As a girl of more than average height and weight, Prudence had received only one marriage proposal in her life.

A thirty-year-old spinster didn't really fit in anywhere. The women in town her age were all married and talked of homes and husbands and children. The younger women had been students of Miss Hofheinz and never felt quite comfortable on a first name basis with their former teacher. Like a governess in an English gothic novel, Prudence had no real position on any level in Rincon—except for her job. She had joined this sewing circle in an attempt to make friends, but she never felt quite right. She had only one real friend in town.

A knock at the door attracted the attention of the quilting circle. A lithe, golden-haired woman of twenty-two came breezing in. She wore a brown corduroy split riding skirt, plain, knee-high riding boots and a red calico blouse modeled after a man's shirt. A flat-brimmed gaucho hat hung by a thong about the throat down her back.

"Prudence," the blonde said with a smile, "you about through here?"

Prudence popped the knot on the thread she was sewing and dropped her needle, thimble and scissors into her sewing chatelaine. "All ready, Arabella," she responded. "Ladies," she said with a polite smile as she rose. The other women mumbled casual farewells as the teacher and her friend, Arabella Morgan, left the parlor. She pinned on her flower-trimmed bonnet and stepped out into the sunshine.

"How can you stand that crew of cats?" Arabella asked as she replaced her flat-crowned felt at a jaunty angle. "They'd as soon gossip as eat." Arabella untied her horse from the hitching rail and walked next to Prudence through the streets of Rincon while leading the mare by the reins.

Prudence looked at her friend. It should have been easy to be jealous of Arabella Morgan. Where Arabella was petite, Prudence was too tall. Where Arabella's hair was the color of burnished gold, Prudence's was brown. Not sable, not chestnut—just plain old brown. Where Arabella's eyes were the color of a clear summer sky, Prudence's were brown. Not gold-flecked, not hazel, not amber—just brown, brown, brown! Where Arabella was slender as a willow with high, full breasts that seldom failed to attract the eye, Prudence might be referred to as pleasantly plump by someone kindly, but her disproportionately small bosom was unimpressive.

Arabella's father, Ethan Morgan, owned the Bar M, so Arabella had been sent to a fancy ladies' academy in New York, so she had only been Prudence's student the first year the older woman taught. The two women were drawn together by their education and their unmarried state. But where every man who was anybody would die for a chance to wed the rich and elegant Miss Morgan, Miss Hofheinz couldn't get the time of day from them.

Arabella even had a better name. Arabella Morgan. It was flowing, poetic and so very American. Who could possibly be attracted to a woman with a virtuous name like Prudence? And who could even pronounce so decidedly foreign a name as Hofheinz?

"Arabella, I doubt the Saturday Sewing Circle gossips about me. What could they say? I think they're just as happy when I leave. I try to fit in, but I don't understand them any more than they understand me. All their talk of husbands and babies reminds me that I'll never experience them myself. I'll just spend the rest of my life teaching other people's children, including yours when you have them."

"God! The men I've seen are enough to put a girl off marriage!"

"Why ever would you say that?"

"Oh, Prudence, you're so lucky you aren't an heiress," Arabella began, never seeing the slight stiffness in Prudence's spine at her words. "Men of every age from twenty-two to sixty-two offer to court me. But it's not me they want, it's the Bar M. I wish my father *had* remarried and had a son!"

Prudence raised an eyebrow. "You're not serious—I don't mean about Mr. Morgan remarrying. I mean about men not wanting you. You're absolutely beautiful and educated..."

"And rich."

Prudence shrugged. "Yes, and rich, but money isn't everything, trust me. If they notice me at all, they act like I'm going to rap them across the knuckles with a ruler. Believe me, the Bar M is far from your only attraction."

The two women reached the small cabin adjacent to the schoolhouse that was the lodging the Rincon School Board provided their grammar school teacher. Stepping onto the porch, Prudence used her latchkey to unlock the door and they entered the neat little cabin that had been Prudence Hofheinz's home for the last nine years.

It was a pleasant house with lots of windows to allow cross ventilation in the heat of summer. It consisted of a main room, a small bedroom and a kitchen and pantry with a pump and a wood-burning stove. The floors were smooth wooden planks covered with braided rag rugs. The windows had calico curtains and real glass panes. The furniture consisted of an eclectic collection of castoffs from well-meaning townspeople. Nothing really matched, but everything was in good repair. Prudence traded tutoring services for carpentry and other repairs to make sure of it.

Arabella sat down on one of the armchairs and threw one shapely leg over the arm. Prudence herself had gone into the bedroom to change into a split skirt of indigo denim, a worn shirtwaist and riding boots.

"I thought we'd ride up along the ridge at Ganados Ravine," Arabella called from the main room. "Papa's been having trouble with rustlers again."

Prudence emerged from her bedroom changed and grabbed a gaucho hat like Arabella's from the hat rack by the front door as the two women left the cabin and entered the shed adjoining where Prudence's horse, Max, and her buggy were stored. Max was no match for Arabella's beautiful mare Horizon, but Prudence was patient enough with the plodding gelding.

Prudence skillfully saddled Max and mounted and the two women set off to ride the ridge. It was a bright afternoon, bearably hot and sunny.

Rustlers were the bane of cattlemen's lives. In the previous couple of months a man named Jack Derry was rumored to be the head of the rustling gang, but nobody had seen Derry in action and he always seemed to have an alibi.

There was speculation that some mining interests were using the Derry Gang to wreak havoc before moving in their mining equipment to work some of the old Spanish mine sites, but this was unconfirmed.

Arabella and Prudence sat on their mounts on the ridge overlooking the Bar M range. Right now, everything looked as it should, but there was an underlying current of ill ease disturbing the otherwise bucolic setting.

"Does the Cattlemen's Association have any idea what they are doing to stop the Derry Gang?" Prudence asked.

Arabella nodded. "I overheard Papa tell some of his friends that he hired a famous range detective named Clint Randolph to rid us of the gang. Randolph should be here in the next few days."

"He hired one man to go against a gang?"

Arabella shrugged. "Maybe he's used to taking on whole gangs of desperados alone."

"Anyone who could take on an outlaw gang single-handedly is someone I'd surely like to see."

Arabella grinned. "Come over for dinner a week from Sunday and I'll introduce you—if he hasn't already captured the gang and gone his merry way."

Prudence grinned back. "That's a deal. Come on, I'll race you back."

Arabella laughed. "Prudence, I know you love Max, but he can't beat Horizon."

Prudence shrugged. "So I lose." She spurred Max into action. Horizon hardly had to breathe hard to catch up and surpass the gelding.

Prudence actually found herself looking forward to that day eight days hence. To meet an authentic Western Hero would be something!

Ethan Morgan stepped onto the veranda and lit up a cigar. He scanned the horizon through a cloud of blue smoke. As far as he could see this land was his. Even the War had not ruined him. He was damned if anyone or anything, even Nature herself, was going to destroy what was his.

He had heard that Clint Randolph was the best there was in settling range problems permanently. If he wasn't the fastest gun in the West he was pretty close to it. He'd leave Jack Derry and his gang of hired thugs bleeding in the dirt.

And nobody would ever figure it out.

The Cattlemen's Association wanted the rustlers driven out of the county—all the way to hell if necessary. But that group of middle-aged men was not about to dirty its own hands forming posses and chasing them down. It was worth paying Clint Randolph his $10,000.00 fee to do the dirty work. In addition, Morgan volunteered to house Randolph and whatever men he hired to work with him on the job.

It was a perfect setup. Everyone's attention would be on Clint Randolph.

In the distance, Ethan saw a dust cloud. As it grew closer the rancher could see two riders in dusters; one in a black Stetson on a black horse, the other in a camel-colored Stetson riding the biggest dun he'd ever seen. The two riders approached the house, stopped and dismounted.

The shorter of the two men pulled a Western Union telegram from his duster pocket and approached the house.

"Mr. Ethan Morgan? I'm Clint Randolph."

Stepping off the veranda, his right hand outstretched, Morgan said, "Very glad to meet you, Randolph. Your reputation precedes you."

Clint shook Morgan's hand. "Thank you, sir."

Morgan looked briefly over Clint's shoulder and said, "I wasn't aware you would begin hiring men before your arrival."

Sam, who had come up to stand beside Clint, stiffened uncomfortably at the remark.

"My partner, Sam Blake, sir." Clint said carefully.

"Partner? I was unaware you had a partner, Randolph."

"Sam Blake is every bit as good as I am." *Better*, he added to himself.

"If he's so good, why haven't I heard of him? The fee doesn't change just because you have a partner."

"What I charge and you agreed to pay includes Mr. Blake and me. We have our own arrangement. Now, sir, if you could direct us to the barn and then our rooms, we'd like to unpack our grip and wash up. Then we'll come in and discuss the situation and begin to map out plans."

Gesturing, Morgan directed them to the barn, saying, "I'm afraid I've only one guestroom, Mr. Randolph. I can hardly imagine that two men your size would be comfortable sharing one bed. One of you will have to stay in the bunkhouse with my hands and whatever men you hire."

Clint nodded abruptly. Leading their mounts, the two detectives headed for the barn.

When they were unsaddling their horses, Sam declared, "This is my last job, Clint."

Clint nearly dropped his saddle in surprise. "Why?"

"I'm tired of being the forgotten man. I'm only your equal partner financially. I've had enough of sleeping in bunkhouses while you lounge in featherbeds and eating chuck grub while you dine at the boss's table. When we're done here I'll have over $30,000.00 in the bank. That's enough to buy some land or start a small business someplace—maybe a print shop or bookstore."

Clint looked his best friend straight in the eyes. Frustration and anger were mirrored, emphasized by the frames of the spectacles on his hair-covered face. "Sam, I have the name, but I'm nothing without you. You're the brains of the outfit."

"And you're its image. If you've ever read a dime novel, you'd know that you even look like a goddamned hero. But don't worry, Clint. Nobody will miss me. After a while, even you won't."

"You're wrong, Sam. Hell, when I was a scrawny ten-year-old kid you came to my rescue more times than I can count. You're the closest thing to a big brother I'll ever know."

"I'm sorry you feel that way, Clint. I'm no great shakes. I only came to your aid because you were as alone as I was."

"I don't believe that for a minute, Sam. Look, I'll sleep in the bunkhouse and you can take the guestroom if you want."

Sam threw his saddlebags and bedroll over a massive shoulder. "I saw the look on Mr. Morgan's face. He would think it's demeaning for you to sleep among the common men, whereas I'm as common as they come. If I want privacy I can sleep in the hayloft. At least my feet won't hang over the edge. I'll go stake out a bunk and meet you at the house." Sam lumbered off to the bunkhouse.

Clint sighed as he slung his own saddlebags over his shoulder. He thought about his relationship with Sam Blake. For the four years between the time Clint came to San Antonio from Ohio with his parents immediately after the War, until Sam left to go east to the University, Sam had always been his protector, his mentor. It was Sam Blake who taught Clint to shoot a six-gun, how to saddle a horse, how to throw a lasso, how to build a rabbit snare and how to light a campfire without matches. Sam had accepted the taunts of "Yankee lover" and "Injun lover" silently and nobly. He never instigated a fight but never backed away from one either. Sam had always been a big kid and had grown to become a big man.

The Sam Blake who came back from the East Coast was changed from the one who left. Not just physically; that was likely to happen to any young man between the ages of eighteen and twenty-two. There was a melancholy defeat in his face from causes he never discussed. Though Sam had earned a degree in civil engineering, he chose instead to join the reorganized Texas Rangers when Clint did. During the five years they served with the Rangers, Clint's hawkish good looks and presence caused him to be noticed and celebrated far beyond the steadier, more thorough and accurate investigations of the quiet, workmanlike Sam.

Clint usually acknowledged—at least to himself—that Sam had been the major contributor in the pair's success as range detectives. But handsome, flashy western heroes were always more celebrated than taciturn, efficient operatives who hid behind eyeglasses and a full bushy beard.

It was only in these last few jobs that Sam began to make his displeasure at his anonymity known. Maybe Clint should have been more conscious of his friend's needs, but over the years he had begun to take Sam's quiet presence for granted. It had struck home most recently on the trail when Clint had failed to notice that Sam had quit smoking.

Now Sam wanted out and Clint was facing working alone or finding another line of work. But unlike Sam, Clint had saved no money. The fee from the El Molino job was virtually every cent Clint owned, and while $5,000.00 was nothing to sneeze at, it was hardly enough money to live on while trying to make a go of something else.

Clint was deep in thought about these matters as he approached the ranch house and was reaching for the front door when it opened to reveal one of the most beautiful women he had ever seen.

Chapter 2

Even in a modest chintz day gown she was elegant and came, as he might have described her, "right up to here" on him. Clint felt an instantaneous tightness in his jeans enough that he was glad his duster was buttoned.

When she smiled at him, Clint felt he had gone straight to heaven.

"Oh," she said," you must be the range detective the Association hired. I'm Arabella Morgan..."

Please don't make her Mrs. Morgan, Clint prayed swiftly.

"Ethan Morgan's daughter."

Clint felt his breath returning. "I'm one of them," he stammered.

"One of them?"

Clint gestured back over his shoulder. "My partner is settling down in the bunkhouse."

Arabella cocked her head in surprise. "But we arranged the guestroom for you."

He nodded with a half smile. "Yes, and I'm using it, but when you meet Sam you'll see that there's no way the two of us can share a bed."

Arabella blushed. "No, no, of course not," she stammered. As if remembering her manners, she continued, "Please, Mr.—uh..."

"Randolph. Clint Randolph, ma'am." He touched his brim politely.

"Mr. Randolph, let me show you to your room and get Consuelo to bring you up a pitcher of water and a towel. I'm sure you'll want to wash some of the trail dust off."

"Thank you, Miss Morgan. I'd like that pretty well."

Arabella led the way. Clint was going crazy watching the natural sway of her derriere beneath her skirt. This job had better be over quickly or he was going to forget that he was supposed to show respect for decent women. He followed her up the stairs like a puppy dog and down the hall to where she opened a door and revealed a sunlit room with a simple double bed and furniture. Clint wondered what Arabella's room looked like. How would she look clad only in that golden hair lying on a feather bed while Clint covered her pale body with his swarthy one? It was all the man could do not to groan with frustration.

Meanwhile, Arabella was finding herself fascinated by the tall, handsome detective. She had watched the glowing silver of his eyes when they caught hers. She was going to have to watch her step or she'd find herself underneath him in no time flat.

Of course, that idea didn't sound so very outlandish to Arabella. After all, the man was glorious! If he looked this good in an ankle-length duster, how would he look in a work shirt and well-worn denims? Or better still, in nothing but the skin God gave him?

Arabella blew some air out of her lungs to dispel the blast of heat her thoughts sent shooting from her breasts to her core. Heavens, but no lady was supposed to feel that way. And yet, there must be something right going on. No other man she had ever met had aroused this kind of response in her.

"I'm—I mean we're glad you're here, Mr. Randolph," Arabella said. "Papa says you're the best at stopping disreputable elements from bothering law-abiding people."

"We do our job well, I reckon," Clint said, moving closer to Arabella.

She could detect the scent of leather, horse, tobacco and maleness. It was a heady feeling, but in self-defense she stepped back.

"I'll just...go down and ask Consuelo to send up some warm water for you. Dinner will be served in about an hour."

"Thank you, ma'am, but I think I'll go eat with my partner. Just because he's sleeping in the bunkhouse doesn't make him any less my partner."

"But of course he'll be included in meals in the main house. I'm terribly sorry the house is so small. Perhaps the Association has another member with a guestroom."

"I'll see how he feels about that, Miss Morgan."

"I'll just leave you now." She slipped out the door.

Arabella was beside herself. He was gorgeous and exciting and even considerate of his partner. What a combination!

After dinner, Ethan Morgan got out an old plat map of the county and showed the detectives the current ranch boundaries. Sam used a pencil and sketched in borderlines and sites of slaughtered cattle as Ethan reported them. The older man was surprised to see Sam taking charge of the strategy session while Clint provided mostly brief comments.

"How many men do you think you'll need to hire, Randolph?" Morgan asked at last.

Clint and Sam surveyed the map and exchanged comments. It was Sam who answered. "If your regular hands can keep a sharp eye out, it's possible to do this with just the two of us. At this stage, it appears if we can catch Jack Derry in the act we can cut the guts out of the gang. Clint will meet with the hands Monday morning and explain their responsibilities to them."

Clint nodded.

"Why not tomorrow?" Morgan asked impatiently.

"Clint and I will want to ride out tomorrow morning to survey the area."

"I'll take them out, Papa," said Arabella, who just now appeared at the door bearing a tray with coffee and cups.

Puffing out his chest, Morgan said, "My daughter knows this ranch as well as any of my hands. Sometimes I can't help thinking of her as the son I never had."

"I'm certain, Mr. Morgan," Sam said stiffly, "that nobody in his right mind would ever mistake Miss Morgan for your son."

Arabella giggled lightly. "Why, thank you for those kind words, Mr. Blake. Shall we say eight o'clock tomorrow morning? I'll have Consuelo pack a late breakfast and we should be back well in advance of Sunday Dinner. I have a dear friend coming here who is just dying to meet a real western hero."

Clint and Sam exchanged weary glances. The last thing they wanted was a gushing little flirt who wanted to squeeze Clint's big, strong muscles. If anyone was going to squeeze his muscles, Clint preferred it be Arabella. As for Sam, he would probably be completely overlooked.

It was better than chuck grub in the bunkhouse and more economical than going to a restaurant, assuming there was a restaurant open in Rincon on a Sunday afternoon.

Prudence was looking forward to this dinner like she might face a trip to the barber to have a tooth pulled. While she had told Arabella she wanted to meet the Great Western Hero, even at informal functions like this dinner, she was so far outshone by her beautiful friend that her presence was barely noticed.

She combed through her wardrobe. Finally, she located a gown of dark pink faille with a modest bustle and some ecru ruching at the modest décolletage and drawn-up overskirt.

For a moment, she sat down at her vanity table and looked at herself.

Just once, if someone would see her, really see her, instead of their expectation of a spinster schoolteacher. Even in woman-short Northwest Texas, she was destined to live her life alone.

"Maybe I should just go back to Chicago," she said aloud, but knew that was a very bad idea. Her father had remarried about five years ago. Better to be alone with a career, even schoolteacher in a small town one-room schoolhouse, than the unnecessary appendage of a married couple. Prudence never begrudged her father remarrying. He had remained a widower for years. She always wondered why he had waited so long.

At least the food would be good.

Early Sunday morning, Arabella, Clint and Sam rode out to survey the property and observe the locations where some of the damage had been done.

Making an expansive gesture, Arabella indicated the distant foothills. "Before Texas independence, the Spanish Conquistadors came to this part of the country looking for the Seven Cities of Gold. The foothills are riddled with mineshafts going back over two centuries. We don't even know for certain how many of them are out there hidden in the underbrush."

"Have you been up there?" Sam asked.

Arabella shook her head. "Not in ages."

"Derry and his gang probably know that the ranchers don't go up there," Sam said. "If there are any structures up there they'd make a good hideout."

"Just what I was thinking," Clint said.

Arabella raised an eyebrow. "You really are full partners."

"I've never denied it," Clint responded defensively.

"Come on," Arabella said. "We've got lots to cover."

They rode the perimeter, Arabella showing them where wire had been cut and cattle slaughtered. Sam and Clint conversed in fractured sentences that seemed to have meaning to them though they were a blur to Arabella. She felt like she was eavesdropping on two generals preparing for battle—but then, in a way that's what they were.

Sam shook his head negatively in response to a comment from Clint. "I don't know. Not like Derry."

"You know Jack Derry?" Arabella asked, amazed.

"By reputation," said Clint. "He's a nasty little man who'd as soon back-shoot you as face you."

"Patrols, I think," Sam said. "With spring calving and branding done Morgan has hands to spare. Until there's another strike we won't have any idea where to chase."

"What are you going to do until someone strikes?"

"Listen and cull information from every available source, Miss Morgan," Clint said. "Sam always says that you can learn as much by listening as you can by chasing around."

"Do you always quote Sam?"

"I do when he's right, and he's right a fairly good piece of the time."

"Amazing. Which, of course, is why so many people have heard of him."

"I'm not responsible for what people think or do, Miss Morgan. Only for my own actions."

"I don't need you to fight my battles for me, Clint," Sam growled.

"Whether I do or I don't, I'm wrong," Clint snapped back.

"I've seen enough." Sam spurred his dun to head back toward the built-up part of the ranch.

Clint watched his partner leave without saying a word until Sam was no more than a cloud of dust.

"For a big man he has an awfully thin skin," Arabella said.

"It's all your doing."

"Excuse me for living, but what just went on has nothing to do with me. It has more to do with him and you." Suddenly Arabella started as if the wind had been knocked out of her. "Mr. Randolph, exactly what is your relationship with Mr. Blake?"

Clint looked confused. "What do you mean?"

Arabella drew her mount closer to Clint's. What she was about to ask him was so sensitive that even though they were alone, she was afraid of prying ears.

"When I was back east I heard of men who...well, it's difficult to say, but they...well, they didn't care much for women."

Clint's eyes widened and the color drained behind his naturally dark complexion. Despite his limited education, he realized what she was saying. "You think I...you think we...son of a bitch. I'll show you what kind of man I am!"

Abruptly, he reached over and dragged Arabella off her horse and onto his. No sooner was she lying across his lap than he wrapped his arms around her and pressed his mouth against hers.

The kiss was punishing and Arabella's first notion was to resist, but then her whole body began to infuse with heat. She found herself softening in his embrace and slipped her arms about his neck.

Clint began to gentle his kiss as he felt Arabella soften. She wore no corset under her riding clothes and Clint could feel the delicate movement of her ribcage as her breathing became deeper. He nibbled on her lips until she parted them to accept the probing of his tongue. He pressed her closer to him as his hand crept up to cup her full, firm breast.

Arabella could feel the growing desire of this man beneath the layers of her clothing and his. She was a virgin, but not so innocent she didn't know what that meant. She pushed herself away firmly, but far from frantically.

"Well," she said between gulps of breath, "it's plain you care for women. I'd better get down or I may consent to something I shouldn't be consenting to."

"Would it be so bad?"

Arabella touched his cheek gently. "No, I'm afraid it might be very good, but while men are allowed their freedom in these matters, eventually I'll have to marry and I'm sure my future husband will prefer an untouched bride."

She slipped off Clint's lap and jumped to the ground. Quickly she stepped the few feet to where Horizon had ambled off and smoothly remounted.

"We'd better go," she said. "We'll need to wash and change for Sunday dinner. Do you and your partner carry more formal clothes with you?"

Clint looked down at his plaid cotton work shirt, leather vest and denim jeans. "I reckon I could come up with something cleaner, but not much more formal. You never know about Sam. For all I know he could have a full set of evening clothes in that saddlebag of his and I'd never know it. He went to college back east, y'know."

"Did he now? He hides it well."

To her eternal displeasure, when Prudence pulled the rags out of her hair, instead of unrolling beautifully formed sausage curls, her hair fell in thick waves that rebelliously had a life of their own. Grumbling in frustration, Prudence brushed her hair away from her face, parted it down the middle, braided the two halves and wound them into a coronet. While it was fancier than usual, it was far from soft. For some reason, Prudence had an overwhelming urge to be softly feminine this evening. She supposed it was because she would be competing for the spotlight with her vividly beautiful friend.

There was nothing to do about it except get dressed and go.

"He probably won't notice me, anyway."

Sam grumbled as he tried for the third time to tie his bow tie around his starched collar. The primary disadvantage of having a full beard, he mused, was it tended to get in the way when he was buttoning on a collar and tying a tie. The simplest solution would be to shave it off, or at least trim it.

"But then," Sam mumbled, "folks would know for certain what a dogface I am."

Finally, Sam managed to get the tie tied as he wanted it. He tucked his shirttails into his trousers, pulled his suspenders over his shoulders and donned his vest, buttoning it and spanning his watch and chain across his middle. Brushing off the frock coat that had been hanging up for two days, he pushed his arms into the silk-lined sleeves and shot his cuffs. Yanking a handkerchief from his back pocket, Sam removed his spectacles and wiped the lenses before putting them back on.

Looking again into the mirror, Sam scowled at his image.

It was hopeless. No matter how hard he might try, he would never be Clint Randolph. He would forever be the invisible man.

"They probably won't notice me, regardless."

Leaving off his hat, Sam Blake raked frustrated fingers through his thick curls and stepped into the late afternoon sunshine to walk the short distance from the bunkhouse to the main house for the Sunday Dinner he had been dreading for days.

Lost in thought, Sam failed to notice the black buggy pulled by the nondescript brown gelding until it was almost upon him.

"Whoa!" cried a female voice as the buggy ground to a stop. Surprisingly quickly for a big man, Sam sprang out of the way.

"You ought to be more careful to watch where you're crossing," said the woman. "A buggy can't stop on a dime."

"Sorry, Ma'am," he mumbled. "May I help you down?"

The woman pulled the brake. "No, thank you," she began curtly, then added, more politely, "Actually I would appreciate it very much if you would."

Sam stepped around to the left side of the buggy and held up his arms to give the woman a place to lean. She lifted the dark pink skirt of her gown, revealing black high button shoes and some ruffled white petticoat, and stepped down from the buggy.

"Thank you..." she began when she looked up into the face of the man she had nearly run over.

Prudence Hofheinz looked at the most compelling face she had ever seen. Though his cheeks and jaw were shrouded by a thick black beard, there was a look of amazing strength. Behind round wire frames were dark brown eyes that showed extreme intelligence coupled with melancholy. A full lower lip of a broad, sensuous mouth was visible—a mouth that made Prudence's own tingle.

The man was huge. Prudence estimated his height at six feet five or so. He had shoulders so impossibly broad as to be described as massive. He looked as strong as an ox. Surprisingly, he was wearing a pristine white shirt with a clean, starched, collar, a black silk bow tie and a frock-coated black broadcloth suit that fit his large frame perfectly. His black, ribbed faille vest was cut to make him look powerful rather than portly and was spanned by a gold watch chain on which hung a small charm. Prudence's eyes widened to see that the charm was a Phi Beta Kappa key. The man had not only been to college, he had excelled beyond the norm.

Prudence felt a wave of heat diffuse through her. Though the man was far from handsome, there was character in his face that made her unable to look away. She felt a strange aching in her most private zones at the sight of this mammoth in men's clothing. She found herself wondering what he hid behind the fancy, well-made suit and began to blush at the random wantonness of her thoughts.

Sam looked down at the woman he had just assisted. She was taller than average; tall enough that he didn't feel like he towered over her. She had big brown eyes that dominated a face with the clearest flawless skin. A thick brush of lashes surrounded the beautiful eyes; eyes that showed intelligence and a melancholy Sam knew well. Her nose was straight and her mouth full and a little bit too wide for classic beauty, yet eminently kissable. There was a sturdiness to her full figure that made her look like she would not blow over in the slightest breeze or crush beneath the strength of a man.

Sam found his thoughts wandering to what it might be like to kiss this woman, to explore the lushness others might just call plumpness and he began to feel an uncomfortable tightness in his trousers.

Sam had been sure he had completely suppressed this sort of feeling because of its futility, yet as he looked at the woman standing in front of him, long buried desires began to overwhelm him. Because of it, he reacted with anger, more at himself than at her.

"What are you staring at?" he growled.

For a moment, Prudence looked away. It was the same as always. Whenever she met an even remotely attractive man, he either ignored her or rejected her. "I'm sorry. It's just that..." She stopped as a deep blush reddened her face.

"What is it?"

No guts, no glory, girl. You've got nothing to lose. "It's just that...well, you have the most amazing eyes I've ever seen."

No way was Sam prepared for that. "What?"

"I'm sorry. That was unseemly of me. I'm quite certain you've heard that before."

No, never.

Prudence reached her hand up near his bearded cheek. "Would you mind taking off your specs for a minute?"

Sam felt a strange heat as her hand fluttered near his face. The urge to rest his cheek against her hand was overwhelming. Instead, he reached up and unhooked the curved earpiece from one ear and pulled his glasses off, holding them in one hand.

Prudence looked deeply into those dark brown orbs. She felt her breathing grow shallow at the sheer beauty of his thick-lashed eyes—despite the evident sadness in their depths. This man had also known disappointment in his life.

"Thank you," she said hoarsely as Sam replaced the lenses.

For a moment they stood in silence, gazing into each other's eyes. Had they not been so accustomed to indifferent responses from the opposite sex, perhaps both of them would have reacted more forcefully.

Max's whickering in the traces broke their concentration.

"I'm sorry," they said in unison.

"What's your name?" he asked.

"Prudence," she replied with a sigh. "Prudence Hofheinz. I'm Arabella Morgan's best friend. And you must be Clint Randolph, the range detective and Western Hero."

He laughed bitterly. "Afraid not, Miss Hofheinz. My name is Sam Blake—and I guess you could say I'm the hero's best friend."

Chapter 3

"The hero's best friend," Prudence repeated, then smiled. "That's funny."

Her smile knocked him out. This Miss Hofheinz might not be a classic beauty, but when she smiled her soft, oval face was heartstopping, at least to Sam Blake.

"I suppose it is—if it wasn't me who had the misfortune to be thought of that way."

"I guess every man secretly wants to be the hero himself. Are you a range detective also?"

"I am."

Gently, she placed her hand on his arm. "It takes a special kind of courage to do a job and watch others get the glory."

If she could have looked through a window into his soul, she had read Sam's deepest thoughts. His heart began to thump so hard he feared it might be visible even through his clothing. God curse him for having his emotions barely beneath the surface! If only he could be calm and collected inside like Clint was.

"You sound as if you understand what that's like."

Prudence nodded. "I've been a teacher for nine years. When your students succeed, it's because they're brilliant. When they fail, it's because you're a terrible teacher. Sometimes you get so frustrated you want to shout..."

"Look at me. *I'm* the one who made it possible," Sam finished for her.

Prudence smiled again. "You understand!"

"Are you two going to stand out there in the dust all afternoon or are you coming in to dinner?" Arabella's voice reverberated in their ears, interrupting the emotional and spiritual link that was beginning to build between these two lonely people.

Prudence backed away from Sam a couple of steps and nervously smoothed her dark pink skirts. Lifting them with her hands, she walked to the porch and stepped up and into the house.

"I see you've met Mr. Blake," Arabella stated when the three of them were inside the house. "I'd like you to meet Clint Randolph, the range detective the Association hired to get the Derry Gang. This is my very best friend in the world, Miss Prudence Hofheinz."

Prudence looked up at Randolph. Absently, she held out her hand briefly and shook Clint's automatically. "Pleased to meet you. You're Mr. Blake's associate?"

Clint glanced at Sam. He immediately noticed his friend was distracted. He looked at the woman he was meeting. She was not much to look at. He would never have pegged this type of woman to be friends with the beautiful Arabella, but then, who was he to judge? Far more interesting was the strange look on Sam's face. The man looked positively poleaxed!

Sunday dinner was a blur. Ethan Morgan kept talking about the Derry Gang and trying to draw Clint into serious conversation about it. He kept touching on areas Clint knew were more Sam's area of expertise, but Sam was being singularly uncommunicative. Time and again the big man's glance was directed at the brunette schoolmarm.

It couldn't be true, Clint thought to himself. Sam had never shown the slightest interest in a woman since he'd returned from college twelve years before. He had said it was a waste of his time to wish for things that could never be. Now, he seemed to be making calf eyes at this woman who had to be thirty if she was a day.

"Mr. Randolph, are you listening to me?" Ethan Morgan's voice interrupted Clint's thoughts.

Clint nodded. "I'm sorry. I was reminded of something."

"What did your tour of my property this morning tell you?"

"Well, um..." Clint waffled, "we were looking for a pattern—um..."

"A pattern?"

Clint shrugged. Being the façade of the partnership was not always easy. Sam was always better at coming up with the explanations. "Maybe I should let Mr. Blake explain it. Sam?"

"Huh?" Sam answered absently. He was so busy watching Prudence slide her food around her plate that he was not paying any attention to the conversation.

Ethan Morgan rolled his eyes. The "huh" coming from the distracted Sam sounded almost moronic.

"Mr. Randolph, I don't care if your associate is a Harvard graduate..."

"University of Pennsylvania," Sam responded automatically now that he was back at full attention, "class of '72."

Prudence looked up. The University of Pennsylvania was a top university, every bit as quality as Harvard. A Penn Phi Beta Kappa was a smart man indeed! What other secrets were hidden behind this man's full beard and wild hair.

"That's beside the point, Mr. Randolph. I hired *you* to do this job and I expect answers from *you*."

Clint expelled some air before he spoke again. He glanced surreptitiously at Sam periodically for approval as he proceeded. "We—that is—*I* believe that in order to escape detection, the Derry gang is actually making strikes close to their hideout rather than travel distances where their movements might be spotted and reported. This morning with Miss Morgan's assistance we mapped the locations of the strikes to determine a pattern. We're not..." Clint cringed at the disapproval in his employer's face at the plural pronoun, "I'm not certain yet what those patterns are. It will take a little more exploration. We'll need to speak to your hands about what they've found and where."

"Mr. Morgan," Sam interrupted, "the kind of men who usually ride with scum like Jack Derry aren't the kind who can keep their mouths shut about their activities. Yet asking around town revealed nobody who has seen or heard anyone identified as belonging to the Derry Gang bragging about the vandalism or thefts. Is it possible the Derry Gang is here as a decoy to camouflage someone else's work?"

If looks could kill, Sam Blake would have been dead right there. "Mr. Blake, my daughter may have been softhearted enough to invite you to share dinner at our table, but I am not interested in your opinions. In future, Arabella, Mr. Randolph's associate can eat in the bunkhouse with the rest of the hands."

"Father!" Arabella protested.

The color draining from his cheeks, Sam threw his napkin on the table and rose to his mountainous height. "Think nothing of it, Miss Morgan. I've sort of lost my appetite after all. Good night, Miss Morgan, Mr. Morgan, Miss Hofheinz. Clint, if you want me, I reckon I'll be around." Sam strode out of the dining room and out of the house, his boot heels clicking on the wooden floor.

Prudence felt the pain Mr. Morgan's insult had caused. Putting down her own napkin, she made a show of reaching for the brooch watch she wore pinned to her bodice. "Oh, dear," she said, not all that convincingly, "has it become so late already? Please forgive me, Arabella, but I must get home before dark. I do have school in the morning. Mr. Morgan. Mr. Randolph. I'll talk to you soon, Arabella." Lifting her skirts, Prudence nearly ran out of the house.

Clint rose. "Excuse me. I'm in sudden need of a cigarette." He strode toward the stairs and his room.

"Father, that was cruel. Mr. Randolph and Mr. Blake are partners. They always work together. It would serve you and the Association right if they resigned and left you to the tender mercies of the rustlers."

Morgan rose and approached his daughter. Without warning he slapped her hard across the face. "Don't you sass me, girl. Just because you went to that fancy New York women's college doesn't mean you can talk back to me. You'll tell Consuelo to clean up in here, then take yourself to your room."

Arabella wanted to rub her reddening cheek, but instead she rose and ran into the kitchen.

"Mr. Blake, Mr. Blake," Prudence called after the retreating form of the large man as she ran after him.

Sam turned. Running after his long strides in a corset had pinked Prudence's cheeks, making her look like a flower in bloom.

Prudence stopped a few feet from him.

"Mr. Blake, I'm so sorry you were treated that way. It was cruel."

Sam kicked at the dirt. "I appreciate the sentiment, Miss Hofheinz, but it's things like that that tell me to get out of this business."

"I wonder what a brilliant man like you is doing playing second fiddle to a empty-headed cowboy like Mr. Randolph."

Sam laughed bitterly. "Maybe Clint is not so empty-headed as you think and I'm not so brilliant."

Prudence placed her arms akimbo. "Mr. Morgan might not recognize a Phi Beta Kappa key, Mr. Blake, but I do. A man who earns that honor at a school like Pennsylvania is brilliant by definition."

"Miss Hofheinz, why did you follow me out here?"

"Well," Prudence began, looking at her feet, embarrassed by her hopeless attraction to this large but fragile man, "I thought Mr. Morgan was wrong and I wanted to tell you so. Besides, I really have to be getting home or I'll be traveling alone on the road after dark."

Sam grabbed her arm sharply. The electric jolt pulsed through both of them. "Weren't you listening? There is a gang of marauders, whether the Derry Gang or someone else, committing all kinds of malicious mischief. How can you travel alone on these roads knowing that?"

Prudence looked down at the big, strong, tanned hand that held her so firmly, yet so gently. In a quiet voice, she replied," Mr. Blake, if I waited around for an escort every time I needed to get anywhere, I would spend my entire life bounded by the schoolhouse and my cabin. If I die, I die."

"There are worse things than death for a beautiful woman."

"Perhaps," Prudence said bitterly, "but then, not being beautiful, I doubt I would be particularly interesting to the average marauder."

Sam heard her bitterness. It was kindred to his own. "Miss Hofheinz, if you'd wait a few minutes for me to saddle my horse and strap on my gun belt, I'd be honored to escort you home."

Prudence knew she should decline, but she didn't want to. So few men had ever shown her even a moment's concern.

"I'd be honored to have you do that," she said with a smile.

A crooked grin crossed his face that even his brushy mustache and beard couldn't conceal.

"I'll only be a minute," he said and nearly sprinted towards the barn.

Prudence stood watching the direction he had gone for a few moments when Clint Randolph walked up.

"Have you seen Sam?"

"He's gone to the barn to get his horse."

Clint thanked her and trotted off after his partner. Prudence went over to her buggy, unhitched the reins and waited.

Sam was nearly finished saddling his mount when Clint found him in the barn.

"Sam..."

Without looking in his direction, Sam muttered, "There he is, my best friend."

"Where are you going?"

Sam yanked at the cinch on his saddle and took the horse by the reins. "It's none of your business where I go, but I'm escorting Miss Hofheinz home. I may take a room for the night in Rincon so I can get to the bank and telegraph office early. I'll feel better when my money's safely on its way to my bank."

"Look, I'm sorry about what happened."

Sam turned to face his friend. "Clint, you're always sorry. It's always the same. You never support me in front of others, then you come out and try to make it up to me later." He sighed. "I'm so tired, Clint. Bearing this gets harder and harder."

"Do you want me to tell Morgan we quit? I'll do it, you know."

"For God's sake, Clint! Where would that leave you? Stuck in *Rincon* with only the money in your saddlebags and a black mark against your reputation. No, we'll finish this job and then I'm through, but I suggest you find a way to save this money. If you'll excuse me, I'm going to escort the lady home."

Sam led his horse out of the barn and hitched it temporarily on a hitching post by the bunkhouse door. He walked in and found the bed he had staked out. He strapped on his gun belt, threw the saddlebag over his shoulder, pushed on his hat and strode out without a word.

When he got back to the house leading his mount, Prudence was already sitting in her buggy, her hat pinned on her head and whip in hand. Quickly, Sam tied the horse to the buggy and began to swing himself onto the seat. The buggy groaned slightly under the unaccustomed weight.

"You're not riding alongside?"

"If you don't mind, I'll drive you home and ride back."

"No, I don't mind at all."

Sam sat to her right in order to leave his gun handy. For two large people the fit was snug. Prudence could not help being aware of the length of well-muscled leg running hip to knee with hers as well as the warmth that spread through her body at his nearness. She handed over the reins and their hands lingered just a moment longer than the transfer took. Prudence's hands were far from dainty, yet they were dwarfed by Sam's leather-hardened, ham-sized mitts. Sam declined the buggy whip and got Max started with just a gentle pull on the reins. The buggy took off with Sam's dun trotting alongside.

They sat in companionable silence, neither knowing quite what to say.

Prudence used the opportunity to examine this giant, decidedly unusual man. Other than the pure physical mass of him, at first, Prudence could not put her finger on the difference. It was then that she realized that he smelled different from other men of her acquaintance.

"Mr. Blake," she began tentatively, "you don't smoke, do you?"

Sam's eyes widened in surprise at the question. "No, not anymore. Why do you ask?"

Prudence blushed unexpectedly. "Most of the men I've met carry certain odors. Leather, tobacco smoke, sweat, bay rum, horse...Oh God, I'm not doing this right!" *Well, girl, in for a penny, in for a pound.* "You smell—I don't know—clean somehow."

For a moment there was an uncomfortable silence. Then, unexpectedly, Sam threw back his head and laughed.

Prudence was confused. She folded her arms across her chest. "What's so funny?"

Still laughing, Sam reached in his back pocket for his handkerchief, removed his glasses and wiped the tears from his eyes, then wiped the lenses and replaced the glasses, all with one hand since the other was on the reins. "I'm sorry, Miss Hofheinz, it's just...it's just that...well, when a man wants to make an impression on a lady, I suppose that *clean* is not exactly the description he wants to hear."

"I didn't mean to insult you, Mr. Blake."

"You didn't. But please, call me Sam."

Prudence's face fell. "But that would mean you would have to call me Prudence."

Sam touched her lightly on the arm. "You don't like your name, do you?" he asked gently.

"No. When you have a name like Prudence, people expect you to be virtuous and untouchable. Can you imagine a man saying 'Prudence, I love you?' It sounds absurd!"

It didn't sound absurd to Sam.

"Why don't I call you Pru," Sam said with a grin, "it doesn't sound quite so virtuous."

Prudence smiled. "I'd like that, Sam."

For a while they drove on, then Sam asked, "Where are you from originally?"

"Chicago. My father was a butcher there. My mother died when I was five. I don't remember her very well and any photographs we had of her were lost in '71 when the city burned."

"The Great Fire. That must have been frightening."

Pru nodded. "Terrifying. Fortunately, I was sixteen, so I handled it better than some of the children in my neighborhood, but my Dad and I escaped with the clothes on our backs and a couple of blankets. If it weren't that Dad thought ahead about such things and had fire insurance, we would have been ruined. He was back in business in a tent within a week. That year between the fire and the time I left for school was exciting in Chicago. It's when I became interested in architecture. There was so much new building going on. It was as if the city fathers decided to rebuild the city on a logical, artistic plan instead of the haphazard way most cities spring up. I would have sold my soul to become an architect."

"Could your father not afford to send you after the fire?"

Pru shook her head. "No, it wasn't that. Dad could afford it. I couldn't find an architecture school anywhere that would take me."

"Because you're a woman."

"Exactly. It took a lot of soul searching to finally give up and apply to teaching college." She sighed. "So now I'm a small town schoolteacher who still drafts architectural drawings to fill my nights. Recently I've taken to designing interiors rather than buildings."

"Interiors?"

"Yes. I'll look at an existing house or store in town and try to speculate on what can be done to use the existing area more effectively or more beautifully. Most people's houses and stores are a hodgepodge without any kind of unifying plan, and everything is so cluttered with knickknacks."

Sam thought about the fine houses he had seen in his life and realized she was right. For himself, he lived in a boarding house with little except a few books, his clothes and his guns. It wasn't that he didn't appreciate the finer things in life; it was just that he was gone so often it never made sense to live more opulently. "What do you see instead?"

Excitement began to fill Pru's voice. "Have you ever seen Shaker furniture? Simple, clean lines, functional, little wasted space or ornamentation. Beautiful in its simplicity. I'm not advocating everyone live quite that simply, but I like the feeling of lots of space and light with limited things to clean and collect dust." Her face filled with light and her hands gestured freely as she described her dreams. "I also like comfortable things. Soft mattresses and sofa cushions, parlors where a family can relax and be comfortable both with their surroundings and each other. One of these days wealthy people won't flaunt their wealth by how cluttered and ostentatious their surroundings, but by how well their furniture is made, by the most modern conveniences—telephones, indoor plumbing, even electric light in the house. Can you imagine how wonderful this world can be if we let our imaginations fly free?"

"The way you describe it, I can almost see it," Sam responded warmly. "Maybe in this new, modern world you see, being a woman won't stop you from doing what you want to do."

"Do you think so?" Pru asked as she saw the sparkle in the glass-shielded eyes, but then she looked away. "It's useless to hope. The most likely thing to happen is I will live and die a spinster schoolteacher, unmourned and forgotten. You know—I *hate* teaching. But what can I do? I can't go home to my father. He'd take me in, I'm sure, but he has a new wife now."

"You could marry."

Prudence laughed bitterly. "I'm thirty years old. I don't want to get married because someone needs a housekeeper or a stepmother for his existing children. I'd only want to marry if I met a man who wanted me for me, someone capable of loving me whom I could love in return. But men like that fall in love with women like Arabella Morgan, not with women like Prudence Hofheinz."

They drove along the road in the waning afternoon until the structures of Rincon could be seen. On the outskirts of the town they came to a large picket fence area in which there were three detached structures. One was a large, rectangular building with a tile roof and a bell tower. The second was a much smaller wooden cabin with a stone chimney and a porch in front. The third was a small shed. Prudence identified this as the school grounds and the cabin as her house. Sam directed the buggy to the shed, which served as the stable, and slowed it until it came to a stop before the door. Handing the reins to Pru, Sam climbed down and unlatched the door. Prudence drove the buggy inside as Sam followed her in on foot. He untied his horse, leaving it to stand while he helped Prudence to unhitch Max.

Standing near him, Prudence again became aware of how big this man actually was, but instead of being intimidated, she was fascinated. A man like this could envelop a woman and make her feel protected. She wondered if his arms were as strong and secure as they appeared in the well-made black frock coat. Prudence wanted to touch Sam's hair and beard. Were they coarse or soft? She had occasionally seen men undressed from the waist up. It was difficult to live in a rural area and not have observed ranch hands working with their shirts off. Pru wondered what this man's chest might look like. He was not one of those whipcord lean, narrow-waisted, spare cowboys. Was his chest smooth, or did he have body hair?

Prudence blushed at the wantonness of her thoughts. She had no right to speculate about this man. And yet—she sensed the loneliness in him, saw the isolation. Perhaps they had both been lonely too long.

Pru wanted to take a chance. It might be the biggest chance she would have to be humiliated by his rejection, but if he did not reject her, he would be gone when the job he and his partner had been hired to do was done, so what would be the harm to her reputation?

The biggest problem was he was most likely to say no.

Then again, the worst thing was that he might say no. Prudence needed the most courage she had displayed since the Great Chicago Fire.

"Sam," she said warily," would you like to come in and sit a while?"

Chapter 4

For a moment the only sounds in the barn were the whickering of the two horses and the surely audible pounding of Pru's heart. Sam's face was a picture of shock. Pru felt the color drain from her face. She had erred terribly.

"I could light the stove and brew some coffee or tea. I'd offer you something stronger, but schoolmarms aren't supposed to touch strong drink, so I have no spirits in the house."

Sam blinked owlishly. He couldn't believe what he was hearing. She could just be being polite, in which case he should immediately decline, mount up and head for the boarding house in town to wait for tomorrow and the bank. Or it could be that she had some attraction to him. That was absurd. Women didn't go for Sam Blake.

What was the worst thing that could happen? She could make him coffee, they could talk a while and then he would leave.

And the best thing? Sam didn't even want to speculate. He had been celibate for so long; it was barely believable that he could ever find satisfaction again.

He had nothing to lose. He had no plans for the rest of the afternoon and evening. What could be so bad about spending a little time in the company of an educated woman?

"Tea is fine, Pru," Sam heard himself say. "I'll brush down your horse while you're boiling water."

Prudence felt a surge of hope at his response. He hadn't rejected her overture out of hand. Quickly, she pointed out the curry comb and brush. Lifting her skirts, she all but danced out of the shed.

About fifteen minutes later, Sam, his frock coat slung over his arm, put down the curry comb and replaced his Stetson on his head. He left his dun saddled, but led the beast into the empty stall in the little shed, loosened the cinch, forked some hay into the feed trough and tossed a couple of bucketfuls of water into the water trough.

As he looked out the shed door, he saw nobody around. That was probably for the best. Gossip could damage a schoolteacher's reputation and he certainly didn't want that to happen to Pru.

He ambled over to the cabin and stepped onto the porch. He rapped a couple of times on the door and a moment later Prudence opened the door.

She had removed her hat and tied an apron around her waist. A small, square wooden table was set with bone china cups and saucers, as well as a sugar bowl. A white damask table cloth covered the table and four ladderback chairs flanked it. Beyond an open door, Sam could see the bedroom, though only the end of the bed was visible within.

"Let me take your hat and coat," Pru said, stretching out her arms. "The tea won't be a minute. Would you like bread and butter? I'm afraid I have no cake."

"Tea is fine."

Pru nodded. "Well, all right. Make yourself comfortable. It won't be but a few minutes."

Make himself comfortable indeed! Sam had never been so uncomfortable in his life. He scanned the parlor portion of the room. In keeping with her declaration, the decoration was simple. She had a large sofa with very soft chintz cushions, two chintz upholstered chairs and an end table. A cluttered desk was covered with large sheets of vellum on which Sam found the architectural design sketches Pru had described. Drafting tools as well as pens and ink were scattered about and a pile of corrected school papers sat in one corner of the desk, clearly showing that—dislike it though she did—Prudence Hofheinz paid attention to her students' work.

The bookshelves were plain. The books in them consisted of school textbooks, architectural digests and some fiction. There were no knickknacks or mementos on the shelf except for two photographs. The first was of a middle-aged man with a square face and pale hair and eyes. His face had the frozen sternness necessary to take the slow exposure photographs of the day, but the pale eyes showed intelligence. The subject wore what appeared to be a well-made suit with a watch chain across his well-fed girth.

The second picture showed the same man with a woman, probably taken at the same sitting. The woman was also middle-aged, but was very thin and wore a fashionable, plaid walking gown and ribbon-festooned felt hat.

"My father and his wife," a soft voice said behind him. "Hans and Agnieska Hofheinz." She was standing so close to him that he could sense the faint tuberose fragrance she wore. "He married her after I left Chicago to come to Rincon, so I don't know her well. It's a little hard referring to a virtual stranger as 'stepmother,' but Dad seems to love her very much."

Sam looked at the pictures and then turned around to face Pru. She was so close to him; all he would have to do was lean down and kiss her. Did he dare?

"Won't you sit down?" she asked, gesturing. He was so near her, she thought. All he had to do was lower his head a bit and he could be kissing her. Somehow that didn't seem like a bad notion at all. "The tea is still steeping," she added quickly to disguise her apprehension. "We could talk a while."

Sam walked over to the cushy sofa and sat. It was soft and cozy and a far cry from wooden chairs and leather saddles.

"May I ask you a personal question?"

Sam's eyebrow raised over his frames. "It depends on the question."

"Well, most men who travel the country by horse have great difficulty keeping tidy. Most of them seem ignorant of hygiene at all. I was wondering how your shirt and suit came to be so clean and pressed-looking. I doubt Consuelo had a hand in it."

Sam laughed. "I learned to appreciate a clean body and clothes when I was back east. When I'm in town, I bathe every day. On the trail it's not so easy, but I do my best. As for my clothes, I had this pouch made that fits in my saddlebag. It's leather lined with cotton and has an oilcloth cover. When I put my suit, shirts and collars into it and fold the flaps correctly, it's very difficult for road dirt to get in. All I have to do is hang out my clothes for a day or have them pressed and I'm ready for any occasion. Most of the time, though, I dress pretty much like ranch hands do. It's more practical for daily use."

While he was speaking, Prudence suddenly found herself thinking about Sam in the bathtub. The thought made her ache between her legs most tellingly and a slow flush crept into her face. To regain her composure she walked around the room picking up books and papers she left lying around because she was not expecting company. "What a wonderful idea. This part of Texas can be so dusty."

"Pru, you don't have to flit around straightening things or trying to entertain me." Sam patted the sofa cushion. "Please sit and talk to me."

Prudence gathered her skirts and sat gingerly on the sofa next to him. She could feel the heat of him and smell his clean, masculine scent. They sat stiffly, uncomfortably on the sofa, unsure what to do next. Both of them felt more than a little stupid. They were both in their thirties. They weren't children.

Prudence smoothed out her skirt and apron. She did it again. And again.

"Do I make you nervous?'

"Um—no," she lied. "Why do you ask?"

Sam reached for her hand. It felt so cool and small in his giant one. Using his thumb, he gently stroked the back of her hand. He raised it to his mouth and kissed the palm.

Prudence gasped sharply from the surprise of it. Immediately, Sam let go of her hand, stood and walked a few steps away from the sofa.

"I'm sorry," he croaked. "It was very forward of me."

Forward of *him*? Prudence couldn't believe how forward *she* was being. How forward she was feeling. She rose and walked over to him. Tenderly, she raised a hand to his thickly bearded cheek and felt the surprisingly soft, silky bristles of his beard. Her thumb lightly brushed over his lips in invitation.

Sam's eyes darkened and rounded beneath his spectacles. Looking into her brown eyes, he could see desire matching his own. Could he trust his impressions of what he saw reflected in her eyes? He had been miserably wrong before and it had nearly destroyed him.

"I don't take kindly to being teased," he said cautiously, fighting the urge to kiss the thumb that was making him crazy.

"I'm not a tease, Sam Blake. I don't understand why I'm feeling what I'm feeling, but I know I want to."

He grasped her hand in his and pulled it away from his cheek while his other hand slipped beneath her chin and pulled her face up as he lowered his head to meet hers.

When he kissed her it was as if lightning shot through both of them. His mouth was hungry for the taste of her, his body hungry for the feel of her soft body against his harder one.

As Sam wrapped his arms around her and drew her against him, Pru could feel his strength and heat. Instinctively, she moved closer into his warmth. Her hands laced through his thick, curly hair. Although the softness of his beard should have given her a hint, she was surprised to discover that his hair was baby fine and silky beneath her fingers. Her lips parted of their own accord and she felt the teasing of his tongue as he tentatively sought to see if she would admit him.

Pru pulled away slightly and took a deep gulping breath. Sam was concerned that he might be overwhelming her. He was becoming harder by the minute and feared that his trousers would no longer conceal his ardor.

"Are you all right?" he whispered.

"You take my breath away, Sam Blake. I've never felt this way before."

The big man grinned crookedly. There was no hint of arrogance in his face, only the wonder of finding a woman who was not repulsed by his size.

His size! Oh, God! If he wasn't already cursed enough in life with his big, ungainly body, homely face and nearsighted eyes, he was larger than average down there as well. He thought of the terrified looks he received from more than a few whores who should have seen everything before. Because of it he had stayed away from all women for nearly two and a half years. He felt the passion in this woman. He wanted her more than any woman since...well, that was another lifetime. Would she turn away from him in disgust?

"Sam, have I done something wrong?" Her hands crept up to cup his face. "Something's wrong. Please tell me what it is."

Sam pulled away from her and walked a few steps away. His back to her, he spoke his heartbreak aloud. "It's nothing you did, Pru. You are so sweet, so fine, so lovely. I want you so badly in ways a fine lady could never know. But you deserve better than an ugly lump like me."

Prudence felt a catch in her throat at the sound of this incredible man calling her *lovely*. Lovely! Though she had never lain with a man, she knew the process and knew the hungry ache at the apex of her thighs was sexual desire. This was whom she wanted inside her, filling her and covering her with his warmth and strength. He had just declared he thought she was lovely. It wasn't exactly *pretty*, but it was another attribute of other women she never imagined hearing about herself. He wasn't the ugly lump, but somehow, he didn't see that was how Prudence usually saw herself. She might never have another chance to learn the secrets withheld from unmarried women. She knew this was the man she wanted to teach those secrets to her. When he left, there would be nobody to know.

She walked quietly up to Sam and pressed her face against his broad back as her arms slipped around his ample waist and her hands pressed against his belly. She could hear the beating of his heart and feel the expansion of his lungs.

"Ugliness is not of the face or body, Sam Blake. It's in the soul. You may not be an Adonis, but there's so much more to you than meets the eye. I doubt I deserve you either, but there's a reason why you chose to accompany me home—and I don't think you had bedding me in mind when you offered."

"It's true, but because you're a lady."

Pru hugged him tighter. "Make love with me, Sam. Touch me all over and let me touch you. Let's turn this terrible day for you into something beautiful."

Sam stiffened slightly. "You went out to the Bar M to meet Clint, didn't you?"

"'The Great Western Hero.' Funny, I barely noticed him. From the moment I saw you I saw only you. Men like your partner are a dime a dozen. Men like you are very rare." Prudence released her hold on Sam, stepped around and took his hand in hers and raised it to her mouth to kiss his palm tenderly. "Please, Sam, I truly believe we need each other. If I'm too bold, it's because I feel like I was missing part of myself until now." Pru stepped away, still holding Sam's hand. "Come to bed, darling."

Like someone in a trance, Sam let her lead him into the small bedroom. He barely noticed the sparse furnishings. Translucent muslin curtains allowed the afternoon light in but not anyone's view. Heavier drapes swagged back would keep light out and heat in when necessary. Prudence guided Sam to her soft, comfortable feather bed and motioned him to sit down. She knelt on the bed beside him and wrapped her arms around his neck.

Sam's own arms circled her body and he fell back onto his back, carrying her along to lie on top of him. Their mouths met, hungrily, passionately, their tongues dueling playfully when he wasn't kissing her eyelids, cheekbones, and ears. She nuzzled her nose in the thick silk of his beard as she gently reached beneath it to untie his necktie and pop the button of his stiff collar.

Sam moved his hands over Pru's back and sides. He could feel the press of her breasts against his chest, even through the layers of clothing. He stroked up her ribcage, feeling the stiff boning of her corset before feeling the rise of her breasts. Pru was neither slim nor grossly obese, but her soft roundness was—to him—angelic and comforting, like making love in a cloud. As he stroked the sides of her breasts, she moved to press against his chest. Sam knew he wanted to feel those soft mounds in his hands and began to pull at the buttons at the back of her bodice until the cool rush of air told Pru her back was exposed.

She rose enough to allow Sam's big hands to smooth her bodice over her shoulders and down her arms, exposing her corset and chemise to his view. Her breasts rose and fell beneath the remaining coverings as Sam began to unhook the front of her corset and untie the tapes that kept her skirt, drawers and petticoats attached at her waist.

Sam pulled the corset away and tossed it to the floor as Prudence took a full, deep breath. He pulled her chemise out of the waistband of her drawers and slid his hands beneath the muslin garment to cup her breasts in his hands.

Her breasts were small, but perfectly formed globes with dusky rose nipples already puckering with arousal as he stroked them with his thumbs. Pru moaned with her desire as his callused hands drew out the most delicious sensations.

She reached for the buttons of his vest and undid them. She was reaching for his shirt buttons when he stopped her.

"Take down your hair, Pru," he said hoarsely.

Pru smiled and reached for the pins holding her braided coronet to her scalp. Unbound, her hair fell in thick waves to her hips.

"Glorious," Sam gasped as he lifted a thick lock to his face. His need surged again and he dropped her hair and quickly divested her of her remaining clothes, also shrugging off his vest. He laid her on her back and pressed his face into her rounded belly as one hand caressed her thighs and the other stroked the skin between her breasts and where he was pressing kisses.

"You are so beautiful," he whispered, not caring that she didn't believe him. "So soft and sweet."

"Sam, please, I want to see you."

He raised his head and looked at her, his eyes stricken behind the round lenses. He rose to a sitting position and buried his head in his hands. Pru could see his massive shoulders shaking as he fought back emotions. Was he crying?

In an instant she was on her knees behind him again, her hands reaching around to caress his arms, chest and belly. "Please trust me, darling. There's nothing to fear from me. I want to see you, touch you. Kick off your boots and let me love you as you deserve."

"I'll frighten you—maybe disgust you. I couldn't bear it."

"How could you possibly disgust me?"

Sam kicked off his boots, then rose from the bed. His movement jerky with fear and self-hatred, he began to tear at the buttons on his trousers and shirt, then his union suit. When his clothes were pooled about him on the floor, he stood up to face her.

"Oh, my!" Pru gasped. Sam stiffened at the exclamation. She climbed down from the bed and approached him. She spread her fingers and pressed them against a chest and belly so thick with soft black hair that the skin beneath was almost completely obscured. His barrel-chested frame was massive from his impossibly broad shoulders to his far from slim hips. His thighs were thickly muscled and hard as tree trunks. Those columns of leg and thigh as well as his forearms were similarly shrouded in dark thick hair all leading to a dense forest of black curls at his groin from which emerged a huge, hardening phallus.

Sam prepared himself for her rejection and so was completely taken aback when she pressed her face against his furred chest and breathed his scent deeply into her lungs. As her hands stroked her way down his chest, then around his back and hips to rest on his buttocks, she sighed into his chest. "Oh, Sam, why didn't you warn me how beautiful you are?"

"What did you say?" he responded, his voice risen in pitch from disbelief.

She gazed up into his bespectacled eyes. "I said you're beautiful. You're fine and strong and furry like a black bear. You smell so good—of nice things like leather and soap. It surrounds me."

Unexpectedly, one of her hands crept down and slid beneath his shaft to cradle it tenderly. Immediately, it began to spring to life. She was a little bit shocked at her own behavior. And yet, not shocked at all.

She looked at his tortured face; the color drained from it. "What would it take to prove to you that your size doesn't frighten me? Would this?" she asked, gently stroking the length of his shaft as the blood continued to engorge it. He gasped at the unbearable agony as he fought within himself for control. God help him if he released like some adolescent schoolboy!

"Or this?" She dropped to her knees before him and pressed her lips to the velvety tip of his iron hot manhood and kissed it while her hair shielded her action from view, leaving him only with blinding sensations.

Sam groaned and hauled her up by her shoulders. As if she weighed nothing, he lifted her into his arms and walked the few steps to the bed. As he laid her on her back, she raised her arms to welcome him home. As he lowered himself on top of her, even she could feel the dampness that signaled her readiness to receive him and her hips rose to meet the lowering of his against hers. The hard length of his rod rested against her thigh as he stared right into her eyes.

"Who taught you to touch a man that way?" he asked huskily.

"You did, Sam. You are teaching me. Please, darling, I need you to kiss me again."

He crushed her against him as his mouth crashed into hers. There was no gentle teasing this time. He took her in almost brutal need, yet she gave him back as good as he gave. Their hearts began to pound and their breathing to grow ragged as he thrust his tongue again and again into her warm, sweet cavern.

Prudence could feel the brush of his body hair against the super-sensitized skin of her straining nipples as his bulk pushed her breasts flat between them and the ache she felt in them and in her most secret place doubled and redoubled in intensity.

"Please, Sam, please. I need you inside me."

Ever conscious of his large organ, Sam lowered his hand and found her sex. His thumb caressed the sensitive nub while his index finger began to stretch her tight muscles to prepare her to receive him. She moaned with building pleasure. She was so unbelievably tight. She couldn't have known many men, he thought absently as he felt the dampness lubricating his finger. He slipped another finger inside her. Her muscles drew his fingers in. He prayed he wouldn't hurt her too badly.

Slowly, agonizingly, he guided himself inside her, feeling her tight sheath and pull against him. Sam had gone a considerable distance when he encountered resistance. His eyes widened in shock. It couldn't be her maidenhead. He was Sam Blake—no woman could possibly choose him for her first lover. He glared at her. She gazed back; her eyes filled with love. Unbelieving the evidence of his senses, he thrust in, hearing her gasp as he pierced the telltale barrier.

Pru's eyes flooded at the initial rending pain, but she blinked them away. She felt awe at the marvelously full feeling she was experiencing and thought there was such a completeness about it.

Sam lay very still, afraid to move, almost afraid to breathe. She had been a virgin. A virgin! Yet she had given her most precious gift to him: Sam Blake, the man no woman ever wanted—before now.

He saw the tears shining in her eyes and felt his own eyes begin to sting. Still deeply embedded within her, he lowered his head and kissed her eyelids, tasting the salty flavor. "I hurt you," he said painfully, guilt chilling his soul.

"Yes—and no. What pain I felt I expected." She smiled warmly. "You feel so good inside me. That part I never expected."

Sam held himself away from her by resting on his elbows for fear his heavy frame would make it difficult for her to breathe easily. He lowered his head again and kissed her tenderly. His beard brushed against her skin, making it tingle.

"Sam..."

"Yes, Pru."

"Aren't you supposed to be moving now?"

The big man laughed. It was the same deep pitched laugh she had experienced in the buggy, full of joy and surprise. He kissed Pru hard again. "Yes, love, if you're ready for me, I should be moving now."

He began to move, pulling out and sliding back inside her while his fingers stroked the pinpoint of her desire. Her hips rose to meet his thrusts. Nobody had to instruct her in how to love a man; it was as natural as breathing. Her body felt a growing tension as if it were reaching for something undefined and indefinable. She grasped the coverlet beneath her for fear she would float to the ceiling. She saw a grim determination on Sam's face as he used all his concentration to postpone his own release until she found her own.

Pru felt her need to reach for something too intense to keep silent. She cried out rhythmically in her growing pleasure, at first concerned that she might worry Sam until she saw a small smile amid his tension and heard him groan encouragement as he continued to move within her.

Without warning, Pru felt as if her body exploded. Wave after wave of the most startling sensations radiated from the place of their joining to the tips of her fingers and toes. A sheen of perspiration coated her and she felt exhilarated and enervated at the same time.

As she was floating back to earth she saw Sam strain once more and a flood of warmth filled her as he emptied himself into her. For a brief moment he collapsed on top of her, spent in more ways than one, then he raised himself and slowly withdrew before rolling over beside her.

The absence of his big, warm body over hers made Pru shiver once. Her woman's parts continued to throb—not painfully but with the intensity of pleasure.

She looked at the man who moments before was one flesh with her. His own body was damp with the exertion and his wide chest rose and fell as his breathing returned to normal. His manhood was soft and diminished, yet still formidable and beautiful in Pru's eyes as it emanated from the thick black nest at his groin.

Prudence rose onto one elbow and looked at him. He looked tired. She leaned over and kissed him again. "What...happens... now?" She asked between kisses.

"Either I get dressed and leave now or I stay the night and sleep a bit and then wake up to make love to you again. It's your choice, Pru."

Grinning, she reached in the direction of his eyes and plucked off his glasses. Carefully folding the ear pieces, she deposited the specs on the side table. She reached to pull down the covers on the bed.

"Wait," Sam said.

He climbed out of bed and went to the wash basin near her dressing table. Pouring water into the basin from the ewer, he took a washcloth and returned to the bed. Before Prudence could lie down on her white muslin sheets, Sam gently washed the virgin's blood and his semen from her thighs. Fortunately, the coverlet was not stained as she had not bled overly much.

"You may not want to make love with me again tonight. You may be sore from this."

"Will you stay even if we don't make love again?"

Sam nodded and grinned as he slipped in next to her. He feet went right to the footboard, but he was used to beds being too short for him. At Pru's urging, he lay with his head at one corner of the double bed and his feet at the diagonal corner, giving him room to stretch out fully.

Prudence rolled against him as he gathered her in his arms and stroked her hair. She traced paths in the forest on his chest and around the nearly hidden male paps until sleep overcame her. Right behind, Sam held her close and thanked God for this woman. He swore to protect her at all costs.

He had fallen in love with Prudence Hofheinz—irretrievably, permanently, eternally. She was the part of him that had been missing, the balm for his broken heart.

If only he wasn't leaving Rincon when this job was over.

Elise Dee Beraru · 38

Chapter 5

The dawn sky was just bright enough to give some light in the little cabin bedroom on the edge of Rincon.

Pru's eyes opened slowly as they usually did. But this morning was unique in her experience. She was lying on her side, her head resting on a warm, muscled shoulder. A furred forearm was draped around her waist and stray ends of Sam's beard tickled her nose. They had made love two or three times during the long afternoon, evening and night and the scent of it was on his skin.

So this is what it feels like to wake up with a man, she thought. *I like it.*

Sam lay on his back, his chest rising and falling calmly in sleep. Prudence took the opportunity to examine his face more closely. He had unbelievably long, thick, straight, black eyelashes. Fine lines fanned from the corners of his eyes from squinting into the sun and two worry creases marred his high brow. His nose was straight and far more finely chiseled than she had first observed it to be. His mouth was full and sensuous. Just staring at it reminded Pru of how wondrous that mouth felt on her skin. True, he did not have perfection of features, but the elements of his face were fine. Prudence began to wonder at the contradiction of this man. Who in his past had thought him ugly? Who had convinced him to believe it of himself?

She knew next to nothing about him. Range detectives were little more than hired guns, often not much better than their adversaries. But this man was a scholar, his deep voice well modulated with only a trace of Texas. He was inventive, as indicated by the protective pouch he created to keep his Sunday best clean. But he wore a gun whose holster was tied around his thigh to enable a quick draw. He believed in cleanliness, yet his baby soft hair and beard were long and wild. He was clearly the smarter of the two range detectives, yet so much in the background that he was nearly anonymous.

Prudence sighed. Whatever her speculations, she had no misgivings about the night just past. Making love with Sam Blake was glorious. Despite her lack of anything to compare it with, Pru found herself unable to believe that the act of sex could be any more fulfilling. The big man had been passionate, arousing her passion; gentle, arousing her tenderness and—most especially—playful, keeping her from feeling any guilt.

Guilt! Prudence realized the day was growing lighter. Within the next hour or so Rincon would be awakening. Being Monday morning her students would begin to arrive around eight o'clock.

She eased herself up and kissed Sam lightly on the mouth. "Wake up, Sam," she said in a hushed voice as she brushed an errant curl off his forehead. "You've got to get out of here."

Sam slowly opened his eyes. Her face was close enough to his to see without his glasses. "What time is it?" he asked groggily.

"I'm not sure; sometime just after dawn. I'll heat some bath water and coffee, but you've got to leave before anyone sees you leaving."

Sam was sitting bolt upright in an instant. "Where are my specs?"

Pru reached over to the table on her side of the bed and handed them to him. Once he had them perched on his nose, Sam bolted out of bed. "You're ashamed of me."

"No!"

"You didn't have to give yourself to me last night."

She nodded. "I know that."

He began to gather his things together as Prudence climbed out of bed and yanked on her dressing gown.

"Your reactions were normal, you know. I know ladies believe they're not supposed to enjoy the sex act."

"It's not that." Pru went over to where Sam stood, somewhat helplessly with an armful of clothes. She reached a hand up and stroked his cheek. "Sam, I'm not ashamed of you or of what we did. I gave myself to you willingly and I don't regret a minute. It's just that—well—it's just that I'm a teacher and this is a small town. Schoolmarms are supposed to be symbols of morality and gentility. What I was yesterday morning—a virgin spinster—is what I'm still supposed to be. Making love with a stranger passing through town, no matter how wonderful it was—if we're found out—could mean losing my job. While I'm not especially enamored of my job, I'd hate to lose it *and* my reputation all in one fell swoop. Whether you were the love of my life or a passing fancy, gossip about us could do that. If you care for me, even a little..."

"Don't you know that I do?"

Pru smiled broadly. "...and I care for you, Sam. Then you understand why you have to leave before you're seen by any of my students who could carry tales back to their parents."

Sam understood. For him to be seen leaving could mean her ruination in Rincon.

"Is there a bathhouse in town?" he asked.

She nodded. "Wing Chan, the Chinaman who runs the laundry, has a bathhouse out back. New water is a quarter, I think. But you could bathe here."

"No. By the time you got the water heated, it might be more dangerous. I'll go to the Chinese laundry and buy a bath, then do my business in town and get back to the Bar M."

"Are you sure?"

"I am. You could make some coffee, though."

Pru grinned and saluted. "Yes, sir," she said as she departed the bedroom.

A few minutes later the stove was lit, two large kettles and a coffee pot all filled with water were heating and Pru had rolled her hip bath out of her pantry and near the stove. Thick slices of bread lay soaking in a mixture of milk, eggs, sugar and cinnamon as butter melted in a large, cast iron skillet.

Using a fork, she lifted the saturated bread and dropped the slices into the sizzling skillet. The table was still set from the afternoon before, when they never got around to having tea, so all she had to do was put out some full-sized plates and her tin of maple syrup.

Pru was putting the plate of golden French toast on the table when Sam emerged from the bedroom. He was fully dressed except for his coat and tie, his vest was unbuttoned and he was tying his tie around his starched collar as he walked into the room.

"I borrowed your hairbrush."

"That's fine. Do you like milk in your coffee?"

"Just sugar. Is there anything I can do?" he said, eyeing the tub.

"No. Just sit down and help yourself to breakfast. I hope you like French toast."

Sam looked at Pru. Her hair was tousled and loose, her mouth swollen from an abundance of kisses. Though her robe was modestly tied, it seemed barely able to contain her lush body. By God, she was lovely in the morning! Sam turned a chair around and, taking her hand, pulled her down against him to straddle his lap.

"I like French kissing more." Lustily he cupped her face and brought her mouth to his. To prove his point, he thrust his tongue into her parted lips as his hands drifted down to reach inside her dressing gown and cup her soft, warm breasts. Her nipples immediately hardened as her breasts swelled into his kneading hands and he brushed at them with his thumbs until she was squirming with delight, moaning into his mouth.

Pru felt completely wanton in her spread-legged position. Her arms went around Sam's neck as her fingers laced in his black hair. Her sex was throbbing, both from last night and present desire. She undulated against his thighs and hips to assuage that need. Beneath her, she could feel Sam's growing erection and that made her wriggle harder.

Sam released her mouth. "God, what you do to me!" He found her mouth again and plunged a hand down, spreading the overlap of her dressing gown and cupping her sex. His fingers began to probe her pleasure center as she jerked in response, her moans of delight feeding into his mouth. She was damp with arousal, honeyed warmth spilling onto his hand. Sam felt around and released his fly buttons and with a quick raise of his hips pushed them down, then lifted his ramrod stiff manhood though the placket opening in his union suit.

Their mouths still joined, Pru's arms still around his neck, Sam thrust both hands beneath her thighs and lifted her onto his pulsing shaft until she was fully impaled. With a combination of his arm strength and her leg muscles, she began to ride his shaft like a wild horsewoman, feeling his mass all the way to her womb. Grunts of straining pleasure rose from both their throats as the pounding grew wilder and more frantic. Pru's entire body felt like it might explode and she nearly bit Sam's tongue in her excitement.

Suddenly, Prudence screamed her pleasure as an intense climax rifled through her, shaking her to the core. As her shuddering began to subside, Sam took a mighty thrust of his hips and emptied himself into her in a warm flood of his own release.

Panting, they sat, still joined, resting their heads on each other's shoulders, Pru kissing Sam despite the covering cloth.

"Now I think I'm ready for some French toast," Sam said quietly, teasingly in her ear.

Prudence looked at him, her eyes glassy in the aftermath of their lovemaking. Through his lenses, his eyes were dark, gentle and full of loving humor. Pru began to giggle.

"How can you think of eating now?"

He kissed her nose. "I'm hungry now. Would you deny food to a man who hasn't had a bite to eat since dinner yesterday afternoon?"

"Of course not." Prudence slowly extricated herself from him invasion and stood on rubbery limbs. "Help yourself. I'll get the coffee." She closed her robe beneath the sash and picked up the potholder to pour steaming coffee into their cups.

Owing to the short time, they ate quickly. After breakfast Sam poured the buckets of water into the bathtub for her. Buttoning his vest and pulling on his frock coat and hat, he kissed her again, hard.

"I'll say good-bye now." His voice was sad.

Prudence touched his cheek tenderly. "Will you come again tonight?"

"You would want that?"

"Uh-huh."

He lifted her chin. "Pru, you know I'm here to do a job. When it's over, I'm leaving Rincon."

She nodded. "I know."

"If we get word on the Derry Gang, we'll be off after them."

"I know."

"What about your reputation?"

"If you're discreet, nobody will ever know except us. Sam, I would very much like you to come back if you can. If you can't because of your job, I'll understand."

Sam crushed her to his chest. "I swear to you, if I'm not here, it's the job. By God, I want you again. You're like a fire in me."

"Then you'll come back tonight?"

"If I can, I'll come after dark. You don't have to wait supper for me...I'd better go so you can bathe and get ready for school."

He kissed her once more, then opened the door a crack and looked out. Seeing no one, he stepped out into the dawn light and walked to the shed.

Prudence leaned against the closed door and listened until she heard the sound of hoofbeats telling her that Sam was gone.

She touched her mouth and breasts where he had touched them, reliving the tingling, aching pleasure of being with him. With a sigh, she dropped her dressing gown and stepped into the steaming bathtub to bathe and prepare for her day. In the quiet of the morning, the day could have seemed like any other now.

But for Prudence Hofheinz, night and morning would never be the same again.

Clint Randolph stood on the porch and rolled and lit a cigarette. The match burned brightly in the early dawn light.

The disagreement with Sam following the set down had disturbed his sleep. He was still uneasy. He took a long drag of smoke, only to find the damned thing tasted like burning dust. With a curse he dropped the butt and crushed it under his boot heel.

He had been to the bunkhouse already this morning to find Sam had spent the night in town. Knowing that his partner was reliable kept Clint from worrying that Sam might ditch the job. The big man wanted the fee as much as Clint did.

"Penny for your thoughts," he heard Arabella's bell-like voice behind him. "Though I'm guessing they're pretty angry ones."

"Last night..." Clint began.

"Last night what my father did was unforgivable—the not apologizing, I mean. What did Mr. Blake say?"

Clint shrugged. "No more than before we started this job—that it's the last one for him. He spent the night in town after he drove your friend home, I reckon."

"He'll be back, though."

"I reckon. He had some errands to run in town. My partner is real cautious with his money. As soon as we get paid for a job he wires his extra cash to his bank."

"He's a good man, isn't he?"

Clint nodded. "The best there is; only he doesn't believe it of himself."

"Sounds like Prudence."

Clint cocked his head. "You think it's *prudent* not to believe in your own worth?"

Arabella laughed. "No, no, my friend is *named* Prudence. She's a good teacher, but it puts her in a peculiar position in town. She can't flirt like the younger unmarried women like me and has nothing in common with the married women her age."

"I'd like to meet her some day."

Arabella sighed. "You did, Mr. Randolph. She was here for dinner yesterday afternoon."

Clint flushed crimson. "I'm sorry. I guess I didn't catch her name."

"Few men do."

Clint turned to face Arabella. She was wearing a split riding skirt, riding boots and a man-tailored shirt that casually emphasized her stunning figure though it was not blatantly revealing. Her blond hair was pulled back into a single braid down her back and her gaucho hat and gloves were in one hand. She would have been perfectly beautiful had it not been for the deep purple bruise on her left cheekbone.

Clint frowned and gingerly touched Arabella's cheek. He could feel the softness of her pale skin and see the brilliant sky blue of her eyes. "What happened to your face, Miss Morgan?"

Arabella looked down. "I made the mistake of telling my father what I thought of the way he insulted Mr. Blake."

Clint's hands curled into fists. "And he struck you for it? The bastard."

"I suppose he thought I was not properly respectful."

Clint's hand returned to her cheek. His callused thumb gently stroked the skin just beneath the bruise. "Sam wouldn't want you to be hurt on his account."

Arabella shrugged. "Are you going to want to continue with this job? If it were me, I wouldn't want to."

Clint threw up his hands. "I haven't much choice. I have to finish this job while I still have Sam working with me. The money I get is going to have to last a while."

Arabella's eyes narrowed. "You're a fraud, Clint Randolph. You're taking money under false pretenses."

Clint's back went up. "I am not. I can't help it if people have more reliance in me than Sam. Appearances are everything, aren't they, Miss Morgan? When Sam and I started working together, we were dead even partners, but I just *looked more* what they expected a successful range detective to look like. After a while it didn't matter that Sam did most of the planning and investigating, it was me they came to with their handshakes. Even the folks who think half-breeds are lower than dirt began to talk about the famous range detective, Clint Randolph. Maybe I should have insisted on Sam getting the credit he deserved, but the money was good and we still split it fifty-fifty. Until the last job ended, I didn't know Sam was so very discontented. I really need the money this job will bring and Sam can use his share to help him set up a business of his own." Clint grabbed up Arabella's hands. "Please don't let the Cattlemen's Association know. Between us, we can do the job. We've been a successful team for years now."

"You'll need my help."

"Say that again," Clint said, dropping her hands in surprise.

"You'll need my help. I know this ranch as well as any wrangler on it. I can ride as well as a man and handle a gun reasonably well."

"It's not a woman's job, Miss Morgan."

"Mr. Randolph, you have very little choice. I help you and you get my cooperation to maintain the illusion that you're the brilliant and brave Western hero."

She walked by him, down the porch steps and headed toward the barn, clapping her hat on her head and pulling on her gloves as she walked. In her riding clothes, her hips swayed provocatively. Though Clint was angrier than a cat thrown in a puddle, he immediately felt himself harden at the sight of that naturally flowing motion.

He imagined she was going riding. He could imagine her riding.

It was not, however, a horse he imagined her riding.

In a small room behind the Wing Chan Laundry, Sam Blake soaked himself in a steaming bathtub.

His knees pointed in the air. Wing Chan boisterously remarked, "You too tall for bathtub. Not wash whole body same time."

"I'll manage," Sam remarked dryly.

The water felt good, particularly on Sam's somewhat overworked shaft. After a two-and-a-half-year hiatus, it felt particularly good to have made love again.

No, Sam mused, maybe he had never made love before. Before, it had only been intercourse. Just thinking about how freely and enthusiastically Pru had shared herself with him made him start to harden again.

Sam ducked his head under the water. Taking the soap, he lathered his hair and beard thoroughly, then soaped his fur-matted chest and legs. When he quit this vagabond existence, he would bathe every day come hell or high water. Just as soon as he figured out what he wanted to do with himself after he retired from detective work, he would buy a small house and settle down. It was too bad, he mused, that he couldn't use his civil engineering training, but in the dozen years since graduation the field had advanced beyond his catching up.

Sam rinsed his hair and lay back in the tub with his eyes closed. Immediately the image of Prudence Hofheinz filled his mind. How could she have become so dear to him so quickly?

She was a forever kind of woman. True, she had given her precious virginity to him, but she was not the kind of girl one fucked quickly and then discarded. It was too bad he wasn't staying in Rincon. He wouldn't mind courting her.

Suddenly, Sam sat up straight in the tub, unmindful of the water sloshing over. What the hell was he thinking of? Why would a lovely woman like Pru Hofheinz saddle herself to an ugly cuss like him? Things hadn't changed in thirteen years. Sam was certainly no prettier.

Well, he'd come back tonight if possible. Might as well take what he was being so freely given. Who knew when he might meet such a special woman again?

It was past 11:30 when Sam rode back into the courtyard of the Bar M. Clint was sitting on a corral rail, a cigarette dangling from his mouth, his arms folded across his chest.

"I see you finally decided to come back," he snarled.

Sam glared at him. "What are you? My mother?" he snapped back as he dismounted.

"Where the hell have you been all night and morning?"

Holding his horse's reins, Sam responded, "I stayed overnight in town and went to the bank to wire my money back to Santa Fe. The bank didn't open until ten. If just once you'd let the grateful town fathers wire our bounties before we leave the previous town, I wouldn't have to go to all this trouble with these small town banker's hours."

Clint jumped down from the rail and strode up to Sam, who was walking his mount toward the barn. "We've got a problem."

Sam cocked an eyebrow. "We do?"

"Yeah, Arabella Morgan."

Sam laughed. "That doesn't sound like my problem. Usually fine pieces like her are your problem. Me they never notice."

Clint laughed slyly. "Oh, I wouldn't mind getting a taste of that one, but that's not the problem."

The two men reached the barn where Sam led the dun into its assigned stall. Clint looked around to see if anyone was around, then dunked his cigarette butt into the water trough. It sizzled dead.

"Miss Morgan has threatened to go to the Cattlemen's Association and tell them that I'm only a front man for this operation."

Sam leaned against the stall divider and folded his arms. "So, what's the problem? It's time I got my due."

"Shit, Sam, we'll be out on our asses so fast your head'll spin. Her price for her silence is to be included in all our planning and to go along on any mission."

"No!"

"Then we've come to the end of this job."

"She gets wounded or killed and we'll be lucky to get out of here alive," Sam cautioned.

"I won't get wounded or killed," Arabella said from the doorway of the barn where she had just entered. "I'm a damned good shot and an excellent rider. Besides," she said petulantly, "if word gets out about this little bait and switch scam you're running, you won't get another job in Texas. You think anyone will hire you alone, Sam Blake?

Or you on your own, Clint Randolph, if people figure out your partner does the thinking for both of you?"

Anger boiled through Clint. He glared at Arabella and she at him until even Sam could see that there was more than met the eye between them.

"You want to be the brains of the outfit, be the brains. I'm going to the bunkhouse to change into working clothes," Sam said as he exited the barn. "You two figure out what you want to do and let me know."

Chapter 6

Clint charged Arabella and grabbed her by the forearms. "You think I'm stupid! I did all right before Sam came back from the east."

"What *did* you do?"

"I joined the Texas Rangers. I lied about my age and joined when I was sixteen. I was commended twice for bravery."

Arabella tried to throw off his hands, but he just gripped tighter. "So you're brave. That's to be expected from a man in your profession, but you don't know this part of the country, either of you."

"We can learn the area better without a girl tagging along. Are you bored, Miss Morgan? Is that why you want to meddle in this?"

Arabella felt the strength of his hands and the heat through the cotton of her sleeves. Clint's steely eyes seemed to be of limitless depth, draining the defiance right out of her. She could sense the scents of leather, tobacco, sweat and man on him and an odd warmth settled where her legs met her body. It surprised her enough that, instead of answering Clint's challenge, she merely blinked in wonder at the wildly wanton feelings. She felt surrounded by him and as odd as it felt, she liked it.

Clint's grasp loosened as he became aware of the confused intensity in the slight blonde's gaze. Though he was looking in her eyes, he could see the rise and fall of her impressive bosom beneath the modest blouse that exposed little more than the hollow of her throat. The thought of leaning down and kissing that hollow occurred to him.

The moment was frozen in time for both of them.

"God damn it," Clint growled and a breath later he crushed Arabella against his length, their mouths mated. His kiss was hungry against her surprised mouth.

Arabella's eyes snapped open and her body stiffened in her astonishment. Her arms came up and pushed against Clint's chest to put some distance between them. They stood a couple of feet apart. Her fingers touched her mouth, which was tingling from Clint's touch. Her breasts were heaving from the strange emotions warring within her.

She shouldn't want this feeling. Ladies didn't feel like this—Arabella just knew it. No other man had ever made her feel this breathless heat in the depths of her. She should slap his darkly handsome face. She really should. She didn't even like Clint Randolph.

Arabella knew she was lying. She was drawn to his lean, hawkish features, his smoke-roughened voice, the way his eyes shot daggers when he was angry. Maybe she was the wanton hoyden every woman in town—except Prudence—said she was. Maybe she really wasn't a lady deep down inside.

"What are you doing to me?" she asked hoarsely.

"I don't know. I don't understand it myself."

He didn't. Clint Randolph never bothered to get serious about women. He knew the effect his swarthy, exotic good looks had on the opposite sex, but he never involved himself with virgins—especially not the employer's daughter! Far better to pay for his pleasure—no guilt, no consequences. A man had needs, after all. Clint was not the kind of man who could go without for two or three years at a stretch like Sam Blake did. A couple of weeks and he was going crazy, but not so crazy to consider one woman over every other.

But Arabella Morgan was making a hash of Clint's brain. All he wanted to do right now was bury himself so deep inside her that no one could tell where she ended and he began.

He couldn't do that, though. Despite her riding clothes, she was a lady. One didn't toss a woman like her in the hayloft, leave a couple of bucks and go off without a backward glance. She was the kind of woman who made a man think of settling down.

Which took money. Which Clint didn't have.

"Get out of my sight!" he roared, though it was the last thing he really wanted.

Arabella's eyes filled with unshed tears. She blinked twice, then turned on her heels and ran from the barn.

Sam was nearly at the barn door when it slammed open and Arabella ran out, her hands over her mouth.

Sam followed her with his eyes, then stepped into the relative coolness of the barn. He saw the stricken look on Clint's face and glanced down at his partner's jeans. Sam Blake knew a full-on erection when he saw one.

"I can see you told her a thing or two," Sam commented dryly.

"Go to hell, Sam."

"What—and leave you here to suffer alone?" Sam handed his pocket handkerchief to Clint.

Clint looked at the bandanna in his hand. "What's this for?"

Sam raised an eyebrow. "Either a cold compress or a wiping cloth. You can get water in the horse trough either way, but I wouldn't go outside with that hard-on if I were you."

Clint's face reddened dangerously. "Just because it's been so long ago for you that you don't remember..."

Sam cut him off. "It's not so long ago that I would forget, but you're a bastard for mentioning it. You'd better go whack yourself off, partner, before someone who might care notices. When you're ready, I'll be waiting outside. We've got some work to do today." Sam led his horse out of the barn, leaving Clint to his discomfort.

"Miss Hofheinz," said the whining, strident voice. "Miss Hofheinz!" it pierced again.

Prudence snapped out of her reverie to look at thirteen-year-old Laura McCreedy, who was standing in front of the wooden teacher's desk in the large, rectangular classroom. She hadn't any idea how long she had been staring out into space while her students worked on some reading assignment.

"I raised my hand, Miss Hofheinz," Laura insisted. "I raised it ever so long." Lowering her voice to a whisper, she continued, "I need to use the privy, Miss Hofheinz. I can't wait until school's out."

"Of course, Laura," Prudence said quietly, "but you be right back. No dawdling."

The girl nodded and walked out of the schoolroom. Prudence looked at the rest of the class. They were busy with their heads hidden in their books. As usual, Tommy Mather was sleeping instead of reading. Poor boy. Only eleven, he was up before dawn to do chores his father was too hung over to do, then walked three miles to school, only to walk home to more chores on the failing ranch until after dark. No wonder he fell asleep in class. To make matters worse, the boy really needed eyeglasses because the eyestrain was making him even more tired, but his stupid father considered glasses a character flaw. *Tommy ought to talk to Sam*, Pru thought. *He's not ashamed to wear glasses.* She sighed.

Sam. Pru smiled when she thought about the powerful but tender mountain of a man. She pressed her thighs together. She was tender from last night, but it was a nice kind of tender. Feeling the slight ache was to bring back a reminder of how wondrous it felt to have Sam Blake buried deep inside her. She had had no idea that lovemaking was such a wonderful thing.

As she dressed after Sam left that morning, Pru wondered if she looked different. She stared in her looking glass trying to discern if people could tell she was no longer a virgin. Certainly she was fallen, but Pru had trouble being embarrassed about it. Sure enough, the rounded face and roundly curved figure with the wavy brown hair looked the same as she remembered them the day before. But did her eyes look changed? Or was it just that she'd had far less sleep than her custom? It was a wonder she hadn't slept in class herself today!

Funny, everything she had overheard about relations between men and women, spoken in a sort of shorthand by the ladies of the sewing circle, had not prepared her for the sensual banquet on which she had feasted last night. If it was that wonderful for other women, why did they speak of it as if it was a duty and a chore? Sex with Sam Blake had not been anything vaguely resembling a chore. Instead, it was something she could see herself looking forward to again and again.

Maybe it was that Sam was very good at lovemaking. With no frame of reference, Prudence couldn't be certain. She wondered how experienced a man who thought himself as unremittingly ugly as Sam did could be.

Pru wondered if he had ever been married. She suspected not. She tried to imagine what it might be like to be married to someone like Sam Blake.

She shook her head. Even a man who thought himself as physically unattractive as Sam wouldn't want her for a wife. By God, she was already thirty years old!

It suddenly occurred to Pru that she should be feeling soiled and guilty about what had happened the night before. If anything, she only felt guilty about not feeling guilty. It had been *fun*—the last thing she would have ever expected. Despite the discomfort she was feeling between her legs right now—it felt wonderful.

Pru wondered again who it was that had convinced Sam that he was ugly. He was bulky, some might even say fat, but there was nothing soft about his huge chest and belly. He had come to be embarrassed about the wealth of hair on his body, but to Prudence it was a wealth. And he had such nice, caring eyes, both with and without his specs.

Just thinking about lying in bed with Sam's strong arms around her and her head resting on his chest made Prudence feel all hot and hungry again.

She had to get through this school day and get home. It was just possible he might come again this night.

Prudence couldn't remember anything in her life more worth anticipating than that.

It was something she could get used to really quickly.

If only he weren't going away eventually. It would be so nice if he could find an excuse to stay in Rincon.

Or ask her to leave with him.

"One of the horses had a cracked shoe," Sam commented. He was hunkered down on his haunches examining the ground near the arroyo where some Bar M cattle had been slaughtered by vandals. "I wonder if he's still tromping around on it or he's been to the smith."

Clint crouched down beside his partner and reached to finger the hoof print. "Rincon is the only town for thirty miles in any direction. If he got the shoe replaced, that would be the only place he could get it done."

Sam rose slowly. He pulled off his Stetson and ran splayed fingers through his fine hair. He replaced the hat as Clint rose beside him.

"Clint, I can't help thinking that this isn't what it appears to be."

"How do you mean?"

"Morgan seems to be the only victim to suffer any appreciable losses, yet that hilly area where the old mines are supposed to be touches on other ranches."

"Do you think someone's out for revenge against Mr. Morgan in particular and is using the rustling as a decoy?"

Sam stroked his beard thoughtfully. "Actually, I was thinking of something even more sinister than a vendetta."

Clint looked up. "A ven-*what*?"

Sam sighed. "*Ven-DET-ta*," he repeated. "A vow of vengeance."

Clint shrugged. "What were you thinking of?"

"Derry's gang. He usually rides with six or eight others, but there aren't enough hoof prints for that many riders. He's a small time rustler. Uses a running iron to obliterate brands and sells off the steers he's stolen. This is more like destruction for its own sake. Everything I know about Derry doesn't point to this."

"Yeah, but if somebody's paying him to do this, maybe it's worth more to him than the price per head he'd make stealing cattle."

"Possibly. You worked cattle, didn't you?"

Clint nodded. "Yeah, before I joined the Rangers. Miserable work."

Sam nodded. "And dangerous, expensive, time-consuming and risky to man and animal. If there's a drought or stampede or Indians or rustlers it could wipe you out before reaching the railhead. Cattle and cowboys die and find themselves buried in anonymous graves along the trails. Then, to top it off, if you get the herd to the railhead and there's a surplus of cattle, the price could drop so far you don't make a profit, but still have to pay your men their wages."

"Yeah, so?"

Sam tugged on his beard. "I've got something to check out in town. Ride with me and check out the blacksmith about that horseshoe. I need to go back to the ranch first before I go into town."

Clint agreed and they mounted up and headed toward the ranch. When they reached the ranch house, Sam dismounted, swung his reins over the rail and strode into the bunkhouse.

Arabella was on the porch, dressed in her riding clothes, when Clint sat on the porch step and rolled himself a cigarette. He was lighting up when she sat beside him.

"Back so soon?" she asked brightly.

Clint blew out a mouthful of smoke. "Sam has a theory."

Arabella smiled with interest. "Yes?"

"Yes."

"So?"

"So?"

She rolled her eyes. "Is there an echo out here?" The comment seemed to go over Clint's head. "What theory?"

Clint shrugged. "He didn't tell me. It has something to do with cattle drives. I reckon he doesn't think I'll understand his theory."

He sounded so vulnerable that Arabella's heart did a flip-flop. She knew what it was like to be thought stupid. Unlike her plain, plump best friend Prudence who was accepted as smart because she wasn't pretty, the beautiful Arabella was often treated as if her brains had evaporated out of the ends of her gold-colored hair.

Empathetically, she touched Clint's shoulder. She was shocked to feel the strange vibratory heat through his shirt and vest into her hand. In the course of dances and socials, she had had occasion to have contact with a lot of different men. None of them had created the electric connection she had around Clint Randolph. It was unexplainable, They hadn't done more than kiss.

As from a burning stove, she pulled her hand away. The tingling sensation in her hand remained. "Clint—Mr. Randolph," she began, her voice a little strained.

"*Clint's* okay."

"Clint, how much schooling did you actually get?"

Clint had just been about to take another drag on his cigarette when the question stopped him in midair.

"Do you think I'm stupid, too?"

Arabella shook her head. "No. I just wondered. Being smart or stupid seems to be such a sore spot for you."

Clint took a last drag and crushed the butt beneath his boot heel. "I reckon it is. I finished grammar school, which is more than some kids in Texas do. School bored me. Now Sam, he was always the smartest kid in school. He tutored me after class when he wasn't breaking up fist fights I got into because my father was a Carpetbagger."

"He's been your friend a long time."

"Twenty years. Used to be nothing I couldn't tell him. He was like the big brother I didn't have. We even wrote each other when he was away at college, even though the other hands used to rag on me about the *love letters*."

"Love letters?"

Clint shrugged and laughed lightly. "A bad joke. It's just that during the years I did ranch work we wrote almost every week and Sam had this real pretty handwriting, like an artist or something. Anyway, I don't think I would've gotten out of grammar school without Sam's help, so when he went to college, I just quit school. My dad was already dead, so there was nothing to keep me in San Antonio anymore. Without tutoring, I figured high school would be a waste of time. I just packed my duds and rode north. I worked on ranches for a couple of years, then lied about my age and joined the Rangers. My height and Indian blood let me get away with claiming I was already eighteen."

"I wondered if you were part Indian."

Clint laughed. "Yeah, I am, but it's always kind of funny. Folks are always giving credit to my Indian blood for my ability to hunt, ride and track, but my grandfather, or maybe it was my great-grandfather, was a Narragansett."

Arabella frowned. "Narragansett?"

"Yeah, they're a tribe from Connecticut; the kind that lived in permanent lodges and owned community farms and grew corn and squash and such. They're as much like the Sioux or Apache as Chinamen are like Frenchmen. They wouldn't know which end of a buffalo eats and which end sh—um—sits. I grew up in Ohio until my dad decided to make a quick fortune on the fall of the South after the War. I might as well be white, but somehow I got the straight black hair and dark skin. That didn't matter so much in the Rangers."

"Did you like being in the Rangers?"

Clint smiled at the memory. "Yeah. I was good with a horse and a gun, so I got a lot of respect. A lot of the Rangers had even less school than me, so I was looked at as real smart." He sighed again. "Sometimes I think my life was better before Sam came back from college."

"What changed?"

Clint shrugged. "Mostly Sam changed. I mean, he was always bigger and taller than anyone else, and never much of a talker; but he came back from college real sad. He was trained to be some kind of engineer—I'm not sure what they call it—the kind that builds bridges and buildings, not the kind that runs locomotives. But he didn't want to build anything. For about a year all he wanted to do was drink and gamble and drift around. When I ran into him he was lying in a jail cell in some pissant West Texas town, sick as a dog, smelling like a brewery, filthy, his hair wild and long, his beard like a piece of hat felt. He was fat and soft and didn't care much whether he lived or died. I bailed him out, took a leave and dragged him to a hospital in Santa Fe. When he sobered up and cleaned up he still wouldn't tell me what happened in Pennsylvania, but I talked him into joining the Rangers because he was the best with a gun I've ever seen. I figured I could keep an eye on him so he wouldn't turn into a drunk again. For the better part of five years we Rangered together and then about five years ago we resigned and went to work for ourselves. At first we were equal partners in everything but Sam was so quiet—almost shy—that folks did more talking to me. Next thing I knew, instead of being partners in folks' minds I became the leader and Sam my sidekick. Then people started to think that Sam was this big stupid hulk and I was the smart one, even though he's the one that makes most of the decisions. I'm just realizing how much it's hurt him and how much he's kept it inside him."

"So now he's leaving you out of the decision-making?"

Clint cocked his head. "I was never really in it, but at least we discussed what he was thinking so I could talk to the folks that hire us and sound halfway smart. I don't know what I'm going to tell your father."

Arabella brightened. "You could say, 'we're exploring several leads right now.' Wouldn't that work?"

Clint grinned. "Yeah! 'Several leads.'" He pulled Arabella to him and kissed her hard. Unprepared, Arabella stiffened for a moment, then relaxed into his arms.

"Are you going to lollygag, or do you want to get to work?" Sam's voice pierced through the haze of desire.

Clint and Arabella pulled apart, Arabella blushing and nervously brushing down her skirt. Clint's eyes narrowed in rage. He rose from the porch steps, his hand instinctively poised over his pistol.

"Clint," Arabella hissed, "he's still your partner."

Clint turned and glared at her.

"Let it go, love," she whispered. "Just do the job and let him go his way when you're through. I'll be here when you want me."

Clint felt himself relax. He walked over to Wind Dancer and mounted up next to Sam. Without a word, the men rode off.

Arabella watched them until they were out of sight. She realized that she had just declared her love for the tall, dark detective.

"That was, without a doubt, the nastiest thing I've ever heard you say," Clint snapped at Sam as they rode toward Rincon. "Even when you were sobering up you weren't such a prick."

Sam rode silently, declining to answer.

"Don't ignore me, you son of a bitch."

"You want to screw the employer's daughter, go right ahead, but if it costs us the fee the Cattlemen's Association put up, so help me, friend or no friend, I'll put a bullet in you."

Clint could not recall ever hearing such venom.

"You're jealous."

Sam blanched. "I am not."

Clint slapped his thigh and laughed. "You are. It's come to that. You're interested in Arabella yourself."

"It's Arabella now, is it?"

"Why wouldn't it be?"

"Why the hell would I be interested in a spoiled little rich girl like Miss Morgan?"

"More likely, why would she ever be interested in you?" Light suddenly dawned on Clint. "It isn't Arabella. It's women in general. Are we busting up this partnership because I can get a girl and you can't?"

"It's everything!" Sam exclaimed. "It's the girls who can't keep their hands off you. It's the mayors and ranchers who treat me like I'm invisible. It's sleeping in bunkhouses while you sleep in the guestrooms. And it's realizing that if I'm right about this case, we're not going to get paid. I'm thirty-four years old. I'm tired of drifting."

Clint halted his horse and raised one hand. "Hold up a minute there. What do you mean we won't get paid?"

Sam halted his dun. "Ethan Morgan's supposedly putting up most of the money, right?"

"Yeah."

"Do you know anything about insurance?"

"You pay a little bit every month and if you die it pays your widow what it costs to bury you and maybe a little bit more."

"That's one kind. But people get insurance for other reasons. Like if a house burns down or a store gets robbed or a ship sinks and destroys a cargo."

"So?"

"Remember what I said about cattle drives when we were out in the pasture?"

"Uh-huh."

"What if a person saw the opportunity to make the same money as he would on a cattle drive without hiring any hands or trekking north to the railhead two or three months. You think he might be tempted to take it?"

"I reckon."

"There's an insurance agent in Rincon. I saw his office when I was there this morning. I want to ask him some questions about insurance. In the meantime, you need to go to the smithy and see if anyone has brought in a horse with a cracked shoe in the last couple of weeks. Then check the land office about who's filed any mining claims in the last six months to a year. Then go to the saloon and listen to see if any of the Derry Gang drops any information about who hired them, if anyone. I'll meet you there to compare notes."

"Okay, but I don't understand."

"If I'm right, we've been hired to be patsies for a little con game called insurance fraud."

Chapter 7

The sign read "George Tyler—Notary Public—Insurance." Sam yanked his vest down—wishing he'd thought to wear his suit again—brushed the dust from his clothes and walked in.

George Tyler was a skinny little man, about fifty, with graying brown hair combed over a bald spot and slicked down with hair tonic. He wore a plaid Norfolk suit and a high, starched collar.

"May I help you?" he said, his hand outstretched.

Sam took the proffered hand and shook it carefully. He sat in the chair Tyler offered.

"I wanted to talk to you about insurance," Sam began.

The little man brightened. With a broad smile, he said, "I've just the thing. It's a $10,000.00 accidental death and dismemberment policy with a double indemnity clause. Only twenty-five cents monthly premiums."

Sam nodded. "That's fine, but I was more interested in insurance on property than on my life right now."

Tyler looked the big man over. "Rancher, huh?"

"Cattle are an interest of mine, but it occurs to me that there are a lot of risks in getting cattle to market. Is it possible to get insurance to protect my investment if something were to happen on my next cattle drive?"

"Young man," Tyler said confidently, "for the right premium, you can insure anything, including a presidential election."

Sam chuckled. "I'll remember that the next time I run for President. But seriously, if I wanted to get insurance on my cattle, where would I go?"

Tyler grinned. "Actually, until a few years ago, there weren't a lot of options. There still aren't. But there's a new company out of Denver called Stockmen's Mutual that's writing all sorts of stock policies, including what I think you may need—and there's always Lloyd's Underwriters of London. They'll insure anything given the right premium. I can wire either company and get you a quotation in a few days now that there's a transatlantic cable between New York and London."

Sam nodded and stroked his beard thoughtfully. "Sounds interesting...Got any references about these companies?"

Tyler wrinkled his brow. "Stock insurance is still pretty new, but I've sold Stockmen's Mutual policies to Ethan Morgan and Pete McKinley in the last couple of years. This year, with the Derry Gang attacking cattle ranches around here, it's possible both of them may have to file claims against the policies. I hear tell that the Cattlemen's

Association hired some hotshot range detective to capture the Derry Gang. I hope he shoots them to vulture meat."

Sam kept his face composed.

"So," Tyler said, picking up his steel pen and placed a piece of paper in front of him, "If you'll give me the particulars about your ranch, I'll be glad to wire Denver for a quote."

Sam tipped his hat politely. "I'm afraid I don't have them handy. I was just inquiring. I should be back in a few days for a quote."

Tyler wished Sam well and the big man left, realizing Tyler had never asked his name. Typical!

Pete McKinley had a spread that touched on the mountains and bordered the Bar M, but based on the Cattlemen's Association record, he had not lost any cattle to vandalism and only a few to rustlers in the preceding six months.

Sam hurried to the telegraph office.

STOCKMEN'S MUTUAL INSURANCE COMPANY

DENVER, COLORADO

REQUIRE ASSISTANCE IN INVESTIGATION STOP PLEASE ADVISE ISSUANCE OF STOCK POLICY FOR ANY INSUREDS VICINITY RINCON TEXAS STOP ALSO ADVISE REWARD FOR PROOF OF FRAUD STOP WIRE RESPONSE RINCON TEXAS STOP S BLAKE B AND R AGENCY STOP

Sam instructed the telegrapher to hold any telegrams for him to collect. He then sent a similar wire to the New York office of Lloyd's Underwriters.

The Rincon saloon was like a hundred other saloons in a hundred other Texas towns. It was dark and smelled of stale liquor, stale smoke and stale sweat. Drinking tables and card tables were scattered around, while the late afternoon's deepening shadows brought down the soiled doves to begin their night's work.

Sam walked through the batwing doors, hearing the faint squeaks that meant they were overdue for an oiling. As his eyes adjusted to the dimness, he saw Clint sitting alone at a corner table, a beer in front of him and a cigarette dangling from his mouth.

Sam walked to the bar and quietly ordered a cup of coffee, ignoring the raised eyebrow of the bartender. Fortunately, the bartender merely poured the coffee and took the nickel it cost.

He sat in a chair next to Clint and waved away some of the cigarette smoke as he set down his mug.

"Find anything?" he said without preamble.

Clint nodded. In a low voice he said, "Checked with the smith. He replaced three cracked shoes in the last two weeks. One was the local preacher's, one was from the undertaker's team and the third belonged to Ethan Morgan."

Sam nodded grimly. "And the land office?"

"There have been several mining claims for mountain lands filed in the name of Morningstone Mining Company. The signatures on the claims all say Peter McKinley."

Sam took a sip of his coffee. It tasted good on his dry throat. "The insurance agent has sold two stock insurance policies; one to Ethan Morgan and the other to Pete McKinley. Morgan's had vandalism, both have had rustling. It all makes sense."

"You'd better tell me straight out," Clint said. "I'm obviously not smart enough to figure it out myself."

Sam ignored the remark. "Depending on the response to my wires, my guess if that our dear host and his neighbor are planning a major insurance swindle. I'm not sure whether they've hired the Derry Gang to do it or are trying to lay off the blame on them because Jack Derry's been hanging around town lately, but one way or another one of them is going to suffer a major covered loss and split the proceeds with the other. It's a new form of dirt-free rustling."

Clint blew out a cloud of smoke in wonder. "But Sam, if Mr. Morgan is going to commit this swindle, why has he asked us to stay on his spread?"

Sam took a deep breath and let it out. "If you're one of the biggest wheels in the Cattlemen's Association and you're the one doing the stealing, what better way to make it seem like simple cattle rustling than invite your detectives right into the middle of it and hope they aren't savvy enough to see below the surface appearance. Which, you have to admit, most of our compatriots wouldn't have the smarts for."

"Including me."

"Clint, in this you would be in the majority. If I hadn't spent most of my last year in college working for an insurance company, it might not have occurred to me either."

Clint frowned. "I thought your old man left you enough money to get through college without working."

"He did, for bare basics. I needed extra money, so I took a job to make up the difference. I learned a little something about insurance while I was working for Great Pennsylvania that I never figured would come in handy again. I just wonder if Miss Morgan knows about the plot. Work on her," Sam finished.

Clint's dark eyes flashed his anger, even in the dimly lit saloon. "Work on her! You think she's involved?"

"I don't know, but she'd be a good decoy if she is. Keep your concentration fixed below your belt buckle while they perpetrate the fraud."

Clint had to admit to himself that a niggling doubt crept over him. Arabella had certainly come on to him far more rapidly than he would have expected a lady to do. Sam was right about so many things. He could be right about this. Arabella claimed to want to become involved in the investigation. Could that be a way to keep him and Sam off track?

Sam finished his coffee and rose from the table.

"Going somewhere?" Clint asked.

Sam grinned sheepishly. "Have to see a man about a dog. Then I'm headed out."

Clint sipped his beer as his partner strode out of the saloon. He didn't want to believe Arabella could be involved in a fraud scheme. He realized he was becoming obsessed with the blond beauty. He decided he had to think of something else.

A poker game was beginning at another table. Picking up his glass, Clint strode over to the table and asked in.

"New in these parts?" asked a bone-slender, mustached man whose fine suit and ruffled shirt marked him as a professional gambler.

"Yeah," Clint said noncommittally.

"Name's Caldwell," said the gambler.

"Randolph."

Another man at the table, a short, unshaven man with greasy brown hair and rat-like eyes said, "Randolph. As in Clint Randolph?"

Clint nodded.

"You're the detective the Cattlemen's Association hired to find out who's been killing cows," said another player, a cowhand who was chewing on a matchstick.

Clint nodded again. No sense denying the obvious.

"You're famous," said the cowhand.

"So they say," Clint responded.

"Does the Association have an idea who's doing it?" Caldwell asked as he shuffled his chips with one manicured hand.

"They say the Derry Gang," Clint said. No sense trying to deal with Sam's complicated insurance fraud theory. The Association plainly suspected Derry, and Clint wasn't so sure he didn't have more faith in them than Sam of late.

The color drained from the face of the rat-eyed man. "What do you think?" he snapped as all eyes except Clint's focused on him immediately.

Clint's eyes narrowed. "Jack Derry?"

"You got it. And I ain't wanted in this here county, Randolph."

"You'll be more than wanted if we catch you near any cattle, Derry."

"Cash me out, Perce," Derry snarled as he rose and pushed his chips at Caldwell. "The air in here just got too thick to enjoy poker." Taking up his cash, he strode to the bar, bought a full bottle of whiskey and strode out the door with it.

Clint rose, but Caldwell grabbed his arm. "He's not going far, Mr. Randolph. In an hour he'll be passed out in his room at Mrs. Lester's. Why don't you just set a spell and play a few hands? Even if he's your man, I doubt he'll be stealing any cattle tonight."

Jack Derry didn't stay long in his room in the boarding house. Instead, he merely sneaked the bottle upstairs—Mrs. Lester didn't allow spirits—came back downstairs and mounted his horse to ride through the deepening darkness out of town.

A short time later he rode up to the Bar M Ranch. He dismounted and stealthily made his way around to the window of Ethan Morgan's study.

Morgan sat at his desk, working on ledgers. A smoldering cigar sat in an ashtray. The rancher pressed his fingers to his tired eyes and rubbed slowly. He looked up when he heard a tap on the window.

His face paled when he saw the outlaw. He quickly walked to the window and pushed it open.

"What are you doing here?" he hissed.

"Let me in and I'll tell you." The outlaw climbed in the window as Morgan went to his study door and locked it. Turning around, he snapped, "Now, what are you doing here?"

"I met that dick you hired, the breed. Where do you get off telling him that I'm in on this? That wasn't part of the plan."

"What do you care? You're being well paid when we're done, more than enough for a good life in Mexico like you said you wanted."

Derry shook his head. "I hear tell Randolph is a hell of a shot. All the money in the world ain't gonna help me if I'm dead."

"You aren't going to be dead," Morgan said, hoping he was lying. He and McKinley had too much at stake to share the proceeds with a greasy little rustler. "In a week the plan is we start rounding up for branding. You and your boys meld into the cowhands, set fire to the range and send the cattle toward Canados Ravine. The cattle fall in the ravine, we fire the hands, file the claims and our financial problems are solved. As soon as the insurance company pays off, we split the proceeds and you're off to *la vida buena*. When the cattle die racing away from a prairie fire, no one will suspect a put up job. It'll happen so fast all that will be left is a pea-wit range detective with an inflated reputation trying to find rustlers that don't exist."

"And while all this planning is going on, his eyes are gonna be on me."

"And most of your gang has hired on as hands for McKinley. We'll have that detective and his big, stupid mountain of a sidekick traveling around in circles—when he isn't sniffing around my girl's skirts."

"She in on it?"

Morgan shook his head. "Not a chance. The more innocent she is, the better distraction for Randolph because she can't tell him anything she doesn't know. By the way, how are your fellows doing on McKinley's spread?"

Derry shrugged. "Idiot bastards. Some of them actually *like* being cowboys. Always knew honest work could ruin a man."

Morgan laughed mirthlessly. "I wonder how you'll handle the honest life."

"Shit, I've got a good little wife in Mexico whose father owns a cantina. With the money I'll get for this job, maybe I'll just build rooms on for an inn of some kind. I'm getting onto thirty. Rustling is a young man's game."

If you live long enough to collect, Morgan thought. "Look, Derry, Randolph is staying here. I had to do that to avert suspicion. You'd better skedaddle before he comes back from town."

Derry was halfway out the window when he turned back. "You double cross me and—so help me—you won't come out of this con alive." He wheeled his other leg out the window and blended into the darkness as Morgan heard knocking on his study door.

"Papa, is everything all right?" he heard Arabella's voice through the door.

Ethan walked to the door and unlocked it. "Of course, sweetheart. I just had some serious accounting to do and didn't want to be disturbed."

Arabella walked over to the desk. A quick glance at the ledger told her the balances were not what they should be.

"Papa, are we in financial difficulty?"

Ethan stiffened. "Why would you ask that?"

Arabella tapped the ledger. "These numbers. I recognize what parentheses mean." She looked again more carefully. "Papa, if these figures are accurate, we're in serious debt."

Ethan laughed nervously. "Nothing you have to worry your pretty head about. A good roundup and cattle drive and we'll be back on top."

"I don't know," Arabella said thoughtfully, fingering the ledger. "You shouldn't keep these things from me, Papa. I'm not a child. You sent me to college."

Laughing condescendingly, he walked over to the desk and shut the ledger. Putting his hand on his daughter's shoulder, he said, "Sweetheart, I sent you to college hoping you'd meet some nice boy from a good family and get married. After all, what future is there for a college-educated girl? You want to end up an old maid like your friend Prudence?"

"Then you think I'm stupid."

"I never said that, honey. But when a girl is as pretty as you, she doesn't have to be a genius. How'd you like to spend the summer in San Antonio with your Aunt Edith? I'm sure you'll find a nice young man."

Arabella pulled away from her father. "Maybe I don't want a nice young man who wants me to be pretty and brainless. Maybe I could run this ranch at least as well as you can."

"Don't be ridiculous, Arabella. This is man's work."

"Everything is man's work until women start doing it, then it becomes nearly worthless as an occupation."

Ethan's face reddened with anger. "Where did you hear that tripe, from that bluestocking schoolteacher? No wonder nobody would look at her twice, even in a part of Texas where the men still outnumber the women by a fair piece."

"That's unkind, Father. Prudence is the best friend I've ever had."

"That doesn't change the truth about her."

Arabella suddenly felt very sad. She turned away from the desk and walked out of the study, needing fresh air very badly.

Ethan Morgan watched her leave. By this time next month, they could both be rid of this ranch and living well in San Antonio, San Francisco or even Europe on the proceeds of the insurance claim. Even if he sold the ranch for the value of the mortgage, it would be enough. He'd find her a wealthy husband and live comfortably the rest of his life.

Prudence sat at her desk correcting papers. She absently played with a stray lock of hair.

She was wearing her hair down. Ever since she got home after school and buying fixings for her lonely supper, she had pulled all the pins from her hair and brushed it out. But instead of braiding it, Prudence left it down. She had taken a bath and put on the silk kimono her father had sent her for Christmas. Even though the sleeves sometimes caught on papers and desk drawers, she loved the ankle-length, heavy silk robe. No wonder Japanese women moved so smoothly if they wore such garments! Although she hadn't seen her father in nine years, he always seemed to know what she would like.

The knock on the door startled her. No one ever came calling this time of night. A brief hope filled her heart as she padded toward the door.

Prudence opened the door a crack. The huge figure in the doorway was unmistakable.

"You came back," she breathed, a small smile playing about her lips.

Sam smiled broadly. "I said I'd try."

"I'm so glad. Did you put—what is your horse's name?"

Sam shook his head. "He doesn't have one. There's an old Indian saying that you shouldn't give a name..."

"...to something you might have to eat. I know it. Well, did you put Nameless in the shed?"

"I did."

Pru drew Sam inside, closing the door behind them. No sooner was the door closed than he dropped the saddlebag from his shoulder and crushed her to him, pressing his mouth against hers and caressing her with his lips and tongue until her knees threatened to give out from under her.

Pru pulled away, gasping for breath and looked at the big man. "You got your hair and beard trimmed."

Sam stroked his beard. "You noticed," he said, realizing she was the only one who had.

Pru stroked his bearded cheek. "I like it. It's sort of *shaped* now. Not that I didn't like it before," she added hastily.

Sam looked at Pru. Her hair fell in heavy waves about her face and the kimono hugged her full figure. To Sam's eyes, she looked quite delicious.

"You look wonderful."

Pru looked down, embarrassed. "That's kind of you."

Sam lifted her chin with a big, gentle hand. "I'm not being kind, Pru. Only truthful. I think you look wonderful. Were you okay today?"

Pru blushed. "Fine, just a little sore."

"I'm sorry."

"I'm not. Except that, instead of concentrating on my students, I kept thinking how I got sore and wishing I could be doing it again. Then I'd feel guilty."

"Guilty. About making love with me?"

"No," Pru responded with a nervous laugh, "guilty about not feeling guilty. Hoping you'd come back, but not being sure you would."

Sam reached down and picked up his saddlebag and opened up one side. He pulled a small, paper-wrapped package and handed it to Pru. "I brought you a present."

Pru smiled broadly. "Oh, Sam, you didn't have to."

"I know."

"I love presents."

"And I'll bet you don't get many."

"No, only from my father on Christmas and my birthday."

Prudence tore off the paper. "*A Midsummer Night's Dream.* Oh, Sam, I love Shakespeare."

"I kind of figured you might."

Pru opened the cover. Sam had written something on the flyleaf in a beautiful Spencerian script.

She read, "*Haply I think on thee, and then my state,*

Like to the lark at break of day arising

From sullen earth, sings hymns at heaven's gate;

For thy sweet love remember'd such wealth brings

That then I scorn to change my state with kings.

"From The Sonnets," she commented. "You write so beautifully. I mean your handwriting."

"Just a little something I picked up along the way."

"You are such a mystery, Sam Blake. So many contradictions. A person could spend a lifetime learning about you."

"I suppose—if one wanted to."

"Sam, are you hungry? I could make you some eggs or something."

Sam grinned slyly. "I'm hungry, Pru, but not for food."

Pru set down the book and reached for Sam's hands. With a sensual smile, she put one of his hands on the obi holding her kimono closed. Taking the cue, he pulled on the sash and the bow came undone, causing the kimono to fall open and reveal Prudence's lush curves to his eyes.

Pru watched Sam's eyes as the pupils dilated slightly when he looked at her. His large, strong hands settled on either side of her waistband and drew up her sides and under her round, firm breasts. She held her breath as his hands brushed across her nipples until they hardened under his touch. She reached her arms around his neck and buried her fingers in his thick curls as she drew his face down to meet hers. His kiss was gentle, almost shy. He nibbled teasingly on her lower lip until she made little moans of building pleasure.

He reached down to lift her into his arms.

"No, Sam!" she cried, "I'm too heavy for that."

He lifted her anyway. True, it wasn't as easy as if she'd been slimmer, but for a strong giant like Sam Blake it was not much of an effort. He carried her into her bedroom and laid her gently on the bed. Pru opened her arms and invited him into her embrace. In a matter of moments, Sam stripped himself of his clothes and spectacles and stood naked and ready for her.

Sam lay down on the bed, halfway over Pru, straddling her with his arms, putting weight on his forearms so as not to put his full bulk on her. Pru could feel the tickle of his chest hair and beard against her skin. He kissed her tenderly again and again, touching her jaw, eyelids and forehead as much as her mouth. Pru could feel the firmness of his arousal against her hip. She reached her hand down his body and stroked the pulsating shaft as her lover gasped with the sensation.

Hoisting himself to his knees, he positioned himself between legs that opened readily for him. He touched her sex, feeling through the dark thatch to find her pleasure center and stroked firmly. She was ready for him.

"Please, Sam," she begged, "I need you inside me."

Sam plunged deeply. Pru's hips rose to meet his as they settled into an age old rhythm neither of them had to be taught. Pru could see the sweat bead Sam's face as he strained and felt herself seem to rise from the bed in intense desire as she met his surging thrusts.

Sam's face showed the strain his control was bringing.

"Please, love," Pru crooned, "come to me."

With a cry, Sam emptied himself deep within her, then relaxed, still inside her, resting on her briefly, even in his ecstasy cognizant of his weight. After a few moments, he rolled off and beside her and took her into his arms. She rested with her head on his shoulder and one hand nestled in the matting on his chest, her hips rolled up against his.

In that position, they dozed lightly for a time, though Sam awoke first to feel Pru's warm breath ruffling his body hair. He would have sworn he no longer believed in fate. Certainly since leaving Pennsylvania he no longer believed in God. To believe that something outside of himself put Prudence Hofheinz and Samuel Blake in the same small Texas town when both were in need of a passionate encounter was hard to fathom. Yet here they were in Rincon, Texas in the spring of 1885. Sam knew he should be wary and watch his heart. Women didn't like him. He was a fat, ugly, oversized man. He wouldn't be staying long in this two-bit town anyway. He should consider himself fortunate he had found a girl whom he didn't have to pay for his pleasure. Instead, he found a girl—a woman, he corrected in his mind—completely and unabashedly sensuous who seemed to find his big, ungainly self attractive. If he wasn't careful, he might find himself in love with her—and that would be too dangerous. He told himself he should just take his pleasure as he found it.

Through her closed eyelids, Pru could sense that Sam was lowering the lantern until the bedroom was almost dark. Funny how she hadn't noticed she had been able to see him in the well-lit bedroom when they'd made love both this night and last. It felt cozy in the dark.

The next sensation was so unbelievable, Prudence wasn't sure she felt it. Then she felt a tickle on the soft rounds of her buttocks and realized that the tickle was Sam's beard brushing against her backside. *My God,* she thought, *it can't be his* ***tongue!***

But he did it again and there was no doubt. The lightning shot through Prudence.

"Sam!" she cried, "What do you think you're doing?"

He pressed a kiss on her mons. Calmly but playfully, he responded, "The Latin term is cunnilingus. It has several vulgar terms, none of which you need to know to enjoy it."

"You like this?"

"Hmmm," he said as he resumed. "I'm liking it very much. Relax. You may like it, too."

He began to lick, kiss and nibble on her soft flesh, swirling around the swollen nub of sexual desire until Pru thought she might go mad. If she had ever thought the sensations she'd experienced before now had been pleasure, they didn't come close to compare to this. Her head twisted from side to side, her hands gripped the sheets in a death grip and her hips rose against his teasing mouth as she moaned out her building pleasure. Vaguely she felt Sam's big hands slip under her buttocks to give himself greater access to her, but it seemed as if her brain was melting into the sensations building like a prairie fire from her sexual center and racing outwards. Long, warm strokes up and down, punctuated by kisses, nibbles and nuzzles raised her temperature until she felt like she was burning hot. Her body shone with sweat and she cried out uncontrollably as he raised her senses higher and higher.

Suddenly, Pru screamed as the most intense pleasure streaked through her and she shuddered in pure sensation over and over again. Her breathing was labored and ragged, as if she had just run a mile.

But Sam didn't stop. For what could have been mere minutes or hours on end he continued to pleasure her, causing repeats of the string of climaxes that shattered every notion of physical love she had ever imagined.

Pru was so completely satiated with pleasure she barely felt the large hardness of Sam's swollen shaft slipping inside her. Through heavy-lidded eyes she watch him moving over her and inside her until, with a sudden stiffness and strain, he flooded her with his essence. Then, resting on his elbows and still lodged within her, Sam leaned down and kissed her eyelids and mouth.

Gradually, he pulled out of her and rolled beside her, lying diagonally on the bed. He gathered her pleasure-limp body against his and stroked her dark hair as she cuddled against him in deep, exhausted slumber.

Sam Blake was in love.

Heaven help them both!

Chapter 8

Sam lay still in the dark, unable to sleep. Pru lay along his side. Her breasts were pressed against his ribcage, one leg thrown across his hips, one hand nestled in the thick, soft matting on his chest as her breathing ruffled his beard. Sam knew he could gladly spend every night in just this manner.

But, restless this night, he gently maneuvered Pru off him and covered her with the sheet and coverlet after he pulled himself out of bed. His love was deeply asleep and snuggled against her pillow with a deep sigh.

Not bothering to pull on his denims or his drawers, Sam padded into the main room. The moonlight was bright enough for him to find the matches to light a lamp. The candle reflected off the mirror reflector behind it, magnifying the light. Lifting the lamp, Sam explored the main room, trying to learn more about the woman who had become so very important to him so rapidly.

He went first to her bookcase. The books a person read said a lot about him—or in this case, her. Pru had a small collection of classic books bound in good leather bindings—the expensive kind, but she also had a collection of cheap, dime Western novels and romances. She had a Bible, but it lacked the well broken-in spine of a book read often. Far more worn were her copies of *Jane Eyre, Huckleberry Finn* and *Tom Jones* as well as several copies of Shakespeare plays. Sam was pleased to note that she didn't already have *A Midsummer Night's Dream.*

He walked over to the kitchen area. Her china was stacked neatly on a couple of cupboard shelves. He picked up a plate. Even the dim candlelight shone through the china. Sam was surprised. Only the best, most expensive bone china was translucent. Curious, he turned the plate over. It was from Limoges, the finest makers of porcelain in Europe—and the most expensive. Her wineglasses were leaded cut crystal and there was a matching set of cut crystal tumblers.

Sam had suspected that the furnishing of this rough cabin were castoffs provided by the town council, but that august body would never provide fine china and crystal and leather-bound books to a mere schoolmarm. Sam wondered who had given Pru those kinds of expensive possessions. She had said her father was a butcher. Sam Blake had no notion of how much money a butcher made, but he doubted it was the kind of money that could provide these luxuries in the wilderness. He felt an unbelievable stab of jealousy at the sight of the photograph. Then he chided himself for his foolishness. He had known her all of two and a half days. Of course she would have had a life before him—as she would have one afterwards. She lived and worked in this town. She would be here long after he was gone.

If Sam was right in his suspicions, he would make no friends in this town. Ethan Morgan's daughter was Pru's best friend. What would Pru say if he proved that her best friend's father was an insurance cheat?

He and Clint would be lucky if they weren't ridden out of town on a rail when this business was through!

Out of curiosity, Sam counted the dishes and glasses. Pru had a complete service for twelve of each. Apparently nothing was broken. That in itself was almost amazing. Carefully, he replaced the plate he had taken.

Sam hadn't even noticed the quality of the china this morning when Pru made breakfast. The Morgans hadn't served dinner on china this fine. The last time he remembered eating on fine bone china was—Philadelphia.

Cynthia.

The name brought forth memories that clutched at Sam's stomach like a vise. All the comfort he felt in this cabin that allowed him to walk around naked fled him and he became aware of his big, ungainly, hairy body with the oversized hands, feet and—whatever.

His clothes were in the bedroom. Sam padded back, picking up his jeans and drawers as he approached the bed.

Pru stretched luxuriously in the bed like a satisfied, well-fed cat and open her dark eyes slowly. A glorious smile stretched across her mouth.

"Is it morning?" she asked.

"No, not yet."

She lifted the blanket to reveal herself to him. "Come back in. I miss you."

Sam dropped the clothes where he stood. He accepted the invitation and was greeted with her arms about his as she drew the blanket over them both and nuzzled her nose against his chest.

"Who gave you the fine china and crystal?"

"You took a good look around, didn't you?" she said defensively. "Just because I'm a schoolmarm doesn't mean I can't have nice things." Pru rolled away from him.

"I didn't mean to offend you."

"I'm not offended," Pru bit out.

"I'm such an oaf sometimes."

Pru hugged herself under the covers. "People make assumptions about schoolteachers. We're expected to be emotionless, genderless, impoverished creatures with no families and no lives beyond our students. My father is a good businessman and we're in regular contact by mail. He makes sure I'm all right and sends me presents on my birthday and Christmas. If I ever wanted to quit teaching and go home to Chicago, I'd be welcome. But there's nothing in particular back home. I don't care much for teaching, but I like the independence of being able to earn my own living. If I choose to spend my money on nice things, isn't that my business?"

Sam rested his hand lightly on Pru's arm. "Of course it's your business. I don't know why I got so damned jealous. It's just that such fine things seem so incongruous in this house. You have to admit this place is little more than one step above a log cabin."

"The use of the house and furniture were provided by the Town Council as part of my wages. I had little choice in them other than reupholstering the shabbiest donations." She sighed. "I suppose most women spend their money on clothes or jewels instead of tableware and upholstery. My clothes are well made and I have enough of them considering what a social butterfly I am," she added cynically. "I sure don't need fancy jewelry in a two-bit town like Rincon. What do I need beyond a reliable watch and a couple pair of ear-bobs?"

A plain gold band might do nicely, Sam thought, but didn't voice his surprising revelation. Sam had sworn long ago he would never marry. Not since the debacle with Cynthia. What was putting it into his head now? Such thoughts were hopeless. He had no chance that a sweet lady like Prudence Hofheinz would want to marry an ugly oaf like him, even if she did enjoy his lovemaking. She was certainly not emotionless or genderless. Her passion was genuine, her femaleness obvious, his attraction to her real. In Sam's eyes she was a lush and beautiful woman—the kind who deserved forever.

He leaned over, brushed a lock of Pru's hair off her cheek and kissed her tenderly. "Pru, sweetheart," he said, "you don't need any enhancements. You are lovely just as you are. I wouldn't change you."

Prudence blinked back tears—tears of joy. No one had ever been so complimentary of her. Why of all times did she manage to fall in love with a man who would be gone from this town and her life within a few days or weeks? A part of her told her that she should ask him to leave her house and leave her alone before his leaving broke her heart. The other part of her screamed to accept from him all the care and loving he could give her as long as he was here, knowing as well as she did that once he was gone, she would go back to being a lonely, undesired spinster. Eventually, Arabella would marry and Prudence would completely inhabit the half-world of unmarried women who care for other women's children.

But Sam Blake was not Edward Rochester. He was just a wandering troubleshooter drifting from job to job and probably gunfight to gunfight. It was already too late. He would leave and her heart would be broken, but it wouldn't be Sam who broke her heart. It was Prudence's own fault if her heart was broken. She had allowed herself to get into this pickle.

"Sam," she said sadly, "would you hold me, please? I need to feel your warmth around me."

"Oh, sweetheart, of course." He pulled her against him so her back rested against his chest and his arms came around her, resting just beneath her breasts. Gently, lovingly, he stroked her ribs and belly as he breathed in the faint scent of her fragrant hair. "Do you think you can sleep a while longer?"

"Um-hmm."

"Good. I didn't mean to wear you out."

Pru leaned against him. "It was a nice kind of wearing out. Do other women enjoy it when you do that to them?"

Sam took a deep breath and let it out slowly before he answered, almost inaudibly. "I don't know. I never wanted to do it with another woman before."

"Sam," Pru said strangely, her voice a caress, her stomach a knot at the import of those words. She linked her fingers through his and squeezed them softly. For the first time she began to think that perhaps her love for him was returned. But he hadn't said so, and she didn't dare voice her own emotions.

All she could do was enjoy their closeness for as long as she could and make the memory of it last a long, lonely lifetime after Sam Blake and his partner rode off into the sunset.

Chapter 9

Prudence awoke the next morning sprawled on her bed, alone. It was just after dawn, judging by the sun through her window curtains.

She sighed deeply as she drank in the mingled scent of herself and the man who had shared her bed last night. *He must have left during the night,* she thought sadly, as she rolled out of bed and yanked on her kimono. She pushed her tangled hair out of her face and pulled the obi tightly around her waist as she walked barefoot into the main room.

To her surprise and delight, Sam was standing in front of the stove, a wooden spoon in one hand and a quilted hot pad in the other. On the back of the stove, the large kettles she used to heat bath water were sitting, steam rising from their spouts. The tub was standing in front of the fireplace with fresh towels hung over its edge. On the front of the stove, two skillets were standing.

Sam was fully dressed except for his hat and gunbelt. He turned with a grin on his face. "Good morning, sleepyhead," he said gaily.

"I hate a man who's so cheerful in the morning!" Pru growled.

Sam quirked an eyebrow above his specs. "Oh, and how many have you known?"

Pru snorted. "Only you. Daddy is a grouch in the morning."

Sam stirred the contents of one skillet with the wooden spoon, then put it down and picked up a fork, which he used to lift strips of bacon onto a plate. Quickly he carried the plate of bacon strips to the table and returned to the stove, picking up the skillet with the hot pad and using the wooden spoon to spoon scrambled eggs onto two plates.

"I hope you like eggs and onions," he said as he moved the two skillets to a pan of water in the sink. "There's tea in the pot under the cozy," he added, gesturing with his head.

Pru sat at the table, feeling very cared for. She pulled off the cozy and poured out tea for both of them. Sam slipped into the chair at right angles from her.

Pru took a bite. "This is delicious. I would never have pegged you for the domestic type."

Sam shrugged. "When you travel as much as Clint and I do, you have to learn to cook. It's a treat to cook on a stove instead of a campfire."

Pru chewed thoughtfully. "Sam, have you ever thought about giving up a traveling life and settling down?"

A relentless hand wrapped itself around Sam's gut and squeezed tightly. Until a week ago the thought had not entered his mind in twelve years. Now it was central in his thoughts, wrapped up in the hopeless dream of reprising such a scene as this, a quiet breakfast in a cheery room with a loving woman flirting with him over a tea cup.

It could never happen. Not to Sam Blake. He was too big and ugly for any woman to want.

"Yeah, it's crossed my mind, I guess."

Pru saw his face close up, shielding his emotions. She knew she shouldn't ask any further. It was obvious it was useless to hope that he could possibly want to settle down with her. Despite his compliments, she was too fat, too plain, too old for any man to want.

Well, breakfast was good anyway.

Before he left, Sam helped Pru pour the steaming water into the bathtub and wash the breakfast dishes. He offered to feed and water Max before he and Nameless set off for the Chinaman's bathhouse and his day's investigations.

Prudence began to soap herself down. Dunking her hand under the water, she came in contact with her mons. Bittersweet memories of the night before, along with that longing she hadn't truly felt until two nights ago, flooded her.

She could only hope that there might be another night ahead of her.

"Do you have any rings?" Sam asked Harmon Jackson as the storekeeper stood behind the counter of the mercantile wiping off the glass top.

The merchant unlocked a cabinet and pulled out a tray of rings of various types.

"What did you have in mind?"

"Something with a stone, I think. A lady's ring."

The merchant pursed his lips and tapped his mouth with a thoughtful finger. "Don't have much call for that kind of ring. Mostly wedding rings here," he said, holding one up. "Do have this one. Gold with an amethyst."

Sam paled. "No," he said too forcefully. "Anything but that."

Jackson sighed. "Give me a hint, mister. What kind of girl is she?"

Sam smiled slightly. "Smart, passionate, beautiful."

"Anyone I know?"

Remembering Pru's rightful concern for her reputation, Sam said, "I don't know who you know."

Jackson held up one hand in surrender. "Excuse me for living." He held up another one. "This was traded to me a few months back. It's Navajo, I'm told."

The ring was wrought of silver with a wide band carved with Indian symbols. A rough-shaped bright pale blue stone was set in it.

"Stone's called turquoise. It's not a precious stone but it's a real pretty color."

Sam took the ring and slipped it on his little finger. It stopped at the second knuckle of his big hand. He tried to imagine it on Pru's hand and decided he liked the idea.

He hoped she would. But experience is the best teacher. "If the lady says no, can I return it?"

"Sure, sure," Jackson assured him. "Ladies can be fickle."

Sam nodded and paid for the ring. Jackson put it in a small velvet drawstring bag and handed it to Sam. "Good luck with the lady."

Sam thanked him and walked out, shoving the bag in his vest pocket.

He poked his head in the telegraph office. The telegrapher looked up.

"Mr. Blake, right?"

"Yeah."

"Two telegrams for you."

Sam took the envelopes and sat down on a bentwood chair in front of the small writing table. The first telegram was from a New York insurance brokerage indicating Lloyd's had no current stock policies in the area. The second telegram came from Denver. It read:

TWO NAMED PERILS PROPERTY POLICIES WITH INLAND MARINE STOCK FLOATERS PLACED STOP ETHAN MORGAN PETER MCKINLEY POLICY HOLDERS STOP REWARD TEN PERCENT OF FACE VALUE FOR PROOF OF FRAUD STOP PLEASE ADVISE STOP ARDEN STOCKMENS MUTUAL.

Sam folded the telegrams and put them in his pants pocket.

"Times good here?" he asked the telegrapher casually.

"Not too. Drought two years running. The grazing lands've been real dry. We don't get some good rain this spring and it could be real rough on the cattlemen hereabouts. Worst part is one spark and the whole range could go up."

It was the perfect setup. A drought shriveling the grasslands might be crisis enough for a man to consider giving disaster a helping hand.

Sam considered this as he mounted Nameless and returned to the Bar M. He was thinking that he and Clint should get rooms in town if Ethan Morgan was now a suspect instead of a victim.

Staying in town would put him closer to Pru. The thought brought a pleasant tightness in his jeans. He patted the pocket that held the silver ring.

She might not marry him, but Sam suspected that she wouldn't laugh at his proposal.

At least he hoped not. Her derision would destroy him.

Jack Derry sat in the saloon, a bottle and glass in front of him. His gut was roiling, and not just from the cheap whiskey. Early this morning he'd ridden out to the Lazy K, Pete McKinley's ranch.

His gang, all seasoned rustlers, was actually enjoying the straight life. They were willing to pull the scam, but Jack had the sinking feeling that he was going to lose these boys and have to start over.

Of course, the money he'd get from Morgan and McKinley when the insurance company paid off would help.

If he got it.

Derry had the premonition he should have gotten the money up front. He had been offered more money to wait, but the rustler realized there was no honor among thieves, particularly when the thieves were amateurs.

Morgan and McKinley could take the money and leave him holding the bag. He was the one with the criminal record, not them. They were respected cattlemen in this town. Between his word and theirs, who would anyone believe?

Jack Derry had to make sure he didn't get cheated.

Pete McKinley had no family.

Ethan Morgan had a daughter.

A daughter was better than any insurance policy.

School let out at two o'clock. Prudence was piling up papers to take into her cabin to correct. Ready, she walked to the cloakroom and grabbed the broom to sweep out the classroom as she did every day.

As she swept, she noticed her lower back was aching. Considering the physical workout she had experienced the last two nights, it was no wonder she was a bit sore.

Prudence was about to open the door to sweep out the debris when it opened and Arabella, dressed for riding, strode in.

"You up for a ride?" Arabella asked as she leaned against the front desk and raised one booted leg casually as she only did in front of this—her best friend.

"No, but if you want to, you can walk with me to the mercantile. I want to see if I got any mail and then go by the butcher shop and buy a couple of steaks."

Arabella's pale eyebrow rose. "*Steaks* plural?"

Prudence grinned.

Arabella straightened. "You've got a gentleman caller?"

"I do indeed."

Arabella squealed in delight and clapped her hands. "I'm so glad. I always hoped you'd find a fella. What's his name?"

Prudence's smile grew enigmatic. "I'd rather not say."

"Oh, come on!"

"Call me superstitious, but until I know his intentions I'd rather not say anything that might cause rumors."

Arabella made an "X" over her heart and held her hand up, palm forward. "I won't breathe a word," she promised.

As Prudence returned the broom to the cloakroom, she responded, "Not intentionally, but inadvertently. You know I have to keep my reputation intact if I want to keep my job." She emerged from the cloakroom pinning on her hat. "You coming?"

Arabella nodded. Prudence locked the schoolhouse door and quickly took the school papers into her cabin while Arabella was unhitching Horizon from the rail. Leading the mare by the reins, she fell into step beside her friend. They headed the short distance from the school property at the edge of town to the center of Rincon. It was a pleasant day for a walk.

"Do you love him?" Arabella asked abruptly.

Prudence sighed. "I think so."

"Does he love you?"

"He hasn't said so, but I think he might."

"You going to marry him?"

Prudence blew out some air in annoyance. "Arabella, he hasn't asked me. I'm not going to send him skedaddling by bringing it up. Is that all right with you?"

Arabella held up her empty hand. "Okay, okay! Peace!"

They walked quietly for a while before Arabella spoke again.

"I think I'm in love, too."

Now it was Prudence's turn to be excited. "That's wonderful. I guess our luck was destined to change."

"Don't you want to know who?" They walked a little bit further. "Clint Randolph."

Prudence stopped dead in her tracks. "You're not serious."

Arabella shrugged. "I know, I know. He's a drifter, a hired gun. If my father knew he'd lock me in my bedroom until Clint leaves town. It was love at first sight, I guess, or close to it. Those things do happen."

Resignedly, Prudence agreed. "I suppose they do." For hadn't she fallen in love with Sam Blake as quickly herself? "But Arabella, he works for your father and when they catch the rustlers they'll be gone."

Arabella raised an eyebrow. "They?"

"Mr. Randolph and his partner, Mr. Blake."

"Of course."

"Be careful, Arabella. You deserve the best kind of man. You're young enough to make a good match and a good marriage."

"So are you."

Prudence laughed bitterly. "Not me. I'm thirty years old and not pretty. That I've even got a man vaguely interested in me is a miracle. I'm so far back on the shelf I'm surprised I don't raise a dust cloud when I walk."

"Prudence, you seem to think you're some kind of ugly old witch. You're not bad looking."

"That's damning with faint praise."

"I'm serious," Arabella insisted. "Your hair is shiny and thick. You have nice eyes and long eyelashes. Your skin is clear and smooth..."

"And there's so much of it."

"Oh, hush," Arabella snapped indignantly. "You're not that fat. Some men like plump women. Your gentleman caller must."

A rose blush suffused Prudence's face as her mind recalled the memory of Sam Blake loving her with his mouth the night before. To her amazement, the thought of it aroused her as she walked along. She could feel her nipples tightening and said a quick prayer that her chemise, corset cover and bodice obscured them from view. Sam certainly seemed to enjoy her plumpness.

"I guess he does," Prudence conceded, "but he's a man in a million."

"Oh, Prudence, when you're in love, they're always one in a million."

They stopped in front of Jackson's Mercantile. Prudence stepped up on the boardwalk. "You coming inside?"

Arabella shook her head. "No, I'm going riding. Maybe this weekend," she added as she mounted.

Prudence nodded. "Maybe. It depends."

"On him?" Arabella had a giggle in her voice.

Prudence laughed in response.

Arabella kicked Horizon's sides and galloped off, a cloud of dust in her wake. Prudence watched her ride down the street before entering the mercantile.

She was completely unaware that across the street, a pair of bloodshot, feral eyes watched.

There was a letter from her father. She would read it later at home. First, she had to get to the butcher shop. Prudence was starting to get a headache and renewed aching in her lower back.

She stepped out of the mercantile and into the afternoon sunshine. She walked along the board sidewalk, stepping into the street to cross to the other side.

Abruptly, she felt the hard feel of metal poking into her side and heard the hammer of a revolver cocking. She drew in her breath and smelled whiskey and stale sweat.

"Do what I say and you'll get out of this alive," growled a rough male voice.

Prudence was no coward, but she was no fool either. She walked ahead of the armed man into the space between the saloon and the building next door. The space was only about a yard wide so when the man instructed her to stop and back up against the wall and stood face to face with her she could feel the length of him against her.

Prudence began to sweat as she felt the barrel of the pistol poking deeper into her ribs.

"Know who I am?" he growled.

"No, sir," she squeaked.

"Name Jack Derry mean anything to you?"

She drew in a harsh breath. "The rustler?"

He ignored the comment. "You're friends with Morgan's girl, ain't you? Don't lie to me. I just seen you talkin' to her before she rode off."

"Then you know," Prudence said. She felt the barrel push harder.

"Don't sass me, bitch. I want you to deliver a message the next time you see her."

"I don't know when that will be."

Derry ignored her. "Tell her to tell her old man that Jack Derry says if he double-crosses me, the prairie won't be the only thing that'll burn. You got that?"

"I don't understand it."

"You don't got to, teacher lady. Just pass it on."

Prudence nodded. She thought Derry would back away now, but instead he pressed closer for a moment. She held her breath. The feeling of invasion permeated her senses, filling her with fear. She became aware of every grimy pore in his nose, every bristle of his reddish-brown stubbled beard, the reek of whiskey on his breath and person. A cramping feeling seized her stomach, legs and back.

Suddenly, Derry stepped back and away. Prudence's knees gave way and she slid down the wall to the ground.

"No," Derry taunted, "I don't think I *will* kiss you. I'd sooner kiss a mule than an ugly, fat thing like you." With that riposte, Jack Derry hitched up his pants and sauntered out of the alley.

Prudence sat in a heap of emotional and physical pain. She was shaking and tears wet her face. Even the Chicago Fire was not as terrifying as finding a gun in her ribs.

A moment later, she felt the unmistakable warm, sticky feeling between her legs that explained her low back pain and cramps. She had forgotten that her monthly was due, but the increasing pain told her this was going to be a particularly bad one.

She rose slowly to her feet. Perspiration rolled off her body. She forced herself through the pain to stand and, using her hand for balance, to leave the alley.

Prudence barely noticed the normal flow of traffic on the street as she walked, head down and arms pressed against her sides. All she concentrated on was the pain and the way home.

Chapter 10

Arabella finished her ride and returned home just before dusk. She had unsaddled Horizon and was brushing the mare down when she saw Sam Blake come in. She greeted him politely.

Sam had his saddle in his arms as he looked up. "Good evening, Miss Morgan. Looks like you've been riding."

Arabella smiled. "Yes, I have."

"Do you ride out on the range?"

"Uh-huh and sometimes as far as the Mystics."

"How is it out there?"

Arabella sighed. "I've never seen it so dry out there. It looks like a careless spark could set the whole range on fire. The hands are going to have to watch cigarettes and campfires very carefully this year or we could lose the entire herd as well as the grazing land."

Sam hummed thoughtfully. Just what he was thinking.

"If that happened, it would be a disaster for Papa," Arabella continued, thinking Sam wasn't listening.

He was, though. What might be a disaster for Ethan Morgan was uppermost in his mind. But instead of commenting, he said, "I'll mention to Clint to be careful with his smokes."

"He smokes a lot, doesn't he?"

"Whenever he has tobacco handy. Does it bother you?" The frequency of Clint's smoking never bothered Sam until he himself quit. Now it bothered him greatly.

Arabella shrugged. "I don't really mind smoking in general, but I've hardly ever seen him without a cigarette in his mouth. It can't be good for him, aside from the fire danger."

"It's his life," Sam replied, but he saw a strange light in her face as she discussed his partner. Something was definitely there. Sam wondered if he should ask. If Arabella was involved in the plot Sam suspected was brewing, what better way to throw them off the scent than to have her cultivate an attraction with Clint? His handsome, not-so-bright and egotistical partner was just the kind to fall for a pretty face and presume it was sincere.

"Let it go, Miss Morgan. Nice, settled girls like yourself don't fall for saddle tramps like Clint and me. Do yourself a favor. Leave Clint Randolph alone. He'll be happier and so will you."

"Mr. Blake," she said, shock and anger flavoring her response, "I'm an adult and my affairs are none of your concern."

Sam tightened the cinch on Nameless's saddle. "Where they involve our assignment they concern me. You're a very distracting woman, Miss Morgan. Women like you turn a man's head and make him forget about his responsibility—then drop him like a hot potato the moment you get bored."

Arabella's spine seemed to stiffen. Had Sam not been at least a foot taller she would have doubtless looked down her nose at him. "Mr. Blake, I'd bet that what a man like you knows about women would fit in your hat and still leave room for your head."

"Undoubtedly," he responded coolly. He tipped his hat. "Good evening, Miss Morgan." He walked Nameless outside.

Clint was headed toward the barn as Sam was leaving.

"Where're you headed?" Clint asked.

"Personal business."

Before Sam could mount Nameless, Clint grabbed him by the arm.

"Are we partners or aren't we?"

Arabella appeared in the barn doorway just then. Sam glanced in her direction briefly. "Not in everything."

Clint's face darkened with rage. How his relationship with his best friend had deteriorated so quickly was beyond him, but there was going to be neither a partnership nor a friendship by the time this job was over. But this! Sam had hardly ever trafficked with women since he had come back to Texas, much less seeming interested in any girl who had already touched Clint's fancy. "Have you lost your mind?"

"Are you fucking her, Clint?"

"No!" Clint shouted almost too quickly. While it was true he had done little more than kissing, he certainly wanted more, enough to be self-conscious of his answer.

"Good. She's a complication we don't need."

"She's a complication *you* don't need. She's not all that complicated."

Sam threw off Clint's arm. "You idiot. She could be in on the scam. McKinley and Morgan both have stock policies. The range is bone dry and everyone's worried about how the drought is affecting the health and price of cattle. While the man's daughter is pulling you off the scent, the cattle and range could end up in a conflagration and nobody could prove it was arson and fraud. Do us both a favor, Clint. Stay away from Arabella Morgan or she'll pull you down with her."

"She's not involved."

"You willing to bet our lives on it?"

Clint glanced over at Arabella, still standing in the barn doorway. She was so damned pretty. But could she be false? Sam was right so often; could he be right this time?

Sam glanced at Arabella for an instant. "If you have to pump her, pump her for information. Find out what she knows—if she's in on the conspiracy."

"Are you sure there's a conspiracy? Are you sure it isn't exactly what we were hired for?"

Sam took a deep breath before he spoke. "You saw Jack Derry in town, just playing poker like a man biding his time. What cattle rustler is going to sit around town as if he's waiting for a signal to go into action. If this was simple rustling or hired mayhem, Derry would be out on the range or hidden in the hills with his gang, but I asked around. He seems to spend most of his days in the saloon, drinking and playing poker. And another thing. The drought conditions run north toward the railhead in Amarillo. Not a lot of grass or water for a cattle drive. If Morgan and McKinley are strapped financially, a failed cattle drive could bankrupt them both. I'll bet if Miss Morgan is as smart as she claims, she has an idea of her father's financial condition, even if she's not in on the scam. You might consider trying, *subtly if that's possible*, to find out. Better a quick settlement from the insurance company than a risky cattle drive. Clint, if we can't prove the fraud, we're not going to see a penny for this job."

Clint ground his teeth. "I'm not ready to leave just yet."

"Neither am I," Sam affirmed. He had unfinished business in town that had nothing to do with the job.

"If we prove this is a put-up job, what will the insurance company pay?"

"Ten percent of the policy limit. That could be more or less than what the Cattlemen's Association—via Ethan Morgan—offered to pay to catch the so-called rustlers. It's difficult to send wires for details since I can't be completely certain how confidential the telegrapher keeps things and I haven't the kind of relationship with the insurance company that would allow for the use of a code or cipher to send confidential messages. Look, if we find out anything and I'm not able to wire, you need to contact Edward Arden at Stockmen's Mutual Insurance Company in Denver. Have you got that?"

Clint nodded. "Stockmen's Mutual in Denver—Arden. Sure, but what could happen?"

"Anything could happen." Sam mounted and rode off.

Clint watched for a few minutes, then became aware of Arabella as she joined him.

"What was that about?" she asked.

"Sam's worried about the drought conditions. Says it might make a cattle drive risky."

Arabella nodded empathetically. "I know. The dry weather is just burning up the grass. I'm afraid if this year's cattle drive isn't successful, we could be in serious financial difficulty."

It can't be this easy, Clint thought. "What do you mean?" he asked casually.

Arabella shrugged. "I got a glance at Papa's books. We're operating on barely a shoestring. With the cattle being stolen and maimed and the high number we might stand to lose if the drought is all along the drive route, this drive could break us. If you and your partner can at least stop the gang that's robbing us, there'll be fewer cattle lost before the drive and we might do all right."

"When did you find this out?"

"A night or so ago. Papa tried to treat it like it was something I shouldn't 'worry my pretty head' about."

Clint came closer to her. "Arabella, has anyone seen any of the cattle while they were being harmed or just afterwards?"

Arabella thought a moment. "Gosh, now that you mention it, I don't think anybody's caught any of it being done."

"Then how did the Cattlemen's Association come to suspect that mining interests hired the Derry Gang to attack the ranchers?"

"I'm not sure. I heard it from my father. Nobody owns the Mystics, but the rumor is that they're filled with veins of gold and silver abandoned by Spanish explorers three centuries ago. The only way to readily get to them is through either the Bar M or the Lazy K. My father came home from an Association meeting and mentioned it in passing over supper, but I have no idea how it got started. Why?"

"I can't say yet. I've got to talk to Sam."

"But he's gone."

Quickly, Clint walked back into the barn and began to saddle up Wind Dancer. "I'll catch up with him on the way to town. Wind Dancer is a swifter horse carrying a lighter load."

In minutes the stallion was saddled and Clint was on his way, leaving Arabella standing in the barn wondering what her father's financial condition had to do with who was committing crimes against the Bar M.

Clint could see the dust cloud from Nameless's galumphing hooves, although he was far enough back that the sound wouldn't carry back nor drift forward. Clint slowed Wind Dancer to remain at an even pace behind Sam. Sam was not looking back; clearly he didn't expect a rider behind him.

As they approached the outskirts of town, Sam began to slow as he reached an area slightly apart from the main part of town where there stood a cabin, a larger building, an outhouse, horse shed and wooden swing set just out of view from the road.

There was a small copse of spindly trees in line of sight of the property. Clint pulled Wind Dancer into the trees and dismounted quietly.

He could not hear anything from that distance and hoped that Sam could not see or hear him. Sam led his horse into the shed and came out a few minutes later without the gelding.

As he watched, Sam removed his camel-colored Stetson, raked his fingers through his thick, unruly curls, rubbed the uppers of his boots against the legs of his trousers, replaced his hat and tugged his vest down. He knocked at the door.

As Clint observed from his vantage-point, after a few moments the door opened a crack. Clint couldn't see who opened the door, the person being obscured by Sam's body. Sam conversed briefly with the occupant. A few moments later he slipped inside the cabin and the door closed behind him.

Clint sat down on the ground out of sight but within view of the cabin door. When Sam came out, Clint would find out whom he was seeing.

As darkness descended, Sam did not emerge. Clint lit another cigarette and continued to sit and wait.

Sam knocked on the door. There was a silence at first, followed by a strained voice calling, "Who's there?"

"It's Sam, sweetheart," he replied, concern reflected in his voice.

Pru opened the door a crack. She was wearing a modest white nightgown and a hastily tied kimono. Sam saw at once her face was drawn and her hand gripped the door with white knuckles.

"Pru, what's wrong?"

She lowered eyelids that seemed more violet than usual. "Nothing's wrong," she bit out and tried to shut the door.

Sam reached out and kept the door open. "You're lying," he said. "Please let me in, love."

She glared at him with pain-glazed eyes, but she pulled open the door just enough for Sam to ease himself inside. He pushed it shut behind him.

Pru walked away slowly as if her entire body was stiff with pain, her arms wrapped about her waist. Her hair hung down her back in tangled waves as if she had merely yanked out the hairpins.

Sam walked up behind Pru and drew her against his big, warm body, his arms around her. She stiffened. At first Sam felt the clutch at his heart that she was rejecting his touch, but it seemed to be something other than that.

"You're in pain." He put his palm on her forehead. Her brow was as damp as was the rest of her body through her nightclothes. "You don't have a fever. Are you ill? Or is it something to do with me?"

"No," Pru grunted, "I'm not ill."

"Did someone hurt you? Did you fall off Max?"

"No," Pru protested, "Sam, it's nothing to worry about. It has nothing to do with you. Please let me go."

Rather than release her, Sam turned her to face him and hugged her against him. She stood stiffly, angling her lower body away from him.

Stroking her back and hair, Sam glanced into the kitchen area. Over the sink he saw a pair of pantalets and a petticoat hanging to dry.

At first he wondered why she would not have hung these items on the clothesline outside, but a moment later he realized the problem. It made him feel both relief and guilt.

"Pru," he began quietly, "is it your female time?"

He felt her nod against his chest.

"Oh, sweetheart, are you ashamed of it?"

She nodded again. "I was looking forward to seeing you tonight, but now I feel so dirty. How can you bear to touch me?"

Sam tucked his hand under her chin and raised her face to his. Tenderly, he lowered his face and touched his mouth to hers. As much as he wanted to crush her against him and take her mouth as his own possession, he knew he must go slowly.

"Pru, darling, you never have to be ashamed about being a woman. Never consider yourself tainted by it...Do you always have this kind of pain?"

"Most months. But Sam, we can't make love."

Sam drew her against him, enveloping her in his arms again. "Pru, I know this is all new to you, but lovemaking is more than just sex. Will you trust me to help you feel better?"

"I'd do anything short of laudanum not to have this pain."

Sam reached down and lifted her into his arms. Ignoring her protest that she was too heavy for him, he carried her to the sofa and set her down. An afghan lay over the back of the sofa; he draped it around her shoulders.

He took off his hat and gun belt and hooked them on the hat tree. He went to the kitchen and pumped water into her bath water kettles, which he then set on the lit stove. He was rolling out the bathtub when Pru remarked, "What are you doing?"

"I'm drawing you a bath."

"I cleaned myself when I got home."

"I'm sure, but this isn't about being clean. This is about your pain."

Pru shuddered beneath the afghan. In the blink of an eye Sam was before her, kneeling in front of the sofa. His big hands slid under the blanket and began to knead her thighs through her nightgown. Through his spectacles Pru could clearly see concern in those dark brown depths. The familiar heat she associated with his nearness flooded her, turning her thoughts away from the pain and toward the secure feeling of his hands massaging her. The feeling was both erotic and homey. Pru knew she could easily spend the rest of her life looking into those glass-shielded eyes. She reached a hand out of the blanket and stroked Sam's bearded cheek. She felt a strong, angular jaw beneath the thick black foliage. For a moment Pru wondered what Sam might look like without his beard. The big man told her he was ugly as sin. He had been living with his face for thirty-four years; he must know. Prudence did not find anything ugly about Sam Blake—but she knew that the eyes of love are biased.

As she watched him, Sam turned his face into her palm and kissed it. He was ready to burst with love, but was afraid to declare it without a verbal declaration from her. He had been burned before.

Speaking of burning, the rattling lids of the two kettles told him the water was boiling. Sam poured the boiling water onto the bath salts, then added cold water until he could bear to keep his hand in the water.

"Now," he said, "undress and get into the tub."

Pru wrapped the afghan about herself like a shield. "Sam!"

He touched her cheek and murmured throatily, "I've seen you naked before," He eased the afghan off her shoulders, then lifted her nightgown over her head.

Instinctively, Pru's hands went to cover herself. Sam saw the muslin strip tied about her waist to which was pinned a thickly folded pad of rags.

"You have more of those?"

Pru blushed, but she nodded. "In my top drawer."

"Fine, take that one off and throw it in the sink and get into the tub." His voice indicated he would take no back-talk from her.

As Sam disappeared into the bedroom, Pru hurried to obey him. Stepping into the tub, she gasped at the heat, but lowered herself gingerly.

The heat began to permeate her muscles and she felt herself drifting as the cramps eased. She closed her eyes. Sam placed a rolled-up towel behind her neck. She felt the tug against her scalp as he drew her brush through her hair with long, soothing strokes. There was a tender healing in the silence.

After a while, the brushing stopped and Pru felt Sam's hands kneading her shoulders, his thumbs pressing against her upper back.

Despite her closed eyes, she sensed him changing position. His hands slipped into the warm water and began to knead her thighs and waist. Pru opened her eyes a crack and saw Sam had removed his vest and shirt to keep them dry. Between the hot water and Sam's strong, caring fingers, the worst of her pain began to fade as she never remembered it doing in the past, replaced with a far more pleasant ache.

As if he read her mind, Sam drifted his fingers to tease at her mound. As he slipped searching fingers into the center of her sex, Pru's eyes flew open.

"Sam!" she gasped. "You can't do that!"

"Do what?" he teased, but did not stop.

She splashed at him. "That. You can't touch me there now."

He stoked the swollen bud again and she groaned. "Why? Because you're bleeding? I can't be inside you tonight, love, but you like what I'm doing."

"Yes," she groaned.

"You like what you're feeling."

"Yes."

"You may be more sensitive now than at any other time of the month."

Lightning streaked through her and her hips rose to press against his probing hand. "Yes!" she shrieked.

He silenced her with his mouth, taking her climax into him. His own groin ached with the erection concealed in his jeans, but his deep love for her helped him sublimate his own need in favor of hers. It would be a long night, but he could bear it for her sake.

While she came back to earth in the cooling water, Sam left her for a moment. Pru heard the pump in the sink and blushed as she realized that this very male man was rinsing out her menstrual pad as if it were the most natural thing for him to do.

Sam Blake was one in a million. Too bad she couldn't keep him. Prudence Hofheinz knew better than to declare her love for someone who would be gone when his work was done.

Before the water cooled, Sam wrapped Pru in a towel and dried her, every touch of his hands enveloping her in the warmth of his caring. Pru pinned on a clean pad and put on the soft, old nightgown Sam found in her bureau. It was then she noticed he had also shed his boots.

Sam slipped a book from her shelf and, arm wrapped around her waist, guided her into the bedroom.

He told her to lie on the bed, stomach down, pillows propped under her breasts. He handed her the book. It was the copy of *A Midsummer Night's Dream* he had given her the night before.

"Read to me, Pru. Just start with Act One Scene One and keep going until you finish."

Pru began to read aloud. As she read the play, Sam's hands massaged her shoulders, back, buttocks and thighs, drawing the pain out of her body. Sam said nothing, only chuckling at the lines as she read, the distraction of concentrating on the Elizabethan language separating her from the pain.

Chapter 11

Pru finished the play slowly. *"...And Robin shall restore amends."*

She felt Sam move her heavy fall of hair aside and kiss the nape of her neck. "How do you feel?" he murmured as he nuzzled her.

Prudence purred at the feeling of warmth that filled her at his caring touch. "Wonderful. No pain. You're a miracle worker."

"No, just something I picked up at college."

Sam leaned against the headboard of the bed and pulled Pru to lie against him while he held her and stroked her hair. As his hand caressed the silken waves, hers made teasing paths through the hair on his chest.

"I thought you studied civil engineering," Pru commented lazily.

"I did," Sam replied, brought back to reality, "But I was convinced to play on the football team because of my size."

"Football?"

"It's a sport they're playing at the East Coast universities. It's a pretty stupid and violent game compared to, say, baseball. You have heard of baseball?"

Pru responded by yanking at a tuft of chest hair. "I *am* from Chicago."

Sam chuckled and kissed her on top of the head playfully. "I only played one year, but it was physically tough and often painful. A lot of players took laudanum for pain, but I didn't want to do that because I didn't want to develop the craving. I read somewhere that heat, massage and distraction could make pain go away, and it usually worked."

Pru snuggled closer. "Well, it seems to have worked for me, too."

"I'm glad. It tore at me to see you in such pain."

She shrugged. "I've had to live with this for nearly half my life and, like you, I didn't want to get addicted to laudanum, so I've just managed the best I could. I asked a doctor once if there was something I could do." Her jaw tightened at the bitter memory. "He told me I could have a baby or I could have a hysterectomy. I was about nineteen at the time. Can you imagine?"

Sam stiffened at her words from the realization that her period meant their love play had not resulted in a pregnancy.

"Pru, I'm so sorry. It was so selfish of me to put you at risk as I have."

She looked up at him. "Risk?"

"I could have gotten you pregnant the last couple of nights."

Pru tensed. "I hadn't considered that."

"Neither did I, but I should have. It was damned irresponsible of me."

Pru smoothed at his chest with her palm. "Sam, Sam, don't blame yourself. I'm no schoolgirl. I'm responsible for my own actions...But I suppose I *should* be glad I'm bleeding then—um..."

"What?"

"It's so lonely sometimes, having all the curses of womanhood but none of the opportunities."

"What are you talking about?"

She sighed. "I can't even be accosted like other women. Even a lowlife like Jack Derry found me too ugly to kiss, even for spite."

Abruptly, Sam sat bolt upright, his hands gripping hard on Pru's upper arms.

"Derry! What did you have to do with Jack Derry?"

"He forced me into an alley this afternoon..."

"Did he hurt you?"

Pru shook her head. "Only scared me. He put his gun in my ribs and gave me a message to relay to Arabella."

Sam ground his molars. "I'll kill him," he mumbled, angry beyond belief that his woman had been assaulted.

His woman! Could he really be thinking of Prudence Hofheinz as his woman? No! It wasn't for Sam Blake to have a woman to call his own. Sam hauled himself out of bed and began dressing.

Pru climbed out after him. "Sam, don't kill him. He didn't hurt me." She reached out for him.

Sam whirled back to her. "Why didn't you tell me earlier?"

Pru shrugged. "My monthly started right afterwards and with the cramps and the bleeding it just drove everything out of my mind except getting home." She paused. "What he said was so cryptic, I doubt if Arabella will understand it if I do tell her."

She hadn't relayed the message yet. Good! "What did he say?"

Prudence closed her eyes to concentrate on remembering the exact words. "He told me to tell Arabella that if Mr. Morgan double-crossed—yes, that was the term—double-crossed him the prairie wouldn't be the only thing that would burn."

Sam's face closed off frighteningly.

"It means something to you."

"It means that Clint and I have been taken for suckers by Ethan Morgan," Sam responded as he plopped down in a chair and yanked on his boots.

"What about the rustlers?"

Sam shook his head. "There are no rustlers. It's a fraud."

"No rustlers?"

"Only those working for Ethan Morgan and his partners in crime, Pete McKinley and Jack Derry. And we were expected to go off chasing shadows while they soaked their insurance company for a small fortune. Or maybe we were supposed to rid the conspiracy of Jack Derry once the fraud was perpetrated."

Sam had gone into the main room while he was speaking. Pru followed him and watched as he strapped on his gun belt and clapped on his hat. He reached for the door and pulled it open.

"Sam!" Prudence cried and ran. "For God's sake, it's three in the morning. Do you have to leave this minute?"

"Yeah, I do."

"Will you be coming back?"

Sam looked at his boots. "I don't know. Seems unlikely."

Pru felt a tightness in her throat. She ran to the doorway and threw her arms around Sam, not caring if anyone saw her standing in the doorway in her nightgown embracing her lover. "Please, Sam," she begged, "kiss me once more before you go."

With a considerable amount of hunger, Sam clasped Pru against him and lowered his face to meet hers. Their kiss was passionate, bittersweet; full of the good-byes neither of them could bear to voice.

It was Pru who pulled her mouth away first. Stroking his beard, she said, "I'll never forget you, Sam Blake."

"Nor I you," Sam affirmed in a voice choked with emotion.

"Please, take care of yourself."

"I'll do my best," he said emotionlessly as he released her and walked away from the cabin toward the horse shed. She closed the door rather than watch him ride away, probably out of her life for good.

Clint was fighting sleep when he saw the cabin door open in the wee hours of the morning. Sam stood in the doorway, then turned back and Clint got a view of a pair of white-clad arms thrown around his partner's torso and Sam lowering his head to kiss the resident.

The kiss he observed was interminable; more than he believed Sam capable of bestowing. Finally, they broke apart and Sam, after saying a few parting words to the woman, left to walk toward the horse shed. Clint looked toward the cabin door once more to see a full-figured woman with long, dark hair glance briefly toward Sam's departing back, then quickly shut the door.

Immediately, Clint mounted Wind Dancer and rode toward the Bar M. He had to get back before Sam saw him.

As he rode through the darkness, it suddenly registered who the woman was. He couldn't remember her name exactly, except that it was one of those virtuous names—Charity, Hope, Patience—something like that. It was the fat schoolteacher friend of Arabella's who had been at the dinner table the previous Sunday.

That's right, Sam. Tell me not to fuck Arabella, while you're putting it to her best friend.

The more he rode, the angrier he got until by the time he reached the Bar M, he was in murderous rage. He had never felt so betrayed.

He had thought Sam Blake to be as close as a brother. It was time to settle accounts with his partner, conclusively.

Before Sam rode off, he glanced at the cabin. A lantern light was still glowing in one of the windows. He touched his lips as if to rub that last kiss permanently into his mouth.

He was well on the road back to the Bar M when he realized his cheeks were soaked with tears. He needed to get this Morgan matter resolved and get the hell out of Rincon before what was left of his heart was shattered beyond repair.

Prudence went back to her bed and lay down. It was three hours before she had to get out of bed and face her students and she had had no sleep that night.

But sleep would not come. The pillows and linens were pervaded with Sam Blake's unmistakable scent and reminded her of every touch of his hands and the completeness she felt when he had been sheathed deep inside her.

She wished she had someone in whom she could confide. But, as usual, she was alone.

Sam approached the Bar M. Everything was quiet. He dismounted and opened the barn door. He led Nameless into an empty stall, unsaddled the gelding and quickly brushed him down.

He walked out of the stall, intent on the bunkhouse, and collided against a murderous fist aimed right at his jaw.

Unprepared for the blow in the darkness, Sam fell backwards with an oath. A large, dark figure jumped on top of him and began pummeling him with both fists. Sam tried to ward off the blows, but he caught one on the cheekbone and snapped his head back while a blow to the solar plexus knocked the wind out of him.

Sam tried to reach for his Colt when he heard a familiar voice growl, "Touch it and I'll kill you, you fat, fucking son of a bitch."

Clint.

Sam froze at the voice and the words long enough for Clint to crack him across the jaw again. Sam could taste the faintly metallic tang of his own blood.

He began to fight back. In the darkness, Sam landed a punch on the younger man's face, then followed up with another. Clint groaned at the blows and Sam levered himself over until it was he who was straddling Clint instead of the other way around.

Once he had the advantage, he found his partner's arms and pinned them under his own knees, then grabbed the lapels of Clint's jacket and yanked him up until he and Clint were nearly nose to nose.

"What the hell is the matter with you, Randolph?" Sam spit out. "Have you lost your mind?"

"Me? You're the one who's crazy, you lying bastard!" Clint struggled against the weight and force of Sam's knees holding down his arms. "Where do you get off giving me orders?" Clint's fury was palpable.

"What's this coming from?"

"You. You. Always telling me what to do, where to go, what to think, how to act. Look to yourself, you bastard."

"You're not making sense."

"Is she good, that schoolteacher, or are you just grateful for any ready cunt?"

Sam hoisted himself off Clint and sat on his haunches in the dark barn. Their scuffle had filled the air with dust that Sam could taste along with the blood. Clint scrambled to his knees, drained by the battle.

Sam said nothing. He couldn't defend himself. The enormity of his guilt at enjoying himself at Pru's expense and acting self-righteous to Clint shattered his soul.

Clint wasn't through with his invective. He wiped blood from his own mouth and spat out, "I'm surprised you were able to fuck her at all without bouncing off each other."

"Enough," Sam responded almost inaudibly. He whole frame was shaking. His abraded knuckles were throbbing as he buried his face in his hands. To Clint's amazement, the next sounds he heard were huge, wracking sobs. "It's over...it's over."

Clint sat in the darkness, completely helpless to respond. His anger had only barely cooled, but he was not cool enough to deal with this reaction. He heard the shifting of straw on the floor as Sam slowly rose to his feet. A second later Clint was also standing.

"We're a couple of suckers," Sam said when he was able to talk rationally again. "Only it's going to cost more than money—at least for me."

"Morgan," said Clint.

In the pinkening darkness, Sam discerned Clint's outline in the barn. "You know."

"I'm not as stupid as you think, partner. You were right. Arabella told me her father's in financial trouble and everyone is afraid of what the drought has done to the range. Your idea about Morgan planning to cheat his insurance company makes sense."

"I got confirming information that Jack Derry's got a premonition that Morgan and McKinley are going to double-cross him. He's made a vague threat to assure they don't."

"But I don't think Arabella's in on it—not from the way she gave me the information."

"I won't argue with you. You know her better than I do." Sam sounded defeated.

"So what do we do about it?"

"We wire Stockmen's Mutual and get them to hire us to uncover or stop the insurance fraud and if they won't, we pack our grip, go back to Santa Fe and chalk this one up to experience."

"How soon do you think the insurance company will let us know?"

"I'll wire Denver this morning. Today's Wednesday. If we don't get a confirmation by Friday, we should just resign and get out of town." Sam had no energy left.

"Did you sleep at all?" Clint asked.

Sam shook his head. "I've been up all night." He chuckled.

"Was she worth it?"

"Yeah. Every precious moment. But she never spoke of love. I may have been no more than a temporary diversion. She'll find somebody new."

"According to Arabella, she's never even been asked to dance at a social."

"Well, it's all water over the dam. She'll be working when I go check for telegrams and I'll have no other occasion to be in town."

"If you want to write out the telegram, I'll take it into town. You could probably use some sleep."

"No, I'd rather it not be in writing any longer than it has to. If I catch a few winks now, I can be in town by noon and back here by 2:30. Then we need to ride out toward the Lazy K and look for anything suspicious."

Sam opened the barn door. The sky was pre-dawn pink. He bent over painfully and swept up his Stetson, carrying it in one scraped hand as he lumbered wearily to the bunkhouse.

Arabella heard the horses ride in as she lay in bed trying to sleep. She knew Clint had ridden off after Sam late Tuesday afternoon and hadn't returned until nearly dawn.

Why she was frantic, she couldn't say. She and Clint had shared a few passionate kisses, but little else. He was a virile, handsome man. He needed more than a few virginal embraces.

The thought made Arabella unreasonably jealous.

When she heard each rider return she looked out her window, but it was too dark to tell who was who. It was nearly dawn before the barn door opened again and she could see the unmistakable figure of Sam Blake trudging toward the bunkhouse.

A moment later she saw Clint emerge and pull the barn door shut behind him. She threw her wrapper over her night rail and flew down the stairs like Nemesis on the wing.

She reached the front porch as Clint stepped up onto it.

"Where have you been?" she asked accusingly.

"The barn," Clint mumbled.

"No, before that."

"Rincon."

Arabella was about to ask him who the woman was he'd seen in town when she saw Clint's swollen and bruised face. "Oh, my God, Clint, what happen to you?"

Clint touched his jaw gingerly. "I had a little run-in."

Arabella grabbed Clint's hand, but his hissed when she touched his skinned knuckles. "Sorry," she mumbled. "Come into the kitchen and we'll put something on that."

They went through the parlor and dining room into the kitchen, where Arabella lit a lamp and pumped out some cold water into a basin. Grabbing a clean towel and some antiseptic, she indicated a chair for Clint to use.

"I hope the other guy looks worse," she said as she began to gingerly dab at the cuts on Clint's face and hands.

"Don't know. It was dark."

Arabella gasped. "He jumped you in the dark. What a coward!"

Clint chuckled bitterly. "Yeah, I reckon I am, since I jumped him." He winced as she applied the antiseptic.

"*You* started the fight! Whatever for?"

"I reckon you could say it was over a woman."

Arabella stiffened and pulled away from Clint. Then she realized she could detect neither liquor nor perfume; only the ubiquitous smell of tobacco.

"The other guy must have won," Arabella said through gritted teeth. "You don't smell like you got the woman."

Clint looked up at Arabella. With her fair hair in a tangle about her lovely face, she looked like an avenging angel.

He grinned grimly. "I didn't want the woman in question. The only woman I want is standing in front of me right now looking too beautiful to be real." He shook his head bitterly. "But I can't have you the way I'd like to."

Arabella's eyes widened and a tentative smile played about her lips. "How is that?" she asked, half-afraid of the answer.

"Enough to want to settle down and think about permanent. Enough to want to ask you to marry me."

For a moment she stood there, flabbergasted.

"But I can't." Clint's words broke Arabella's reverie.

"Why not?"

"Because I'm broke. Because I'm part Indian. Because I'm stupid. Because you could get hurt by this job I'm doing and hate me for it."

"I could never hate you, Clint. You could use the money you get when you're done helping my father to buy a small place. And your being part Indian matters nothing to me."

"I'm still stupid."

"What has being smart done for your partner? He takes second place to you in everything for all his brain. Darling, you're smart enough for everyday purposes. I don't need a genius. I need a man who's just smart enough to love and care for me." She reached out her hand. "Come."

"Where?" He surrounded her small hand with his larger one.

Quietly, she led the way upstairs and into her room, shutting the door behind them.

"Your father..."

"I don't care." Arabella cut him off and threw herself into his arms. Even this early in the morning she could smell the unmistakable scent of the cigarettes he had smoked during the night. She pulled his face down to meet hers and pressed herself against him.

Immediately, Clint's body came to attention. Foreplay was not exactly his style. He scooped Arabella up in his arms and deposited her on the narrow bed.

Arabella stifled a giggle as the tall cowboy hopped around trying to get his boots off and tore at the buttons on his shirt and fly. In moments he was naked, the naturally coppery skin of his torso smooth, hairless and unscarred. A sparse thatch of raven hair crowned his already erect manhood. She gasped slightly, never having seen a completely naked man; not even an infant.

"You're beautiful," she exclaimed, careful to keep her voice down.

He chuckled in response as he joined her on the bed. Arabella's bed was not built for two to share and Clint, although lean, was not a small man. He wasted no time putting her on her back and caging her amid his limbs. Lowering himself with his elbow, he kissed her thoroughly, his tongue searching the warm, sweet inside of her mouth as he felt the fullness of her breasts against his chest.

Arabella welcome the onslaught of his kisses as she raised her arms around his neck to lower him against her and felt the urgency of his hardened shaft against her thighs. It seemed to be going so quickly, like wildfire, when Clint yanked up her nightgown and wrapper and urged her legs apart, settling himself between them, his manhood poised for entrance.

He reached one hand down between them.

"Damn," he muttered, "you're dry as a bone."

"Huh?" Arabella had no idea what he was talking about.

Clint took a deep breath and let it out. Then he spit into his hand and dampened the area around Arabella's sex. She shuddered in distaste and braced herself, teeth gritted as she felt Clint begin to insinuate his shaft inside her. Her nails dug into his back as she felt the abrasive force of his entry.

Part way in, Clint stopped, as the barrier of her virginity was perceptible. He looked down at his partner. She was lying beneath him, eyes tightly closed, jaw set.

Virgins, he thought as he drove through the membrane and buried himself within her.

If Arabella was stiff enough in apprehension, the sharp pain of her hymen rending stiffened her more. But then, Clint began to move in and out, thrusting within her as his body broke out in a fine sheen. A few quick thrusts and she felt a warmth flood her as Clint sighed and collapsed on top of her.

If that's all there is, I can see why married women avoid it.

Clint levered himself off Arabella. He kissed the tip of her nose and said, "Thanks, honey, that was great," as he yanked his clothes back on. Pressing his ear to the door and hearing no one stirring, he silently opened the door and slipped out.

Arabella lay on the bed, her nightgown and wrapper wadded up around her waist, feeling damp, sticky and sore between her thighs. Carefully, she eased herself out of bed and went to the washstand. She poured the tepid water from the ewer into the basin, wet her washcloth and gingerly sponged herself to remove the evidence of her indiscretion.

Unbidden, tears filled her eyes and spilled onto her cheeks. She wished she had someone to talk to about whether that was what lovemaking was all about, but to whom could she talk without revealing what she had done? She could not even tell her best friend, for what would Prudence know about lovemaking?

As much as she loved Clint Randolph, this was not an experience she wanted to repeat often.

Or maybe ever again.

Chapter 12

Ethan Morgan knew nothing of the activity going on in his daughter's room. His mind was on sneaking downstairs and getting to the Lazy K before the ranch hands stirred. He tiptoed downstairs, pulling on his boots when he got to the porch. After saddling his horse, he rose across his land, making it to the Lazy K ranch house in about two hours.

Morgan stepped onto McKinley's porch. A wizened Mexican housekeeper answered the door and directed Ethan into the study. McKinley greeted him cordially and offered him coffee and a cigar, both of which he accepted. Once the housekeeper exited, Morgan felt free to speak.

"We've got a problem."

McKinley took a long draw on his cigar. "In what regard?"

"Derry. I don't trust him."

McKinley gestured dismissively. "I wouldn't worry about him. He won't live long enough to collect. I'm more worried about your bright idea to hire that range detective Randolph as a decoy."

"Randolph is an idiot. He thinks he's still looking for rustlers. You should see the two of them, him and that big oaf of a partner, chasing all over the range looking for clues and following Derry in town. We'll be halfway through spending the insurance drafts and they still won't have figured out they've been had, unless Derry shoots off his big mouth to one of them."

"And risk jail. I don't think so."

Morgan rose from his chair and paced toward the window. He stopped and stared out at nothing in particular. A curl of smoke wafted from his cigar. "Maybe you better run it all by me again."

McKinley sighed. "It's real simple. This Thursday, before dawn, Derry meets up with the members of his gang about a mile from Ganados Ravine. The gang will have begun to round up the cattle this week and led them towards the Mystics in search of better grass, it being so dry and all. They set off torches to the grass and head off in separate directions. The fire stampedes the cattle into the ravine and certain death at the bottom and the fire takes care of the grassland as well as the evidence. What Derry won't know is that you and I will be following behind them with your patsy range detective and will shoot Derry and whoever else of his gang is still around. The rest will have scattered, thinking Derry is coming with their cut. We file our claims and within a few weeks Stockmen's Mutual sends us the bank drafts. You and Arabella can head east and I'll be on a boat to Australia with more than enough money to start over again in grand style. By the time Derry's boys realize he's not coming with their cut, we'll be long gone. And if, by chance, that hotshot range detective gets caught in the crossfire and 'accidentally' killed, when then, you've saved yourself ten thousand more right there."

Morgan closed his eyes. The game was escalating beyond his original thoughts. "Arabella seems to be following Randolph around."

"Hot for him, eh?"

Morgan winced. "God, I hope not. The man's a breed."

"Hmm. Didn't know that. Well, then, he's better off dead anyway than sniffing around your little girl."

Ethan realized what a cold-hearted bastard Pete McKinley was. "I'm concerned that she might follow at the wrong time and get herself hurt."

"You have a sister in San Antonio, don't you? Send her there for a visit this week. Use her interest in the breed as an excuse if you have to."

Morgan nodded thoughtfully. He'd find a way to keep his daughter safe.

"Stockmen's Mutual's hired us," Sam told Clint Friday afternoon. "Twenty thousand, that's ten percent of the two policy limits, if we prove insurance fraud. They're sending down an investigator to follow up with us. The man will have authority to issue us a draft on the spot it we succeed."

"That's twice what the Cattlemen's Association offered."

"Which we won't see, because if the fraud works out, it'll look like a prairie fire and if the cattle are lost, we won't have succeeded—which they'll use as an excuse not to pay us."

"Now, all we have to do is find out when they're going to pull it off," Clint said as he rolled himself a cigarette and lit it. "I'm worried about Arabella," he commented after a drag. "If her father is caught, the scandal would ruin her. She could lose everything."

"A pretty girl like Arabella Morgan always winds up on her feet somehow," Sam commented cynically.

"You don't like her, do you?"

Sam shrugged. "I don't know her." He snapped his fingers. "She doesn't mean this to me nor I to her."

"I love her."

"That, my friend, is your problem."

"I'd marry her if she'd have me."

Sam leaned back in his chair and crossed his legs at the ankles. "Well, ten thousand is a good start, if you're frugal and don't marry a girl who's used to expensive things."

Clint released a chest full of smoke. The Morgan house was filled with high-class knickknacks. Arabella's clothes were high quality. The bed linens were fine—as were the china and silver. "We'll manage," he said through gritted teeth. "What about you?"

Sam sat upright. "What about me?"

"You and the schoolteacher. You fucked her that night, didn't you?"

"No," Sam answered truthfully, "although it's none of your damned business. But she'd never marry me. I'm not the kind of man women marry. I've known that for years."

"You think less of yourself than any man I know."

"I have reason and long experience...We've got to find out when they're planning to set the fires."

"How do we do that?"

"We follow and we listen. Keep an eye on Derry, another on Morgan. Keep priming Arabella for information. The old man may let something slip. Above all, be ready to ride at a moment's notice. Our lives and our fortunes may well depend on it."

"Why, Papa?" Arabella cried.

She stood in Ethan's study, her face flushed with anger as her father told her she was leaving on the Wednesday afternoon stage for San Antonio to spend some time with her Aunt Edith.

"I've decided. You're a beautiful, educated girl and you're not going to meet the right kind of man in a two-bit town like Rincon. My sister can introduce you to decent, stable men with a future. I'd hate to see you throwing yourself away on some worthless cowboy or homeless drifter."

Arabella felt a pain near her heart. "This is about Clint Randolph, isn't it? You're afraid I might have feelings for him."

Morgan was a bit surprised at her directness, but it did made things easier. "Exactly who I mean. He may be good at what he does, but I don't want you following him around. His kind'll end up leaving your reputation in shambles. And you'd never be accepted in polite society with someone of his upbringing."

"What part of his upbringing, Papa? That he's from the North? That his father was a carpetbagger? Or is it his Indian grandfather that troubles you?"

"All of those, since we're putting all our cards on the table. Randolph has a job to do and I don't want you interfering. If you aren't out of town on the Wednesday afternoon stage, so help me, I'll tie you to your bed and lock you in your room until this is all over and Randolph is gone. I won't have you here on Thursday next."

"Thursday next? What's so special about next Thursday?"

Morgan blanched. He'd said too much. "Nothing. Just a gut feeling."

Arabella shuddered. She turned and began to leave the room.

"Where are you going?"

"To town to see Prudence."

"Prudence, I don't want to go away," Arabella whined as she helped her friend shop in Jackson's Mercantile.

"I appreciate that, Arabella, but it won't hurt you to spend some time there. In one way your father's right. Clint Randolph is a drifter who'll likely never settle down. Neither of them," she added bitterly.

"Papa wants me to leave on Wednesday afternoon's stage. He says he doesn't want me here on Thursday."

The word *Thursday* caught the attention of another shopper who hung just out of sight in the next aisle. Jack Derry realized his ace in the hole was slipping out of his grasp.

Damn him, Derry thought, realizing he'd better work fast.

Prudence paid for her purchases and the two women loaded them into the boot of her buggy next to her laundry. She had reluctantly taken her sheets to the Chinese laundry, knowing that once cleaned, Sam's scent would be gone forever.

They rode back to the school grounds.

"God, I wish I were a man."

Arabella's eyes widened. "Whatever for?"

"Damn it, Arabella. If I were a man, I could do what I wanted; be what I wanted. I wouldn't have to teach school because it's one of the few jobs open to me. If I wanted to be an architect or a lawyer or President of the United States, no one would dare say I couldn't. And if I met someone I could love, I could court that person publicly without it ruining my reputation. I would stay with her or ask her to follow me wherever I went and she would go. Go to San Antonio. Meet a high-class Southerner whose blood is pure enough to pass muster. Get yourself out of Rincon while you're still young. It's Saturday, Arabella. Take the stage going south tomorrow. Don't wait until Wednesday. And don't *ever* fall in love." The tears fell now.

Quietly, Arabella touched her friend's arm. "I'm sorry, Prudence. Like you, I'm afraid it's too late."

They rode silence until they got to the schoolyard. Prudence unhitched Max and the two women went into the cabin where Prudence made some tea and took out a plate of tarts she'd made that morning.

Arabella toyed with her spoon in her tea. "Prudence, in those Sewing Circles, do the wives ever talk about—um—intimate things? You know, things they do with their husbands?"

Prudence shrugged. "Sometimes, when they've forgotten I'm there. Then they blush and apologize for offending my maidenly sensibilities."

"What do they say about making love?"

Prudence sat straight up. "Arabella! You haven't had intimate relations...Clint Randolph."

Arabella nodded miserably.

So we've both made the same mistake. "Well it won't go farther than this cabin, but weren't you running the risk of finding yourself in the family way?"

Arabella paled. "Oh, God, I never thought of that. But you can't get that way on the first time, can you?"

Prudence looked upwards to the heavens.

"What was that look for?"

"I can't believe you're that naïve about such things. If you're old enough to have monthlies, once will do it." Prudence shuddered herself, realizing that her own actions could have landed her in the same predicament. Arabella might not be so lucky.

Arabella pulled at her hands. "How will I know?"

Prudence folded her hands on the dining table. "If you have your monthly next time, you're safe. If you miss it, chances are you're expecting."

Arabella sat silently for a while. "It seems hardly worth it."

"What does?"

"The risk. I mean, it wasn't all that much fun. Just a lot of grunting and sweating and pain."

"I beg your pardon?"

"Um—the—you know—I didn't like it much. I guess that's why women consider it a marital duty to submit to it."

Prudence thought back to three gloriously intimate nights with Sam Blake. That was a duty she'd never shirk—and might even volunteer for extra! "I'm afraid I don't understand."

"When it was over I felt so—I don't know—used. I was almost surprised Clint didn't drop a few coins on my dresser as he left. Be glad you're a spinster and never have to submit to such humiliation...And what makes it worse is even though I love him, I can't imagine a lifetime of that. The thought makes me shudder."

"So maybe getting away for a while will be good for you. You can sort out your feelings about Clint Randolph and sexual intercourse and so forth without his being around to confuse you. If you and he are meant to be together, you'll soon know it."

Arabella sipped her tea and sighed. "I suppose you're right. I'll leave Wednesday afternoon. While I'm gone, will you ride out to the ranch occasionally and exercise Horizon?"

"If I can. The days are getting longer now."

And all the longer now that Prudence felt Sam's absence keenly.

Jack Derry sat in his room in the boarding house, a half-empty bottle of whiskey cradled in his arms. Ethan Morgan was sending his daughter away before the scheme went down.

Derry took another drink. He was certain now that Morgan and McKinley were going to make sure he never saw a penny of the money.

So, the girl would be in town Wednesday to take the stage.

Sometimes, in an insurance fraud, a man needs a good insurance policy.

All day Saturday Prudence mulled over what Arabella told her.

Thursday. Ethan Morgan wanted her to leave town Wednesday because he didn't want her in town on Thursday.

Whatever was going to happen—that insurance fraud Sam mentioned—was going to happen sometime on Thursday.

Pru didn't sleep well Saturday night. Sunday morning she dragged herself out of bed, bathed and dressed in her riding clothes, saddled Max and headed for the Bar M.

Most of the hands were sleeping off Saturday night drunks, but she did see young Bob Bonetti sitting in a chair outside the bunkhouse reading a book. The nineteen-year-old cowboy had been once of Prudence's students. He was a handsome boy who still had some filling out to do and had grown a sparse mustache in an attempt to look older than he was.

"Bob," Prudence called out lightly.

The cowboy looked up and a pleased smile crossed his lips. "Miss Hofheinz!" He would not forget that Miss Hofheinz told him a man could read books as well as handle cattle—that learning was a lifelong pursuit. He marked the book with a strip of leather and closed it.

Prudence smiled. "I didn't mean to disturb you on Sunday, Bob."

Bob nodded. "Oh, that's okay, Miss Hofheinz. Miss Arabella's gone with Mr. Morgan to church this morning. I'm surprised you didn't pass them on the way."

"I rode off the road this morning. You didn't see Mr. Randolph or Mr. Blake this morning, did you?"

"Yeah, I did," Bob answered slowly, wrinkling his brow as if trying to remember where. "Sam rode that dun of his up toward the Mystics. I didn't see Mr. Randolph with him."

"What do you think of Clint Randolph, Bob?"

Bonetti shrugged. "He doesn't talk much. I guess he's doing a lot of figuring and planning. I hope they catch whoever's been killing our cattle, though I truly hate to see Sam go when they're done."

Pru's eyebrow rose. "Why do you say that?"

Bob smiled. "I think you'd like Sam Blake, Miss Hofheinz. He's real well-read but he knows how to survive in the West. He's just like I'd like to be in a lot of ways."

"Have you told him this?"

Bob shook his head. "Nah. I figure it'd embarrass him. One thing surprises me, though."

"What's that?"

"Well, Sam seems so much smarter than Mr. Randolph. I'm surprised he works for Randolph instead of the other way around, except..."

"Except?"

"Well, Mr. Randolph looks like a hero is supposed to. Sam looks kind of like a big bear. I reckon seeing is believing."

Prudence nodded. "Unless you've learned to look beneath the veneer to the wood beneath."

"Like you taught us in school, Miss Hofheinz."

"I hope so...You said you saw—um—Sam heading toward the Mystics?"

"Yes, ma'am."

"Thanks, Bob. Enjoy your book and your Sunday." She mounted Max and headed in a northerly direction.

She needed to find Sam Blake. For more reasons than one.

Chapter 13

Prudence kicked Max into action—well, action for him. She rode the gelding as fast as he would go until she reached the base of the Mystics.

She was nearing Ganados Ravine when she sighted Nameless grazing nonchalantly in the dry grass.

"Sam!" she yelled, loud enough—she hoped—for him to hear. "Sam Blake!"

She headed toward the ravine calling his name until she sighted him standing not far from the edge of the ravine.

He turned, pistol drawn, until he saw her. He holstered his gun and waved to show he recognized her. Sunlight glinted off his spectacles like a pair of round mirrors.

Quickly, Prudence dismounted and ran toward him. Before she could say a word in greeting he collected her in his arms and kissed her possessively.

"God help me, I've missed you," he groaned hoarsely before crushing her mouth with his again.

Raggedly, she repeated his name between kisses as she wrapped her arms around him and pressed against him as if to merge into him. If he didn't love her, he certainly wanted her.

"By God, I would take you right here under the sky," he whispered in her ear.

"And I would let you," Pru whispered back, "but when I tell you what I'm about to say, you may not want to."

Sam released her, pain in his eyes. He stalked away like he had been slapped.

"Sam, that was clumsy of me. I can't imagine anything more exciting than making love to you, What I meant was you may need to meet up with your partner and move on what I've heard."

Sam turned, uncertainty replaced by a crooked, boyish grin when he saw the loving smile on Pru's face. He came back and, taking her upper arms in his big hands, kissed her gently on the forehead.

"What have you heard, sweetheart?"

She filled him in on what Arabella told her the day before. "She said he was specifically insistent that she be away before Thursday. I know it's not much to go on, but if Mr. Morgan is working on the scheme you suspect, it seems he wants Arabella out of harm's way before the day everything happens." She cocked her head. "Is any of that useful?"

Sam grinned. "If you ever decide to quit teaching, you'd make one hell of a detective, Pru."

How about tomorrow, my love, she thought.

"Do you know anything about this part of the ranch?"

"They call this Ganados Ravine." Pru pointed to an eroded piece of a mountain ledge. "Normally in spring that's a waterfall. They say the Mystics are laced with small underground trickles of water the Conquistadors used in their mining operations. For years, cattle have heard the rush of water from the fall. Mr. Morgan and Mr. McKinley regularly lose a few head that walk over the edge smelling water. That's why they call it Ganados Ravine."

"Spanish for *cattle*."

"Exactly. I'm surprised they don't lose more each year to this, since this area sort of bottlenecks up to the edge of the ravine. Cattle are such stupid creatures. With the right spooking they would follow the herd into oblivion."

Sam watched the way the hills narrowed to the edge of the drop, then turned back to look deep into the ravine, then up into the Mystics. Men with combustibles could set the prairie ablaze and spook the cattle to stampede right into certain death, and if arson couldn't be proven, Stockmen's Mutual would have to pay the claim.

The low mountains seemed to have rock formations and trees sufficient to conceal people and horses. If he and Clint could find a hiding place a little higher up, they could catch the arsonist in the act and prevent the fraud from occurring.

"Ride up with me a bit, Pru. I need to reconnoiter."

They mounted and rode up into the Mystics. When they had gone up several hundred feet in elevation, they dismounted and began to walk around, keeping Ganados Ravine within sight. Finally they sat on a boulder. Pru felt Sam's arm affectionately wrap around her waist and she leaned against him, loving the simple nearness of this big man she seemed to understand more than anyone else did.

"Why do they call these the Mystic Mountains?" Sam asked after a while.

Pru laughed. "They're not much as mountains go, but in land as flat as this part of Texas, these pass for mountains. Folks around here say these hills were sacred to medicine men of an extinct Indian tribe. The Conquistadors used them as slaves in their search for the Seven Cities of Gold and white men's diseases eventually killed them. You have to be careful. The hills are riddled with mine shafts overgrown with brush and fallen tree branches. No one knows for sure how many holes were dug and where they all are or how deep or in what condition, only that little if any precious metal was found. It's shameful."

"Shameful?"

"Yes, that a whole tribe of Indians was destroyed and their sacred ground defiled for nothing."

"You don't think like most people."

Pru laughed. "Tell me something I don't know. Most Texans figure the only good Indian is a dead Indian, but that's shortsighted at best and at worst the most insidious bigotry. I know you don't think that way since your partner is part Indian."

Sam stiffened slightly. "I don't really want to talk about Clint."

She touched his bruised face. Most of the discoloration had faded to yellow-green since his set-to with Clint. "You fought with him."

Sam grunted in affirmation.

"Why? You two have been friends forever."

"He followed me into town Tuesday night," Sam said dully.

Pru closed her eyes. "Oh, God."

Sam's hand dropped from her waist. "You *are* ashamed."

"No," she protested.

Sam climbed down from the boulder and strode away. "You don't have to lie to me, Pru. I fooled myself for a few days, but..." He stopped speaking as the pain of his reality filled him.

"Sam..." How could she tell him she wasn't ashamed of him or anything she felt about him, but afraid of what disclosure would mean to her. In most parts of the West female schoolteachers couldn't even be married, much less conduct extramarital affairs with strangers, no matter how special. An unmarried woman's reputation was her most important possession. A ruined woman couldn't hope to hold even the most menial of honest jobs. Even a friend as loyal as Arabella would have to shun her. "You don't understand."

"I think you'd better go, Pru. I appreciate the information you gave me."

Pru climbed down from the boulder and reached out her hands to him, but he walked away.

"I don't think we'll be seeing each other again."

"Sam, you don't mean that."

"I'll have a lot of planning to do the next few days and I'll probably be gone from here by the end of the week."

Tears filled her eyes. There was nothing she could say to remedy the situation. She stood there helplessly.

"Oh—and don't worry about Clint. I'll shoot him myself before I let him spread any word of what he saw that night."

"Oh, Sam!"

Sam's big hands fisted until the knuckles were white. "Just go, Pru. *Leave me alone, do you hear?*"

Pru ran to where Max was tethered, untied the reins and mounted. Carefully she led him down the mountain and back onto the plain.

She turned around. Sam was plainly visible where he was standing, the sun glinting off his lenses. He stood stiff and motionless, a dark shadow against the late morning sun.

"Take care of yourself, my love," Pru said, though she knew Sam couldn't hear her. "I'll be waiting for you if you change your mind."

She rode back towards Rincon.

"Don't go, Arabella," Clint pleaded as he held her against his chest.

"I must." Her voice was thick with tears.

"Couldn't you hide in town somewhere?"

"Where would I hide?"

"Couldn't that friend of yours—what's her name—the schoolteacher help you?"

Arabella stiffened. "She wouldn't. She already suggested I leave this afternoon instead of waiting until Wednesday."

"The bitch," Clint mumbled. Another nail was driven into the coffin of the friendship between himself and Sam Blake.

Arabella pulled back. "Don't say that! I'm sure she's just jealous of me."

"No reason. She's getting hers."

Arabella's eyes widened. "I beg your pardon?"

"Oh, not from me, darlin'."

She shook her head as if to clear it. "Are you implying that my friend is having an affair?"

He'd already said too much. "Forget it. I'm just spouting off."

Arabella folded her arms. "You'd better be careful before you say such things, even in jest. A girl's reputation is always at risk, and a schoolteacher's more than anyone."

Clint held up his hands. "I give up. My lips are sealed."

Arabella got back to the main subject. "I can take the stage as my father wants, but instead of changing to the train for San Antonio when we get to Big Spring, I can catch the return stage and be back in Rincon by Saturday afternoon. If you've finished the job, you could get a room in town and wait for me to get back."

"You want me to wait?"

"I want to go with you, wherever you go."

Clint opened his arms and Arabella came back into them. "It won't be easy. All I'll have is the pay for this job."

"We'll do fine. If I'm with you I don't mind roughing it for a few years."

"It's more than just that, you know. I'll be going it without Sam for the first time since I left the Texas Rangers."

Arabella lay her hand against Clint's smooth cheek. "Darling, you don't need Sam. If you stop the rustlers, maybe my father will forget his objections to you and let you help manage this place."

Clint stepped away. He had not dared tell Arabella that Ethan Morgan was suspect in the crime. He dared not tell her now, but if Sam was right, there was no way Ethan Morgan was going to forget—or forgive.

"Go to San Antonio, Arabella," he said instead. "See your aunt and get away from here. If what we feel for each other is real, it'll stand the test of time and distance. If when the job is done you still want to be with me, I swear I'll come to San Antonio and claim you myself."

"You want me to go?" Arabella sounded incredulous.

Clint's hands fisted with tension. "No—and yes. I love you and want you, but I want you to be safe. I'm dealing with criminal acts here. That could mean shooting and killing. As your father's daughter you could easily get caught in the crossfire and hurt or even killed. I don't think I could live if that happened."

"You love me?"

"I said it and I won't take it back."

"Oh, darling, I love you so," Arabella cried and ran back into his arms. "We'll do fine together, you'll see."

"Then you'll go to San Antonio?"

"Yes, on the Wednesday afternoon stage."

Wednesday, April 23, 1885

Prudence taught her class as usual. The nice part about having a job was that it made it possible to get her mind off the previous Sunday's heartbreak and rejection. The weather was pleasant but dry. A slight breeze blew through the open windows of the schoolhouse.

School would end at two o'clock and Prudence would ride over to the stage office to see Arabella off. Then she planned to return to her cabin and correct papers. After supper she would read until she got tired and went to bed.

Just as she had done almost every school night for nine years.

As if the previous week had never happened.

Arabella finished packing her valises. Her ability to take a full breath was stifled by the corset she wore with her pearl gray traveling suit. Having double-checked that she packed everything she would need for a short stay in San Antonio, she secured her gray felt, ribbon-trimmed chapeau with a long hat pin, pulled on her gray cotton gloves and took her reticule and valises downstairs. One of the hands would drive her into town in the buckboard and leave her to wait for the stage.

She had not seen Clint Randolph all morning. She would likely not see him again until everything was over.

Clint and Sam left the ranch just after daybreak. Wind Dancer and Nameless were packed down with everything necessary for an overnight stay in the Mystics: their bedrolls, cooking equipment, guns and ammunition, lanterns, dusters, coiled lengths of rope and whatever else they could think of. Each detective put his hunting knife in his boot sheath. Neither left much more than extra changes of clothing and Sam's books in their sleeping accommodations.

They reached the lookout position above the rise in the Mystics that Sam had scouted that fateful Sunday past. Hobbling the horses just above them, they laid a fire, loaded their guns and waited. They were not readily visible, but if the arsonists meant to start their prairie fire in order to spook the cattle into Ganados Ravine, they were in the perfect position to stop it.

Now they just had to wait.

The members of the Derry Gang working on the McKinley property were getting nervous. When darkness began to lower, they were supposed to ride out with their torches and whips and begin to move the cattle toward the ravine. Now they had, with the help of the regular wranglers, already moved the herds further toward the Mystics in search of better grass. On Ethan Morgan's orders, the Bar M cattle had also been moved further north, ostensibly for the same reason.

It wouldn't take much to stampede the cattle. A few well-placed whip cracks, a few bullets shot into the air and a fire behind them would send the brainless bovines up and over to their doom and bring Morgan, McKinley, Derry and his gang their big payday.

Ethan Morgan loaded his rifle. He had never killed anyone before, but there was always a first time.

With his debts, he couldn't afford to split the money with Jack Derry. Somehow, in the confusion of the night, a bullet would have to find its way into Derry's brain.

If it couldn't be accidental, then it would have to come from him.

He was just glad Arabella was going to be safely on her way to San Antonio when it all happened.

Jack Derry was hung over, but he refused to drink this day, even to stop the pounding in his head. He would need to be cold sober if this day's work was to be done and he was to survive to see the next dawning.

The stagecoach south was scheduled to leave Rincon a little after three o'clock with Arabella Morgan on it.

The stage *will leave at three. That part won't change.*

About 1:30, the southbound stage arrived in Rincon. It would lay over for ninety minutes while the driver, shotgun and passengers got some lunch and a chance to use the necessary and would leave around three. Nobody really noticed the nondescript man with the short blond hair and briefcase who took his valise out of the boot and walked to the boarding house, there being no hotel in Rincon.

Mrs. Lester greeted him brightly.

He politely greeted her in return. "I understand that you have the only rental accommodations in town."

"That's the truth. You'll be needing a room, sir?"

"Yes, for a few days to a week."

"I have a nice, sunny room I think you'll like." Mrs. Lester pulled out her guest register and opened it to the current page.

The blond man dipped the pen in the inkwell and printed, then signed *Edward Arden, Denver, Colorado,* in the register.

"Tell me, ma'am," he said casually, "do you know where I might find a Sam Blake?"

"Blake, Blake? Sorry, no, but there are lots of ranch hands whose names I don't know. He could be out at one of the ranches."

Arden nodded absently. The telegrams from Sam Blake were from Rincon, as were the two suspect policy-holders. As he claimed his key and walked upstairs with his valise and briefcase, he decided to get some lunch and then try to find the mysterious Sam Blake.

2:15pm

Prudence dismissed her class, pinned on her hat, put Max in the traces and set out for the center of town in the buggy. She would have close to a half-hour to talk to Arabella before the stage left.

Arabella had given her valises to the stage line clerk to put in the boot of the stagecoach. Carrying only her reticule, she walked about under the wooden awning of the stage office to wait for the driver to return. No sense boarding the stage until just before they were ready to go.

Sam was lying against a boulder, trying to catch a brief nap. When darkness fell, there would be no time for sleep, but plenty of time for a tired man to die.

Clint was gazing over Ganados Ravine, one of an endless chain of cigarettes dangling from his mouth. He and Sam, in turns, had been watching the herd of cattle moving toward the Mystics since early this morning. Later in the afternoon, Sam would take over the watch and Clint would grab a few winks.

Edward Arden ate a quick lunch and walked to the telegraph office. The telegrapher quickly identified Sam Blake as a big, black-bearded stranger who had sent and received several telegrams over the preceding week. The telegrapher couldn't tell Arden exactly where Sam was staying, but guessed, from gossip around town, that he was staying at the Bar M.

Arden thought it strange that his informant lived on the premises of the insured under suspicion, but then, how better to get the information? He would have to find a livery stable and hire a rig to travel out to this Bar M Ranch.

Ethan Morgan was finally starting to breathe easily. By now, Arabella was waiting at the stage office to leave town. Ethan took a large tumbler of whiskey and drank it down quickly. By this time tomorrow he would be on his way to becoming a wealthy man again.

Jack Derry was looking out the window of his room. His saddlebags were all packed and his six-shooters loaded. He saw Arabella Morgan in her gray traveling suit, pacing in front of the stage office impatiently.

The time was now.

Derry headed downstairs and out the back door where his horse stood, saddled and ready. He threw his saddlebags over the back of the saddle. When he was behind the stage office, he tied off his horse and stepped quietly around the building to where his target was in sight.

Arabella was pacing back and forth. Her mind was on Clint. What was he doing? Would she see him again when his job was over? Did he really love her as much as she loved him?

"Just walk casual-like, like I was an old friend, and you won't get yourself hurt," said the rough voice close to her ear.

"Who are you? What do you want from me?" she said in a panicky whisper.

"Who I am is none of your business. What I want is insurance. Now move."

Shaking inside, Arabella had no choice but to follow the man around the back of the building. Still holding his gun on her, he swung up into the saddle.

"You can ride behind me on your arse or your belly—your choice," he snarled.

With the grace of one who has spent nearly as much time in the saddle as on her feet, she stepped in the stirrup and mounted, holding herself to the back of the saddle. She was not going to argue with a man with a gun.

Derry spurred his horse into movement as he headed out of town in the direction of Ganados Ravine.

Prudence stood on the boardwalk in front of the stage office, arms akimbo. It was 2:30 and there was no sign of Arabella. The stage was standing in the street. Curiosity piqued, Prudence looked in the boot. There were two valises marked with tags identifying them as her friend's.

Prudence poked her head inside the stage office. The clerk was busy doing paperwork. He heard the door open and looked up.

"Miss Hofheinz?"

"Mr. Rodgers, good afternoon. Was Arabella Morgan here?"

The clerk nodded. "Sold her a ticket to the train depot at the end of the line and loaded her bags. Isn't she outside?"

Prudence shook her head. "No, I expected she would be waiting in front."

Rodgers shrugged. "She was out there a little while ago. Maybe she went to Jackson's or The Bluebird to get something to eat before the stage leaves."

"I'll try there. May I leave my buggy tied up outside?" On receiving an affirmative reply, she continued, "If Arabella comes back, tell her I'm looking for her and I'll be back before the stage leaves."

"Sure," Rodgers answered as Prudence ducked out and shut the door behind her.

She went to Jackson's. Arabella had not been there that afternoon. It was the same at The Bluebird.

It occurred to Prudence to try the telegraph office. Perhaps Arabella has sent a wire to her aunt to let her know when she expected to arrive.

She was stepping onto the boardwalk in front of the telegraph office when she nearly slammed into the conservatively dressed, blond stranger. He tipped his hat and apologized.

"Did you just come from the Western Union office?" she asked.

"I did."

"Did you see a pretty blonde about five feet four wearing traveling clothes? I think her suit is light gray. She's the kind of woman who turns heads."

Edward Arden grinned. "I'm sure I would have noticed someone like that, but no one meeting that description was in the telegraph office."

Prudence's brow wrinkled worriedly. "It's not like Arabella Morgan to just wander off."

Arden's ears pricked up. "Morgan. Any relation to Ethan Morgan?"

Prudence started and stared at the stranger. "His daughter. You have business with Mr. Morgan?"

Arden cocked his head. "In a way. And with someone else out there. I need to get out to his ranch. Do you know the way?"

Prudence looked at the man. He was about Sam's age and dressed for the city. With the leather briefcase he looked like a lawyer or accountant.

"I certainly do. I have my buggy parked by the stage office. I'll drive you out there once the stage leaves." She glanced at the small watch pinned to the breast of her dark blue shirtwaist.

"That's very neighborly of you, uh, I don't believe I caught your name."

Prudence smiled. "That's because I didn't throw it. Miss Prudence Hofheinz."

"Edward Arden, just in from Denver."

Prudence snapped to attention. "Denver?" She looked at the briefcase. Lawyer? Accountant? Insurance man? "Are you with the insurance company in Denver?"

Arden's color seemed to drain from his face. "How do you know about the insurance company?"

"Sam Blake is a friend of mine. Mr. Arden, I'm worried about Arabella. It's not like her to disappear like this. I need to get back to the stage office and see if she's come back."

Prudence lifted her skirts slightly and half-walked, half-ran back toward the stage office, Arden barely a step behind her. The stage was still parked, but there were a couple of people inside now. Prudence glanced inside the coach. Arabella was not there. She was not inside the stage office nor was she waiting out front.

Prudence began to feel the cold chill of fear trickling down her spine. Her breathing felt harsh within her lungs—and not just from running all over town. She looked at her watch again. It was 2:55. The stage was leaving in five minutes and there was no sign of Arabella save her luggage. Three more people boarded the stage, none of them Arabella. It had been nearly three-quarters of an hour since anyone remembered seeing her.

"Are you all right, Miss Hofheinz?" she heard Edward Arden ask her.

"No, I'm very worried."

Mr. Rodgers came out of the office. He went into the boot and retrieved Arabella's valises. He looked sheepishly at Prudence and said, "If she shows before the stage leaves, I'll put them back. Otherwise, they'll be here in the baggage room."

The time passed both too rapidly and inexorably slowly. Finally at three o'clock, the driver shut the stagecoach door, he and the shotgun climbed on top and the coach drove off to the south, absent the only passenger Prudence cared anything about.

Frustrated, Prudence flounced down on the bench in front of the stage office. It was then she saw the envelope with the badly written legend *Ethen Morgen—Persinall.*

She picked up the envelope and stared at it.

"What is it, Miss Hofheinz?" Arden asked.

Prudence's hands were shaking. "I'm afraid it's the answer to where Arabella Morgan's gone. And I'm afraid it's not good news."

Chapter 14

Arden immediately sat down next to her. Prudence turned over the envelope. It was not sealed; rather, the flap had just been tucked inside the envelope.

"I'm opening it."

"Good idea," Arden affirmed.

Prudence flipped open the envelope and removed the paper. In a clearly uneducated hand, it said:

"Ethen Morgen—

"I dont believe you and Mr. Mckinly are going to keep your end of the bargen, so I took sum insurence that you wil. My boys wil do your fire and wen you giv me the mony I wil giv you back your dotter. But if you dubble cross me and the boys, wat I giv you back wont look much like wat I took. Shes real purty and I bet shes real gud too, if you no wat I meen.

"Dont think Im kiding heer, cos I aint."

Prudence handed the letter to Arden. The missive wasn't signed, but its authorship was unmistakable.

"Blake was right," Arden commented.

"Arabella's in danger." Prudence clasped her fingers together.

"Do you know who wrote this note?"

"A small-time rustler named Jack Derry. He made this threat a week ago, but it looks like whatever they have planned is going to happen tonight, as we suspected."

"What do you have to do with it?" Arden asked suspiciously.

Prudence shook her head. "Nothing really. I discovered information I gave to Sam Blake that led him to conclude Mr. Morgan has been setting up some scheme to defraud your insurance company. You're an investigator of some kind?"

Arden pulled out a business card from a metal case in his inside pocket and handed it to Prudence. "I'm head of the claims investigation department for Stockmen's Mutual. Where would Mr. Blake be now?"

"He and his partner, Mr. Randolph, are either at the ranch or they're already up in the Mystic Mountains to head off the arsonists."

"We'd better get out to the ranch, Miss Hofheinz. On the way there you can tell me what you know about what's going on."

Using her buggy whip to get as much speed out of the plodding Max as she could, Pru and Arden headed out to the Bar M. Prudence related what she knew, as well as what she surmised but had not confirmed.

She wondered what Edward Arden was going to do. If they were trying to catch Ethan Morgan actively involved in the fraud, Arden showing his hand might hamper things.

Unless things had already gone too far for it to matter.

It certainly no longer mattered to Prudence.

And it certainly no longer mattered to Arabella.

Prudence barely pulled the brake on her buggy before she was dismounting. She saw a number of Bar M hands coming out of the stable covered with dust from a day's work. Except for Bob Bonetti, she knew none of their names. The men were laughing and talking like nothing out of the ordinary was happening.

"Bob, Bob Bonetti," Prudence called. "Where's Mr. Morgan?"

"Search me, Miss Hofheinz. This morning he ordered us to drive the cattle up to near Ganados Ravine and we all just got back. That's awful close—I mean awfully close to the ridge and the grass is pretty near as—nearly as dry up there as it is down here. Did you try the house?"

"Not yet, Bob. Thanks."

Prudence beckoned to Arden as she darted toward the house. Under her breath, she said, "It's starting, Mr. Arden. Ganados Ravine is a deep divide in the Mystics. A strategically placed fire could drive the whole herd off the edge."

On reaching the front door, Prudence knocked loudly. Consuelo answered the door.

"*Señorita* Prudence," the housekeeper exclaimed, "*Señorita* Arabella has gone to San Antonio."

"Something's happened, Consuelo. Where's Mr. Morgan? It's important."

"I don't know. He ride away about an hour ago and did not tell where he go."

"Mr. Randolph?"

"Him and *el gordo* go at daybreak. Do not know where they go."

Consuelo referred to Sam as *the fat one*, which made Prudence shudder. Quickly she thanked Consuelo and gestured Edward Arden away as she returned to her buggy.

She was starting to climb into the buggy when the insurance investigator grabbed her by the arm and hauled her down. She stared at his smooth, pale, long-fingered hand with the manicured nails and thought of the contrast between this and Sam's big, tanned and callused hands with the tufts of black hair between the knuckles and on the backs and her heart hurt for missing him.

"Where are you going, Miss Hofheinz?"

She tilted her head up slightly to look into his very ordinary blue eyes. "Back into Rincon, Mr. Arden."

"Have you any idea where Mr. Morgan might be?"

She shrugged. "Mr. Morgan? Not exactly. But I've a pretty fair idea where Sam Blake and Clint Randolph are and I can't get there in a buggy. If Sam's right, Mr. Morgan may be near there as well." She threw off his arm and climbed into the buggy. "I would suggest you come back into town with me and hire yourself a good horse and tack."

Arden climbed into the buggy beside Prudence and she urged Max into action. On the way back to town she described the way to get from town to Ganados Ravine.

"My contact on this case has been with Sam Blake, yet you asked the housekeeper about a Mr. Randolph."

"Sam's partner. Most folks consider Clint Randolph the leader of the operation, but they're equal partners in all of their business dealings."

She halted the trap in front of Mrs. Lester's boarding house to let Arden off.

"I *know* where we're going, Mr. Derry," Arabella growled from her place behind the rustler on his saddle. It didn't take a genius to tell they were headed for the Mystics.

"I don't give a rat's ass whether you know or not," he snapped back. "I want your old man to be able to find us."

"Why are you doing this? My father doesn't have much cash to pay a ransom..."

"He soon will. You're here to make sure I get the cut he promised me for the job I'm pulling for him."

"You're pulling a job *for* him? Why would my father want to rustle his own cattle?"

"Shut your damned mouth or I'll gag you," Derry said.

Arabella shut up. The last thing she wanted was a dirty bandanna shoved in her mouth.

They continued to ride toward the Mystics.

Prudence realized she had to reach Sam and Clint as soon as possible to let them know about the kidnapping. She was sure it would change their plan of action. Even if Sam and his partner were on the outs, she could not believe Sam would intentionally do anything to harm Arabella Morgan.

Prudence unhitched Max and led him out of the traces. She brushed him down lightly and put him in his stall with hay and water. She would saddle him before she left again.

She changed from her shirtwaist and skirt into her riding clothes. She belted the split skirt with a sheath for her hunting knife. She plaited her hair into a single braid down her back, tying it off with twine. On a chair near the front door she laid a man's fringed buckskin jacket that would protect her from wind and weather and which, layered with a shirt and cardigan, would keep her reasonably warm at night.

Rifling her drawer, Prudence took out an extra pair of socks and some bandannas. One she tied around her neck, the remainder and the socks she put in her saddlebag.

From her linen chest she drew out the blankets and sheet she used when she and Arabella went camping out on the range and a large length of unbleached muslin to use for bandages. With a kidnapping and potential arson and stampede, she reasoned that there might be shooting and injuries.

In the kitchen, Prudence filled her two canteens with water from the pump. She dumped several cupfuls of raisins into cloth napkins and stuck in her can opener and several cans of beans and potted beef along with her tin of tea. She had a small cooking set for camping out in a canvas drawstring ditty bag along with a metal tin of matches waterproofed by dipping them up to the sulfur in melted paraffin.

Prudence took along a candle lantern and several extra candles. She took a small sewing kit. She wished she had a pistol.

She also wished she had a bottle of laudanum, but she didn't. She would have settled for a bottle of whiskey, but all she had was a bottle of Dr. Brown's Sure Cure Tonic, which she had bought two years before at a medicine show. Later, she found out Sure Cure was about sixty percent whiskey and about forty percent herbal tea. It might not be a sure cure, but it could render a person just tipsy enough not to care about his aches and pains.

Just before she left, Prudence made herself a sandwich and ate it with a glass of water. There was no sense trying to be up all night on an empty stomach.

It was already dusk when Prudence threw her saddlebag over one shoulder and her jacket over her arm. Hat on head, she left her cabin and headed for the shed.

She saddled Max; tied on her saddlebags and bedroll. A coil of rope hung on the shed wall. She took it down and tied it to the saddle. It was already cool, so she put on her jacket and gloves and led the horse out of the shed. After closing the door, she mounted and headed toward the Mystics. She glanced at her watch. It was nearly seven o'clock.

It would be close to two hours before the plodding Max could get to the north range. Galloping was not in his repertoire.

Prudence hoped two hours would not be too long. Lives depended on her getting there now.

Arabella's for one. Sam Blake's for another.

Her best friend and her dearest love.

As darkness descended, the Derry Gang began to converge on the north range. None of the Bar M hands or the honest Lazy K hands were around, all of them having been sent back to their respective bunkhouses.

All they were waiting for was for Jack Derry to arrive and give them the order to start stampeding the cattle toward Ganados Ravine and setting the fire.

Ethan Morgan was hiding near an outcropping on the near side of the ravine. His rifle was poised; he was within range of the ledge to shoot Derry before the night was over.

Sam Blake and Clint Randolph were concealed behind boulders on the far side of the ravine; both of them armed with rifles. They could not see Morgan, nor he them.

"Morgan!" a voice echoed through the night. "You out there?"

Ethan was shocked to hear his name called. "Derry, you son of a bitch, where the hell are you?"

"I'm here," Derry called back, "and I have a little surprise for you!" To Arabella he growled, "Say something, or you'll wish you had."

"Papa!" she called out. Her misery-filled voice echoed.

"Arabella?" Clint gasped.

"Arabella?" Morgan cried out. "Are you all right, Baby?"

"I'm all right, Papa, but I'm scared."

Clint started to stand up, but Sam yanked him down, hissing, "What, are you crazy? You want to give up our position?"

"But..."

"I know. I'd feel the same if it was Pru, but stay calm and let Derry give up his position first."

Clint felt cold sweat along his spine. This wasn't just a job anymore. He couldn't stay detached when the woman he loved was involved. Anger seeped into his heart. He vowed if Derry hurt even one hair on her head the rustler was dead. He tried to discern the locations of Morgan and Derry, but the echoes of the voices within the ravine walls and through the hills distorted the sound.

The sound was further distorted by the lowing of cattle being driven toward their eventual doom in the ravine. Torches held by the Derry Gang members created points of light in the darkness.

Morgan's voice split the night. "What do you want from me, Derry? More money?"

"Nah," Derry yelled. "I'm just makin' sure you keep up the bargain you already made. My boys are out there, ready to burn you and McKinley's cows right into the ravine. Only change is, I keep your girl until I get the money you promised."

"That could be weeks, Derry. It's not like I can write you a check. The insurance company has to pay the claim first. You planning to keep her that long?"

Derry grabbed Arabella by the arm and pulled her against his chest. "She's a real looker, Morgan. Could be a few real good weeks for me."

Clint started to rise again, but Sam dragged him down again. "Give them a little more rope, partner; they'll put themselves both in prison in a moment. Derry's bluffing."

"How do you know that?" Clint whispered back.

"Because he knows Morgan will kill him for sure if he hurts her."

Morgan yelled back, anger making him shake. "You son of a bitch, you'll get your money. You harm my daughter and you're food for vultures. Let Arabella go and I'll protect you from McKinley. Just get those goddamned fires started or none of us will see a penny."

"We've heard enough," Sam hissed at Clint. Rising to his feet in the darkness, he called out, his deep voice resounding through the Mystics, "It's over, Morgan. The insurance company knows about the fraud. They won't be paying any claim."

"Shit," Derry mumbled.

"Clint!" Arabella shouted. "Clint!"

"Arabella!" Clint yelled back, "stay calm. I'll save you."

Sam groaned. How stupidly gallant!

"The game is over, Derry," Sam called into the night. "Let the girl go and call off your boys and all you'll face is conspiracy charges."

In the darkness, nobody saw or heard Pete McKinley ride up, skirting the herd. He heard Morgan betray him and his reason left him. Straining to discern Morgan's location, he raised his rifle toward the sound of his erstwhile co-conspirator's voice and squeezed the trigger.

The shot rang off the rocks above Ethan's head. A moment later, hell broke loose.

Ethan, unsure where the bullet came from, assumed it came from Derry. He raised his rifle and fired.

"Jesus Christ!" mumbled Derry. He grabbed Arabella by the arm. "We're getting out of here." He dragged her to his horse, threw her in the saddle, mounted behind her and took off.

"Clint!" Arabella cried. "Help me!"

"Arabella!" Clint called back. He raised his rifle and shot into the darkness. The bullet echoed in the canyon.

McKinley shot; then Ethan. Bullets were flying everywhere. The sounds of gunfire began to panic the cattle, who began moving in all directions. The Derry boys, not accustomed to handling stampeding cattle, didn't know what to do. Seeing the force of the herd heading towards them, most of the rustlers took off into the night, their torches lighting the way.

In the darkness, one of the horses stumbled and the rustler, trying to keep his seat, dropped his torch. It landed in the drought-stricken grass and flared up. The rustler didn't stop to retrieve the torch; he just rode off to safety as flames began to spread in all directions.

Unaware that Derry was gone, Morgan rose and fired again. McKinley fired where he thought Morgan was and Morgan fired back. Clint fired his rifle, his mind more on Arabella than what he was doing. He fired in the direction of the shots.

Sam rose in the darkness and raised his own rifle. Before he could squeeze the trigger, a shot from Morgan's rifle struck him in the left shoulder. With a cry he stepped backwards, off-balance into the darkness behind him onto a patch of overgrowth.

And kept falling into the darkness, for the overgrowth concealed one of those abandoned Spanish mineshafts.

Hearing Sam fall, Clint shot in the direction of the shot that felled his partner. The bullet was true. It had Ethan Morgan's name on it and struck him right between the eyes.

In the sudden cessation of gunfire, McKinley realized he'd escaped harm. He mounted and turned his horse to run, but the horse panicked in the stampede and ran toward Ganados Ravine instead of away. The stampede carried Pete McKinley over the ledge into the ravine to his death, landing beneath his own horse and the dying steers.

Into the stygian darkness Sam fell, unable to right himself or determine how deep was the hole into which he had fallen. He tried desperately to curl himself into a ball, but his sheer size prevented it. Sam had to settle for throwing his right arm over his face to prevent his glasses from breaking, knowing that shards of glass from his lenses could blind him if his glasses broke when he landed.

Thus it was that he was halfway curled, facedown when he landed on the floor of the shaft on a slag pile of broken rock left in the hole when the mine was abandoned. He landed, propelled by the force of a nearly twenty-foot drop compounded by his 275 pound frame.

Unbelievable pain spread through his body. His gunshot shoulder was bleeding. Sam had no idea of the extent of that injury, but the pain in his shoulder was minor compared to the agony in his legs. He could tell that some of his bones were shattered; it felt like his legs were bent unnaturally, but shock made his perceptions vague. He pushed himself with his sound arm until he rolled over off the slag heap and landed on his back.

"Sam!" Clint shouted, "where are you?"

In a voice harsh with pain, Sam called back, "I fell down a mineshaft."

"I've got to find Arabella before Derry hurts her—or worse. Are you hurt?"

"Not too badly," Sam lied. "Go after her. Derry probably... headed...deeper...into the Mystics."

"You going to be all right, Sam?"

"I'll...be...all...right. Go find her. I'll...just...stay put...until morning."

Going to Wind Dancer, Clint lit a lantern. He went over to Nameless and released Sam's rope. Carefully, he wended his way back to the hole in the hill. He peered down into the shaft, but couldn't see in the darkness.

"Sam, I'm lowering a lantern on a rope now." Clint let the coil slide between his fingers until he heard the lantern hit stone when it landed on the slag pile. "Sam, have you got it?"

"Yes," Sam bit out, though it wasn't the truth. "Go get Arabella, partner. I'll be all right."

"You sure?"

"I'm...sure."

Clint hesitated, but finally he rode off deeper into the Mystics in the direction he presumed Jack Derry had taken Arabella.

Sam heard the faint sound of his partner riding away. He lay his head back and closed his eyes.

He was going to be all right.

After all, he was going to die before the sun rose.

His life was one full of regrets. His principal regret was that he had never told Prudence Hofheinz he loved her.

Now he was going to die without ever being able to say the words.

Chapter 15

Prudence rode through the darkness, the redoubtable Max plodding at his own, leisurely pace. Pru could have kicked the old gelding's sides until they bled and he wouldn't go a trot faster.

It was dark—darker than she ever remembered. Her arm was getting tired holding her lantern to try to light the virtually moonless way. A stiff, dry breeze was blowing. She rode through Bar M property toward the Mystics.

Suddenly, she heard in the distance the sound of hooves and shouting and saw torches. The sound was definitely stampeding cattle—and coming closer.

It was happening as they expected. Prudence realized she would need both hands to control Max if the stampede got him skittish. Quickly, she blew out the candle in her lantern and hooked the wire over the pommel. She grabbed the reins with her now empty hand and edged Max further north.

The torches came closer, revealing about half a dozen cowboys riding hell bent for leather amid a herd of stampeding cattle. Prudence kept moving Max back, hidden in the darkness.

Skirting the outside of the stampede, trying to control Max, who was beginning to panic himself, she saw a glowing light closer to Ganados Ravine.

"My God, the fire," she gasped.

With the wind and dry grass, the conflagration could swallow the entire range. Pru realized that her only chance at safety was to get up into the Mystics. Riding back to the ranch would put her in the middle of the stampede. Heading directly for the ravine would put her in the fire.

Prudence knew from where she was that Ganados Ravine was to the northwest, but the Mystics began directly north. Glancing up in to the clear, starlit sky, she located Polaris and turned Max to ride toward the North Star and the relative safety of the foothills.

She could feel the terrain grow steeper as she began to ride up into the hills. She rode up a few hundred feet when she remembered that the Mystics were riddled with abandoned mineshafts. Neither she nor Max could see well in the dark and to lose the old gelding to a broken leg could be fatal to her as well.

She pulled Max to a halt and relit her lantern. The area was not familiar, but looked like much of the rest of the hills. Still holding her lantern, she dismounted, then stroked Max's neck and crooned gentling words to try to calm him more.

Quickly she hobbled Max and untied her blanket roll. Even with her buckskin jacket, cardigan and shirt, the wind was making it very cold. Prudence found a spot as much out of the wind as she could and wrapped herself in her blankets. To conserve candles, she doused her lantern. She was grateful she had taken time to eat before setting out. She could hold out until morning on water from her canteen.

Sitting huddled in her blankets, Prudence began to worry. Not about herself. She was as safe as she could be, but if the cattle were stampeding and she could see the fire in the direction of the ravine, had Messrs. Morgan and McKinley succeeded in committing their fraud? What had happened to Arabella? She wasn't sure about Clint Randolph's feelings toward her friend, but she knew Mr. Morgan would want revenge if Jack Derry hurt Arabella.

And Sam. Was he alive? Had he gathered the evidence he needed to prove the fraud? Was he all right?

Prudence shivered, as much from fear as cold. She knew so little of what was going on and here she was, huddled in the dark, unable to find out any more until a long morning away.

"What kind of monster are you?" the whore screamed at the sight of his huge, hairy body. "Get out of my crib!"

"I paid my two bucks."

"I don't care if you paid two hundred bucks. I ain't lettin' you stick that thing in me. You'd likely rip me in two."

"But..." It had been too long between women, even this kind.

"No buts, Mister." She grabbed a letter opener and held it like a dagger. "Come near me and I'll kill you, so help me!"

With an anguished cry, Sam woke from his fevered dream. Movement sent unbearable pain through his shoulders and legs.

He lay back. It was so dark in the pit into which he'd fallen. Only in sleep was there any relief from the pain, but sleep brought nightmares.

But nightmares or no, sleep was his only relief.

His eyelids felt so heavy.

When, oh when, was he going to die?

He drifted into oblivion again, his last conscious thought the sweet, sad face of Prudence Hofheinz.

Clint's arm was aching from holding a lantern to light his way. Accepting Sam's word that he was all right, all Clint's thoughts were concentrated on finding Arabella before Jack Derry could do her any harm.

Though he knew that even the feeble light of the lantern was like a lighthouse beacon in the darkness, Clint was smart enough to know it was folly to ride through unknown terrain without some light. Fortunately, the wary Wind Dancer was walking slowly, as if sensing his master's ill ease.

He rode on through the reclaimed land of the Mystics hoping to find some clue as to the direction the rustler and his hostage were traveling. He began to see some evidence of trampled foliage on the ground. Halting Wind Dancer and dismounting with the lantern, Clint saw deeply cut tracks of a well-laden horse.

Figuring that Derry would not go far in the moonless night hoping that the others would have all shot each other while he escaped with Arabella, Clint remained on the ground and led his horse, holding the lantern low to illuminate the hoofprints.

As he walked, he got to thinking. After Sam fell into the hole, Clint had fired a shot in the darkness. Almost immediately after, there had been a man's scream over the lowing of cattle and then all the shooting stopped.

What had happened to Morgan? To McKinley? Was it possible they were both dead? Clint had taken the last shot. Had he shot and killed Ethan Morgan? How was he going to tell Arabella her father was probably dead and he had likely killed him?

Would she reject him now, turn him away from her as one might a murderer? Would explaining about the crime he and Sam had uncovered be excuse enough for her to forgive him for the misadventure that had probably cost her father his life?

Clint sighed. He stopped walking for a moment and rolled himself a cigarette. The strong smoke seemed to calm him as it flooded his lungs. Well, rejection or not, he owed it to Arabella to rescue her. If she never wanted to see him again, he'd just go on as he always had, moving from town to town finding detective jobs to earn a few bucks.

No, it wouldn't be the same. Clint would be on his own for the first time in a dozen years.

A cold shudder shook him. He couldn't do this without Sam. He would have to look for a new line. Maybe he could get a sheriffing job where he could trade on his reputation and quick draw. He wouldn't have to be brilliant, just solid and reliable.

His life was about to change. The question was would it be for the better or the worst?

He wanted to talk to Sam about what to do. But Sam and he had barely spoken to each other since their last fight.

And he didn't know how Sam was, really.

Clint returned his attention to following the trail of hoofprints in the kerosene illuminated darkness. Sam could take care of himself.

Clint wasn't as certain about Arabella.

Arabella didn't know how long she and Jack Derry had ridden, but it felt like about an hour. She had lost her hat and hairpins somewhere and her hair was falling in tangled disarray over her shoulders and down her back. She felt gritty and dirty and very frightened, but realized that her relative safety depended on her cooperation with the rustler.

Her mind was reeling with the realization that her father had conspired to get money from an insurance company for the loss of his herd. It was obvious to her he had convinced the Cattlemen's Association to hire the detectives as a ruse to cover his illegal activity. When she heard the incriminating words flying through the air at Ganados Ravine, a tight knot formed in her stomach.

Clint hadn't told her that her father had become a suspect.

Did he think she was involved? What would that do to their relationship? Would he reject her and ride away? Or had he only been playing the lover to get information from her? Was it all to cover the work he was doing?

And more fool she; she had let him make love to her in her own bed. And she hadn't even liked it much.

Finally, Derry halted the horse, dismounted and hauled Arabella down after him. It was pitch black and cold. Arabella wrapped her arms about herself and rubbed herself to get warm.

"Where are we?" she said as calmly as she could.

"Shit if I know for sure," the rustler replied, "but if I don't know, it's a cinch nobody else does."

"What are you going to do with me?"

"Girl, don't you sass me and I ain't gonna do nothing. You ain't no good to me dead and it sounds like that half-breed boyfriend of yours'd be standing in line behind your pa to skin me alive if I did anything else. Right now you and me're gonna sit right down here and get comfy and wait until morning. As long as you're real quiet-like, I won't have to gag you and we're gonna get along okay. You got me, girl?"

"Yes," Arabella hissed out.

"You cold? I know it's colder'n the North Pole, so don't go getting all brave on me."

"Yes, I am cold," she admitted.

A few moments later a stiff, mildewed blanket was tossed in her lap. Arabella shook it out and wrapped it around her, covering her head. She was grateful to be wearing her soft kidskin traveling gloves. They would help keep the heat in her hands.

She heard footsteps near her in the darkness. Jack Derry crouched and thrust a canteen and some jerky into her hands.

"I reckon you need this, too. Go easy on the water. I ain't got that much and we both'll be needing it."

Mumbling thanks, Arabella began to chew slowly on the salty dried beef. She could hear the creak of his boots as he hunkered down with another blanket not far from where she was sitting.

"No fire?"

"Can't take a chance on being seen."

It took Arabella a while to work up her courage. "Mr. Derry, may I ask you a question?"

He grunted in response.

"My father—did he hire you to destroy our herd?"

"Hmm."

"It was for the insurance money?"

"Yeah."

"I never heard of such a thing before," she commented quietly.

"Me neither 'til they brung it up to me," Derry admitted. "Stupid idea, huh?"

Arabella shrugged. "I don't know. Maybe not, until my father decided to hire detectives to distract everybody. I guess he never thought they would figure it out."

"Yeah, I guess Randolph lives up to his reputation again," Derry said bitterly.

Arabella sighed. She knew it probably wasn't Clint who figured it out but his big, taciturn partner—but that hardly mattered now. Her father was a criminal, as much a criminal as the foul-smelling man sitting barely an arm's length from her.

She was safe—for now. Derry seemed disinclined to hurt her. It seemed all his suggestive comments about using her sexually were just threats to secure her father's cooperation. Right now he sounded more depressed than evil.

Arabella gathered the blanket tighter around her shoulders. It was warmer than nothing, but only barely, and it smelled of mildew and stale sweat and horses. She wished she was home in her safe, warm bed, or even on her way to San Antonio. Instead she was somewhere in the Mystics, lost and in the dark with a desperate, defeated rustler.

Right about now she'd be happy to have Sam Blake show up to rescue her—and she didn't even like him much. Gradually, exhaustion overcame her and she nodded off to sleep.

Huddled in his own blanket, Jack Derry tried to fight off the sleep that threatened to overtake him. Finally he could no longer keep his heavy eyelids open and drifted off to sleep.

First light awoke Prudence. She realized it was Thursday morning and she was miles from town. Her students would show up this morning and find their Miss Hofheinz gone. In nine years in Rincon, she had never missed a day of school.

What had happened at Ganados Ravine?

Prudence crawled out of her bedroll and stretched her stiff muscles. Quickly she rolled up her bedroll and lashed it to Max's back. She took a drink of water from her canteen and ate the contents of one of the raisin-filled napkins.

She pushed her hat back on her tousled hair.

When she mounted she got a rather unpleasant surprise.

"Oh, my God!"

The sky as dark gray with smoke and the range was ablaze. She was trapped in the Mystics, unable to return to Rincon.

There was only one way to go—that was further into the hills toward Ganados Ravine where she and Sam had parted so miserably.

It was too quiet.

She pressed on to the northwest, not sure what she would find.

Arabella was shaken awake by a bleary-eyed Jack Derry. He thrust the canteen into her hands.

"Take a slug and use the bushes. Then mount up, we're moving."

She took a drink and stood stiffly. Every part of her body ached from sleeping sitting up. She handed the blanket back to her kidnapper, who rolled the two blankets back together and tied them to his horse. She looked around, but realized that she had no idea where she was. It was a part of the Mystic Mountains in which she had never been. The sky was strangely dark making it was difficult to tell where the east was.

Not knowing where she was, Arabella realized there was no place to run. Without food or water, clad in high-heeled shoes and a long skirt with no hat, trying to escape was suicide. She was safer with Derry for now. She slipped her foot in the stirrup and hoisted herself into the saddle.

The rustler followed her into the saddle and spurred the horse into action as they climbed higher into the hills.

Jack Derry had no idea where he was going at this point. The two detectives had pretty much assured that there would be no insurance claim. With all the shooting going on, he had no idea if Ethan Morgan was still alive. Morgan had told him he had no other money.

Jack had about twenty dollars in his pocket. It was all the money he had in the world. It occurred to him his best plan was to get to a way station or town, leave Arabella there and get the hell out of Texas. If he didn't hurt the girl, maybe he'd escape hanging one more time.

"What's north of here?" he asked.

"Amarillo eventually, but I don't know how far it is...Mr. Derry, please let me go. If my father is broke enough to try to cheat his insurance company, I doubt he'll have any money to ransom me."

"I can't let you go, girl, not yet anyway."

"If you let me go and they catch you, I'll testify that you didn't do any shooting at Ganados Ravine."

"Yeah, but I snatched you and put a gun to your fat friend's ribs..."

Arabella stiffened against Derry's back. "What!"

"She didn't tell you?"

"No."

"The breed," Derry muttered.

"Clint?"

"She must have gone running to the half-breed."

Or his partner, Arabella thought, but kept her mouth shut.

On they rode, neither of them sure where.

Clint Randolph found where Derry and Arabella spent the night. In the daylight the trail was far easier to follow. Derry was making no effort to hide his trail.

Clint wondered if Derry had a hideout somewhere in the Mystics where he planned to stash Arabella until he received the money he would now never see.

With the two of them riding double, it was only a matter of time before Clint would catch up with them.

Prudence reached the hills above Ganados Ravine about an hour and a half after she arose. She could see the wild fires burning below where she rode. She was almost to the spot where she had been with Sam the previous Sunday when she spotted something moving behind a thicket of high brush, boulders and trees.

She dismounted and looped Max's reins over a clump of brush. It was enough to keep the docile gelding standing in place.

The area was littered with rifle cartridges. Prudence felt a pain clutch at her heart. There had been shooting. But it was over now. Who was alive? Who was dead?

There were the remains of a campfire, a coffeepot and skillet sitting on the circle of stones. There were footprints around.

Prudence heard the sound ahead of her again. Her hand on the hilt of her hunting knife, she crept around the large boulder. She took a few more steps and saw that the animal was the hobbled Nameless, calmly munching at some brush. There was no sign of another horse.

"Sam!" She began to fear he was dead, or else why would Nameless be standing here alone?

But if Clint was bringing his body back to town, wouldn't he have tied Sam across the dun's saddle? Prudence took a quick look at Nameless. The horse seemed sound.

Terror-stricken, she began to look for Sam's body. She returned the way she came, looking for some sign. She called out Sam's name over and over again. She saw no sign of a body.

She went a few steps farther and found a large hole in the ground partially concealed with tangled brush. By the hole she found a rifle.

Her heart pounding, she dropped to her knees and peered down into the hole.

"Sam!" she cried. "Sam Blake!"

Sam opened his eyes. He heard a voice calling his name. He looked up and saw a beam of light. Could it be the voice of death at last?

"Sam!" He heard it again. It sounded like Pru.

Through dry, cracked lips he croaked, "Pru?"

Pru heard the weak voice and called down, "Sam, are you hurt?"

He could lie to her, but he suspected she would not just leave him alone to die.

"Yeah," he croaked, "pretty...badly...I think."

"Is there a ladder somewhere down there?"

Sam moved his head from side to side in the feeble light. "I can't tell."

"How far is it down?" she called down.

Sam closed his eyes and responded painfully. "About fifteen, twenty feet. Clint threw me a rope, but it's useless down here. Is there a rope on Nameless?"

"I'll look. Hold on, darling."

Sam lowered his head back, defeated and in exquisite pain. Of all the people to find him, it would have to be Pru.

Pru ran to Nameless. There was no rope, but she had brought one herself. She untied her own rope and released her saddlebags as well. Her lantern and what little medical supplies she had were in those bags.

She got back to the hole and stood there for a moment. It occurred to her she could not climb up and down a rope. She was not strong enough to pull herself up and down hand over hand. If she had hand or footholds...

She sat down for a moment and began to tie knots in the thick rope about every foot and a half. She found a crack in the boulder nearest the mineshaft and threaded the rope into the crack. Tying knots until she had a large hemp clot at the end of the rope, she created a stop.

She grabbed hold of the rope and yanked with all her body weight. The rope went taut through the crack, the knot stop holding it. She yanked at it several times to test it.

There was no margin for error. If Sam had fallen twenty feet he must be pretty badly banged up. If the rope gave way, they might both be trapped down the mineshaft.

Prudence slung her saddlebags over one shoulder. She said a little prayer and threw the loose end of the rope down the hole.

She prayed that she would get safely down the shaft.

Sam's life—and her own—hung in the balance.

Chapter 16

Prudence was definitely not the athletic type. The prospect of climbing down a knotted rope into twenty feet of near darkness was frightening. But Sam was down there and needed her help. That gave her courage.

She would have to carry her saddlebags down on her shoulder. With glass in them she could not take a chance on dropping them and following them down and she only had the one rope, so she had no way to lower the items down first because she had no idea how badly injured Sam was.

She crouched beside the hole and gingerly lowered herself, holding tight onto the uppermost knot until she found a lower knot and clamped both feet together above it.

Then slowly, one knot at a time, she moved her hands down, then her feet, hands, feet, hands, feet, barely able to breathe for fright and balancing the saddlebag on her shoulder.

Sam saw her figure as a shadow in the beam of muted light filtering into the shaft. He found himself holding his own breath at the enormity of what she was doing—for him. He should have told her not to bother, that he was dying anyway, but a part of him realized that would not have stopped her.

"Be careful, Pru," he said hoarsely. "The bottom of the shaft is a slag pile. It may not be stable."

Prudence grunted in response, but she'd heard the warning.

Her feet soon touched down on the pile of broken rock. It had been the longest two minutes in Prudence Hofheinz's life. Still clutching the rope in her gloved hands, she steadied herself and eased her way off the slag pile into the darkness.

Quickly she found her box of matches and lit her lantern. Her first sight was of the slag pile. It was a mound of jagged, rough stones and dirt and dead vegetation. The rope Clint had thrown down lay at her feet also, the lantern attached to it burned out. To have fallen twenty feet and landed on those rugged rocks! No wonder Sam thought himself badly hurt. She held the lantern higher.

The mine was a large cavern, littered with debris. There was a tunnel that seemed to wend into the darkness.

"Sam?" she called out.

"Behind you."

Pru turned, lantern in hand. Her free hand flew over her mouth when she saw him.

"My God, Sam," she gasped.

Sam lay flat on his back, his face filthy. The left side of his shirt and the legs of his jeans were black with dried blood.

"Your legs are all cattywampus," she exclaimed.

Instead of lying straight, his legs were bent in places where legs didn't normally bend and both of his knees seemed bent in the opposite direction from where knees should go. The denim jeans were taut from the swelling of the skin beneath and torn in one place where Pru could clearly see the broken end of one femur.

Her entire body went cold. Still holding the lantern, she dropped to her knees and bent over Sam's face. Through his spectacles, which miraculously had remained intact and on his face when he landed, his dark brown eyes were glassy with pain. Pru lowered her face and kissed him gently on the mouth.

"What hurts?" she said with quiet concern.

"What doesn't?" he responded with a wry chuckle.

"Can you feel your legs?"

"Yeah. They hurt like the devil."

She smiled slightly. "That's good news. It means your back's not broken...Sam, I'm going to have to get you out of your clothes to see what I can do for you. Have you a change in your saddlebag?"

"I don't think so. I left my other clothes in the bunkhouse."

Leaving the lantern on the ground, Prudence rose and returned to the knotted rope. Taking up the other rope, she slipped it over her head and stuck her arm through.

"I'm going to get my blanket roll."

"Pru!" Sam called after her.

She turned. "Yes?"

"This is hard to say..." Sam closed his eyes. "I've been lying here all night unable to move. I know this is indelicate..."

"What is it, Sam?"

"I have to—uh—urinate something fierce."

Pru started, knowing how difficult it might be for a proud man to admit that, even to a woman who had been his lover.

"Oh, Sam." Coming back to the floor of the shaft, she opened her saddlebag, yanked out the dittybag containing her cooking kit and pulled her wire-handled saucepan from the kit. Returning to Sam, she knelt down at his waist level and unbuttoned the fly on this jeans, then unbuttoned the bone buttons of his union suit. As dispassionately as she could, she reached inside and guided his penis out.

"Do you want to try to sit upright?"

"If I can."

Shifting her position, Pru slid one arm behind Sam's back and began to raise him up. Though he groaned with pain, she got him more or less upright with that lift and held the saucepan in position with the other.

Sam looked at the woman he loved. She hadn't shown any delicacy about helping him. He reached his right hand down, took hold and relieved himself in the saucepan. When he was finished, Pru put the pot aside and lowered him back down. Before she returned to the knotted rope, she again kissed him.

"What was that for?"

"Just because you needed it. I'll be back down in a few minutes."

She uncoiled the second rope, tied one end to the handle of the saucepan and climbed up the other rope—far more assuredly than her initial descent. A moment after she reached the surface, Sam saw the saucepan rising into the air.

Alone again, he raised he right hand to his mouth where she had kissed him. He felt a tingling sensation like he had only before sensed those three nights in Pru's bed. She was right; he did need her kiss, even more than food and water.

He felt a surge of arousal. He groaned, but realized her comment about his back was true. Whatever happened to him, he was not paralyzed.

A sense of relief shot through him.

A few minutes later two blanket rolls, his and one he assumed was hers came tumbling down the hole. Being soft, they fell without breaking. Then Sam saw his own saddlebag lowering tied to the extra rope. These were followed immediately by a much more self-assured Prudence Hofheinz down the knotted rope.

In a flash she had one of the bedrolls untied and gathered a blanket in her arms. She walked around to Sam's left side and knelt down, a worried frown on her face.

"What's wrong?"

"I need to get the blanket under you, but I don't know how to do it without causing you pain."

Sam actually laughed. "Pru, darling, I'm in so much pain now a little more isn't going to make much difference. I can use my right arm to help you some."

Pru reached over and undid Sam's gun belt. Sam raised himself as much as he could with one hand to let her slide it out from under him. His face broke out in a sweat as pain assailed him, but he gritted his teeth as Pru drew the blanket under his shoulders and hips and smoothed it out as much as possible. On her direction, he lowered himself again.

"Now the worst part."

Although Sam could not imagine anything worse, he knew she was going to have to move his legs and that would be worse.

"Go ahead and yell if you need to. I'll never tell."

As carefully as she could, she slid her arm under his knees and lifted them.

An unearthly scream shattered the quiet. Sam barely realized the scream came from him before he passed out.

Pru started at the scream and deathly quiet that followed. Frightened, she turned her head and was relieved to see the rise and fall of his massive chest. Realizing that unconscious it would not be as painful, she straightened the blanket and laid his shattered legs atop it.

Change of clothes or no, Pru realized there was no way she was going to be able to draw his jeans over his legs. Besides the broken bones and swelling, dried blood had glued his pants to his skin. There was nothing to do except cut his clothes off. She reached for her hunting knife and slid it under the hem of his jeans leg. Sawing carefully, she cut up the leg.

When she got to his knee, she could see how purple his legs were with subcutaneous bleeding. His own knife was in its boot sheath, the skin swollen around it. She pulled out the knife and saw immediately that it was far sharper than her own. His knife sliced through the heavy denim like butter. His union suit sliced even more easily.

In short order she cut off everything he wore except his boots. Dried blood covered his legs and left shoulder and glazed his body hair. She tried to get his boots off, but couldn't do so without jarring his injured legs. With a sigh, she began to cut through the leather of his large, well broken-in boots until she could slide them off his feet, followed by his socks. While he lay unconscious, Pru covered him with another blanket. She was surprised how unembarrassed she was to see his naked body. Would she have felt this comfortable two weeks ago?

His shoulder wound appeared to be just a deep laceration. It had stopped bleeding, but needed stitching. Going through her saddlebags, she drew out her chatelaine, a bandanna and her bottle of Dr. Brown's Sure Cure Tonic. She had to be cautious of their water or she would have tried to wash his body. She dampened her bandanna with Tonic and swabbed down the bullet wound. She threaded a needle and stitched closed the laceration. She again swabbed the stitching.

Sam slept through the stitching, but opened his eyes as she daubed him with tonic.

"Is that whiskey?"

"Mostly. It's medicine show tonic—whiskey and herbal tea. I didn't have anything else and we have to be careful with our water until we know whether I can find us more...Sam, I'm going to have to try to set your leg bones and stitch up where the bones have gone through the skin."

"Have you got anything for splints?"

"I don't know. I'll have to look around up top."

"It's too much to ask. Maybe you should leave me here and ride back for help. You could ride Nameless and make better time than on Max."

"I can't. Even if I wanted to leave you here, I can't. The whole range is on fire. It could burn for days. I'm as trapped here as you are. Please, Sam, just stay covered up and I'll be down again in a few minutes."

"Why not take the lantern and look around down here first? Maybe the Conquistadors left things you could use."

Pru crouched to get the lantern. Sam reached and touched her cheek with his hand. "You don't have to do this. I've accepted that I'm going to die."

Pru grabbed his hand and squeezed it hard. "Shut your mouth, Sam Blake. You're not going to die if I have anything to say about it."

"You're wasting your time."

"I'll know when I'm wasting my time. You're not going to breeze into my life, make me fall in love with you and then go off and die on me. Do you understand me, Samuel Blake?"

"What did you say?"

"I said I love you and I'm not going to let you die. Now, shut the hell up and let me look around."

Prudence stood up and stomped around the slag pile.

Sam lay quietly, blinking away tears that welled up in his eyes. Even said in anger, Pru had said she loved him. It was impossible. Nobody loved Sam Blake. He simply wasn't lovable. He'd known that for years.

Prudence wandered into the depths of the mine. She could hear her own footsteps as she wandered into places that had not seen a human being for two centuries.

She heard something that sounded like running water. She followed the sound and found an eroded piece of wall down which ran a trickle of water. Prudence grinned. It wasn't much, but it could mean the difference between life and death.

She went a little further into the mine and found a mound of debris. There was a spade with a broken handle and some broken furniture. Lastly there was a ladder with some broken rungs.

Putting down the lantern, Pru tested the abandoned wood. Despite sitting in a trash pile for two hundred-something years, being underground and not exposed to the elements, the wood had not rotted and many pieces were planed and straight. These would make splints. The smaller pieces could be used for firewood if necessary. Carrying the heavy load, she trudged back to Sam.

Grinning broadly, she said, "We're in luck, Sam. I found some good wood to use for splints. And a ladder that may be tall enough for me not to have to climb up and down the rope. And better yet, an underground water flow."

She set down her treasures and returned to Sam's side.

"Sam, have you ever set a broken bone?"

"No."

Pru frowned. "Neither have I. If bones break likes sticks do, they should fit back together along the breaks. I would need to pull on your legs and try to pop the bones back together. But I haven't any laudanum for the pain and I need Dr. Brown's Tonic for antiseptic. It may be unbearable."

"If you don't do it, gangrene could set in and either kill me or cost me my legs. You're the only chance I've got. Just do your best. If there's no gangrene, maybe there won't be. Besides, if the pain gets too intense, I'll probably pass out again."

Pru smiled ruefully. She reached into her saddlebag and pulled out the length of muslin. She tore part of it into strips to make ready. She threaded another needle and dropped it into the bottle of Tonic.

For a moment she surveyed the damage. There were bones broken both above and below his knees. Should she set the lower bones first or the femurs? There was a risk if she set the femurs first that they would pull out again when she pulled on the calf bones.

She took off her gloves and tried to keep her hands from shaking.

Sam lay stiffly on his back, preparing to bear the unbearable. The only thread of hope in his heart lay in her declaration of love.

"Did you know you have the biggest feet I've ever seen?" Pru said brightly from that end of him.

Sam laughed. "I have the biggest feet anyone's ever—ARRGH!" he yelled out as she grabbed one foot and pulled hard. Exquisite pain and the feel of tearing shot through his knee and Pru's other hand manipulated the broken tibia and fibula back into place.

Sam began shaking with pain, but he maintained consciousness. Those bones had not broken through the skin, so Pru took a couple of pieces of chair leg and wrapped them tightly against his calf with strips of muslin.

The femur had broken through the skin. Holding his thigh just above the knee, Prudence again pulled with all her strength—ignoring Sam's scream—pushing down on the bone until it disappeared under the skin and she felt it snap back into place in the other end of the break. Moving the bone caused the thigh to start bleeding again. Pru swabbed the open wound with a stinging, tonic-soaked bandanna and stitched it closed. She wrapped his thigh in muslin strips and splinted it with two more pieces of flat wood.

On Sam's other leg it was one of the lower leg bones that had broken through, but Pru got that leg set, stitched and splinted as well.

She covered his legs with the blanket. She could only pray that infection would not set in—or the dreaded gangrene—and that Sam would recover completely.

Using a strip of muslin, she bandaged Sam's shoulder and used another to tie his left arm against his side to keep the shoulder still so as not to rip out the stitches.

Even in the lantern light, she could see that Sam's face was bloodless. She took a canteen and lifted him slightly. The skin of his back was sweaty, but fever was still a possibility. She urged him to drink a little. He did, slowly.

After she laid him back down, she pulled off her cardigan and folded it into a thick rectangle. She put the sweater under his head for a pillow and removed his spectacles. Smoothing sweat-soaked curls away, she kissed his eyelids gently and then his brow.

"Sleep now, darling," she said quietly. "I'll see what I can do about scaring us up something to eat."

Sam closed his eyes. "Just don't use your saucepan."

Pru looked at him saucily, though without his glasses he could not see her clearly. "You'll be all right, if you can joke."

As the day grew older, Clint Randolph reduced the distance between himself and his quarry.

Finally, he saw the double-ridden horse less than five hundred yards away, down the backside of a hill.

Derry, looking behind him, saw the rider on the black stallion reach the rise. He darted behind a rock formation and dismounted, pulling Arabella down with him.

"It's the breed," he growled. "He's found us."

"Then leave me right here and ride away," Arabella pleaded. "You'll make better time alone and Clint will probably stop chasing you once he has me safe and sound."

"He'll kill me."

"Only if you fire at him, Mr. Derry. I don't think he's the vengeful type. You didn't hurt or violate me and you didn't take any shots in the gun battle. I'm sure I can get Clint to let you go if you just mount up and ride away. Look, while you're arguing with me, he's getting closer. You're losing valuable time while you stand here."

Derry looked at Arabella, then at the closing-in detective, then at his escape route. Clint rode closer and closer while Derry made up his mind.

"Derry!" Clint yelled when he got within earshot, "You're food for vultures!"

"Jesus!" Derry swore before yelling back, "Randolph, I've still got the girl!" He pulled Arabella in front of him.

"Don't do this, Jack," Arabella hissed, using his given name to get his attention.

"Come any closer, breed, and I'll shoot her—and you!"

Clint halted Wind Dancer and dismounted nearly on the run, drawing out his rifle from its scabbard and darting behind a boulder for cover.

"Let her go, Derry, and I'll let you live."

"You think I can trust you, breed?"

"Send Arabella out and over here alone and I'll let you ride off. I only want her."

Arabella felt Derry's hand tighten about her arm. "For God's sake, Mr. Derry, do as he says. Get on your horse and go."

The rustler released his hostage's arm and pushed her out away from him. Arabella walked toward where Clint was hidden as Derry ran for his horse.

"Clint," she called, "I'm free."

But as Derry broke for freedom, Clint Randolph raised his rifle and dropped the rustler from his horse with one shot. With Arabella's back to the outlaw, she didn't see whether he had drawn his gun or not. Astonishingly, she ran back toward the fallen man, who was bleeding profusely from a bullet wound to the chest. Rivulets of blood already were forming at the corners of his mouth as his life drained out of him.

Arabella dropped to her knees beside him. She noted his guns were still holstered. He had not tried to draw on Clint.

"He...lied."

"I know. I'm sorry."

Jack Derry struggled for breath as his lungs filled with blood. "Beats...hanging...I reckon."

"Have you any family?" she asked quietly.

"A...wife in...Mexico," he rasped. "Can...you...get me a...Christian burial?"

"I'll do my best, Mr. Derry."

"One...more...thing..." His eyes were already glazing over. He didn't see Clint stride up behind where he lay, nor did Arabella sense him, concentrating as she was on the dying outlaw.

"I...always...dreamed of...dying with a...pretty...girl's kiss on...my...lips."

Arabella took a deep breath. She didn't like this man. He had kidnapped and frightened the hell out of her, but somehow he seemed so pathetic as he lay dying. She leaned over and kissed him lightly.

"Thanks," he rasped out, then rattled one last breath and died.

"Very pretty," Clint remarked.

Arabella stared at him. "You didn't have to kill him."

"I couldn't let him go. Not only is the reward on him dead or alive, the Cattlemen's Association did hire me to stop the cattle rustler. I mean to get that ten thousand besides what the insurance company might pay."

Arabella reached over and closed Jack Derry's eyes. She had never seen anyone die before. She rose slowly and came into Clint's arms. "I was so frightened when the shooting started. I was glad Derry pulled me out of there."

"Yeah, him being a coward saved your life. Bullets were flying from everywhere."

"My father?"

Clint shook his head. "I don't know, Arabella. All I know is it got very quiet all of a sudden. He could very well be dead, but I don't know for sure. The moment it got quiet I went after you."

"He was a criminal," Arabella said miserably. "Why didn't you tell me?" Anger crept into her voice.

"Sam wasn't sure you weren't involved. The fewer people who knew what we suspected, the better."

Arabella broke away. "Sam, Sam, Sam! Everything is Sam with you. Don't you ever think for yourself?"

Clint kicked at Derry's fallen body. "Sometimes I do. And I will from now on. Sam and I are through."

"Where is Sam?"

"He fell down a hole of some kind. He told me he was all right and sent me off after you."

Arabella looked at him. "A hole? In the Mystics that could be an abandoned mineshaft. Some of those holes are fifteen to thirty feet deep. If he fell down one of those, chances are he's badly hurt."

Clint shrugged. "Well, that's his problem. Mine is to get you back to town and collect my rewards. Then we probably should get married."

"Married?"

Clint untied Derry's bedroll from his saddle, wrapped the dead man in his blanket and threw him across the saddle. Rolling and lighting a cigarette, he said, "Seems I already proposed, and you'll be pretty well compromised by the time I get you back to town, besides which I could well have knocked you up that time we did it. You might as well marry me. I do love you."

"That's so romantic." Sarcasm dripped like honey.

Clint shrugged again. "It's the best I can do in a pinch."

"I think if we head south from here we'll wind up in Hereford. You can turn in your corpse for the reward and there's a justice of the peace, too. Hereford is about a half-day's ride from Rincon. We can go home from there."

Arabella mounted Wind Dancer and Clint climbed on behind her. Leading Derry's horse with its carrion burden, he turned his stallion southward. He was already thinking that the reward bounty on Derry would be his alone. He wouldn't tell Sam about that part.

Or share it with him.

Chapter 17

Edward Arden, George Tyler and Sheriff Murphy rode out to the Bar M. In the distance, the sky was dark gray with smoke.

The Bar M hands were no help. Most of them had been back in since late Wednesday afternoon. None of them could admit to being near Ganados Ravine during the night because none of them were. Neither hide nor hair had been seen of Ethan Morgan, Arabella nor the two range detectives since some time on Wednesday and here it was, Thursday afternoon and nobody knew where they were.

It had been the same at the Lazy K. The remaining hands had not seen Pete McKinley and the recently hired hands had all disappeared during the night.

Both sets of cowboys reported the remnants of a stampeding herd, some marked with Bar M brands and some with the Lazy K, careening down the range with the fire behind them. They had managed to round up several hundred head, but that was a fraction of the estimated total.

The real concern was the fire. There was only one way to cope with the blaze—let it burn itself out and just do whatever was possible to make sure it didn't burn to the outbuildings. It was not safe to approach the Mystics until the fire was out—and that could take days if not a week.

There was another mystery in Rincon. The schoolteacher, Miss Hofheinz, did not appear for school this morning. Her horse and saddle were missing as well, but nobody had seen her leave town. The minister's wife had volunteered to teach school until they could figure out what happened to their teacher.

George Tyler was beside himself. His reputation as an insurance agent with Stockmen's Mutual rode on his having sold the two policies to Morgan and McKinley. Blustering, he kept assuring Arden and the sheriff that he had had no idea the two ranchers were planning to commit any fraud. He had known them for years. They were both upstanding citizens of the town.

There was only one thing known for certain: Jack Derry had kidnapped Arabella Morgan. The letter the rustler left at the stage office was proof of that.

With the fire blazing, nobody knew if any of the missing people were alive. They would be unable to send out any search parties until it was safe to venture out onto the range, unless they went several days out of their way to come up on the Mystics from behind. In the time that would take, the fires would be out and they could travel directly through the burned property.

Edward Arden was convinced the fire was arson. Even without the information directly from Blake and Randolph, the partial information he had received from the schoolteacher and the timing of the blaze sold him, along with the incriminating letter from Derry. He didn't care much whether the sheriff pressed criminal charges—his job was to prevent fraud and save the insurance company money.

He overheard the cowhands talking about how many cattle remained. Arden felt a little sorry for the kidnapped woman. If her father went to jail, she would be left with a failing ranch with few cattle and a burned out range to add insult to the injury of her kidnapping. Most of the hands were talking about moving on.

As for Miss Hofheinz, his impression was that the schoolmarm probably rode off to warn Ethan Morgan of his daughter's kidnapping.

Only time would tell who was alive and who was dead.

Sam awoke to a cool, wet cloth on his forehead and a kiss on his mouth. He groaned.

"Sam, you have a fever," he heard Pru's voice in the darkness. "Do you think you can drink something?"

His face felt like it was on fire and his lips were so dry. "Can I have my specs?" He sounded like a dehydrated frog.

Pru wiped them off and hooked them over his ears. She used her left arm across his back to help him sit up and held an enamelware cup to his mouth. "Careful, it's warm."

The warm water tasted beefy and a little bit salty. "What is that?"

"I guess you could call it beef tea. I boiled some of your jerky in water. Between us we don't have much to eat and with the fires raging below, I don't know how long we'll be here before help arrives, so I'm trying to conserve."

Sam drank the remainder of the cup as well as a considerable quantity of water. "What did you eat?"

She smiled at his concern. "Roast loin of beef with little potatoes, corn bread, asparagus, and crème brulée for dessert."

He roared with laughter and raised his right hand to bring her face down to his for a mirthful kiss. The kiss lingered, first playfully, then hungrily, until Sam felt a tightening in his loins he knew he'd better suppress. "The truth." His voice was husky.

Pru was as aroused as he, but managed to answer. "The same as you, plus a handful of raisins. Do you want some?"

Sam told her he did and used his arm to prop himself upright while Pru rummaged around in her saddlebag for the napkin of raisins. She gave him a small handful that he ate out of her hand, licking her palm playfully as he did, which made her giggle.

"How long did I sleep?"

"Close to ten hours. But your fever's up and I'm going to need to swab you down to keep you from getting delirious. How do you feel?"

"Like I fell down a hole and broke both my legs."

"Funny you should feel that way. I can't imagine why."

She helped him to lie down again and lowered the blanket covering him to his waist. Using a water-soaked bandanna, Pru swabbed Sam from face to waist, avoiding the bandaging of his wounded shoulder. The water dried from his body almost as quickly as she could moisten him. His fever was higher than she first believed. Right now he was lucid, even teasing, as she ministered to him. How long he would stay so was a cause for concern. She had a little practical training in teachers' college, but only enough to handle basic emergencies. The only thing she knew about fevers was that the patient needed plenty of water inside and out—ice if possible. Sufficient water was not a problem, but there was little food to feed a large man. While both of them had spare fat on their bodies, he would need food to help the healing process and she would need it to maintain strength to care for him until help arrived.

Pru continued to swab him down. Suddenly Sam shifted slightly and groaned with pain. Pru's eyes burned with unshed tears. If she could have drawn his pain into her own body she would have done so. She loved him so much. She had said so, but she wasn't sure he believed it. Spontaneously, she trailed the nails of one hand through the thick mat on his chest.

"Talk about something, Sam."

"What?" It was more a groan than a word.

"Who was she, Sam?"

"Huh?"

"The woman you loved who hurt you so badly."

"What makes you think there was a woman?" His voice was strained.

"Call it intuition. You're a gentleman, strong and caring. You have a superior education and scholastic honors, yet you never did any work related to your degree. You don't believe me when I tell you I love you. You hide your face behind wild hair and a beard and you've become subordinate to a man not fit to shine your boots. If what I've pieced together makes any sense, something occurred while you were at the university. Now, what kind of occurrence could make a man hide himself the way you have? The only logical thing I can think of is that someone hurt you badly. If it was a man, I think you would have fought him, but you might not fight a woman who hurt you."

"It's ancient history, Pru. I don't want to discuss it."

"Sam..."

"I want to sleep now."

Pru sighed. She offered him the use of the makeshift chamber pot again, covered him and took off his glasses. After putting a cold compress on his forehead again and putting his spectacles in his saddlebag for safekeeping, she carefully climbed back to the surface.

The ladder she found in the trash heap was tall enough and basically sound. It had a couple of broken rungs, but enough were intact that Pru could climb up using the knotted rope in place of a banister.

She took the broken spade she had found and dug a small hole into which she threw the contents of the saucepan chamber pot. She blew out the candle in her lantern after settling herself by the campfire. Pru could see the flames in the distance and wondered how long they would burn.

Tomorrow she would have to unsplint Sam's legs for a short while and check for infection. Pru's two greatest enemies right now were infection and Sam's own stubbornness. For all his teasing, he was in great pain and willing to die.

Prudence resolved, as she stared into the dying flames, to do everything in her power to keep him alive and get him well. She had no idea the extent of his injuries except to know he still had feeling from head to toes and full control over his bodily functions. A paralyzed Sam Blake would certainly wish to die and she would not blame him for wanting to. For right now, it appeared the most serious injuries were the broken bones and with any luck they might heal normally.

Regardless of whether Sam loved her, she loved him and would love him back to health if she could.

It was becoming cold again. Without the cardigan under her buckskin jacket, Pru was beginning to shiver. With the dry conditions and the fire danger, she was going to have to smother the campfire. It would be better to sleep underground for a number of reasons, the most important was to be near Sam if trouble threatened.

After relighting the lantern, Pru used the spade to shovel dirt on the campfire until it was fully smothered. She took a quick check of Max and Nameless, who were huddled together beneath a tree, covered in their horse blankets but unsaddled.

Cautiously, Pru climbed down the ladder to the bottom of the shaft. She unrolled her bedroll a little over a foot from where Sam lay. She held up the lantern to get a look at him. She could hear no sign of the congestion that might mean pneumonia. She sat on her saddle and pulled off her boots, then removed her socks and laid them on the back of her saddle to let them dry in the night. She took off her buckskin jacket and tucked it under her blanket for a pillow and took off her belt and knife sheath.

Before lying down she soaked the compress on Sam's forehead with water and put it back in place. She blew out the candle, plunging the mineshaft into darkness. Pulling the sheet and blanket over herself, she closed her eyes.

Arabella lay in bed in a small hotel in Hereford staring out into the darkness. The night was quiet, except for the sound of Clint's steady breathing beside her.

She fingered the ring, so newly slid on her left hand. She and Clint reached Hereford Thursday afternoon. He dropped Arabella at the hotel and told her to take a bath. Then he took his grisly burden to the sheriff's office. There the sheriff wired the U.S. Marshall's office for him to claim the $2,500.00 reward. Clint instructed the Marshall's office to wire the money to the bank in Rincon. If Sam could do it, so could he. He wired Sheriff Murphy in Rincon to tell him that Arabella was safe and Derry was dead. Unaware that Edward Arden was already in Rincon waiting for him, he wired the insurance company in Denver to advise them he had evidence of the insurance fraud.

Then he went to the mercantile and bought a wedding ring.

By 3:30 he returned to the hotel where Arabella waited. Her traveling dress was stained with dirt and blood, but she had no other garment. She had borrowed a brush and comb from the hotel maid and managed to get her blond hair into a neat braid down her back.

By four o'clock she became Arabella Randolph. Clint said the haste was to protect her reputation.

Dinner had been meager. They dined on the remains of the twenty dollars Jack Derry had on him when he died. There was no money for clean clothing, Clint said. Arabella was too tired to eat.

She was also wondering about this man she married. A part of her was still reeling from the way he dispatched Jack Derry this morning. He barely said a word to her all the way to Hereford and little afterward. He looked jumpy.

Arabella's wedding night was little different than that dawning when she gave Clint her maidenhead. After a few perfunctory kisses, he entered her harshly, pumped a few times and ejaculated. The only difference was that this time he stayed in the bed and just rolled over and went to sleep.

She felt tears gather in her eyes. Her wedding day was not as she had envisioned it growing up. Instead of feeling loved and cherished she merely felt used and tired.

Added to that, she had no idea if her father was alive or dead. Was he lying in a heap in a pile of rocks above Ganados Ravine or on a plank in the undertaker's parlor or was he riding for his life to safety in Mexico to live the life of a fugitive?

It had all happened too fast.

Sheriff Murphy located Edward Arden and advised him that Clint Randolph's wire said they would be returning to Rincon on Friday.

Arden himself had received a wire from Denver advising him that Randolph had wired evidence of the fraud and to issue a draft if he could verify the evidence.

With any luck, he could be on a northbound stage by Monday and out of this dusty, uncivilized town.

That was the best news of all.

News of the fraud spread through Rincon faster than the fire could eat the grassland. The members of the Cattlemen's Association were flabbergasted that two of their founding members could have drawn them in as a decoy to their nefarious acts.

They reluctantly agreed to put in shares and have the bank issue a draft payable to Clint Randolph for $10,000.00, to be delivered when he arrived back in Rincon. The sooner the detective was out of Rincon for good, the sooner they could begin to live down the shame Ethan Morgan and Peter McKinley had brought to their little town.

There remained a few mysteries in the aftermath of the shootout at Ganados Ravine.

When would the range fire burn itself out?

What had happened to Morgan and McKinley?

Where was Prudence Hofheinz?

And Clint Randolph's partner, that fat, hairy fellow? What had happened to him?

What the hell was his name, anyway?

Chapter 18

He screamed in his sleep and his scream echoed painfully throughout the mineshaft.Prudence was awake and beside him before the echo died. She gathered him in her arms, careful not to jar his wounded shoulder. She held him against her chest while he continued to scream until he had almost no voice left. She stroked his hot, dry back and hair with a gentle, caring hand as she held him, crooning loving nonsense words into his ears as his screams dissolved into sobs. She held him like a baby while he cried out his fear and misery against her shoulder.

"Sam, Sam," she whispered. "Come back to me, darling." More than she ever loved him before, she loved him now.

"Tell me what you dreamt," she commanded quietly. "Please."

"I'm going to be a cripple, a worthless man."

Continuing to stroke his hair, she said, "We don't know that. Nightmares are fears, but they're not real."

"No one could love me now," he said, still caught in the thrall of the nightmare.

"Tell me about the woman, Sam."

"Cynthia?"

"Cynthia. Tell me about Cynthia. If you tell me, the nightmares will go away." She gave him water and continued to hold him.

He began to talk about things he'd kept secret for years.

Things that shaped the life he was living now.

Philadelphia, Pennsylvania, 1872

He met Cynthia Depardieu at a house party to which her brother Horatio invited him. He was a senior at the University of Pennsylvania, first in his class, Phi Beta Kappa—a rare honor for the son of a traveling salesman from San Antonio. The two young men were both studying civil engineering.

Sam was a loner. Wounds from the Civil War were still raw. When he committed the unpardonable sin of quitting the football team after one very unhappy year, and added to it being the best student, he made enemies a lonely young man could not fight.

He had always been larger and heavier than the boys his age. He appeared lumbering and clumsy with his head-down, slump-shouldered walk. So he stuck to his books and his guns—literally. Sam Blake might be a big, clumsy oaf, but he could shoot the eye out of an eagle in flight. His well-read, quiet nature he kept to himself, seldom speaking up in class, never seeking praise from his professors. It was bad enough to have needed spectacles since he was ten. He didn't want to be thought a bookworm, too.

He'd received a small legacy that enabled him to go to school. It was a chance to be more than a cowboy or clerk.

The elegant mansions and Colonial public buildings were a revelation after the Spanish influence of Bexar County. But Sam was as different from his classmates as the architecture of home was. He was as rustic as "Our American Cousin," even with his gun belt rolled up safely in his valise.

It was autumn of his senior year when he ran into Horatio Depardieu. Horatio was the self-appointed social arbiter of the class, always in fashion, blond hair slicked back, well-trimmed mustache. His clothes never looked rumpled; there were never ink blotches on his white, manicured hands. He never even seemed to sweat, even on the muggiest days.

"Blake, my man."

Sam looked up suspiciously. Depardieu seldom spoke to him.

"Depardieu." He had worked hard to soften his drawl down to almost nothing. "Listen, I'm sorry about the football team. Maybe when they work on the rules so it's less dangerous."

Horatio waved off the apology. "I say, old man, what are you doing next weekend?"

Sam frowned. "I have no specific plans." He never had any plans except to study.

"I'm hosting a little house party at our place in the country. I'd be pleased if you'd come."

"I don't understand. In three years here you've never invited me to attend any of your fabled parties. Why this sudden interest in me?"

Horatio had the good grace to color at the question. "Truth is, Blake, we're planning to do a little shooting and I hear that you Texans know your way around a gun."

"I don't shoot skeet, and I don't hunt for sport. What makes you think I'm any good with a gun?"

"If you weren't, you'd probably be bragging about how good you are. So are you any good?"

With quiet confidence, Sam said, "Some may outdraw me, but few can outaim me. But I haven't done any shooting since I left home. After all, this is the civilized East, not the Wild West."

Horatio reached around to clap Sam on the shoulder, stopping awkwardly when he realized the six-inch difference between them. "Here's the deal, Blake. There's sure to be some wagering and I like to win. I bet on you and we split the pot when you win."

"Bet how you want. I can bet on myself."

Sam packed his best black suit, which would have to serve since he had no evening clothes. He had taken his gun to a secluded place and practiced until he had his eye back. Wearing a gray suit and vest with a black silk tie he met the group of Horatio's friends who had hired a carriage to take them to the country. His presence among these elite seemed to surprise them.

The other young men bragged about their prowess with firearms while Sam sat back and listened.

"Any of you met Cynthia Depardieu?" one of them asked. "I hear she's invited some of her friends out by assuring their mothers there would be proper chaperons. But you better all keep your pricks inside your pants around her because they say she's selling it high."

Nothing in Sam's experience prepared him for the conspicuous opulence of the Depardieu country house. His guestroom was larger than his two off-campus rooms combined. The "light buffet" set out for the guests filled the huge dining room table to groaning.

Sam carried his gun belt, shifting it from hand to hand. He had made numerous bets on himself and was nervously waiting for the contest to begin.

"Do you ever wear that thing?" he heard a saucy feminine voice say.

He looked down and saw a petite, slender blonde whose hair was daffodil bright. Her lime green and yellow gown was as bright as she was; her blue eyes like a summer sky. Sam's heart leapt to his throat. He had never seen such a pretty girl in his life—or if he had, she hadn't spoken to him.

He looked at his hands. Gesturing with the gun belt he replied, "Um—yes, ma'am, I do. I mean I will. Just not in the house. Um—I mean, this isn't San Antonio, ma'am."

The girl giggled. "*Ma'am*?" she teased. "Do I look so decrepit you'd think I was married already?"

Sam blushed crimson above his beard. "Um—no, ma'am—um—miss—miss..."

She touched his arm with slender, manicured fingers. Sam felt sure his heart was going to pop out of his chest.

"Cynthia Depardieu," she said in a saucy, breathy voice. "And you are?"

"Sam Blake, Miss Depardieu."

Cynthia giggled. "Oh, you, you're being so formal." In a conspiratorial whisper, she added, "you're Horatio's ringer, aren't you. I've heard he's bet a small fortune on you."

"I'm flattered, Miss Dep..."

"Oh, please, do call me Cynthia. Calling me Miss Depardieu makes me think I'm an old lady." With another giggle she flitted away, taking Sam's heart with her.

He had fallen in love.

Sam won the shooting competition easily, hardly missing with either his revolver or a borrowed rifle. He won more than three hundred dollars on his own bets and Horatio, who won nearly fifteen hundred dollars, gave Sam seven hundred of it. Sam resolved to have some shoes made and put the rest in the bank.

At the dancing that evening, Cynthia flirted with him shamelessly, insisting that he dance with her. Having never had so much female attention in his life, he wasn't sure how to handle it. He was so afraid anything he said would mark him as a hopeless rustic he was nearly silent.

When it came time for the guests to part, Sam drew Cynthia aside for a moment.

"Miss—um—Cynthia, when are you planning to return to Philadelphia?"

She smiled blindingly and asked him why.

"Well—um—I would be honored if you would allow me to call on you in your home."

She giggled. "Why, Sam Blake, that's so sweet."

Sam rode home on a cloud.

Sam knew the thousand dollars he had won and his stipend would not be enough to court Cynthia Depardieu. He took a job after classes with the Great Pennsylvania Casualty Company collecting premiums and investigating claims. Some nights he slept only a few hours, trying to go to class, study, work and maintain his class standing.

He called on Cynthia regularly, enduring little gilt chairs too small for his frame, holding china cups that seemed too fragile for his hands. She was always so sweet to him, polite and giggly. She treated everything Sam said as if it were the most brilliant thing she had ever heard. Sam spoke of the great buildings and bridges he would build once he had his degree. All he would need was to get a position with one of the large engineering firms, which with his class standing should not be difficult.

He didn't understand why Horatio, who was also present, sputtered and nearly choked on his mouthful of wine at the comment.

Just before graduation, Sam bought a dainty gold and amethyst ring and came to call on Cynthia, prepared to ask her to marry him. He felt strange in his new black leather dress shoes he was wearing in place of his well-worn, comfortable boots.

His heart was in his throat. Married to Cynthia, he would be happy to live in Philadelphia. He would throw away his boots and wear these awful shoes the rest of his life.

Directed by the butler to the parlor, Sam stood outside the doors listening to a remnant of a conversation between Cynthia and Horatio.

"Mother says they'll be here after the Fourth of July. How is your gown coming?"

"You can be such an old woman at times, love. It will be ready in plenty of time."

Sam entered the parlor. Cynthia extended her hand. Feeling very gallant, Sam pressed a kiss on the back of her hand. He cleared his throat. "Cynthia, I have something very important to ask you."

"Shall I leave you two alone?" Horatio asked.

"Yes, please," Sam said.

"No, please," Cynthia countered. When Sam looked at her peculiarly, she added, "Anything you have to say to me you can say in front of my brother."

"Well, okay," Sam said nervously, "Cynthia, we've known each other for quite a while now and we've dealt quite well together..."

"Indeed we have, Sam. I never thought when I met you that you would turn out to be so amusing."

Sam dropped to one knee and took her hand in his.

"What's this all about, Sam?" Cynthia's voice had an odd edge to it.

"Surely, Cynthia, you must have realized how I feel about you..."

"What are you saying?"

Screwing up the last of his flagging courage, Sam swallowed and said rapidly, "What I'm saying is I'm very much in love with you and would be honored if you would consent to be my wife." He took a deep breath.

For a long, painful moment the parlor was silent.

Then Cynthia laughed.

It was not her usual giggling, girlish laugh, but a deep throated, derisive, almost sadistic laugh. "Oh, Sam," she choked out, "you are too funny. Isn't he funny, Horatio?"

Sam stood up. He was starting to feel ill, for Horatio was laughing as well.

"I never figured you for a sense of humor, Blake." Horatio was holding his sides.

The color drained from Sam's face.

"Oh, my God," Cynthia cried, "I do believe he's serious." She stood up and walked over to the window. Then she turned around, a cold look on her face. "What in the world would make you think I could ever consider marrying you? Who are you? You have no money, no family, no social position. You're little more than a cowboy. You haven't a chance to be accepted in a major engineering firm. Men like that simply don't hire outsiders..."

Sam felt his soul collapsing, but Cynthia wasn't finished.

"...If you were handsome, it might be different, but you're as ugly as those battered boots you wear."

"Besides, old man," Horatio said, "Mother and Father have already arranged for Cynthia to marry the Earl of Winshire. The Earl is already on his way here for the wedding."

Sam stumbled out of the parlor, a hole in his soul. He knew now what he had always feared. He was ugly, fat, unlovable, a laughing stock.

He received his diploma, but never unrolled the sheepskin. The next day he went home to Texas.

As Sam finished, he could feel Pru tightening her hold on him, her hand stroking his hair.

"For a year or so afterward all I did was drink, smoke and gamble. It's a miracle I didn't get into any gunfights or I'd've been killed for sure because I didn't much care if I lived or died. Clint found me by accident and got me dried out. I hardly ever drink anymore. I stopped smoking about a year ago. But none of it matters; not how I dress or how clean I keep myself or how much money I save. None of it alters that when you get down to it, I'm still as ugly as a pair of old boots and that will never change."

A gentle voice pierced the darkness. "And you think that means nobody will ever love you." Pru kissed his temple as she continued to stroke his hair. "You're wrong, Sam. I love you." She touched his chest. "I love what's in here and in here," she added, kissing his temple again. "I'll never love anyone so much as I love you. I'll never reject you. Whether you can ever love me, I will still love you."

"I'm not sure I'm capable of loving anyone again."

"You don't have to, Sam. I have enough love for both of us."

Pru rocked him against her, heart swelling with love. Suddenly she rubbed her hand across his belly. "Sam, you're sweating." She kissed him again. "Your fever's broken. Oh, darling, you're going to be all right."

Sam felt a different kind of pain. Until he knew how badly he was hurt, he could not make any promises to this woman. She said she wouldn't reject him, but would she feel that same way if his injuries were crippling?

When Pru set his leg bones he felt the most horrible tearing sensations in his knees. Every move felt like gravel cutting into his knees from within.

He would put her away from him if he thought he would be crippled. Pru Hofheinz was too vibrant, too alive to be saddled for life with a cripple.

But right now she was the only lifeline he had.

"Pru, I think I can sleep now."

She guided him to his back and covered him with the blanket. She was returning to her own bedroll when Sam said, "Pru, I don't want to presume, but I would like very much to feel you lying next to me. Would you mind very much?"

Pru's voice sounded choked. "Of course not, darling."

She pulled her blankets over to him. His good arm came up to meet her in the darkness and found the softness of her cheek, then trailed down and under her jaw until he found the hollow where her neck met her chest. Pru felt him fumbling clumsily in the dark at the button of her shirt. She reached up and unbuttoned her blouse and the tiny buttons on her chemise.

She lay down so her breasts rested against his ribs, her left hand went beneath his neck and her right arm drifted to rest across his belly, the fingers finding their way under his waist. Sam's right arm encircled her and slipped under her clothes to touch her back. From her hips down she veered away so she would not jar his legs.

Sam had told Pru that sex was the smallest part of lovemaking. Pru knew now that it was the truth.

In a matter of moments they were both asleep, as entwined as his battered body would allow.

And as entwined as his battered heart would allow.

Chapter 19

Saturday afternoon the newlyweds arrived back in Rincon, looking the worse for wear. They rode into town, Clint on Wind Dancer, Arabella on Jack Derry's horse. They dismounted when they reached Sheriff Murphy's office.

The sheriff saw them through his window and came outside quickly. He had known Arabella most of her life.

"Miss Arabella, thank God you're all right," Murphy said. "What happened to Derry?"

Arabella stiffened and, glancing at her new husband, said, "Mr. Derry is dead."

"That bastard didn't hurt you, did he?"

"No," she bit out, "he didn't. Sheriff Murphy, is there any word of my father?"

Murphy shook his head. "We can't get anywhere near Ganados Ravine. The whole range has been burning since early Thursday. Your father, Pete McKinley, Mr. Randolph's partner and Miss Hofheinz are all unaccounted for."

"Prudence?"

"There's an insurance company investigator named Arden here who tells me Miss Hofheinz found a letter from Jack Derry confessing to kidnapping you. We think she was heading out to tell someone and may have been caught by the fire."

Clint's interest sparked. "Arden from Stockmen's Mutual? He's here in Rincon?"

"At Mrs. Lester's."

Clint took Arabella firmly by the arm. "Darling," he said quietly, ignoring the sheriff's raised eyebrow, "I'm going to take you back to the ranch. You need a good night's sleep. I have some business to conduct with Mr. Arden. We'll take the stage to San Antonio tomorrow afternoon and wait for news of your father."

Arabella nodded. "My bags," she said. "Did they go on to San Antonio or were they taken off the stage?"

The sheriff didn't know, but a visit to the stage office found her things waiting for her. It made no sense to take them back to the Bar M for the night.

They rode back to the ranch, silent except for the sounds of hoofbeats. They were nearly back to the Bar M when Arabella pulled her horse to a halt.

"Clint, do you really think it's such a good idea to leave town right now? With my father and Mr. Blake missing, wouldn't it be better to stay here?"

"Are we going to begin like this?" Clint snarled. "Arabella, you're overwrought. You've been through all kinds of hell the past few days. The last thing you need is the sheriff, that man from the insurance company and all your father's hands harping on you to make decisions about the ranch and the fire. We'll take a week or two in San Antonio and come back when things cool down."

"But my father..."

"Your father was a criminal, Arabella, face it. He was up in the mountains shooting at every sound. Chances are he and Sam are dead. And if there's that big a fire going on, chances are there won't be much left of the range to rebuild a herd on."

"So what do I do? Give up? Abandon my father's ranch?"

Clint felt heat rising under his collar. "I'm not saying that. What I'm saying is give yourself some time to recover. It's going to take a lot of money to rebuild the ranch once the fire burns out. Our finding out about the plot your father was involved in makes it damned sure the insurance company is not going to pay for any of this. My share of the reward money will only go so far, but it'll be all you have besides whatever your father had in the bank. We'll go to San Antonio, have a honeymoon and then come back and see where you stand. If your father's alive he's going to jail and if he's dead—well, either way you'll be in charge of the ranch. Do you believe you're ready to do that right now?"

Arabella took a ragged breath. She was so tired. "No, I guess not."

"Then let's get you to the ranch so we can get everything done in time to leave tomorrow afternoon."

They rode on. As they got closer, they could see the smoky grayness of the sky. When they reached the ranch house, flames could be seen in the distance. The air was full of ash.

The hands gathered around Arabella as she wearily dismounted.

"Any word on my father?"

"Nothing," said Bill Porter. "We haven't been able to get anywhere near the Mystics."

"How many cattle survived?"

"We ain't sure, Miss Arabella. A few hundred head, I reckon. We'll know better when the fires burn out, but I don't know what the hell we're gonna do to feed 'em."

"Bill, are all the hands still here?"

Porter took off his hat and ran his fingers through his thinning hair. "Well, Miss Arabella, it's like this. We got five of us left. Anderson, Sully, Sweeney, Bonetti and me. The rest all took off Friday. I ain't sure how long the other boys'll stay on, 'ceptin' for Bonetti, on account of his being local. None of us is hurtin' for money right now, but if you can't make the next payroll, we may just have to move on."

Arabella sighed. Now she knew why Clint wanted her out of here right now. She had to check her father's books to see if he had enough money to pay the five hands plus Consuelo's pay for another month.

"Bill, tell the boys I should be able to keep them on another month. I need your help. My husband..."

"Husband?" Porter said with a start.

Arabella nodded wearily. "Mr. Randolph and I were married in Hereford. Mr. Randolph believes I'm on the verge of a physical breakdown because of what I've been through the last few days. I'll need you and the boys to do a couple of things until I get back. Once the fires are out, round up and tally the surviving cattle. Wire me about how much of the range survived, too. Then take the wagon out to Ganados Ravine and look for my father, Mr. Blake, and Miss Hofheinz. Mr. McKinley is also missing, so if you find him, you may need to bring him back, too."

Bob Bonetti blanched when he heard Miss Hofheinz was missing. "I'll go, if nobody else will."

The others agreed to stay on at least the additional month.

Clint led the horses into the barn. They were as weary as he was, so after Arabella went into the house, Clint saddled Horizon to take a look around.

Things looked bleak. There was no way his wife was going to rebuild on his share of the reward money. The $2,500 bounty on Derry was all Clint's. If he could get the rewards from both the insurance company and the Cattlemen's Association, that would be $30,000, which by all rights was only half his. Clint still had the $5,000 from the El Molino job. But $22,500.00 wasn't going to be nearly enough to help Arabella recover.

But $37,500 would make a lot of difference. If Sam was dead, Clint would get it all.

They said Sam was missing. If he died...

Or if Clint could convince the money men Sam was dead...

Then Clint slapped himself on the forehead. For years now, they paid him, then he and Sam would ride out of town and divide the funds. All Clint had to do was what he always did.

Except not to split the funds with Sam when he finally showed up, if he ever did.

Arabella need never know what the amounts of the rewards were so he need never tell her what he had done.

Clint strode into the ranch house. Consuelo told him Arabella was in her room waiting for bath water. Clint went into the kitchen and washed up in a basin. He went upstairs to his room and changed into clean clothes. As he returned down the hall, he passed the master bedroom and looked in.

He would worry about moving into this room after they returned from San Antonio. He could take Arabella in her own room again or have her in the guestroom this evening. It didn't matter. She wasn't all that great.

Clint rolled and lit a cigarette as he proceeded downstairs and outside to the barn.

It was time to go to Rincon and prove he wasn't so stupid after all.

"What's it like up top?" Sam asked wearily. He was still in great pain, but more than that, he was unremittingly bored. He could only sleep so much.

Pru was just coming down the ladder. "I can still see smoke and flame in the distance, closer to the Bar M." She paused a moment. "God, I hope the ranch buildings aren't threatened. I'd hate for Arabella to lose everything."

"There's not much we can do."

Pru lit the lantern. She knelt down near Sam's legs armed with a bandanna and her bottle of Sure Cure Tonic. "I'm going to unwrap you and check your legs for infection. I'm afraid it's going to hurt."

"Pru, the only time it doesn't hurt is when I'm asleep." He smiled slyly. "Or when you hold me."

Pru laughed sweetly. "If that's so, I'll do it more often."

She turned to her task, happy that he enjoyed physical contact with her despite his infirmity. If she could just convince him she wanted him regardless of his physical condition.

Carefully, she began to unwrap the splints that immobilized Sam's legs. She lifted the lantern with one hand while she gingerly probed at the wounds. The skin was pink and puckered around the stitches and there was no sign of further bleeding.

"Good news," she said casually. "There are no red streaks or blackening. That means no gangrene, and the discoloration around your knees has faded to greenish. With a little luck you'll be perfectly fine."

Sam gasped at the probing. "But you're not a doctor."

Pru shrugged, a little hurt. She began to resplint and rewrap his legs. "I know, but I just have a good feeling. All we have to do now is wait for the fires to die down. I feel confident enough that I'm not afraid to leave you for a few hours to go for help if no one comes looking for us."

Sam made a fist with his right hand and slammed it on the ground next to him. "This is maddening. I feel so helpless lying here, stark naked, unable to move, completely reliant on you..."

"I don't mind caring for you, Sam."

"I mind. I don't feel like a man somehow."

Finished rewrapping, Pru crawled around to where she could look Sam in the eyes. She picked up his hand and laced her fingers within it. Her own eyes were swimming in unshed tears. "Sam, Sam," she said, using her other hand to caress his blanket-covered torso, "never since the day we met have I been unaware that you are very much a man. But just as you cared for me so tenderly when all I was suffering from were the same woman's problems I've suffered since I was thirteen, so I want to care for you now that you're hurt. That's what people who love each other do. It isn't a thing of being a man or not. It's like you said to me, sex is only a part of love. More of it is caring and being there for the other person. Never feel less than a man with me."

Sam's fingers curled around hers. If he was sound, he'd have pulled her under him and made love to her until he took her breath away. He would bury himself deep within her and become one with her. He would taste all her textures and bury his nose in her sweet-smelling, if somewhat messy hair.

Abruptly, he released her hand, rammed his fingers in her hair and pulled her toward him. Pru bent until their mouths were a hair's breadth apart. Then she let Sam bring her face to his and kiss her.

Sam Blake was a man all right! He kissed her luxuriantly, nibbling on her lower lip, teasing her mouth open with a teasing tongue, thrusting into the warm, sweet cavern of her mouth as he wished he could thrust himself into the sweet warmth of her womanhood. Her hands tangled in his hair and stroked his beard as she returned his kiss. She ached with desire that couldn't be satisfied. He had awakened her to passion, taught her she was a desirable woman. But there was more. He made her feel protected and safe. She wished she could give the same feeling of security to him.

Men were so much more fragile than women, she thought.

She continued to kiss him, their tongues dueling playfully. How she loved him!

"Lie by me," Sam rasped. "I need you so much."

He ached with hunger, both physical and sexual. Feeling the length of her body alongside his was not enough, but it was all he could have right now.

He wondered if that was all he would ever have again.

That he was capable of an erection was painfully obvious. Whether he would be able to do anything about it was an unanswered question.

A frustrating, unanswered question.

Prudence lay alongside her beloved and let him press her against his body with his good arm. She rested her head on his shoulder and made paths through the thick hair on his chest with her fingers.

"Talk to me, Pru."

"What should I say?"

"Why did you leave Chicago?"

"I wanted to go to teaching college." Her voice was stiff.

"You hate teaching; you've told me so."

She sighed. "What options does a woman have?"

"You could have married."

She laughed bitterly. "No one wanted me—well, almost no one."

"What happened? Please tell me."

"I wasn't exactly the most desirable woman in Chicago. I was the epitome of wallflowers; fat and smart and not pretty. My school friends were pairing off one by one and I was alone.

"One day a friend of my father's came calling. He was about twenty-five or thirty years my senior with grown children. He always called around suppertime and never took me anywhere. When we parted after a call he never touched me more than to shake my hand. I never even got a gallant kiss on the hand. He never brought flowers or sweets or gifts. He spoke of the grandeur of his house, how fortunate he had been that it survived the Great Fire and how difficult it was for a widower to maintain it and still run a business now that his children were all married and out of the house.

"The summer I turned eighteen, we were invited to his house for a reception of some sort. It blurs what the occasion was, but I remember having a new gown made. My old curse hit that morning and I really didn't feel up to going, but I didn't dare stay home."

Pru sighed sadly. "As usual, my dance card went unfilled. Finally I felt bad enough to look for some place to lie down. I went down the hall and found a library. There was a window seat, so I sat with my back against the sill, pulled the curtain closed and shut my eyes.

"Voices got my attention. It was Mr. Dannesh and some other man. Dannesh was telling the other man he was going to ask my father for my hand.

"The man said, 'But she's a fat, homely little nothing.'

"Mr. Dannesh said, 'But she has a generous dowry and she knows how to keep a house. I won't have to worry about infidelities because I can't imagine anyone wanting to sleep with her. I've had my family. I need a housekeeper and hostess, not a bed partner.'

"The other man asked him why he didn't just hire a housekeeper. He said, 'Do you know how expensive it is to have a housekeeper? I'd have to pay wages and give her days off. If someone offered her more money, she'd leave and I'd have to start all over again. This way I get twenty-four hours a day service for free and she'll never leave. On top of that, her father will be paying me to take her off his hands. And since I'll never bed her I won't have to worry about any more children.'

"I wanted to throw up. I wanted to throw open the curtain and hammer on him with my fists. But instead of charging like some Fury, I just sat there until Mr. Dannesh and his friend left.

"My father always said the decision to marry or not would be mine to make. When Mr. Dannesh did propose that evening, I told him I wouldn't marry him if he were the last man on earth. I told him I'd rather work for a living than be his unpaid housekeeper and if that meant I never married, it was just fine with me.

"I realized for a respectable woman, teaching or nursing were my only real options, since becoming an architect was going to be impossible." She laughed painfully. "I couldn't see myself as a nurse, so I applied to a teaching college. When I graduated I answered the advertisement for the teaching job in Rincon and I've been here ever since.

"Until I met you, Sam, nobody ever treated me like a pretty or desirable woman. I know right now I must look like something the cat dragged in, but when you kiss me, I feel beautiful."

Sam kissed her tangled hair. "To me you are beautiful. That nobody else can see it doesn't matter. I just wish I was more man for you."

Pru kissed his chest, laving at a flat nipple. "You're plenty enough man for me, Sam Blake."

There was nothing else to do except lie in the darkness of the mineshaft and hold each other.

But for now, it was enough.

Chapter 20

Clint rode into Rincon, trying to reconcile himself to what he was planning to do. He knew it was reprehensible. He knew that if it weren't for Sam Blake he would still be chasing bandits with the Texas Rangers.

But if Sam was still alive he had plenty of money in the bank. Enough, he'd said, to open a business of his own. Clint needed the money. He had a wife to support now; a wife whose father's treachery had left her on the verge of bankruptcy.

He had to harden his heart against his oldest friend. It wasn't so many days ago that the two of them had come close to killing each other. While it made Clint sad at heart to think of the love lost between himself and Sam Blake, there comes a time in a man's life when he must think of himself and his own before others.

On arriving in Rincon, Clint went straight to Mrs. Lester's boarding house. A blond man in a tan tweed suit stood leaning against one of the uprights, a dark hardwood pipe in his mouth. He looked overdressed to be a native of Rincon.

Taking a chance, he addressed the man, "You Mr. Arden? I'm Randolph. My partner was shot and killed during the gun battle with Ethan Morgan." For emphasis, Clint took off his hat. "Morgan was also killed in the gunfight, but before the shooting started, he confessed to planning with McKinley to cheat your company by setting the range on fire and driving the cattle into Ganados Ravine. Then the shooting started and the fire was set. When the shooting stopped I set out after the third conspirator, a small-time rustler named Jack Derry, who kidnapped Morgan's daughter to assure that Morgan would go through with the plan. Derry's dead, too."

Arden took the information in thoughtfully. He was bored to death in this tank town. This was information enough to defeat any claim against the insurance policy Miss Morgan might try to make. Having saved the carrier $200,000, the claims investigator could issue a draft for $20,000 to Clint Randolph, pack his valise and be on the three o'clock northbound stage to connect up with the train back to Denver.

"If you'll wait here, Mr. Randolph, I'll get my draft book and issue you the reward." He wheeled around and headed inside.

Clint rolled himself a cigarette and let the hot smoke calm his nerves. He couldn't believe it was this easy.

He was almost finished with his cigarette when Edward Arden returned, valise in hand, hat on head. He opened his briefcase and withdrew a completed insurance draft payable to Clint Randolph in the amount of $20,000. "Stockmen's Mutual thanks you for your invaluable services to our company and may I offer you our condolences on the death of your partner."

Clint took the draft, folded it and put it in his vest pocket, looking down with the appropriate amount of moroseness. "Thank you, Mr. Arden."

Arden tipped his hat. "Now, if you'll excuse me, the northbound stage leaves in half an hour. I'd as soon be on it than wait until Tuesday for the next one."

"I understand. Rincon isn't much, I reckon."

Arden nodded and strode toward the stage office. Clint patted the pocket that held the check.

One down; one to go.

Clint walked down the street to an office building marked "Bennett Palmer—Attorney at Law, Randall County Cattlemen's Association." He walked in.

A clerk was sitting at a desk behind a carved rail partition. He looked up when he heard the door close behind Clint.

"May I help you?"

"I'm looking for Mr. Palmer. Tell him it's Clint Randolph."

The clerk's eyes widened. He saw the tall, dark man with the gun strapped to his thigh. He must have never seen a real life Western hero before and all but tripped over his wastepaper basket in his haste to get his boss. He knocked on the half glass door marked "Bennett Palmer – Private," and was admitted. A few moments later he re-emerged and signaled Clint to enter.

The prosperous-looking attorney held out his hand to Clint. "Mr. Randolph, I'm glad to see you. The Association is deeply sorry that the treachery of Messrs. Morgan and McKinley brought you here for nothing."

Clint was prepared He pulled out the paper from Hereford's sheriff certifying to the death of Jack Derry. "The Cattlemen's Association hired me to rid your county of Jack Derry and his gang. Derry is dead and the gang scattered. I've completed the assignment you hired me to do. If Morgan induced you to hire me under false pretenses, that doesn't make a hell of a lot of difference to me. I've lost more than the measly ten thousand you offered me could ever repay."

Mr. Palmer opened a box of cigars and offered Clint one. Never being one to refuse a smoke, Clint took the cigar, bit off the end and lit it.

"You're a lawyer, Mr. Palmer. Somehow, I don't think with you advising the Cattlemen's Association on legal matters you let them make a contract for my services without having the money available to pay me. I'm planning to leave town on tomorrow's stage. The basis of my hire is payment in full when the job's done. Well, the job's done and I expect to be paid today—at once, as agreed on."

Palmer let out a mouthful of smoke. "Do you want cash, or will a draft on our bank here in Rincon suffice?"

"You got the cash?"

Palmer nodded. He turned to his bookcase and turned the combination of a safe kept there. The door sprang open and Palmer pulled out an envelope. He shut the safe door and handed the envelope to Clint.

"I believe, Mr. Randolph, that you'll find the entire sum in there."

Clint opened the envelope and quickly counted the money. It was there—in cash. No waiting for a draft to clear.

Palmer handed him a receipt to sign. No surprise. He signed one after almost every job. He picked up the pen and signed his name with a flourish.

"Thank you, Mr. Palmer. I appreciate your good faith," Clint touched his hat in farewell. He walked out of the attorney's office feeling almost jaunty. Between cash and drafts he had well over thirty thousand dollars to start a life with Arabella. Once in San Antonio Clint would go into a bank and open an account. If Sam survived, he'd never know where to find Clint, would never suspect him of returning to Rincon. If he died, he wouldn't have any use for the money.

"Now remember what I said," Arabella instructed Bill Porter. "As soon as the fires are out, go into the Mystics and see if you can find my father, Mr. Blake, and Miss Hofheinz."

"Yes, Miss Ara—I mean Miz Randolph," the old cowman replied.

"Arabella, we haven't got all day," Clint complained from where he stood beside the buggy.

"Bill, if my father's alive, you'll have to turn him in to the sheriff. I don't know what else you can do. If any of them are dead, make sure they get Christian burials. Take them to the undertaker and tell him to send me the bill. If Miss Hofheinz is dead, I'll write to her father. I don't think Mr. Blake has any relations. Wire me and let me know about my father. I'll be—I mean we'll be staying with Aunt Edith in San Antonio."

"Arabella!" Clint's voice was laced with warning.

"And send someone into town to get the buggy. We'll leave it at the livery stable."

"Yes, ma'am."

Arabella broke away and let Clint hand her into the buggy. Clint picked up the buggy whip and set the horse in motion. Wind Dancer and Horizon were safely stabled in the barn while smoke still tinted the sky.

They headed into town. They would arrive about a half-hour before the stage left at three. They would stay out of town until everything blew over.

On Sunday Pru saw buzzards flying over the ridge and swooping into the ravine. How easily it could have been Sam who was food for vultures or dying, forgotten, in a hole in the ground.

She went down the ladder. "I saw buzzards just now."

Sam nodded. "Speaking of buzzards, how is our food supply holding out?"

Pru shrugged. "We have one can of potted beef and two cans of beans—and some tea. Everything else is gone. We have plenty of water, though."

"Pretty bleak, huh?"

She sighed and tugged at her loosened waistband. "Not if one was trying to slim down."

Sam laughed and imitated a medicine show barker. "Ladies and gentlemen, are you obese, adipose, chubby, corpulent, fleshy, pleasingly plump or just plain fat? Are you looking for a surefire solution to your present dilemma? Allow me to present, for your edification, education and satisfaction, the one, the only, Dr. Hofheinz's Sure Cure Slimming Plan..."

Prudence began laughing.

"...Wait, I'm not finished yet. Ladies and gentlemen, are you skeptical? Have you tried everything? Steam? Tape-worms? Massage? You haven't tried anything until you've tried Dr. Hofheinz's method. She'll hog-tie you and keep you down a hole, there to feed you on beef tea and raisins in carefully measured doses until she..."

Prudence skittered down the ladder and tried to stop Sam with her lips.

"...until she..."

She kissed him again, still laughing.

"...until...ladies and gentlemen...until she..." he continued, his voice getting husky with need. He slid his arm around her shoulders to pull her closer.

"...until she just plain loves the fat right off your body."

Monday morning, Bob Bonetti rose with the dawn, dressed and stepped outside the bunkhouse to survey the morning sky. The usual pinkness was dulled by the smoke that still filled the sky. Bob had been born and lived his full eighteen years in Rincon but had never seen a prairie fire like this one.

He had been so proud to get a job working for Ethan Morgan. The pay was fair and he could live in the bunkhouse instead of the crowded cabin where his parents lived with his five brothers and sisters, yet still be able to go home and visit.

He worried about Miss Hofheinz. She had always told him he was smart enough to go to college and be anything he wanted to be, but there was no money for luxuries such as tuition, so when he left grammar school at age sixteen he took a job at the Bar M. Now that job might be gone if the Bar M failed because of the fire. If he had to pack his grip and go elsewhere, it was likely he'd never see his family again. Just like his father left Italy and would never see his own family again.

It seemed even the clouds were covered with soot on their undersides, their white cottony puffs tinted nearly silver.

They couldn't be *rain clouds* now, could they?

Tom Sully came out, looking like he'd paid a long visit to the saloon the night before. He scratched at his chest through the placket of his union suit.

"Morning, Bobby," Sully said in his gravelly voice. "Want some coffee?"

"Sure, in a minute. Sully, look at those clouds. Do they look like rain clouds to you?"

Sully looked up, squinting against the early morning sunlight. "Could be. Be real nice if they was, but it could be just the smoke from the fires."

"Rain could put the fire out."

"Rain this winter might've kept them from burning in the first place...Come on, Bobby, get yourself some coffee. We got chores to do."

Lubbock, Monday, April 27th

Arabella stood on the platform of the train station waiting for Clint to join her with the tickets to San Antonio.

The further away she got from Rincon, the guiltier she felt. She desperately wanted to know what had happened to her father, but until they got to her aunt's house in San Antonio, there would be no way for Sheriff to reach her by telegram.

She looked up into the sky. The unremitting blue she had seen for the last few years was grayer, full of dark-bottomed clouds.

"Oh, my," she said, "are those rain clouds?"

She could hardly remember the last time she saw rain clouds. She said a silent prayer that these clouds would dump a healing rain on the range above the Bar M.

Clint arrived on the platform and slipped Arabella's hand into the crook of his arms. "What are you looking at?"

Arabella pointed up.

"So?"

"Clint, it could rain. If it rains as far north as Rincon it could put out the fire and maybe save the ranch."

"Darling, if it does, I'm sure the sheriff or your foreman will wire. Come on now, we have to get on the train."

Arabella rubbed her temple. She had a terrible headache that wouldn't go away. She was beginning to wonder if it had been such a wise idea to marry Clint Randolph. Maybe she could have saved her reputation without having to marry a man she really hardly knew. The man who had poured out his heart to her just after they met was gone, replaced by a tight-lipped, secretive and unfeeling man who seemed to have no affection in his lovemaking or anything else. In addition, he seemed to be smoking constantly and last night when he climbed into their bed she could smell whiskey on his breath.

She wished she had someone to talk to. Usually she would have poured out her heart to Prudence Hofheinz. But she was miles from home—a home from which Prudence was missing.

Maybe her Aunt Edith could help her. But to talk to Aunt Edith meant they had to get to San Antonio.

With a sigh, Arabella boarded the train on her husband's arm. A couple more days and perhaps she could relax.

It also occurred to Arabella she might need to buy mourning clothes.

She would deal with that when they got to San Antonio.

Lightning streaked across the sky in long witches' fingers. The air crackled. Thunder followed, deafeningly loud.

It was about six Monday evening. The hands had gathered around the kitchen table in the main house of the Bar M. Sated on home-made tortillas, beans and *arroz con pollo* flavored with chilies and hot as a pistol, washed down with good strong coffee, they heard the ominous roar in the heavens.

In a flash, Bob Bonetti ran outside. Once he was off the porch he gazed up at the sky. He could feel the electricity in the air. He held out his arms, closed his eyes and said a prayer to the Virgin.

As if in answer, another bolt of lightning shot through the sky, followed closely by thunder. Another moment later the sky opened up and sheets of healing, soaking rain fell from the sky.

Bob was so overjoyed he didn't notice he was getting soaked to the skin. He would have fallen to his knees in gratitude had he not had his slicker and hat been thrust in his arms by Bill Porter.

"Get mounted, Bobby. We can't afford to lose any more cattle to panic now we've got a storm."

Bob clapped his hat on his dripping black curls and pulled on his slicker. *Finally*, he thought. Tomorrow, he'd insist they take the wagon to Ganados Ravine. If Miss Hofheinz and the others were out there, they'd find them.

As he ran to the stable to saddle his horse and grab his lasso, he prayed that everything would turn out all right.

But right now, he had a job to do.

From underneath the ground, the thunder shook the land. Sam and Pru were immediately alert.

"Earthquake?" Sam asked, trying to rise.

Pru shook her head uncertainly. "Not around here as far as I know." She was on her feet. "Lie back down. I'll go up top and see."

Before Sam could say another word, Pru was climbing the ladder. Sam watched her move with self-assurance. The woman who swallowed her fear and climbed down a rope to find him had grown in the last few days to a tower of strength, capable of anything. Not that she'd been any kind of fragile flower, but she was a city girl. In the past few days she had become athlete, cook, nurse, improviser as well as lover, confidante and friend. Though her hair had become a rat's nest and her face and clothing were nearly black with dirt and soot, he had never seen anyone more beautiful.

If Sam Blake loved her before, it was an inch to a mile compared to how much he loved her now. This was a woman who could survive anything.

Even marriage to a cripple.

Which, in Sam's opinion, would be like clipping the wings of an angel.

As much as he loved her, he loved her too much to chain her down to a helpless man.

As much as he loved her, he would have to let her go.

A few moments later, Pru came tearing down the ladder, her teeth unnaturally white against her dirty face. Water dripped off her nose and saturated hair and her clothes were sodden.

"Oh, Sam!" she cried as she hit the bottom of the ladder and bounded to where he was still propped up on his good arm. She threw her arms around him; her tears mingled with nature's. "Oh, darling," she said, covering his face with kisses, "it's raining. It's raining. We're saved. If nobody comes looking for us I'll be able to ride back to the ranch and get some help for you."

Sam let her hold him and kiss him and cry her joy against his neck.

Because he knew their time together was limited.

His pain wasn't getting any less. Sam had no idea what sort of work he would be able to do if his legs were crippled or he lost them. He wouldn't force her to live with a man who couldn't support her.

The woman in his arms was strong enough never to need a man to support her, but Sam couldn't let himself become dependent on her. He had never had much pride. Disappointment and rejection had driven most of it out of him. But he had too much pride to put her through the hell of life with a helpless man.

Letting Pru go would be the hardest thing he would ever do, but he had to.

He would find out if a man could live without his soul.

Chapter 21

Pru awoke the next morning feeling safe and protected. Even before she opened her eyes she could hear the steady beating of Sam's heart beneath her ear and feel the baby soft fur of his chest on her cheek. Lazily she let her hand stroke his belly and opened her eyes to see him staring at her intently, squinting down to focus. The look on his face was enigmatic; both loving and unaccountably sad.

"Have you been up a while?"

"A bit."

"Why didn't you wake me?"

He smiled kindly. "I enjoyed watching you sleep, even if it was a blur."

Pru moved the blanket and sat up. She blushed, remembering she had taken off her wet clothes and slept naked, if chastely, by Sam's side. She smiled to realize how wonderful it was to sleep skin touching skin, feeling the strength of his presence enveloping her.

She rose from the blankets and stepped carefully to where her clothes were spread. During the night they had dried completely.

She held up her skirt and laughed.

"What is it?"

"My clothes are so dirty they could stand up without me in them. I must look a sight."

"A wonderful sight."

Pru grinned lopsidedly, though Sam could not see far enough without his specs to discern it. Once dressed, she handed Sam his glasses, which had been tucked securely in his saddlebag.

"Do we have anything left to eat?" Sam asked after Pru assisted him with the chamber pot.

"One can of beans. I'll go up top and try to get a fire started to heat it and some water for tea. I'm more concerned that we've only got one candle left. Sam, I'm going to have to go for help today. I hate to leave you like this."

"Well," he said, half joking, "at least I'm out of the elements...You may want to go to the trash heap where you found the splint wood to get some dry fuel for the fire."

"Good idea." Lighting her precious candle, Pru ventured back into the tunnel. She took the two coffeepots from their place gathering water from the trickle, then went deeper to the trash pile. She picked up some pieces of wood and was tucking them under one arm when she lost her balance for a moment. Her shoulder brushed against the wall and kept her from falling. But when she stood upright, she was surprised to see a black streak on the shoulder of her shirt.

She grumbled, not that her shirt wasn't already beyond laundering. But when she looked up at where she fell, she saw the dull gleam of dark gray.

Tugging a bandanna from her pocket, Pru rubbed along the wall, taking more black tarnish off what looked like it could be a three inch vein of silver ore. She followed the vein into the tunnel a ways until the vein disappeared into the rock wall of the tunnel.

The history of the area indicated the conquistadors had not found precious metals in the Mystic Mountains and abandoned the sites after the loss of many Indian lives. It appeared the Spaniards had not known what they were seeing and had missed the vein entirely.

Wouldn't it be funny if she had found the hidden treasure that had eluded prospectors for two centuries—by accident? She gathered up her wood again, tucked it under her arm, picked up the two coffee pots and returned to the shaft. As soon as she could, she was going to go to the land office and find out if anyone owned this part of the mountains. If not, she would file a claim, then write to her father about financing a prospector to determine if the vein was of any extent and if the metal was of any quality. She hoped the land had not been claimed by either Morgan or McKinley, since with the probable legal tangles, it might be years before anything could be done with the claim.

Making several trips, Pru carried the wood, chamber pot, water and can of beans up to the surface. The ground was muddy, but she laid the dry wood in the campfire circle and using tinder and kindling from below, got a fire started. She opened the can of beans and set it directly on the flames next to the water-filled pots. She would make tea with one pot of water, the other boiled water would be poured into the canteens.

While the food cooked, Pru saw to the horses. Nameless and Max were nibbling on dampened grass and drinking rainwater from puddles. The two beasts had been astonishingly patient with standing around for days, leather hobbles restricting their movement. They would be fine. There was plenty for *them* to eat.

She wandered back to the fire and used her bandanna to take the can of beans off the fire. There were about two cups of beans in the can, plus little bits of pork and sauce. It was not much for two large people, one injured, to consume for the day. Pru dumped tea in one of the kettles and let it boil while she carried the other coffee pot and can of beans down the ladder.

She set the pot of water and can down to cool and traveled up again. She brought down the tea and poured it into two cups. She brought the can of beans, a single spoon and the two cups of tea to where Sam lay.

"Dinner is served," she said gaily.

She helped him sit upright and held the can while he took up the spoon in his right hand and took a bite of the salty, sweet beans. He took another spoonful and held it for her. It seemed so natural for him to feed her as she had fed him. It made the meager fare more sumptuous. Still, it didn't take long to finish the can and drink a couple of cups of strong, unsweetened tea.

When they were done, Sam asked to lie down again. "You better get upstairs and take care of the fire."

Pru was surprised. He sounded strangely detached. She supposed he must be in worse pain. She reached the surface and smothered the fire. She dumped and buried the contents of the chamber pot. Everything was damp from the rain. She sat on a boulder and looked out in the distance. For the first time since Thursday morning there was no smoke darkening the sky. Hope filled her. It seemed that the rain had extinguished the fire.

The sky was filled with cirrus clouds streaked with gray. It might rain again before nightfall. She realized she ought to saddle Max and get ready to go to the Bar M for help.

She went down the ladder to get her tack. Sam was lying on his back, covered with a blanket to his chin, glasses on his nose although his eyes were closed.

Pru smiled. Every minute of sleep he got was healing. She didn't begrudge him a second of it.

Five very tired cowhands had worked all night to round up the remainder of the cattle. They were wet and hungry and there weren't that many cattle left in the first place, but they'd kept those few from stampeding again and there had been no more lost.

Bob Bonetti looked up at the striated clouds. "It may rain again before nightfall. We ought to go up to the Mystics and look for the missing people."

The other four, warming themselves on the porch with Consuelo's strong coffee, groaned and swore.

Sweeney complained, "If they're dead, it don't much matter when we go."

"Yeah," said Anderson.

"That's true," Bob conceded. "But if any of them are alive, we shouldn't wait any longer. Besides, we promised Miss Arabella we would look for Mr. Morgan and the others as soon as we were able."

Porter conceded that this was true. A half-hour later the buckboard was saddled and some blankets and coils of rope were tossed in the back. Tom Sully took the seat of the buckboard. The others rode their mounts.

They set out through the burned-out range. It had been so dry the past couple of years that the thirsty ground had sucked up almost all of the rain water, leaving surprisingly little mud.

It was a grisly sight that met their eyes as they headed towards Ganados Ravine. Charred carcasses of dead cattle, some picked over by scavengers once the flames had consumed their fill. The stench of smoke and death was overwhelming. Eventually, all of them tied their bandannas over their mouths and noses in a futile attempt to filter out the foulness around them.

"Bonetti," Anderson growled, "there better be survivors."

Bob stared from above his bandanna. He made a sacred vow not to take second helpings nor eat desserts for six months if Miss Hofheinz was alive. For a still growing youth with a powerful sweet tooth it was a powerful vow to make.

They rode up through the carnage until they got to the ridge overlooking the ravine. There the stench was worse because it had not burned in the ravine and several hundred decomposing carcasses lay in a sickening heap.

"Shit," muttered Bill Porter as he looked down, "what a mess!"

The others agreed. Bob Bonetti rode his horse up the south side of the ravine. He saw a buzzard and a cold chill shot down his spine. He went in the direction of the vulture.

A sight worse than the dead cattle greeted him. With a shudder he dismounted and bolted away where he promptly vomited until his stomach was empty.

He pulled his gun and fired twice in the air.

"What is it?" someone yelled.

Taking a deep breath, he yelled back, "It's Mr. Morgan—or what's left of him. Shot between the eyes! It's pretty awful."

Bill ordered, "Sweeney, grab a blanket and go help Bobby bring Mr. Morgan's body down."

Ted Anderson was lying on his stomach overlooking the ridge. "Bill, there's another body down in the ravine. It's hard to tell, but it could be Mr. McKinley."

Bill looked where Ted was pointing. "Yep, it looks that way. It's too small to be Blake. Well, he stays where he is. I'm not risking one of you to go down and get him. We'll just let sheriff Murphy know we found him and let him decide what to do."

Up on the south ridge, a morose Bob Bonetti and Ben Sweeney, holding their breaths, wrapped Ethan Morgan's remains in a blanket and threw the body over Bob's horse to walk down to the buckboard.

Prudence had saddled Max when she heard the gunshots.

She sprinted back to the shaft and down the ladder.

She picked up Sam's gun belt. "Is it loaded?" she muttered.

Sam's eyes popped open. "What!"

"I heard shots. Close together, like a signal. I have to let them know where we are. Is your revolver loaded?"

"It should be. Just be careful. Aim away from the horses."

Pru took the pistol and climbed up the ladder. She fired three shots as quickly as she could pull the trigger.

On the ridge below, the shots were heard.

"Who's up there?" yelled Bill Porter.

"Prudence Hofheinz," she yelled back. "Sam Blake is with me, but he's badly hurt and can't walk. Who's there?"

"Bill Porter and the hands from the Bar M. Hang tight and we'll be up in a moment."

"Have you got a stretcher or travois poles?" Prudence called.

"No, ma'am, but we'll figure something out."

Pru raced down the ladder. "Sam, they're here! The men from the Bar M. We've been rescued."

A fist clutched at Sam's heart. This peculiar idyll was over. "We have a problem," he said calmly and dispassionately.

Pru was starting to put things back in their saddlebags. "Well, they don't have a stretcher, but..."

"Do they have a change of clothes for me?" Sam asked sarcastically. "If you'll recall, you cut my only garments off me."

Pru felt the color drain from her face. She had become so accustomed to Sam being naked under the blanket it did not bother her.

"Oh, God, Sam. I didn't think." She squatted and assessed the situation critically. Suddenly, she brightened. "It's not much, but it's the best I can do, my love."

She crouched down next to Sam and began to tuck the upper blanket under Sam's body but above the blanket he was lying on. Sam grimaced when she touched his splinted legs, but only the change in his breathing hinted at the pain.

Pru took the last remnants of the length of muslin and tore it into strips. She threaded the strips under him until she could tie them around his waist, thighs, knees and ankles. She put his socks back on his feet to keep them warm. He was now wrapped from shoulders to feet in the blankets, completely concealing his nakedness.

"Miss Hofheinz, Miss Hofheinz," called a voice from above.

"You'd better go up," Sam said.

Pru climbed the ladder and popped her head above the surface. "We're down here."

It was Bill Porter who turned around. His eyes widened at the surprising sight of the dirty, disheveled woman whom he had never seen dress in a less than pristine manner.

"Miss Hofheinz?"

Pru put her hand to her wild hair. "I guess I look a sight." She climbed out of the shaft.

"How bad is Mr. Blake hurt?" Porter asked.

"I'm not sure, but both his legs are broken badly and he's got stitches from a bullet wound in his shoulder. He has no fever, but I'm not sure how well I set his legs."

"*You* set them?"

Pru bristled. "Well, someone had to. Anyway, there's an old ladder down here, but he can't climb or walk. Did you bring a wagon?"

"Yep."

"How many men are you?"

"Five."

"Good. Maybe you can lift him out and carry him on a blanket down to the wagon. Two or three lifting and two guiding to make sure he isn't hurt worse may do it. Where are the others?"

"Sully's with the wagon. Sweeney and Bonetti are on the other ridge bringing down Mr. Morgan's body."

Prudence started. "Mr. Morgan's dead?"

"Yes, ma'am, and Mr. McKinley, too. McKinley's at the bottom of the ravine."

"Any news about Arabella?"

Porter laughed cynically. "Oh, yeah. She's fine and dandy. She's on her way to San Antonio with her new husband..."

"*Husband*?"

"Yes, ma'am. Didn't even wait to find out what happened to her old man."

Or her best friend. "When did this happen?"

"Well, they left on Sunday's stage, so it must have happened sometime between Thursday and Saturday, but I ain't sure."

"Who would she...oh, don't tell me. She married Clint Randolph, didn't she?"

"Yes, Miss Hofheinz."

Pru took a deep breath and let it out. "I'm going to go back down and start putting things away. You will take Mr. Blake right to Doc Richards' place, won't you?"

"Sure, we have t'go to Western Union and wire Miz Randolph about her father."

Pru clambered down the ladder again. "It'll be just a little while longer, Sam." She paused. "Sam, Ethan Morgan's dead and Clint married Arabella."

"Fool," he snorted.

"Her or him?"

He snorted another laugh. "Take your pick."

Pru continued to pack the saddlebags. She filled the canteens with boiled water from earlier in the morning.

Sam thought about Clint marrying the pretty blonde. One way or the other he had fallen in the honey pot, as always. He was even going to ride off into the sunset with the prettiest girl in town.

Sam wondered if Clint had the presence of mind to collect their fees. Whether he recovered completely from his injuries or not, he was going to need the money to live on while he healed.

"Miss Hofheinz!" called down a younger voice.

"Bob?" she called up.

"Yes, ma'am. Thank God you're okay."

Bonetti and Anderson descended the ladder. In the pale light they assessed the situation.

"If we tie him to the ladder, we can pull him out and haul him to the wagon, then bring the ladder back," Ted called up.

"Pru," said Sam, "saddle Nameless and have one of the hands tie a rope to his pommel. He's strong enough to pull me up."

Pru hauled the dun's tack up the ladder and saddled him, then brought him to the lip of the hole.

Meanwhile, Anderson and Bonetti pulled down the ladder and laid it down next to Sam. The big man gritted his teeth, damned if he was going to yell. The two ranch hands took Sam's suggestion that they move his hips and shoulders and then move his legs afterward. The pain Sam was suffering was beyond belief, but they managed to get him lashed to the ladder with another rope.

At the signal, Prudence guided Nameless back from the shaft. The ladder lifted and, with Anderson and Bonetti guiding it from the hole and Porter and Sweeney working up top, they managed to bring the ladder out of the mineshaft with Sam on it. Then Bob and Ted climbed the knotted rope that was still there, one of them with Sam's Stetson caught in his teeth.

The ladder was too narrow and fragile to use as a travois, so the four cowhands lifted it like a stretcher and carried it down the hill to where Tom Sully waited with the wagon and the blanket-wrapped body of Ethan Morgan.

They unlashed Sam from the ladder and laid him as gently as they could in the wagon. Pru crawled in the wagon bed beside him.

"Are you all right, Sam?"

"I'm fine, Pru," he responded in a cold, strained voice. "Look, sweetheart, I want you to do me a favor."

"Anything," she said, leaning over to kiss him. To her surprise, his lips were unresponsive.

"Take the ladder back to the mine and bring the rest of our things out, then leave the campsite as if nobody's been there. Take Nameless and go to the bunkhouse and get the rest of my gear and bring it to the doctor's office. Can you keep Nameless in your shed?"

"Sure, Sam."

"Don't tell Clint I'm this badly hurt, please."

Pru wondered why, but agreed.

"Now then, Pru. The doctor may have to operate on me, so I may be under ether or something for several hours. You might as well go back to your cabin after you get my things. Take a long hot bath, wash your hair and get dressed in your town clothes—maybe even take a short nap—before you bring my things to the doctor's office. A couple of hours won't make much difference to me, but I doubt you want any more people than necessary to see you looking like a ragamuffin."

Beneath the dirt on her face, Pru flushed. "All right, darling. I'll see you in a few hours...Mr. Sully, you'll take him straight to Dr. Richards' office?"

"Yes, ma'am."

"Bill," Bob interrupted.

"What's up?"

"Can you transfer Mr. Morgan's body to your horse? I'll stay here with Miss Hofheinz and help her clean up the campsite."

They tied the body to Porter's horse and Bill climbed on the buckboard seat next to Sully.

Pru gave Sam one more lingering kiss, to which he again failed to respond, other than to ask her to please put his hat on his head. She jumped out of the buckboard and stood next to Bob Bonetti as the wagon and cowboys headed toward town.

Bob and Pru watched the buckboard rattle out of sight, Pru wincing at the pain that Sam must be feeling with the jostling. She felt a gentle hand on her shoulder.

"Come on, Miss Hofheinz. The sooner we get back up the hill the sooner you can get home and see how he is."

They lifted the ladder together and headed back up the mountain to the mineshaft.

Prudence finished packing the two pairs of saddlebags, separating Sam's things from her own. She gathered the rags of Sam's clothes and found his money clip, a metal calling card case, a pocketful of change, his watch that had miraculously survived the fall intact and a small, red velvet bag. She opened the bag and out fell a silver and turquoise woman's ring. She recognized the bag as being from Jackson's Mercantile. Sam had bought the ring in town.

Could he have bought it for her? She slipped it on her left ring finger. It fit pretty well. Was he planning to give it to her when his job was done? Or was it for someone else?

Since he hadn't given it to her, she slipped it off and put it back into the bag. She tucked his valuables in his saddlebag, but left the torn, bloody clothes where they were in a corner of the mine along with the saucepan she had used as a chamber pot. She knew she could never bring herself to cook in it again.

Meanwhile, Bob buried the remains of the campfire and scattered the stones. A few windy days and some seeds blowing in the wind would soon make the place look virgin again.

After bringing up the saddlebags, the lanterns and her bedroll, Prudence took one more look around. Tears came to her eyes. In many ways, the time she'd spent in this hole in the ground with Sam had been the most intimate, even more than the nights they had made love. Except for the ragged remains of his garments and a few tin cans, there was little evidence of their presence. The ladder and broken spade were returned to the trash pile near the silver vein. Prudence used the knotted rope to climb out for the last time.

The only exception to leaving the place as they found it was that Prudence brought up two stakes tied with pieces of Sam's shirt. These she hammered into the ground on opposite sides of the shaft so no unsuspecting person would fall through again. The breeze fluttered the rags as she mounted Nameless, took up Max's reins and rode beside Bob Bonetti back to the Bar M.

Chapter 22

Between the blankets and the pain, Sam was drenched in sweat by the time the wagon lumbered into Rincon. He slept for part of the journey, but with his hat over his eyes, he could not see anything.

Finally, mercifully, the buckboard came to a stop. The seconds crawled like hours before he found himself dragged onto a stretcher and carried into the office of Dr. Thomas Richards.

His hat was removed and he saw the doctor, a man in his late fifties with spidery veins in his nose hinting at long familiarity with a whiskey bottle. As the doctor bent over him, Sam was relieved not to smell spirits on the man.

The doctor grabbed a pair of scissors and began to cut at the bindings around the blankets.

"Doctor, I'm not wearing anything under the blankets..." Briefly, Sam explained what had happened and what treatment Pru had performed.

"Miss Hofheinz set your legs?" By now Dr. Richards had removed the blanket and was unwrapping Sam's shoulder. "She saw you like this?"

"You mean undressed? Of course. Who do you think cut me out of my clothes?"

Dr. Richards glanced over to the door connecting his office from his living quarters. Mrs. Richards was standing in the doorway looking as if she'd seen a ghost.

The doctor probed the shoulder wound first. He used a fine pair of scissors and tweezers to remove the stitches from Sam's shoulder. "That looks fine. No evidence of infection."

Sam began to move his left arm gingerly. It ached from disuse, but wasn't really painful anymore.

Then the doctor began to unwrap the splints from Sam's legs. As he probed and prodded, the doctor's face showed more and more concern. He snipped the stitches out of Sam's legs but he was shaking his head.

"Doctor, tell me the truth."

Richards shrugged. "I'm just a country doctor. There's nothing I can do for your legs, Mr. Blake."

Sam felt his life leave his body. "Do you have to amputate them?"

The doctor blinked uncomprehendingly. "That would be a solution, but there's no gangrene, so I don't think so. You need surgery for certain on your knees, but I haven't the expertise and if I botch it, either I could kill you or it could cost you your legs after all."

"I'm not sure which would be worse." Sam contemplated life without his legs. That fear made him determined to let Pru go. How could a legless man support a wife?

And even worse, what if she couldn't bear to have him touch her?

"There is another solution," Dr. Richards voice interrupted Sam's tortured thoughts. "A few years ago a doctor back east performed an operation where he opened up a man's knee and wired his patella—his knee cap—back together and the man survived. I was reading in a medical journal about a doctor in Amarillo who opened a hospital for people with those kinds of injuries. He's apparently had some success avoiding amputation and rehabilitating patients with serious limb injuries..." Dr. Richards went to a bookshelf and sorted through a few journals, muttering to himself as he searched. Finally, he brought one over to where Sam lay and opened to one page. "Here it is, St. Giles—hmm—hmm—Dr. David Maris. I could send you there. You'll be no worse off than you'd be in my care and maybe better."

Sam thought about that. Being in Amarillo would put him far away from Rincon and Pru, but maybe that was a good thing—at least for her. If there was a chance he might recover, he ought to take it.

"How am I supposed to get to Amarillo, Doctor? I can't get on my horse and ride there myself. Also, I'm not exactly dressed for travel."

"Miranda!" Dr. Richards called out. His wife answered the summons. "Miranda, get yourself to Jackson's and buy the largest men's nightshirt they have for sale, a blanket and sheet and a cheap chamber pot. Tell Harmon to put it on my bill. And Miranda, don't talk to anyone."

Mrs. Richards agreed and left.

The doctor pulled out his watch. "The northbound stage leaves in about two hours, Mr. Blake. Amarillo is its last stop. If you can travel strapped to a plank, I believe I can get the driver to deliver you to St. Giles. The only problem is you'll have to sleep in the stagecoach because I doubt there'll be anyone at the way station to carry you out to a bed and back."

Sam laughed. "Yeah, Doc. I'll give it a go. Just one thing; Miss Hofheinz will be bringing my grip along in a few hours. Take whatever money you need for your bill, the tickets and so forth and send the rest to me at St. Giles. And please, doctor, don't tell Miss Hofheinz where I've gone, or Clint Randolph if he comes back to town."

"Why would you want me to do that?"

Sam sighed. "Pru Hofheinz is a beautiful, charming woman..."

"Miss Hofheinz?"

"Miss Hofheinz. I don't want to saddle such a lovely woman with a cripple."

"She may want to write and see how you are."

"Tell her to give the letters to you and you mail them to me at the hospital."

"Well, I don't know about that..."

"Please, doctor," Sam begged, tears in his eyes splashing on his lenses. "It'll kill me to have her see me if I'm going to be crippled. She can't know where I am."

The doctor looked hard at his patient. He had never seen such emotional torment. "Don't you think she's strong enough?"

Sam shook his head dismally. "Oh, she's strong enough to handle anything, even this, but I couldn't subject her to such a commitment. It's not like we were married."

"All right. If she or Randolph finds out, it won't be from me."

The doctor left Sam in his office and walked to the stage office. The northbound stage was already there, as the driver and passengers were having a dinner break. There were only two passengers heading north, so Dr. Richards bought two tickets and explained to the agent that there would be a plank stretched across the seats to accommodate the injured man. The doctor went to the lumber yard and bought a plank long enough to stretch across the seats and some straighter splint material.

By the time he returned with the tickets and the wood, Mrs. Richards had returned with her purchases. The doctor helped his patient put on the big nightshirt. He re-bandaged and re-splinted Sam's legs and pulled the nightshirt down to cover him. With Sam helping to lift himself, they got the plank into place, then the doctor covered Sam with a sheet and tied him to the plank. Finally he covered Sam with the blanket and handed him his hat.

About fifteen minutes before the stage was scheduled to leave, Dr. Richards got a couple of men to help him take the plank with Sam strapped on it to the stagecoach. The doctor handed Sam an old carpetbag containing Sam's two other blankets, some food, a canteen and the chamber pot. The plank was put inside the stagecoach and pushed to the extreme end. With the blanket pulled up to his chin and his Stetson pulled low over his eyes, all that could be seen was the thick blackness of his beard. The doctor gave him a bottle of laudanum and suggested he take some and sleep through as much of the journey as possible. Sam took a spoonful and re-corked the bottle, putting it in the carpetbag that sat next to him.

He was already half asleep when the stagecoach pulled out of Rincon. His last conscious thought before the opiate lulled him to sleep was that he would never see the woman he loved again.

It made him unbearably sad.

On the way back to the Bar M Bob Bonetti filled Prudence in on the events as he knew them. He was angry that Arabella would leave town before finding out her father's condition.

"If it was my father, I wouldn't run out like that."

"I'm sure you wouldn't, Bob, but maybe Clint knew what was best for her."

"Were you frightened, Miss Hofheinz?"

"Of the fire? Yes, but it's not the first or the worst fire I've lived through. When I was sixteen my father and I watched everything we owned burn to the ground in the Great Chicago Fire. We barely escaped with our lives. I was much more afraid Mr. Blake might die of his injuries. What surprises me is that Mr. Randolph didn't ask about Mr. Blake's condition."

"Yeah, that kind of surprises me, too. He was putting all kinds of pressure on Miss Arabella to leave. He looked real nervous—really nervous—looking over his shoulder like—as if—someone was following him."

"Well, I suppose it's not for us to speculate on the goings on between a husband and wife."

"No, ma'am. I reckon—guess—it isn't."

Ted Anderson and Bill Sweeney were already back at the ranch when Prudence and Bob arrived. Consuelo was aghast at how sooty and disheveled Prudence was, but was glad to find her in good health. She insisted Prudence eat some lunch, and, having been on short rations for several days, Prudence didn't say no.

Her hunger sated, Prudence went into the bunkhouse. Only six bunks were being occupied. Anderson pointed out the bunk Sam had been using.

Sam hadn't left much—a few books, two extra shirts, an extra pair of jeans and the waterproof pouch containing his black suit and best white shirts. There were also several pairs of socks, extra union suits, his duster and a case with two extra pairs of spectacles. There was not an additional pair of boots. Pru wondered what he would put on his feet when he was ready to leave the doctor's office.

Then she said a quick prayer that he would need boots when he left the doctor's office. The thought that Sam might still lose his legs filled her with dread. She would stand by him through anything, if he would let her. Men were so prideful, she learned from observation, expecting perfection from themselves so they could demand it from their women. Sam had been an exception—an imperfect man willing to love an imperfect woman.

But he had been a whole man, able to stand on his own two feet. What would he do if he had no feet on which to stand? Prudence shuddered.

"Oh, Sam," she said, unaware that she voiced her sadness.

Prudence packed Sam's remaining things in his saddlebags and brought them out to where Nameless and Max stood waiting for her. She tied the saddlebags onto Nameless's saddle and took the reins as she mounted Max and rode into town.

Once she got home she could see activity through the windows of the schoolhouse. Prudence felt a moment's panic. She had lost track of time. It was Tuesday and class was going on without her. She supposed Mrs. Foley, the minister's wife, was substituting. That was the contingency plan, although it had never been used before.

Quietly, she led Max and Nameless into the shed, unsaddled and brushed them down and put hay and oats into their feeding troughs. She spent extra time with Nameless. She didn't know if horses really knew their masters and missed them.

Pru put Sam's saddlebags and duster in the boot of her buggy, then took her own into the house. Everything was as she left it. The milk was spoiled, so she dumped it down the sink and poured water after it from the pump before filling her bath kettles and setting them on the newly lit stove. She rolled the bathtub over in front of the fireplace and went into her bedroom to undress.

"Oh, my God!" she exclaimed when she caught a glimpse of herself in the mirror. "I look like a minstrel show refugee!"

Her hair was in a straggly braid with almost more pulled out than still plaited and was impossibly snarled. Between soot, dirt, dried blood and tarnish, her face and clothes were almost black. Even her chemise and underwear were soiled beyond cleaning. Prudence slipped her belt and hat off, yanked off her boots and completed undressing. She threw the clothing in a pile on the floor. She would give Wing Chan one chance at laundering them. If he couldn't get them clean, she would dump them in the ragbag and buy new ones.

It seemed every pore was filled with ground-in dirt. No wonder Sam didn't want her coming into town like this! How could he have stood to have her lying so close to him when she looked this bad? She was so filthy she didn't even want to put on one of her dressing gowns until after she bathed.

While the water was heating, Prudence unbound her hair and attacked it with her brush and comb. Eyes tearing, she managed to torture the knots and snarls until it hung in relatively smooth, greasy, sooty, lank waves so dirty her hair looked almost as black as Sam's. How people could routinely go weeks at a time and not bathe was beyond her.

The water was finally boiling. Prudence poured the kettles into the tub and added cold water until she could bear to sit in it. She scrubbed at her hair, skin and nails until she was sure she had taken a layer of skin off with the dirt. She rinsed her hair two or three times until it squeaked and brushed her finger- and toenails until all the dirt was gone from under them. She brought a hand mirror into the tub to make sure she got her face clean.

While she was bathing, the clock on the mantel over Pru's fireplace struck three. A few minutes later the northbound stage rolled past up the road. Pru's only thought about the stagecoach was that the driver be watchful of children leaving school about that time.

Feeling clean at last, Pru wrapped her hair in a towel and put on her kimono, then dumped the bath water down the sink. After towel drying her hair, she sat over a cup of tea and a sandwich and brushed her hair until it dried.

She walked back into the bedroom and looked in the mirror again, trying to see what Sam saw. For the first time in her life, Pru tried to look for what was right with her instead of what was wrong. Between being outside for five days and the scrubbing she had given herself, her skin was all pink and golden. Her face was a soft oval. Pru smiled. Her teeth were straight, white and even. Her eyes seemed lighter than she remembered, almost like dark amber instead of boring brown, and her eyelashes seemed longer than she ever thought. With the natural blush in her cheeks and her hair waving about her face, Prudence Hofheinz saw herself as almost pretty.

She wasn't a pure beauty like Arabella Morgan—*no,* she corrected herself in her mind, *Arabella Randolph,* but few women were. But she wasn't the plain, invisible woman she had always thought herself.

"Sam Blake," she said, her eyes welling with tears until they sparkled with them, "you gave me a great gift. You gave me new eyes with which to see myself. Now, let me do the same for you."

In the end, Prudence took out a rose pink silk gown she hardly ever wore because someone suggested it was too daring for a schoolmarm. Its mock fichu crossed over the breasts; the collar was high in the back, but dipped under the fichu to show the hollow of her throat but no décolletage. The skirt had a cascade of layered ruffles down the back instead of a bustle and a false overskirt in the front that looked like a continuation of the fichu, all tied together with an emerald green velvet sash. The sleeves were fitted to the elbow with ruffled lace to the wrists; the lace shot through with green velvet ribbon.

As Pru was dressing, she noticed her corset was a little easier to hook up than it had been a week earlier. She had not been mistaken. She had lost a little weight—not enough to show in her clothes, but enough that she would have some breathing room in her corset for a while.

She put on the dress and looked at herself. Even trying to be critical she felt good about the way she looked. Maybe being in love changed self-perception.

The skies had looked threatening all day, so Pru took her dark gray woolen cloak and threw it over her shoulders.

With an extra candle in her hand, Prudence left her house and went to the shed. She put the candle on the shelf next to the lantern. She didn't need it now, but it would be dark when she returned. She raised the bonnet of the buggy, bridled Max and led him into the traces. Once outside the shed, she climbed into the buggy. A slight snap of the whip and they were off to the center of town to Dr. Richards' office.

It was nearly five o'clock.

"I can't believe the stage line would let someone in his condition ride a public conveyance unaccompanied," whispered one of the northbound passengers as she glared at the blanket-wrapped, sound asleep Sam Blake.

"From what I overheard, ma'am," said another, "he's being sent to a specialist in Amarillo to keep him from losing his legs—um—lower limbs—excuse me, ma'am. There was apparently considerable haste to get him on this particular stagecoach rather than wait another half week to send him with a companion. I think he must be in considerable pain since the doctor gave him a bottle of laudanum to make him sleep through the journey."

The woman shuddered. She said a little prayer that the stranger would keep his limbs.

Sam Blake slept on in dreamless, drugged oblivion. Had he not, the jostling of the coach would have been too much even for a hero to bear.

Prudence arrived at the doctor's office a few minutes later. She removed Sam's things from the boot and carried them to Dr. Richards' door. She knocked assertively.

The door opened. Dr. Richards was standing in the doorway in his shirtsleeves and vest. It took him a moment to recognize his caller.

"Miss Hofheinz? Forgive me—you look so different in that frock."

Prudence flushed slightly. She would take it as a compliment. "I'm here to see Sam Blake and bring him his things."

Dr. Richards' eyes wandered guiltily away from contact with hers.

"I'm sorry, Miss Hofheinz. Mr. Blake is gone."

Chapter 23

His words hit Prudence like a punch in the stomach. Both her eyes and voice filled with tears.

"Gone?" she echoed, stunned. "He's dead?" Suddenly she couldn't breathe and dropped Sam's duster and saddlebags on the boardwalk in front of her.

Dr. Richards grabbed her before she could fall. "Miss Hofheinz, you misunderstand. He's very much alive, but he's left town."

It took a moment for that news to sink in. Then disbelief with an overlay of rage filled her. "Left town? How could he leave town? He couldn't even walk. Where could he possibly have gone?"

"Miss Hofheinz, calm yourself. I know you acted the Good Samaritan when you found him in the mineshaft, but it's no reason to be so overwrought. I sent him to a specialist who knows more about injuries to the extremities than I do."

"Where?"

"Mr. Blake specifically asked me not to tell you where he had gone. He requested I take his things and forward them to him."

Tears were running down Prudence's cheeks. "Then you do know where he is?"

"I'm sure if he wants you to know he will write to you."

"Doctor, if I wrote to him, would you be willing to mail the letters for me?"

"Of course. Just bring them around to my office and I'll take care of it. I'm sure he would appreciate some nice, friendly letters. I'm sorry I can't break this confidence, but if I did, my patients could never trust me to keep their secrets."

"I understand. Thank you." She turned to go.

"By the way, Miss Hofheinz, for an amateur under difficult conditions, you did a masterful job on Mr. Blake's injuries. There was no evidence of gangrene and the stitched areas were showing healthy, healing skin. If you should ever decide you want to be a nurse, let me know."

Prudence smiled defiantly. "Doctor, if I ever decide to go into medicine, believe me, I won't settle for being a nurse." She turned on her heel and walked back to the buggy.

She was halfway home when it began to drizzle. By the time she had Max unhitched, a light rain was falling. It had progressed to a steady downpour by the time she changed into her nightgown and crawled into bed, matching the steady downpour of the heartbroken woman crying her eyes out into a pillow that would never adequately substitute for the man whose arms she missed.

"You can't just leave him out there in the stagecoach all night," said the drummer.

"Between the plank he's on and the size of him, I ain't a-gonna lift him alone and neither will my shotgun. It ain't in our contract."

"Will you carry him inside if I help and take care of him for the night?"

The stage driver spat a wad of tobacco into the nearby spittoon. "Ah, what the hell. If'n he gits sick, it'll be my neck in the noose anyway."

With the way station operator, the driver, shotgun and drummer all assisting, they managed to get Sam, now awake but groggy, off the stage and onto a cot inside.

The other three left, but the drummer stayed by the cot.

"How you doing, big guy?" he said cheerily.

Sam shook his head. "I've been better. I appreciate your help in bringing me in, Mister..."

The drummer held out his hand. "Basil Mercury. Used to be Vasilis Mercouris, but I changed it."

"Being Greek bad for business, eh?"

Basil looked surprised. "You recognized it? I was born in Piraeus, but we came to America when I was a kid. I'm a drummer for the Novelty Corset Company of New York, makers of the Perfect Fit Corset."

Sam raised an eyebrow at the enthusiastic sound in the young man's voice. "Sorry, don't use 'em myself."

Basil laughed. "Didn't think you did." He turned and drew closed the curtain that gave each cot a little privacy. "Seriously, Mister..."

"Blake. Sam Blake. Always was and will be, I guess."

"Mister Blake," Basil affirmed, then lowered his voice to a near whisper, "I don't want you to take this the wrong way, but I was thinking with you all strapped in like that, well, you might have a problem using the privy. I can't imagine you going two days to Amarillo without going." Behind his Mediterranean darkness, he flushed. "But I'd be willing to lend you whatever assistance you need."

"You'd do that for a complete stranger?"

"Even if you don't wear corsets," he said with a slight laugh. "I would hope someone would do me the same favor if I was in similar straits."

It occurred to Sam that sometimes help comes in the most peculiar packages. He would accept this young salesman's help because he really had no choice and he would be eternally grateful that he hadn't had to beg for help.

"How old are you, Basil?"

Basil grinned and played with the ends of his thick mustache. "Twenty-three."

Sam laughed.

"What?"

"I was just thinking that I was never that young, even when I was that young."

"So what are you, Mr. Blake? Perhaps thirty-five?"

"Nearly."

"So, you've got yourself a good forty years left. You got plenty of time left to be young before you're old. My father, he's still young and he's nearly sixty. I can only hope I'm as young as him when I'm that age."

Sam thought the young man's attitude marvelous. It was almost too bad he'd need to be drugged to bear the rest of the coach trip. Basil Mercury would make a welcome companion, even on a trip such as this.

Exactly one week ago Prudence had stood before her class as usual. Now it was Wednesday again.

It was a week that guaranteed her life would never be the same.

Prudence looked at the rose pink gown, again hanging in a corner of the armoire. She had no idea when she'd have the opportunity to wear it again. Today she pulled on one of her plain white waists and her plaid walking skirt. Her hair was drawn back in her usual plaited chignon. Only her slightly sunburned cheeks indicated that anything was different from any other weekday.

She ate a quick breakfast, knowing that despite her singular lack of appetite, she would not make it until noontime on an empty stomach. The soda crackers, applesauce and tea sat on her stomach like lead, but they were easy and not spoiled. This afternoon she would have to shop for food.

The schoolyard began to fill with students when the door opened and Mrs. Foley walked in. She was a stick-thin woman with a pointed chin, long nose and hair of indeterminate color. It was almost surprising to Prudence that this woman had borne six children, three of whom were still in grammar school. The thought of Halloween witches always crossed Prudence's mind when she saw Mrs. Foley, though the woman would have been shocked.

"You're back."

"Yes, ma'am," said Prudence respectfully, even though Mrs. Foley was less than a decade her senior. The schoolteacher did not know the woman's first name. Rev. Foley referred to her as Mrs. Foley and her children merely called her Mother.

"I'm surprised—considering your recent ordeal," the older woman continued in a voice that was stiff and unsympathetic.

Prudence shrugged. "It wasn't so bad, Mrs. Foley. I was relatively safe, but I couldn't get back through the prairie fire."

"So they say."

Prudence cocked an eyebrow. She and Sam had been found less than twenty-four hours ago and she had spoken to nobody except Dr. Richards.

"If you wish, Miss Hofheinz, I'll take the class for one more day to allow you to recover."

Prudence shook her head. As much as she wanted to crawl back into bed and wallow in self-pity, work was the best thing for her. "I'm quite all right, Mrs. Foley. If you'll just show me where you left off, I'll be able to pick up from there."

Mrs. Foley looked suspiciously unconvinced, but she showed Prudence where the class was. Then, out of nowhere, she asked sharply, "Miss Hofheinz, do you consider yourself a good Christian?"

Prudence's eyes widened. "I've never thought about it. I'm not very religious, I suppose."

"You never come to church except for Christmas and Easter."

"Nor do a lot of other people."

"Those *other* people don't teach young minds."

"I've been teaching here for nine years and nobody's ever had cause to complain about the young minds I've taught." She looked at her watch. "If you'll excuse me, I'd better start letting the students in. I'm sorry if my absence caused you and the town inconvenience. I never intended to be gone so long."

The minister's wife looked down her long nose at the seated teacher and then turned and walked out without another word.

Pru sat for a moment wondering what that discussion was all about, then she rose and threw open the door. Her students were in the schoolyard, some playing, some gathered in small groups talking. Nothing looked amiss. She rang the bell and the children began walking in and taking their seats.

She began every school day with a reading from the Bible and a patriotic song. When the children were done singing, she apologized for her absence and settled down to begin class.

During the morning, Prudence noticed an unusual restlessness in her class. It seemed every time her back was turned the noise level rose. After lunch it was worse. There seemed to be whistling and giggling. She turned quickly.

"What is going on here?" she asked a sea of guilty faces. "Martine Calleia?" Martine was the mayor's daughter and incapable of keeping anything secret.

The girl stood up, face ashen.

"What were you whispering about?"

The child looked down at her desk. "Everybody's talking about it. We heard you were found yesterday...in the mountains with a..."

Martine's face was a bright crimson and she looked up, her eyes filled with apprehension.

"Well?"

"Well, Miss Hofheinz, they said you were with a *naked* man!" She couldn't even voice the word "naked." She had to whisper it.

At the forbidden word, the other students began to nod and mumble and giggle. Prudence began to feel nauseous.

A little probing traced the source of the gossip to the Tuesday evening quilting circle to which the doctor's wife belonged. From the quilting circle it had spread to husbands and children. By this afternoon it would be all over town. Her reputation was ruined.

She pulled her chair from behind her desk and set it in front of the class. Sitting, she asked, "Have any of you ever broken your arm or leg?" A couple of boys' hands went up. "When you went to the doctor, did he cut your pants leg or sleeve off before he put the splint on?" One of the boys conceded that had happened to him. "Well, when I found Mr. Blake, he had broken both his legs and they had swollen so badly he was in terrible pain. In order to help him, I had to cut off his trousers and since he didn't have another pair with him, I had nothing to replace the pair I cut. Do you understand this?"

She got scattered yesses and nods.

"It is usually improper for a woman to be in the company of a man to whom she isn't married when the man has no clothes on. If anyone tells you something different, they are wrong. But there is an exception and that is when the man is sick or injured. It would have been improper for me to say, 'I'm so sorry, Mr. Blake, I'm going to have to let you die or get gangrene and have to have your legs cut off because it's not proper for me to touch you because we're not married.' Does that make sense to you?"

The children admitted that it made no sense.

"Mr. Blake has left Rincon. I hope wherever he went he will get help for his broken legs. I also hope you will help me by not repeating this story about him and me to others. People will get the wrong idea about what happened and I will be the one to suffer for it."

Donnie MacGregor stood up and lisped through his missing front teeth. "We're thorry, Mith Hofheinth. We won't tell anyone. We promith."

While Prudence believed Donnie was sincere, there would be no keeping this quiet. She would have to confront the adults as time progressed.

After school was out and before going into town to shop, Pru wrote a letter to Sam. She dropped it at Dr. Richards' office. Doc told her he would put it with Sam's things when he sent them off.

Gossip is like a prairie fire. All a person can do is let it burn out and hope not to be burned by it. Prudence went from a little benign anonymity to hearing the buzz of voices everywhere she went. Men who barely noticed her before seemed to be undressing her with their eyes. Women who barely noticed her before looked at her with undisguised distaste.

She even began to feel ashamed of the times Sam had spent with her in her cabin. Loving Sam had been easy while he was here. Now that he was gone she was left to deal with her feelings in secret and alone. There was also the nagging fear that Clint would tell Arabella what he knew and one of them would spread it around and destroy her reputation completely.

Prudence had lived through the prairie fire without any real fear for her own safety. Now she was afraid her world would come crashing down around her and she would be completely alone.

ETHAN MORGAN DEAD STOP IMMEDIATE BURIAL REQUIRED STOP SAM BLAKE INJURED STOP CONDITION UNKNOWN STOP THREE HUNDRED HEAD SURVIVED STOP PLEASE ADVISE STOP BILL PORTER.

Clint had to pry the telegram from Arabella's fingers to read it. She was staring into space, alone with her grief.

Clint was more worried about Sam Blake. If his condition became more "known," he was sure to ask about his share of the money. Tomorrow, Clint would open a bank account and deposit the cash.

Maybe Sam would still die. Otherwise, Clint would try to stall as long as possible until he could figure out a way to avoid his erstwhile partner.

Clint made a decision. He was out of the range detective business. Married to Ethan Morgan's heir, he was now the owner of the Bar M Ranch. He could learn to be a rancher. He'd been a cowboy. How difficult would it be?

Amarillo, Texas, Friday, May 1, 1885

"We need the coach turned around right away. Number 36 has a broken axle," the stage agent declared as the driver hauled the last of the baggage from the boot.

The driver hooked one thumb in his belt and gestured toward the coach with the other. "What am I supposed to do with this guy? I agreed to take him to St. Giles Hospital."

The agent looked inside the coach. He saw the blanket-covered passenger in the battered camel Stetson, then looked back at the driver. "What are we, a hack service?" he screamed at the driver. "You there," he called into the coach, "come out of there at once."

Sam tipped his hat back and glared at the agent. "I'd gladly oblige, sir, if I could walk."

The agent whirled on the driver. "You took a cripple on as a passenger?" completely callous of the epithet's effect.

"He paid double."

"Well, get him out of there now."

"What am I supposed to do with him?"

"I don't give a damn what you do. Leave him on the sidewalk if you have to, but get that coach to the barn and back here in fifteen minutes or you'll be looking for a new job."

The agent walked away, leaving the driver in a dilemma. He stepped into the coach.

"Nice guy," Sam said. The driver snorted derisively in agreement. "Seriously, you're going to need at least two men to help you, between my weight and the wood."

The driver nodded. "I'm real sorry about this, Mister."

Sam shrugged, then pulled the blanket up again. "*You're* sorry!"

The driver buttonholed his shotgun, nodded to the agent and they rounded up two bystanders. The four of them lifted Sam and his carpetbag out of the coach and set him on a bench in front of the stage office.

The driver turned to Sam and said, "Look, I have to get this coach to the barn, like Clyde said. You gotta understand, I need this job."

Sam folded his arms. "I do. Don't worry about me."

The bystanders walked away and the driver and shotgun climbed on the coach and drove it toward the coach line's livery barn for fresh horses.

Sam closed his eyes and felt the misery flow over him. Was this what being crippled was going to be like? Helpless, treated like a piece of unclaimed baggage, ignored?

He would rather the fall had killed him.

The future could not have looked so bleak.

Chapter 24

About an hour later, a buggy drove by the stage office and pulled to a halt. Basil Mercury climbed out of the buggy and rushed onto the sidewalk.

"Sam Blake, what are you doing here? I thought the driver was taking you directly to St. Giles Hospital."

Sam shrugged. Every line of his face and body showed a defeated man. "Something more important came up."

Basil lifted an eyebrow. "What could be more important?"

"The flow of commerce. The coach left here about a half hour ago with a full load."

"And they just left you here?"

"As the agent said, they aren't running a hack service."

Basil looked at the big man strapped to the board, then to his hired buggy, then to his wiry self. He removed his bowler and scratched his dark hair thoughtfully. "Are you in pain?"

"I haven't been without pain and what's worse, these are the only clothes I have, so I'm sitting here in the middle of Amarillo half naked with about ten dollars to my name."

"I hate to leave you sitting here any longer, but it's a cinch I'm not strong enough to haul you into this buggy. What I *will* do is drive over to St. Giles Hospital and get them to send over an ambulance." Basil shrugged. "It's the best I can do."

Sam's eyes burned with tears he refused to shed. His voice embarrassingly thick, he responded, "It's a hell of a lot to do for a stranger. Thank you."

Basil reached into his jacket pocket and took out a business card case. "Here's my card. If you need anything, write or wire me. I'm staying at the Mills Hotel while I'm in town. They're on the telephone exchange if you need to reach me."

Sam took the card and slipped it inside the carpetbag. "You'll never know what this means to me."

"Return the good deed to someone else someday. Like maybe that girl you called out for in your sleep."

Sam's head jerked upwards. "Girl?"

"Yeah, you were calling out for someone named 'Pru.' I assumed it was a girl's name. Was I wrong?"

Sam looked down at his hands. "No, but that's over now."

Basil saw the man's misery and decided not to pursue it. "Anyway, pass on the good deed when you can. My father always told me it eventually gets back to you." He climbed into his buggy and headed in the direction of the hospital.

About a half hour later a white, enclosed ambulance with the words "St. Giles Orthopaedic Hospital" painted on its sides pulled up to the stage office. While the driver stayed on the seat, two burly men got out of the back and approached Sam.

"Mr. Blake?" said one. "Your friend told us to come get you."

Sam silently blessed the young Greek corset drummer again for his kindness.

"If we'd known you'd be arriving, the ambulance could have met the stage when it arrived."

The other orderly brought over a stretcher to the bench. Sam unbound himself from the plank at their instructions and they expertly moved him onto the stretcher.

As they carried him to the ambulance, the lead orderly said, "Dr. Maris is waiting to see you. Where are your bags?"

Sam raised the worn carpetbag. "This is it. My other things will be sent along after me."

The stretcher slid into the ambulance and the orderlies climbed in, lifted the tailgate closed and signaled the driver. The ambulance took off with a jolt. A grimace crossed Sam's face as pain shot through his legs. The lead orderly, who introduced himself as Joe Babcock, mumbled an apology.

Barely ten minutes later the ambulance slowed to a stop. Babcock and his associate pulled the stretcher out of the ambulance and carried it up a ramp and into a large, three story building with a sign announcing it as "Saint Giles Orthopaedic Hospital, Est. 1875."

Even from a recumbent position, Sam could see utilitarian, whitewashed walls and practical furnishings in the reception area. He was surprised to see electric lights. Sam had read about them, but had never been in a building that had them. Behind the reception counter were two nuns in cream-colored habits.

Babcock greeted one of the sisters by name and told her he was to take the patient directly to an examination room for Dr. Maris. The nun stopped them for a moment while she took down Sam's full name, address, date of birth and next of kin.

"Put down for next of kin: None."

The nun scribbled it down without even raising an eyebrow. It was obviously not the first time she had heard that response. She released the stretcher to go its way.

The orderlies brought the stretcher to a corridor. Babcock pushed a button and a few moments later a gate opened and they brought the stretcher into a cage about eight feet square. An older black man moved a lever on the floor and the cage started moving upwards.

Sam's eyes widened in shock. He swore under his breath.

Joe Babcock chuckled. "First time in an elevator, Mr. Blake?"

"Yeah."

"You'll get used to them after a while. At St. Giles they're a necessity."

The elevator stopped at the next floor and the orderlies took the stretcher to a small examining room. Carefully, they lifted Sam to the examining table and went to wait outside.

"Dr. Maris will be in to see you soon," Babcock said as they left.

A few minutes later a tall, square-faced priest in his early sixties with a shock of thick, white hair, came into the room.

"Samuel Blake?"

"Yes, Father. I'm Sam Blake."

The priest removed the socks and blanket from Sam's legs and began to examine the splints and the condition and coloring of the unbandaged skin beneath.

Sam raised himself on his elbows and remarked, "Excuse me, I don't mean to be rude, but I'm supposed to be waiting for Dr. Maris."

The priest nodded. "I'm David Maris."

Sam flushed. "Forgive me."

The priest grinned. "Nothing to forgive. I was a surgeon long before I became a priest. Someday maybe I'll tell you all about it. For now, are you able to describe how you were injured?"

Sam related the entire incident while Dr. Maris unwrapped the splints and cut off the bandages. In a careful, businesslike manner, he examined Sam's legs, occasionally interrupting Sam's narrative to ask specific details before having him continue.

"You say a female schoolteacher set your broken bones?"

"Under the most difficult circumstances imaginable short of a battlefield."

He saw a cloud pass over Dr. Maris's face at the mention of battlefields. Sam knew immediately that the doctor had likely been a field surgeon during the Civil War.

Dr. Maris examined Sam's knees with particular interest. This part of the examination was unbearably painful. To Sam it was like his knees were full of sharp pointed bits of gravel and seemed to bend both forward and backward.

"When this lady was setting the bones, did you feel a popping or tearing sensation in your knees?"

"Yes, but also when I first landed on the slag pile." Part of Sam's answer was delivered through gritted teeth, so intense was the pain.

Dr. Maris removed from his pocket a flat metal object that looked like the handle of a dinner knife and ran it along the soles of Sam's bare feet. He nodded when he saw his patient's toes curl. "Any numbness or loss of control of bodily functions?"

"No, and I've had some erections, too."

"Good, very good." He put the metal tester in his pocket. He pulled up a high stool and sat next to Sam. "You look like a man who's able to accept the unvarnished truth."

Sam's heart froze, but he nodded.

"All right, here goes. Your schoolteacher friend did an admirable job of setting the fractures. The femur, tibiae and fibulae are in perfect alignment and should heal properly without having to rebreak and reset them. There appears to be no evidence of paralysis or damage to the spine. You have full feeling and reflex in your feet and, based on your description, no loss of bodily function control. Also positive is there is no evidence of necrosis, what you would call gangrene, nor any visible sign of infection. All of this is good.

"However, it appears that both your patellae—your kneecaps—have been shattered into fragments. It's hard to tell without surgery, but I don't believe I can wire the kneecaps back together; they are too badly damaged. The best I can do is go in and pick out all the pieces so they aren't floating around in there causing you unnecessary pain.

"Also, while your leg bones will heal perfectly, through a combination of the initial impact when you landed and the lack of expertise of the woman who set your bones, there appears to be substantial damage to the tendons and ligaments that hold your knees together. Basically, your muscles may be partially detached from the bones and the network of tissue that connects them, in conjunction with the patellae, to make a normal knee swing in only one direction seems to have been torn away."

Sam could barely breathe. "Am I going to lose my legs?"

Dr. Maris smiled. "Probably not, however, I will have to perform surgery on both your knees, so there is always risk, even in St. Giles where we practice anti-sepsis."

"What kind of surgery?"

"A relatively new procedure. Under anesthetic, I will have to cut open the skin of your knees and use forceps to remove all the bone fragments of your shattered patellae. Unfortunately, we have yet to be successful reattaching severed tendons and ligaments, though I may be able to repair any muscle tears. Then, once the bone fragments are removed, the skin is stitched closed. This will greatly reduce your pain, but I cannot fully repair the damage to your knees."

Sam felt cold. "Then I'll never walk again," he said morosely.

"That depends on you, Mr. Blake."

Sam looked the doctor in the eye. "What do you mean?"

"One of the purposes for founding this hospital is rehabilitation of orthopedic injuries. Your knees are unlikely ever to be stable again. You will have to wear metal leg braces that will provide an external hinge to replace the natural hinge. You will probably start on crutches, but if you put your full effort into it, you will progress to where you will be able to walk using canes with the braces. You may even be able to sit and control a horse again. You will have to learn to live with a certain amount of pain, but you will find yourself quite ambulatory."

Sam drank that in. "Then I am crippled for life."

"How you deal with your injury is entirely up to you. It's true you will never walk without assistance again. But in many ways you will be able to lead a relatively normal life. There's one more thing, Sam. I estimate you weigh about 270—275 pounds."

Sam nodded. "That's about right, I suppose."

"If you want to have a minimum possible level of pain and prevent additional damage to your knees, you will have to lose a considerable amount of weight. That may be the hardest part of your rehabilitation."

Sam raised an eyebrow. "How much weight?"

Dr. Maris folded his arms. "One hundred pounds, maybe 120."

Sam was flabbergasted. "If that's even possible, I would be skin and bones."

"Skin and bones may not be enough to prevent further damage. You might still end up in a wheelchair in twenty or thirty years. If you don't lose the weight, it will be much sooner than that before you can't walk. But if you're willing to undergo it, my staff and I will do everything modern medical science will permit to get you well. The rest is up to you."

Sam paused. "How long will it take?"

"If we operate on Monday, you can be starting rehabilitation in four to six weeks. You can probably be discharged in six to nine months. It may take up to a year to lose all the weight, providing you remain on the food regimen I prescribe after you leave the hospital...Well, Sam, what do you think?"

Sam thought about it. His life as a detective—the life he had already wanted to leave before his accident—was over. Any chance of having a normal life with a wife and children was probably over as well. What woman would want a cripple for a husband? He could live alone just as easily in Amarillo as Santa Fe or anywhere else. He had no occupation anymore—certainly none he could do if he didn't undergo treatment.

Still, Sam realized he wanted to go on living. He needed a goal. If his goal was walking, well then, so be it.

"How much will this all cost?"

"Our charges are based on ability to pay. St. Giles never turns away a patient for want of money."

"I have money in the bank. Let's give it a go—do you prefer Doctor or Father Maris?"

"Whichever is more comfortable for you, Sam. The orderlies will come in a few moments to take you to the ward...One more thing, Sam. One of the reasons we are successful at St. Giles is we practice anti-sepsis. The wards, operating theatres, examining rooms and so forth are kept scrupulously clean and sterile. We also insist that our patients keep as clean as possible and are bathed daily by members of our staff if they cannot wash themselves. Unless you have a religious reason for your beard and long hair, it will be easier for you to keep clean if you're clean-shaven and your hair is short."

Sam had been a daily bather whenever possible, so that was no daunting prospect, but he had worn a beard since age sixteen and hair shoulder length or longer since returning to Texas after college. He wasn't even sure he remembered how he looked clean-shaven.

"Nice thing about hair; it grows back. If your staff can stand to look at this face, I guess I can."

Dr. Maris held out his hand. "Good."

Sam took it and they shook on it.

"Welcome to St. Giles. I'll have the kitchen send you up some coffee once you're settled. I hope you like it black."

"I guess I'll get used to it."

Before bringing Sam to the ward, the stretcher-bearers brought him to a steam-filled room. There were a number of bathtubs in a neat row with movable curtains for privacy. Sam noticed that several of them had netlike hammocks on pulleys over them.

Now he knew why his legs had not been re-splinted. He had not had a bath since before the gun battle.

Using infinite care, the orderlies aided Sam in undressing and lifted him into a hammock with his legs stretched out in front of him. Slowly they lowered him into the steaming water.

It felt marvelous! Sam took off his glasses, swished them in the water to clean them and laid them on the soap tray. Declining assistance, he reached for soap and washcloth and began to scrub his body. The heat of the water permeated his muscles and even relieved the pain in his legs although they were still painful to touch. It felt wonderful to be clean again. It was wonderful to sit in a bathtub long enough and wide enough for his giant frame.

Sam soaped his hair and beard. He rubbed his face slowly, thoughtfully as he examined the soapy, chest-length beard that had been his camouflage for so many years. It was as if letting go of his beard was conceding that he was turning a corner in his life and would not be going back.

Having washed himself as thoroughly as he could without being able to bend his legs, and feeling really clean for the first time in over a week, Sam lay back against the end of the tub and just relaxed in the heat of the water. He closed his eyes and allowed himself to drift in his mind.

As he drifted, he recalled the image of Pru Hofheinz, herself in pain, relaxing in a hot tub as he brought her to an unexpected sexual fulfillment. The gentle passion of that night filled him with overwhelming sadness of things that would never be again. He tried to drive the lovely image out of his brain and quiet his raging, hopeless need. Erections or no, that part of his life was over forever.

He supposed he would have to talk to Father Maris about how a man adjusted to a celibate life. Pru was the first woman he had ever made love with—the first for whom it was not a business transaction but an act of shared passion.

She wouldn't want him now.

"Mr. Blake," said a male voice from behind the privacy curtain, "are you ready yet?"

Sam returned to reality. "Yes," he said as he put on his specs.

The orderlies came in again. One of them turned a hand operated winch that raised the hammock until Sam was level with a gurney. They helped Sam onto the gurney and gave him towels to dry himself, only assisting when asked.

Sam was given a hospital issue nightshirt and bathrobe, both scrupulously clean and smelling of strong laundry soap and bluing. Once dressed, he lay down on the gurney and was covered with a sheet and taken into a treatment room where his legs were splinted again. Then he was taken into a ward with ten beds, some of them surrounded with privacy screens. The orderlies brought him to a bed at the extreme end of the ward, almost at the wall. There was a small bedside table with drawers for keeping personal belongings, an electric reading lamp—the first Sam had ever seen—a pitcher of water and glass tumbler. Sam was assisted in removing his robe and laid on the bed. One of the orderlies covered him with a sheet and blanket and showed him a string he could use to ring a bell if he needed assistance while the other moved the privacy screen to shield Sam from the other patients. The bed was cranked until Sam was in more or less a sitting position.

"There's a Bible in the drawer and a library cart comes through once a day if you want to read."

Sam thanked him. He poured himself a glass of water and sipped it slowly. The Bible was not his favorite reading, but he supposed it beat sitting doing nothing.

He was reaching for the drawer when he saw the privacy screen move. A small cart preceded the entrance of a petite nun in a cream-colored habit and a white apron. The nun had an almost angelic beauty. Her eyebrows were pale, hinting at blond hair beneath her wimple and veil. Her eyes were a cheery blue, her face unlined and ageless, although Sam guessed she was probably near his own age. She smiled impishly in greeting.

"Good afternoon, Mr. Blake. I'm Sr. Mary Grace. I'm one of the ward nurses." She held up a pair of scissors. "I'm also known as the Barber of St. Giles," she added with a sweet laugh.

Sam rubbed at his chin. "If I'd ever had so pretty a barber before, I might not have gone so long between shaves."

Sr. Mary Grace blushed at the compliment.

"And you might as well call me Sam. I'm going to be here for months, so we might as well be friends." He held out his hand. The nun took it and shook it amiably. "Well, this sheep is ready to be shorn."

Sr. Mary Grace took out a brush, comb, toothbrush and tooth powder, mirror and shaving equipment and placed them on Sam's night table. "When we unpacked your carpetbag I saw you didn't have any of these things. I'm sure you'll want to take care of your own hygiene. I'll also leave a jar of talcum powder. It will help prevent rashes that come from sitting in bed and perspiring. You'll appreciate it as summer rolls along."

Sam thanked her and took off his glasses. The industrious little nurse wrapped a sheet around his neck completely covering both him and his bed and clipped it closed with clothespins. She ran a brush and her fingers through his hair with a barber's professionalism. "You have very fine hair, fine and curly. I think you'll find it easier to care for short."

Sam shrugged. "What first, the shave or the haircut?"

"Oh, the hair first, I think. It should be easier to work on your face once those curls are under control."

She picked up a pair of barber scissors and proceeded to work. Sam felt the gentle tugging on his hair and heard the metallic rip of the scissors blades closing while soft black corkscrews tumbled into his lap. Even Sam was amazed at how long his hair was, considering he had had a trim not two weeks ago in Rincon.

As Sr. Mary Grace worked, Sam asked her questions about the hospital. He found out St. Giles had been founded by Father Maris using a generous gift from a local Amarillo businessman whose son Maris had treated in a battlefield hospital while a Union Army surgeon. Although the young soldier was Confederate, supposedly Dr. Maris had operated when other army surgeons were willing to let him die. The hospital was as modern as possible, even having its own boilers and electrical generators to supply piped-in hot water and electric lights. The hospital was a teaching hospital and was supported more by generous charitable donations than medical fees. They only handled orthopedic injuries and ailments. Sr. Mary Grace told Sam that Dr. Maris was loath to amputate any extremity unless there was no other way of saving the life of the patient. Many of the nurses were also well trained in the pioneer rehabilitation techniques used to help injured people regain as much normality as possible. Sr. Elizabeth, another of the nurses in this section, was one of the best rehabilitation nurses in the world and would be handling a large portion of Sam's physical therapy.

"Sr. Elizabeth reminds some people of an army drill sergeant, but she does get people up and walking again if they want to."

Finally, Sam felt a comb running through his hair and a few random snips. Curious, he raised his hand and raked his fingers through it. Even more than the thick pile of black curls in his lap, he could feel his hair was quite short over his ears and the nape of his neck, a little longer and fuller on the top. It was longer than a military cut, but shorter than he had ever worn it in his life. Still, the top curled around his fingers and seemed to follow the shape of his head.

"Let me take care of your beard and then you can view the entire package."

The little nun moved in front of him. She smelled clean, of plain soap and perhaps a little disinfectant. She was attractive in a pixyish way, like one might observe one's sister. She used her scissors to severely trim Sam's beard. He shuddered as he saw the long strands fall on the sheet to follow his hair.

"Did I hurt you?"

"No, no. I guess it's just the realization I've been bearded half my life."

"Judging from the length, you've trimmed it very little in that time."

Sam nodded. Once trimmed, Sr. Mary Grace opened a corked bottle and poured warm water into a basin and a mug. She stirred up a warm lather with the brush and smoothed it over his face and jaw. Draping a towel over Sam's shoulders, she picked up her razor and set to work.

As Sam felt the unfamiliar sensation of the razor scraping over his cheeks and jaw, he felt himself hardening beneath the sheet. He hoped that the nun didn't notice his arousal. He groaned, then tried to suppress the sound.

"Oh, don't worry, Sam," she said calmly, her experienced eyes missing nothing, "a lot of men are aroused by being shaved by a woman."

Sam flushed crimson. "But you're a nun."

"I'm a nun, but I'm also a nurse. Just because I'm celibate doesn't mean I'm stupid." She chuckled. "Don't worry, you'll get used to me and the rest of us. I'm afraid you're not going to have much privacy for the next few months. It's the nature of hospitals, I'm afraid. You can socialize with other patients as much or as little as you want and you can have visitors during visiting hours. We'll also take care of posting any letters you may want to write. Of course, any letters you receive will be given to you unopened. The only thing we can't let you keep in your area is weapons, so if you have any guns or knives, we'll put them in a locker until you're discharged. I hope you understand, but some people become suicidal following severe injuries and we don't want them hurting themselves or anybody else."

"If they come with my things, I'll turn them over," Sam affirmed. He wondered if he himself would be one of those people who would want to kill himself.

Finally, Sr. Mary Grace finished with her barbering and wiped Sam's face with a damp towel. Carefully, she unclipped and removed the sheet, taking care to keep all the clippings inside the sheet and out of Sam's bed.

She handed Sam his glasses and waited for him to hook them over his ears. She handed the mirror to him saying, "Behold, the new Sam Blake."

Chapter 25

Sam stared in the mirror in disbelief. Cynthia had been wrong! The bespectacled face that stared back was not that of an ugly man. True, his cheeks were pale from half a lifetime of being shielded from the sun compared to the sun-darkened forehead and cheekbones. A few months in the hospital would even that out. It was a squarish face with a strong chin and jaw.

Was he handsome? Sam could not make that judgment, but one thing was certain. His was not the face of a repulsive ogre.

An errant curl fell over his high forehead. Absently Sam brushed it back, now seeing that his new haircut complemented the shape of his head and the curl of his fine hair.

Maybe he wasn't so hard to look at.

For what it was worth. Sam sighed. Finding out now that he had been wrong about himself for so many years was like finding out after signing a quit claim deed that your cabin was sitting on a gold mine.

"You worked a miracle, Sister," he said solemnly.

"Oh, no," she protested, "only Our Lord works miracles. I'm just a barber. What you're seeing was under there all the time."

Sam put down the mirror. "Now what happens?"

Sr. Mary Grace was putting her barbering tools in order as she spoke. "Fr. Maris said to start you on your eating regimen immediately. I'm afraid you're going to feel hungry for quite a while until you get used to it. Then you can read or write letters or sleep. Doctor would prefer you not use an invalid chair to wander around the hospital until after surgery because he doesn't want the bone fragments moving around any more than necessary."

"I could use some writing paper and pen."

Sr. Mary Grace said she would bring him a lap desk and stationery after lunch and with a cheery smile, she wheeled her cart around the privacy screen and disappeared from Sam's view.

Sam needed to write some letters. To his bank to arrange for funds to pay his hospital expenses. To Edward Arden at Stockmen's Mutual about payment of the reward for uncovering the Morgan-McKinley-Derry insurance fraud scheme. He assumed the Cattlemen's Association would not be paying their fee. To his landlady in Santa Fe to crate all his personal belongings and ship them to Amarillo. The place had only been convenient as a centrally located base of operations for the detective work he would do no longer. Finally, to Dr. Richards advising him of his safe arrival at St. Giles and to forward his things there if he had not already done so.

There was one more letter he should write, but would not.

He would not write to Prudence Hofheinz.

She had declared her love for him. Sam would not see her love turn to pity.

Better she never know.

For Pru, finding out where Sam was became an obsession. She realized a northbound stagecoach left the day Sam left town, but she couldn't be sure he left that way. It seemed unlikely the coach line would take someone in Sam's condition. If he left by some other conveyance, he could have gone anywhere. The stage line was the place to start.

She went to the stage office. Mr. Rodgers confirmed that a big man strapped to a board had been put on the stage on a ticket purchased by Dr. Richards with a destination of Amarillo.

But Amarillo was the railhead. It was not uncommon to travel to Amarillo by stage and then take the train to points north, east and west. Prudence did not have enough money readily available to engage a Pinkerton to pick up the trail from Amarillo. She would have to write home and ask her father for assistance.

In her letter she described the situation and requested assistance. Unfortunately, it might be a month before she had an answer. By then, school would be out for summer and Pru could take the stage to Amarillo and get some answers for herself.

Dr. Richards had promised Sam not to tell her his location, but he had to buy stamps to send her letters and Sam's things to him. If she could just be at Jackson's when the doctor mailed something to Sam, she might overhear where.

Unfortunately, Prudence was not much of a detective. When she tried to linger in Jackson's on the afternoon before the northbound stage went through, Dr. Richards saw her and left the store, returning in the morning when school was in session. Mrs. Jackson took her postmistress job seriously, so she wouldn't tell Prudence the addresses of any letters the doctor posted.

All she could do for now was wait—and write to Sam.

School let out June fifth, less than five weeks away. She just had to get through the term without losing her mind.

On Friday, May first, they buried Ethan Morgan in the churchyard next to his wife. The only people present besides the undertaker and gravedigger were Consuelo Lucero, the five Bar M ranch hands, Prudence and Rev. Foley. Arabella was in San Antonio, it was assumed. The funeral was over in less than fifteen minutes.

Sheriff Murphy had sent a detail of remaining Lazy K hands to retrieve Pete McKinley's body. It was plain his death was caused when he was carried over the ridge into Ganados Ravine by the cattle stampede. The parsimonious McKinley had made no provisions in his will for his employees, so his hands rode on immediately after retrieving his body. He didn't inspire any loyalty and received none.

Prudence returned to the schoolyard in plenty of time to begin the school day.

After the trouble with her class two days before, normality set in and she conducted classes as usual. Afterwards, she ran errands, corrected papers or wrote letters to Sam. She had no interest in the quilting circle anymore. From the way the rumors had flown about her week in the mine, she was afraid to face the matrons of Rincon.

Now her absent best friend would be joining the ranks of the matrons of Rincon.

Prudence would be truly alone.

Monday, May 5, 1885, early evening

Sam opened his eyes slowly. They weighed a ton. He saw a figure come into focus. To his surprise it was not Sr. Mary Grace. It took him a while to realize it was Pru standing in front of him.

"Pru?" he croaked. "What are you doing here?"

She leaned over to kiss him tenderly on the lips. "I told you I would never leave you, my love."

But when he reached out to put his arms around her, the image faded like a fog dissipating in the sunlight.

"Pru!" he cried out...

And slowly opened his eyes. He was still groggy from the ether. It was dark in the room except for a single, shaded lamp. Everything was out of focus, but that was to be expected without his glasses. A dull, nagging pain assailed his lower extremities.

Oh, yes, the last thing he remembered was lying on a table in an operating theatre. Dr. Maris and some associates were around the table, all of them wearing white cotton coats over their clothes and white cotton masks over their faces. A handkerchief-covered sieve was placed over his mouth and nose and he was asked to count backwards from one hundred.

Sam didn't remember anything after ninety-eight until now. He felt around him. He was wearing a nightshirt and was covered with a blanket.

He felt a tingling in his toes. He smiled groggily. He still had toes.

Then he remembered that amputees had phantom sensations in limbs that were no longer there.

"Sister," he croaked out hoarsely.

"Mr. Blake," he heard the gruff, formal voice of Sr. Elizabeth. "Are you thirsty?" She raised his head with a firm, competent hand and helped him sip some cool water.

"My specs," he said, still groggy. "Can't see."

Sr. Elizabeth unfolded Sam's glasses and helped him put them on. His arms felt like lead weights. In the dim light Sam peered down the length of his body, a cold sweat from dread chilling him. He could see huge lumps under the blanket where his knees should be, then focused further down to where the blanket seemed to rise over the foot rail of the hospital bed.

He tried to move his toes, praying all the while.

The end of the blanket moved!

"Please, sister, blanket, feet," he mumbled in a panic.

Sr. Elizabeth realized what he wanted and carefully lifted the bottom of the blanket and folded it back.

To Sam's relief, poking out from the bottom of the blanket were a pair of bruised and swollen, but very much still attached, size fourteen feet.

"Still there," he said, curling his toes in relief.

Sr. Elizabeth smiled and said in her gruff but compassionate voice, "Yes, Mr. Blake, they're still there. But I should cover them again to keep you from catching cold. Do you want any more water or to use the bedpan?"

Sam said yes to both, then added after he had some water and relieved himself, "Hungry."

"I'm sure, but Doctor says nothing but water until the anesthetic wears off completely. It's for your safety."

Sam mumbled something, then asked, "Where's Pru?"

"Pru?"

"Pru. She was here when I opened my eyes."

Sr. Elizabeth put her hand on Sam's brow. "I'm sorry, Mr. Blake, nobody was here when you woke up except me. Sometimes when ether wears off it causes hallucinations."

"But I saw her."

The nun shook her head. "Without your glasses?"

"Yes."

"How far can you see clearly without your glasses?"

Sam slowly held his hand about six inches from his face.

"Then it must have been a dream. I'm sorry. If she's on the phone exchange I can call her or have one of our messengers send her a note to be here in the morning."

Sam shook his head slowly. "Not here. Never here. She mustn't know."

Sr. Elizabeth had seen this before. Many men who suffered crippling injuries rejected their wives and sweethearts.

With her assistance, Sam drank another glass of water, then let Sr. Elizabeth remove his glasses and put them by his bedside so he could go back to sleep.

Basil Mercury visited the next morning. By the time the little drummer came calling, Sam was fully awake. The traveling salesman brought a vase of flowers, the day's Amarillo *Star* and a couple of books.

"Boy, Sam, you look like a completely different person without all the hair."

Sam smiled. "I noticed that myself."

"You know, you ought to stay clean-shaven. The girls'll love you with that face."

"And hate me with this body."

Basil shrugged. "The doctor saved your legs, eh?"

"Well, he didn't have to amputate them. What happens to me now is anybody's guess."

"You ought to let your girl know."

Sam stiffened. "I don't have a girl."

"The one with the strange name; Pru, was it? Whoever she is she's special to you. You ought to let her know how you are."

Sam shook his head. "She can't ever know. If she were repulsed by me now I couldn't bear it."

Basil folded his arms. "So you won't give her a chance to accept you as you are. If she loves you, she'll accept you."

Sam's hands fisted on the bed. "Since when are you an expert on women, Basil?"

The little Greek laughed. "Since I started selling corsets. You're going to be in here for months, right? I'm leaving town on Wednesday, so I won't see you for at least three months. You're going to need friends. Give the girl a chance."

"No." The subject was closed as far as he was concerned.

"Suit yourself. Look, Sam, I bought you a six-month subscription to the *Star*. Just because you're in the hospital doesn't mean you should be cut off from what's going on in the world. They'll deliver it here to the ward every morning."

Sam smiled. The wiry little salesman had, in a short time, become a true friend. He thanked Basil for his thoughtfulness.

"No problem," said Basil in his most winning way, showing Sam how he had become a crack corset drummer at so young an age.

"Mercouris," Sam called after him. "How do you say 'thank you' in Greek?"

"*Sas efharisto.*"

"And 'so long?'"

"*Andío.*"

"*Sas efharisto,* Vasilis. *Andío.*"

Basil grinned. "See you around, Sam."

Sr. Mary Grace came in the following morning with Sam's familiar, battered saddlebag and duster. She laid a towel over Sam's lap and handed him the saddlebag and the newspaper she also carried.

"These just arrived by post, and at the front desk they said this paper is yours."

"A gift from a new friend."

"We've put your gun, knife and rifle in a locker. You should look these things over to see what you want to keep here and what you want to put away for now."

Sam went through the pockets of the duster. They were empty. "That can go."

He opened the saddlebags. He pulled out camp cooking equipment and his oil lantern, last seen when he was in the mineshaft. His oilskin pouch was still closed, protecting his Sunday best. A couple of extra work shirts, undergarments and another pair of jeans. He would not need any of these for quite a while and designated them for the locker.

He found his bandannas, clean and folded. He opened one of the drawers in his side table and put them in. A small wooden cigar box was in the saddlebag. He opened it to reveal two spare pairs of spectacles. His money clip, minus sufficient money to pay for his coach fare, doctor bill and the cost of sending his things to him, was in there. Pru must have searched the pockets of his cut up garments when she packed. He put the money clip in the box with his glasses. His gold watch, the Phi Beta Kappa key dangling from the chain, followed and found its way into the wooden box. Finally, out came the small velvet bag. His hands shaking with emotion, Sam could not open the bag. He merely fingered it to make sure the ring was still there. He put it, along with his dreams, in the wooden box and slipped the box into his drawer. A last look revealed a few books and his bankbook, which he kept.

Before he packed everything back into the saddlebags to go into the locker, he found an envelope with his name written on it. When he turned over the envelope to open it, he could not be sure whether the initial on the wax was an R or a P. He handed the saddlebags back to Sr. Mary Grace, still holding the letter.

"Once I lock these up I'll be back with your lunch..."

"Or what passes for my lunch."

"Ah, but it's working already," she assured him. "It's showing in your face and neck...You read your letter and I'll be back before you know it."

"What am I getting today, Sister?"

She cocked her head. "I don't know. Raw lettuce and carrots, bread, some fruit."

Sam's stomach growled in response to the growl that escaped his throat. Sr. Mary Grace smiled and bounced away.

Sometimes Sam hated the little nun. She was just too damned cheery!

He slipped a finger under the seal on the envelope and broke it. He pulled out sheets of fine stationery and opened them.

Wednesday, April 29th, 1885

Dearest Sam,

The letter was not from Dr. Richards.

Dr. Richards will not tell me where he sent you, but has promised to forward any letters I might write.

I thought my heart would break when Doc told me you were gone. I was relieved beyond belief that "gone" meant literally. I think if you had died I would not have wanted to go on living...

Sam felt a clutching hand around his heart.

I hope beyond hope that when you get this letter you are well on your way to a complete recovery..."

"Wrong again," Sam mumbled morosely.

But, my darling, whether you recover completely or not, I love you and wish to be with you. I know you are frightened of what the future will bring. Give me a chance to be part of that future...

How could she be sure? She didn't really know how she would react when she saw him. It was better if she never did.

The school term will be over on June fifth if I last that long. It's funny what people consider moral. I have been your lover and reveled in it, but this is known only to us (and Clint) and is doing no damage to my reputation. Yet by daring to be in the same mineshaft with you undressed (your leg splints notwithstanding), local gossip would have us involved in some kind of five day long orgy...

He again read the line, "*I have been your lover and reveled in it.*" It was hard to believe any well-bred lady would be so bold. It was as hard to believe that a man prostitutes turned away could have a woman who reveled in his lovemaking.

But he worried about what unchecked gossip would do to her. He knew any denials on his part would make matters worse. He loved Pru too much to do her any more damage. Better for him to remain silent.

I hope you will change your mind and let me know where you are. Even if I can't come to you, I want to keep writing to you. I hope you will write back and let me know how you're doing.

Regardless of what happens, I love you completely and without restriction. You must always believe that.

All my love,

Pru Hofheinz.

She had actually written "Prudence" but had lined it out and written "Pru." Suddenly, a large water splotch appeared on the paper, then another. Sam didn't even realize they came from his eyes.

"It can never be," Sam said, his voice thick.

He had done the noble thing, the right thing, the only thing.

So why did it hurt so damned much?

Monday, May 18, 1885

Arabella Randolph took off her black-veiled bonnet and looked around. The house in which she grew up seemed smaller somehow.

Arabella had not missed the looks on people's faces when she and Clint got off the stage. Distrust and betrayal were painted there as if she and not her father had perpetrated the fraud.

She also had not missed the guilty look on Clint's face when Sheriff Murphy told them Sam Blake was alive, and the relief when the sheriff added that Sam had left Rincon immediately after being pulled from the mineshaft.

Sheriff Murphy told them Sam was injured, but didn't say to what extent. How injured could he be, Clint reasoned, if he was able to leave town so soon? Nobody knew where Sam had gone, so Clint had a further justification for not sharing the reward money.

But the worst part of returning home, Arabella thought, was the horrible conversation she'd just finished with Prudence.

It came partly as a result of an argument she'd had with Clint about their lovemaking...

He had just finished doing whatever it was he did and had rolled off Arabella to lie beside her.

Instead of lying still, Arabella sat up and swung her legs over the side of the bed. She put her head in her hands.

"What the hell is the matter with you?" Clint growled from his side of the bed.

"Nothing," she said thickly.

"Like hell. Tell me."

"Well," Arabella began with trepidation, "I was always under the impression that it only hurts the first time."

"What hurt?"

She gestured indistinctly. "This—um—what we just did."

Clint leaned on his elbow. "Hell, I don't know, Arabella. I never had a lady before. Maybe they're different than whores. Maybe that's why wives don't enjoy it."

"I certainly don't," Arabella said under her breath.

"What?"

"Nothing."

"Didn't you ever talk to anyone about these things before?"

Arabella turned. "Who was I supposed to talk to? My mother's dead and I didn't have time to talk to a married lady in town. It's not the kind of thing you discuss before you're engaged."

"What about that girlfriend of yours? The schoolteacher."

"Prudence is a spinster. What would she know about it?"

Clint laughed. "She must have everyone fooled. She's got the perfect set-up. A cabin at the edge of town, a horse shed to keep a fellow's horse out of sight. She's probably been fucking every drifter in pants for years."

Arabella blushed at the language while she chilled at the accusation. "You don't know what you're talking about. Prudence Hofheinz is a lady."

Clint sat up. "Really? Well, she was sure spreading 'em for Sam Blake, though why anyone would want to fuck that fat, hairy ox I don't know."

Arabella shuddered. She had thought when she first met Clint Randolph that he respected and liked Sam Blake. When had his respect turned to such venom? And why was he directing his invective toward Prudence? "You mean while they were trapped by the fire? I understand Mr. Blake was injured. Knowing Prudence..."

"No, no," Clint snapped, "before that. Almost from the day we rode into town. If they didn't do it in the mountains it was probably the only time they weren't going at it. And the son of a bitch warned me off you while he was putting it to your best friend."

Suddenly Arabella screamed and launched herself at Clint, fingers clawed, nails ready to inflict whatever damage she could manage. He saw her action and captured her wrists in his. He flipped her over onto her back and held her captive.

"Sheathe 'em, wildcat!" She continued to struggle against his superior strength. "Ask her. If she's your best friend, she won't lie to you, even if she will lie to everyone else in town, unless she's afraid you're just another nasty little gossip like every other damned Rebel whelp in this town."

Arabella was beyond words, so great was her anger. She continued to struggle against his hold on her, but he had her pinioned securely.

Suddenly, he let her loose and stood. Yanking his jeans over his naked legs, he pulled a blanket from the chest at the foot of the master bed and started to leave the room. Before leaving, he turned and snarled, "Maybe if you'd show that kind of life when we're fucking, you'd enjoy it more. I know I would."

He walked out to sleep in another room, slamming the door behind him...

Chapter 26

Arabella hitched up the surrey the next day. She wanted to ride Horizon, but was afraid of gossip if she appeared anywhere in town in other than mourning apparel.

She arrived at the schoolyard about fifteen minutes after school let out. There were still some children playing in the schoolyard as they often did when the weather started to warm. Prudence was nowhere in sight. Arabella assumed she had gone into her house.

She tied up the surrey and knocked on the cabin door.

"Who's there?"

"It's Arabella, Prudence."

The door opened. Prudence looked harried. "What do you want, Arabella?"

"Can you talk a while?"

Prudence frowned. "I've got to get into town to take a letter to be posted so it will go out tomorrow."

"You've never been so particular about letters to your father before."

"It isn't to Papa," Prudence said defensively. "Arabella, if this can wait for another day..."

"It can't. If I don't get this off my chest, I'll burst."

Prudence signaled her in and indicated that she should sit on the sofa. The schoolteacher turned her desk chair and sat facing her friend. "I'm surprised you still have any commerce with me. After all, you're a married woman now and I'm a fallen one."

"Fallen? How?"

Prudence leaned back in her chair and thrust her feet out. "Oh, haven't you heard?" she said sarcastically. "I spent five days in a mineshaft with a naked man who had two broken legs and a gunshot shoulder. I'm positively ruined. No decent woman should have anything to do with me."

"I should talk. After all, my father was a criminal."

Prudence didn't mention what she'd heard from Sheriff Murphy. Of the retrieved guns, only Ethan Morgan's, Pete McKinley's and Clint Randolph's had been fired. This meant there was a fifty-fifty chance Ethan had shot Sam and the same chance Clint had shot and killed Ethan.

"You couldn't have known that beforehand, could you?"

"Do you think I would have stood for it?" Arabella protested.

"No, you would have told me because you aren't the best secret keeper in the world..."

Arabella paled.

"...Even Martine Calleia is an amateur compared to you. I've known that since you were my student...Why are you here, Arabella? I'm not in the mood to chat."

Arabella took a deep breath. "It's about Clint and me."

"You're expecting?"

Arabella's head snapped up. "No, no, it's nothing like that. It's about our—um—personal life."

Prudence sighed. She really wanted to get the letter to Sam to Dr. Richards' office. "I can't help you regarding your personal life if you're referring to what I think you are. Why don't you ask Mary or Christa or Laura? They're all married and closer to your age. You should be cultivating friendships with them now anyway."

"But they don't know Clint."

Prudence cocked an eyebrow. "And I do?"

"No, but he says you were sleeping with Mr. Blake and..."

Prudence felt a wave of nausea fill her. "Get out of my house."

"Then it's true."

"I've said all I'm going to say on the subject of Sam Blake. We were in a mineshaft, he was shot and badly injured."

"I believe you about the mineshaft. I mean before that."

Prudence stood and walked toward the door of her cabin. "My private life is my business. If you're having a problem with your sex life, talk to a married woman, not to me. My feelings about Sam Blake are between him and me. If I hear any of this around town I'll know it came from either you or that miserable excuse for a husband who's too stupid to know how to wipe his own nose if Sam Blake wasn't there to tell him how to do it. I suggest you leave now."

Arabella rose. There was something radically different about Prudence Hofheinz—a spirit that had been tamped down somehow. She started to leave.

She was nearly at the surrey when Prudence opened the door to her cabin again.

"One more thing, *Mrs. Randolph*. You tell your husband if he spreads around such accusations about Sam Blake and me again I will remember that my father was a butcher. When I'm done with him you won't have to worry about any sex problems anymore, if you get my drift."

"You're not serious!"

"Shall I get out my cleaver and prove it?"

Prudence slammed the door so hard her windows rattled.

Friday, May 22, 1885

Sam got three letters that day. One was a penny post card from Tucson from Basil Mercury. It was just a two line greeting, but to a man who expected no visitors and was bored from sitting in a bed all day while his surgical scars and broken bones healed, it was more than welcome.

There had been no complications following surgery. Dr. Maris got all the patella fragments out and there had been no infection or necrosis. Apparently Anti-Sepsis worked. The stitches came out after ten days and the swelling had reduced considerably. Sam was still in splints, but once the stitches were out he had been able to have the splints removed once a day so he could take a bath.

But Dr. Maris's prognosis was confirmed by the surgery. The damage was both permanent and irreparable. His knees would never be stable again. Already measurements had been taken of his legs and feet for braces and shoes so they would be ready when his bones healed enough to start rehabilitation. Fortunately, Sam made the decision the morning after he discovered his legs were still attached to his body that he wasn't going to spend the rest of his life in a bed or invalid chair. He would walk by whatever means were available. He would worry about working once he was walking.

Other than the boredom and the constant hunger from the very restricted diet, the hardest part of Sam's convalescence was learning how to shave himself again. It had been so long he had nearly forgotten. Sr. Mary Grace lent her most attentive assistance and Sam only made a complete mess of his face the first two days.

His face seemed to be changing daily. The color was evening out as his tan faded and his cheekbones were becoming more prominent. In the three weeks he had been at St. Giles he had lost nearly thirty pounds on the food regimen Dr. Maris recommended. His belly was becoming flatter daily and even the cuffs of his nightshirts were looser. The snug nightshirt Mrs. Richards bought for him his last day in Rincon fit perfectly now. If he only wasn't hungry all the time! How much water was a man expected to drink when what he wanted was a thick steak with grilled onions and fried potatoes?

Sam took a look at the second letter. It was written on one of those new-fashioned typewriting machines. It was from Stockmen's Mutual.

Sam was already concerned. He'd heard from his bank that the last deposit to his account was $4,500 on April thirteenth. That was the amount Sam deposited following the El Molino job. The $300 he had in his money clip was the balance of that fee he had kept out for spending money. Perhaps the letter from the insurance company would clarify when and if the reward money was going to be paid. He opened up the envelope and read the neatly typed page.

May 11, 1885

Dear Mr. Blake:

In re: Your letter of May 1, 1885. Although surprised to discover that Mr. Randolph's report of your death was erroneous, we are happy that you are alive and recovered enough from your injuries to write to us.

I am advised by Mr. Arden that, based upon Mr. Randolph's assertion that you had died as the result of injuries received while you were contravening the conspiracy against our company, the complete reward of $20,000.00 was paid to Mr. Randolph on April 25th.

While we appreciate your efforts on our behalf, Stockmen's Mutual Insurance Company is not obligated to double pay any portion of any reward. You will have to obtain your portion of the bounty directly from Mr. Randolph.

Again, may we express our hope that you will make a swift recovery from your current hospitalization.

I remain,

Your obedient servant,

Zebulon P. Doran, President, Stockmen's Mutual Insurance Company.

Clint had had the money for a month and had not sent it to Santa Fe. What was going on? He had told Arden that he—Sam—was dead two full days before he and Pru were located.

Sam didn't need an answer to his question. He already knew.

Clint had no intention of ever sending him his share of the money—money they would not even have earned if Sam had not figured out it was an insurance scam rather than a rustler gang.

Sam crushed the business letter in one fist. He would get even with Clint somehow. He opened his hand and smoothed out the letter, returned it to its envelope and put it in his top drawer along with the growing pile of letters from Pru and the small pile of postcards from Basil.

Then he opened the letter from Pru.

May 18, 1885

Dearest Sam,

I am beside myself with anger! I just had a distressing conversation with Arabella wherein she told me that Clint revealed to her that we have been lovers.

While I wanted to shout out that it was true and I wasn't the least bit ashamed of it because I love you, the sensible part of me kept my own counsel.

I knew Arabella when she was one of my students and she could not keep a secret. To have confirmed our intimacy would have made the information common knowledge within days. I told her I never wanted to speak to her again.

In my anger I also threatened to make a gelding of Clint Randolph if I heard even a peep about this anywhere in town. My only guilty satisfaction is that it appears that Arabella and Clint are already having trouble with their marriage.

Sam, it becomes more and more obvious that my days in Rincon are numbered. If I have any hope of remaining employable as a teacher anywhere, I will probably have to resign at the end of the school term.

Please, my darling, let me know where you are. If I leave Rincon I will be unable to keep giving letters to Dr. Richards. Please do not let stubborn pride keep us apart.

All my love,

Pru.

Sam felt an impotent anger fill him. Clint had stolen his money and now was impugning the reputation of his woman. It was intolerable. Were he sound, he would have been able to take action. Now it was more than a vow to get even. Sam swore to himself that if he ever saw Clint Randolph again, he would kill him.

But he still wouldn't write to Pru.

May 29, 1885

Miss Prudence Hofheinz

Your attendance is required at the meeting of the Rincon Town Council Meeting Monday, June 1st at 4 o'clock on the subject of the renewal of your contract for the Fall 1885 term.

John Calleia, Mayor

For the preceding eight years this summons had been pro forma. She had appeared, negotiated a raise in salary for herself and left with a new contract.

With everything going on, Prudence was not certain her contract would be renewed—or that she wanted to renew it. The only thing really keeping her in Rincon now was that it was the only pipeline to Sam.

Her most recent letters from home had been far from promising. Hans Hofheinz was unwilling to wire her the money to hire a Pinkerton to locate Sam Blake. He even suggested that if Sam wanted to see her he would not have slunk away without leaving a forwarding address, and that perhaps he had merely been using her.

Hans suggested she had spent too much time in Texas and should forget about this "cowboy" and come home to Chicago where she might find a better man among "civilized" people. Otherwise, there were plenty of schools in Chicago that would welcome an experienced teacher if that's what she wanted to continue doing. Of course, she didn't have to work if she didn't want to. It wasn't as if the Hofheinzes were poor.

In the two weeks since her confrontation with Arabella, Prudence had said nothing to her friend. Emotionally she was separating herself from the town already.

Immediately after school on June first, Prudence returned to her cabin and changed into her most businesslike clothes, a dark gray walking skirt and jacket worn over a high necked white cotton waist, a flat straw boater trimmed only with belting ribbon, black shoes and her leather driving gloves. She hitched up the buggy and drove Max to the church where the Town Council held its regular meetings.

Her insides shaking, she held her head high and walked in. By God, she was Hans Hofheinz's daughter and she would be damned if she let a bunch of yahoos make her quail.

"Gentlemen." She nodded at all of them.

Mayor Calleia began to shuffle papers nervously. "Um—Miss Hofheinz. It's about your teaching contract."

"Yes, Your Honor?"

"Well, you know your contract contains a provision regarding being of good moral character..."

"Yes, sir. I'm aware of that. It's pretty standard in teaching contracts, particularly for female schoolteachers."

"Well, well, well, yes, we can't be having immoral women molding young minds."

"No, I suppose you can't."

Mayor Calleia kept phumphing, afraid to get to the point, when Rev. Foley spoke.

"Miss Hofheinz, we are all concerned with your recent disappearance without notice between April twenty-second and twenty-eighth."

"Yes, Rev. Foley. I've explained what happened a dozen times. I never intended to be gone for more than a few hours."

The minister readjusted his *pince nez* and cleared his throat. "We have heard that when you were found by the Bar M ranch hands you were alone with this Mr. Blake and that he was—well, indecently dressed."

"Yes, sir," Pru replied honestly. "His injuries were severe. I've explained this quite a few times also. Nothing of an immoral nature happened."

"And you were the one who undressed him?"

"There was no one else around to do it. Even if I had been able to get past the fires prior to when we were rescued, Mr. Blake would not have survived untreated."

"Why did you go into the hills yourself in the first place?" asked Sheriff Murphy. "Why didn't you come get me?"

Prudence sighed. "I thought it would save time. I knew where the detectives were staked out and could get there directly without the delay of having to describe their location to you."

"How did you know their location?" the minister asked.

"From Mr. Blake. I met him at Ganados Ravine a few days before the fire."

"Why you?"

"He'd met me at the Morgans for dinner and must have thought me trustworthy and of *high moral character*. Gentlemen, I have taught in your school for nine terms now. Until April twenty-third I never missed a day of school for any reason. If my disregarding convention to provide medical treatment to a seriously injured man has so clouded my reputation that you cannot renew my contract, so be it, but I suggest you look at my entire record before you make a decision. If Dr. Richards were here, I believe he could testify as to Mr. Blake's condition when he was brought into the doctor's office and if Mr. Blake were here himself, he would assure you that absolutely nothing of an immoral nature occurred between us while we were caught in that old mineshaft."

"And where is Mr. Blake now?" the Reverend asked.

Pru shrugged. "I haven't the faintest idea."

The men at the council table eyed each other.

Mayor Calleia spoke, "Miss Hofheinz, will you please wait in the vestibule for a few moments?"

Prudence squared her shoulders and walked out. She paced for a while, then sat on an abandoned pew.

About ten minutes later, the door opened and one of the council members asked her to come in.

Mayor Calleia spoke for the council. "Miss Hofheinz, it is the decision of the council not to renew your contract for next term. Since there are only four days remaining in this term, you will be permitted to finish out the term and will be paid in full for your contract. You will be given until June thirtieth to vacate the municipally provided housing."

Prudence felt the sting of tears behind her eyes. Though she halfway expected this to happen, it was still a harrowing rejection. She was not about to let them see her cry. Holding her head high, she thanked the Town Council and strode out.

She went to Dr. Richards' office and begged him to let her know where Sam Blake was. He refused to give her the information, although he was very sorry she had been let go.

Dejected and despairing, Prudence climbed back in her buggy and drove back to the school property. She wanted to go where Sam was, but she didn't know where that was.

Her only option was to sell the buggy and poor Max and return to Chicago. She hated to let Max go. He was getting old and would probably not last too long with the kind of treatment old horses received in this part of Texas. Having been non-renewed for poor moral character was not the kind of sterling reference that would get her a teaching job anywhere else.

Prudence was home barely an hour when there was a knock at her door. She was still dressed in her shirtwaist and skirt, but had taken down her hair and was barefoot.

She was very surprised to see Bob Bonetti standing in the doorway in his Sunday best, a bunch of wildflowers in his hand.

"May I come in, Miss Hofheinz?" he asked in a voice that combined the best of man and youth. He held out the bouquet. "I picked these for you. I hoped you might like them."

Touched by the kind gesture, Prudence beckoned him in. She found a vase, pumped some water into it and arranged the flowers as she talked.

"I appreciate the flowers, but I don't know. It's not exactly the best time and, well, you see, I was fired today."

Bob looked stricken. "Fired? How could they do that?"

"Apparently unmarried schoolteachers are not supposed to help injured, wounded men if it requires being in contact with any parts of their bodies."

Bob let out a quick breath. "You mean Sam Blake? That's so unfair."

"Yes, but it's done. I'm not returning in the fall."

"Where is Sam now? I still have the book he lent me."

Prudence sighed. "Only Dr. Richards knows and he won't tell me. You could give me the book to him to forward to Sam."

She noticed Bob was looking at her peculiarly. "Is something the matter, Bob?"

He shook his head as if to clear cobwebs. "It's just that I've never seen you with your hair down before, Miss Hofheinz. You sure are pretty that way."

Prudence smiled. "Thank you, Bob. That's such a nice thing to say."

Bob came closer. "I've always thought it was true. I used to see you standing by the wall at socials, nobody asking you to dance and well, I always wanted to ask you, but you know how the kids are."

She nodded. Bob had been a shy, bright student. The boys his age would have ripped him to shreds with their taunts if they caught him asking their teacher to dance. They had always considered him to be the teacher's pet as it was.

"What are you going to do now, Miss Hofheinz?"

Prudence shrugged her shoulders, defeated. "I don't know. I'm going to finish out the term. I have to be out of this house by the end of the month. If I don't get another job before then, I suppose I'll have to go home to Chicago."

Bob came very close until he was standing directly behind Prudence, and placed his hands gently on her shoulders.

"There's another solution. You could marry me."

Chapter 27

Pru's heart froze in her chest and she stepped forward, away from Bob's hands. Flustered, she blurted out, "That's very flattering, Bob, but you're not serious."

She looked at his face to see deadly earnestness.

"But I am, Miss Hof—Pr—Miss Prudence. I love you."

Prudence felt her face flame. "Oh, Bob," was all she could say.

Bob came closer and gathered her into his arms and lowered his mouth to hers. His kiss was gentle and questioning, his tall, young body hard and wiry, his arms strong. He was in no way repulsive. His kiss was even faintly arousing.

But he wasn't Sam Blake. Prudence raised her hands between them and pushed him away. For a long moment they stood staring at each other. She could see the love in his face.

"Oh, Bob, this is so wrong."

"Why is it wrong? I love you."

"You're eighteen..."

"Almost nineteen."

Her shoulders slumped. "And I'm thirty. And I'm leaving Rincon."

"I'll go with you. We could lie about our ages a little so the difference doesn't seem so bad. I know you care for me."

"I care *about* you. You're a nice, smart young man..."

"You mean a *boy*, don't you?" he blurted, crestfallen.

Prudence touched her mouth and smiled. "No, Bob. Anyone who can kiss like that is no boy."

Bob walked over to the fireplace and leaned, resting his hand on the mantel. He stared into the cold hearth. "I reckon I knew that. When I wanted to be called Bob instead of Bobby, you were the first to do it."

She walked over to the young cowhand and rested her hand on his shoulder. "That's because I respect you. It's always saddened me that you couldn't go to veterinary school as you wanted because of the cost. You were the brightest student I ever taught."

He turned around and put his hands around Prudence's upper arms. "I swear I'll work hard for you. You'll never have cause to regret marrying me. I'll love you forever."

Prudence lifted one hand and placed it on Bob's cheek. "Bob, I like you very much. I don't reject what you say you feel about me, but it isn't just a question of age or whether you can support a wife." She dropped her hand and walked easily out of the young man's grasp. "I'm in love with someone else."

"Sam Blake."

She turned in surprise. "How did you..."

Bob shrugged. "I reckon I knew when we found you up in the Mystics. It was written all over you. But he left and didn't tell you where he was going."

"He was hurt and scared. If you thought you were going to be crippled for life, would you be standing here proposing to me?"

Bob shook his head. "No, I wouldn't want to burden you."

She smiled knowingly. "And you're eighteen, without a life of hurt behind you. Can you imagine how Sam, who's known only rejection and loneliness, must have felt?"

Tears began to glitter in Prudence's eyes and her body began to shake. Bob rushed forward and took her into his arms again, holding her like a cherished friend.

"Have you told him how you feel?"

She nodded against his chest. Proper or not, she needed his warmth and strength right now when she had none of her own. "I've written him letters, hoping he would write back. But what makes me desperate is once I leave Rincon, I won't be able to do that."

"How are you doing it now?"

"I give the letters to Dr. Richards and he mails them. I tried to sneak into Jackson's, but he found out and now he only mails them during the school day."

"And if you find him?"

"Then I'll go to wherever he is. I know if I can talk to him I can prove that I'll stick, no matter what."

"You really do love him, don't you, Miss Prudence?"

She nodded.

"I'd better go."

"I suppose you'd best. My reputation is already a shambles."

Bob drew himself up very proudly. "Nobody will ever hear of this from me. I swear by the Virgin."

"I trust you, Bob."

Just before Bob left the cabin, Pru said, "Bob, if there was a way for you to go to veterinary school, would you go?"

He grinned. "In a flat Texas minute."

"I want you to know you're the first man who's ever proposed to me out of love. I won't forget that easily."

Bob walked back and kissed her once on the forehead. Tipping his hat, he said, "Good night, Miss Prudence."

She watched him mount his mustang and ride towards the Bar M. Her mood was wistful. Bob Bonetti had been the first man to propose marriage for the right reasons.

If only life weren't so damned complicated.

Pru turned to her desk. She wrote a letter to her father telling him of her firing and that she might be returning to Chicago in early July if nothing changed. She added a special request.

Taking another piece of stationery, she wrote to Sam.

June 1, 1885

Dearest Sam,

I was fired today. I will be leaving Rincon by the end of the month.

I beg you please to tell me where you are. If I leave without knowing, I will never be able to contact you again.

I have no more words to express how I feel. I would bear any hardship to be by your side. If I could take your pain into my body and bear it for you, I would. If I could trade my legs for yours, I would. I have no more pride left.

Write to me, my darling. The silence is more than I can bear.

All my love,

Pru.

She sealed the letter and wrote Sam's name on it. Braiding her hair quickly, she changed into her riding clothes and saddled Nameless. Mounted on the big dun, she rode quickly into town.

A dark figure on a brown mustang watched her from the small copse of trees across the way. The rider did not follow her because he knew where she was going. Instead, he turned his horse around and returned to the bunkhouse he now called home.

He rode, armed with the determination to do something special for the woman he loved.

It might take a little time, but he would find a way.

Prudence explained to her students the next day that they would have a new teacher in the fall. There was an almost funereal quiet. For most of these children, Miss Hofheinz was the only teacher they had ever had.

She was erasing the examination questions from the blackboard after school when Donnie MacGregor tugged on her skirt.

Prudence looked down at the redheaded eight-year-old who lisped from two missing front baby teeth. "What is it, Donnie?"

"Mith Hofheinth, are you leaving becauth you don't like uth anymore?"

Prudence eyes burned with unshed tears. "Oh, no, Donnie. It's because the Town Council decided they want a new teacher."

"But you could thtay in town, couldn't you?"

"I could if there was a job I could do, but there isn't."

"My ma doethn't work."

Pru smiled. "That's because your father makes enough money so she can stay at home and take care of you and your family. Married women don't always have to work."

"Oh," the boy said, taking in this information. Then his face took on a solemn cast. "You could marry me, Mith Hofheinth. Then you wouldn't have to work and you could thtay in Rincon."

Prudence laughed at the earnestness imprinted on the boy's serious face. "Oh, Donnie, you don't want to marry me. I'm old enough to be your mother."

"That'th okay. I don't mind if you don't."

She didn't know whether to laugh or cry. In two days she had received two heartfelt and sincere marriage proposals.

They were from an eight-year-old and an eighteen-year-old, but each was flattering in its way.

She stooped and gathered Donnie into her arms and kissed him lightly on the forehead. "Donnie," she said gently, "I am deeply honored by your proposal, but I have to say no."

Donnie's brow wrinkled with distress. "But why? I love you, Mith Hofheinth."

"Oh, sweetheart, I love you, too, but as your teacher I think it's better if you wait until you graduate from school before you marry someone. It's very hard to go to school and have a wife at the same time. I'll tell you what. If when you graduate from school you still want to marry me, you can ask me again. Now you better get on home or your mother will worry where you've been so long."

Donnie smiled. "Okay," he said and darted out of the schoolroom.

Prudence knew that by the time Donnie MacGregor was sixteen, he would be so busy courting girls his own age he would not even remember a childhood marriage proposal made to his schoolteacher. A part of her would like to come back in eight years and see what kind of young man he would turn out to be.

That afternoon she wrote a letter to her alma mater requesting placement as a grammar school teacher for the Fall term and mailed it.

Later that day she took Nameless out to exercise him. She rode along the northern road toward the Lazy K, intentionally avoiding traveling on Bar M property. Prudence heard that what remained of McKinley's livestock had been bought from the estate for a song by Clint and Arabella Randolph. The McKinley ranch now stood vacant and haunted in its stillness.

Pru sat on a corral rail, staring into nothingness while she considered her options. She had written to her old school, but she wasn't sure she wanted to teach anymore. While she had the occasional exceptional student, they were rare compared to the desultory students who dragged their way through their education. Maintaining a lifestyle above reproach was stifling. Her much vaunted independence had not achieved her anything except loneliness.

She decided not to waste another minute worrying about what the people of Rincon felt about her. She would begin to crate her things to ship once she knew what she was going to do with her life.

She snapped her fingers and declared aloud, "I don't give that for you, good citizens of Rincon! I'm not afraid of anything!"

She was lying. She was very much afraid she might never see Sam Blake again.

She whistled for Nameless and he trotted over to her. She mounted and rode home, new resolve in her mind. Even if Sam Blake didn't want her, she would survive. If the Great Chicago Fire didn't get her, and the Great Rincon Prairie Fire didn't get her, then no mere setback like being fired was going to get her.

Tuesday, June 2, 1885

Dr. Thomas Richards sighed. He had made a promise he would keep, but he wished he had not been brought into the middle of it. The damned schoolteacher wrote to the man three and four times per week and even though she paid the postage, it was getting to be a damned nuisance. Fortunately, her contract had not been renewed and she would be leaving town by the end of the month, releasing him from his obligation.

Her latest missive in his pocket, Doc dragged himself into Jackson's Mercantile. His first patient would be arriving in a few minutes, so he didn't have much time to look around to see who was shopping. He just walked directly to the U.S. Post Office cage.

He didn't see Mrs. Jackson around. Harmon was at the counter, showing a tray of watches to young Bobby Bonetti. He'd known the boy since birth, so paid him no mind.

"What kind of watch did you have in mind?" Harmon said.

"I'll know it when I see it."

"Harmon," Doc interrupted. "Where's Amelia this morning?"

"Oh, I don't know. I think she's over at the Chink laundry picking up our sheets."

Richards puffed out some air in frustration. "I've got patients coming in and I've got to mail this letter so it goes on the coach this afternoon."

Jackson looked from the doctor to Bob. Picking up the tray of watches, he said, "Bobby—um—Bob, can you wait just a minute while I help the Doc?"

Bob nodded. "Sure thing, Mr. Jackson. I'll just wait here."

Jackson closed and locked the counter and went behind the Post Office cage. "Amelia has a fit when I take over her job, Tom."

Harmon took the letter and dropped it on the postal scale. "One ounce," he said, then looked at the envelope. "Mr. Samuel Blake, St. Giles Hospital, Amarillo, Texas," he read aloud. "Say, Doc, wasn't he the partner of that fellow who married Arabella Morgan?"

"Yeah. This letter needs to go to him."

Jackson quoted the price of postage and Richards paid. Jackson stamped the letter and tossed it into the mailbag. Doc quickly walked out of the store.

Bob Bonetti was putting down a pencil and slipping a piece of scrap paper into his shirt pocket. "I'm going to have to sort out a few things in my head about which watch to buy."

Harmon sighed as Bob left the store. The boy would probably order a watch from the Montgomery Ward catalogue.

June 8, 1885, Amarillo, Texas

Sr. Mary Grace was bringing Sam's lunch tray when she saw him crumple a letter written on the familiar fine stationery she had been seeing for the past month.

"Good news, Sam," she said with characteristic brightness. "Father Maris said your splints can come off for good tomorrow and in a week or so you'll be ready to start rehabilitation."

"That's fine," Sam said absently.

"What's wrong, Sam? Bad news from your lady friend?"

"She's not my lady friend—not really—not anymore."

The nun sighed as she placed the lap tray over Sam's thighs and set down the tray of fruit and raw vegetables in front of him. "Fine then. Bad news from the lady in Rincon?"

"Yeah, she lost her job over helping me because she had to undress me to set my legs. Seems that's considered poor moral character."

"That makes no sense."

Sam cocked an eyebrow. "That's an understatement." He looked down at his plate. "This is *lunch*?"

"You should be used to it by now."

"I'll never get used to being hungry all the time."

Sr. Mary Grace smoothed the blanket covering Sam's feet and plumped his pillow. "But you're doing so well. You're healing well and getting so nice and slim. I'll trim your hair this afternoon if you like."

"That's fine."

"Sam, why don't you write to your friend and ask her to come for a visit. I'm sure we could find her a place to stay with a local family for a few days. If she's lost her job, I'll bet she's feeling really low about now."

Sam shook his head vehemently. "No, absolutely not. She's too fine, too special for an ugly cripple like me."

Sr. Mary Grace always got angry when Sam referred to himself in that manner. He was clearly not an ugly man—if only he could see it. As to being a cripple—the nun hated how the description was used as an epithet.

"You're not giving her a chance. Have you written to her at all since you've been here?"

"No, Sister, and I'm not going to. She'll just go on to the next teaching job and maybe she'll forget about me."

Sr. Mary Grace opened Sam's top drawer and looked at the pile of letters, all in chronological order, all saved. "Yes, but Sam, will you ever forget about her?"

Sam gave her a stricken look. He didn't answer in words, but she knew the answer to her questions.

"Sister, did you ever fall in love?"

"You mean with a man?"

"No, with a wheel of cheese. You're pretty enough to have had suitors."

"I had a few while still in school, but I realized my vocation early. I've never regretted my choice. Working at St. Giles is a wonderful way to serve Our Lord. We have a chance to make people's lives so much better."

"Like mine?" Sam's voice was laced with sarcasm.

Sr. Mary Grace set her arms akimbo. "That doctor in Rincon. What would he have done for you?"

"Probably amputated."

"Instead he sent you here and Fr. Maris saved your legs. If he could have fixed your knees, he would have. You have the chance for a normal life. You have a woman two days travel from here who would come here in a flat Texas minute if you asked her. If I were a betting woman, I'd bet she wouldn't reject you. She loves you enough to write many times per week. You love her, too, or you wouldn't be keeping her letters more carefully than your gold watch. Send for her, Sam. If she's for you, she'll come."

"I can't do it."

"You won't do it. You're a stubborn man, Sam. I'm not sure what you want from this world. I can't believe you want to spend your life alone. But suit yourself. It's your happiness. Now you better eat your lunch because that's all you're getting until dinnertime," she added before leaving.

Sam picked up his fork and stabbed into the sliced raw tomato on his plate. Pru had lost her job and it was all his fault.

He had no way to make it up to her.

Chapter 28

Tuesday, June 23, 1885

Prudence was on her knees in her cabin, nailing the lid on a crate containing her good china, carefully packed in straw and wrapped in her winter scarves and extra sheets.

Already her books and papers were packed, her cold weather garments and her good crystal, also packed in straw and cloth. All she had left out was what she would need until the end of June. She could cook and eat on her camp cookware. It would take about a half day to pack her last things. She had made tentative arrangements to sell Max and her buggy and board Nameless.

She was emptying the drawer of the night table when she found the copy of *A Midsummer Night's Dream*. Seeing it made her melancholy. It was her only reminder of her time with Sam. She did not pack it with her other books. Instead, she sat on her sofa and opened the play. Fighting tears, she began to read.

She was interrupted by a knock at her door. She brushed an errant lock of hair from her tear-swollen eyes and opened the door.

Bob Bonetti stood there, dressed in his working clothes. He came in and removed his hat. Shifting from foot to foot nervously, he accepted Prudence's invitation to sit at the table while she set water to boil on the stove.

He looked around at the nailed wooden crates. Compared to the neat but busy cabin he had seen before, everything was barren and sad. He could see the ashes of papers in the hearth.

"I guess you don't have much to show for nine years here, do you, Miss Prudence?"

"No, I guess not."

"I was thinking, if I stay a ranch hand, I reckon I won't have much to show for my life either."

"Well, I have memories."

"Something wonderful's happened and I wanted to talk to you about it."

Prudence poured tea and offered Bob the bowl of sugar. He helped himself to a couple of spoonfuls and stirred. She sat down opposite him.

"I got a letter today from Boston, Massachusetts. There's a big veterinary school in Boston, Miss Prudence. Apparently you wrote them a letter of recommendation when I graduated from grammar school two years ago."

"I thought your family couldn't afford to send you there."

Bob pulled a letter from his pocket and handed it to her. "This is from the dean of the veterinary school. Some meat packing company in Chicago has set up a scholarship foundation and offered me a scholarship, all expenses paid."

Prudence scanned the letter and looked up with a broad smile. "Bob, this is wonderful. I'm so happy for you. Will you accept it?"

"My family is telling me to go. They're so proud about it, they're fit to burst."

"So when do you leave for Boston?"

"Well, that depends. I'm going to accept their offer, but when I leave depends on you."

Pru's head snapped up. "On me, why?"

Bob pulled a gaily, though clumsily wrapped parcel from his pocket and handed it to her.

"What's this, Bob?"

"Open it."

Pru untied the ribbon and removed the colored paper to discover a small, cardboard box. When she opened the box, it contained only a folded scrap of paper. Wrinkling her brow, she looked strangely at Bob. "What is this?"

He gestured at her. "Open it."

She picked up the piece of paper and opened it. Scrawled on the paper in pencil were the words, *St. Giles Hosp., Amarillo, Tex.* "Bob, what is this?"

Bob looked away. "Sam Blake's address."

"How..."

"Don't ask. Call it a thank you gift."

Pru's face paled. "Thank you?"

Bob picked up the letter from Boston. "There is no foundation, is there? This wasn't because of some recommendation letter you wrote two years ago. I don't know how you did it, but you arranged this for me." He held up his hand to stop her protest. "Don't bother to deny it. I'm not too proud to reject my fondest dream, and I love you all the more for making it possible."

"Bob," Prudence's voice was filled with warning.

Bob smiled. "I won't ever mention my marriage proposal again, but I will escort you to Amarillo when you're ready to go. That way you don't have to sell your buggy or old Max. We'll travel the stage route. From Amarillo I can take the train to Boston. And I promise you I'll be a perfect gentleman."

"Oh, Bob, are you sure?"

Bob raised an eyebrow. "That I'll be a gentleman?"

Pru laughed. "No, that you want to escort me."

From his sitting position, Bob made a bow and said in his best Texas drawl, "Why, Miss Prudence, I'd be honored. So, when do you want to leave?"

"As soon as you confirm to the school that you've accepted."

"If we leave Monday, I'll have a chance to give notice to Mrs. Randolph that I'm quitting...Miss Prudence, are you going to write to Sam Blake and tell him you're coming?"

"No," Pru said, shaking her head, "I think I'll just have to surprise him."

Sam looked warily at the heavy black leather shoes with the metal receptacles in front of the heels. Tentatively he kneaded at the stiff leather and ran his fingers over the bent metal tabs under which he was to thread the bootlaces. The shoe tops ended about where his boots always had, but were designed to lace tightly against his legs.

Even more ominous were the shiny steel braces. They consisted of two flat rods with hinges at knee height attached to padded leather and metal rings that buckled around the ankle, calf and about two or three inches above the knee.

"We can paint them black later if you prefer," Dr. Maris said. "For now, we'll keep them as is."

Sam worked the hinges on the knees of the braces. They were meant to replace the unstable joints. He ran his hands over the cool, shiny metal and leather contraptions. Like them or not, they would be a part of his life from now on. The only alternative was life in an invalid's chair.

Sam chewed on his lip and raked splayed fingers through his short hair. *Well,* he thought, *in for a penny, in for a pound.*

"Let's do it."

At Dr. Maris's direction, Sam put his hands under his thighs and drew each leg up until he rested his heel on the bed. He held his breath at the pain in his knee and closed his eyes as sweat beaded his brow and upper lip, but even through the pain he noted how much closer he was able to get his foot to his buttocks than he ever had. In the six weeks since coming to St. Giles, he had lost close to sixty pounds and his paunch was nearly gone, although his belly was still soft from six weeks of being bedridden. The face that stared back at him in the mirror when he shaved showed prominent cheekbones and lean cheeks and was more oval than square now with a long, corded neck.

Sam reached for his socks and pulled them on. The white cotton lisle stockings rose higher than the shoe tops, but not quite to the knees. He attached the braces to the insertion points on the shoes, opened the buckles and yanked the shoes onto his feet. He reached for the bootlaces and pulled them tight to fasten the shoes. Finally, he buckled the braces around the shoes at his ankles and below and above his knees. He lowered his feet to dangle off the end of the bed and yanked down his nightshirt and dressing gown.

"Now what?"

An orderly brought an invalid chair into view.

"Now you take a little ride to the rehabilitation room. Sr. Elizabeth is waiting for you to give you your first walking lessons."

The orderly brought the wheelchair close to Sam's bed and took him by the upper arm. Cautiously, under Dr. Maris's supervision, he started to ease Sam off the bed.

Sam looked at Dr. Maris. "Doesn't he need assistance?"

The priest smiled. "No, Sam, you're slim enough now that Tinker here can handle you alone."

Sam looked at the doctor with disbelief imprinted on his face. He took a quick glance downward at himself. Even though he was not nearly as thin as Dr. Maris wanted him to be, nobody could look at Sam Blake now and call him an ox. For a moment he closed his eyes and drew a hand over his forehead and nose, fighting the emotion that threatened to spill over.

"Come on, Sam," Tinker said. "You've got a full day ahead of you." The orderly helped Sam to get his shod feet to touch the floor and held him for a moment. For the first time since that horrible night nearly two months prior, Sam Blake was standing on his own two feet. The pain in his knees nearly brought tears to his eyes, but he was standing!

"It's hurting you, isn't it?" Dr. Maris asked knowingly.

Sam grunted in affirmation.

"It'll be easier when you're lighter still."

"I...don't...mind. It's...a...start."

Tinker helped Sam to sit in the wheelchair and put his feet in the footrests. He wheeled his patient through the ward and over to the elevators to take him up to the third floor.

The rehabilitation room consisted mostly of sets of parallel wooden bars set at various heights and low-lying padded benches with what looked like circus strongman's dumbbells beside them. There were also walls of mirrors and racks with crutches and canes. Already there were other patients hard at work, supervised by nurses and a retired strongman who served as a trainer.

"Good morning, Mr. Blake," sounded the gruff, no-nonsense voice of Sr. Elizabeth.

"Good morning, Sister. What shall we do to begin?"

The middle-aged nurse gave a nod of approval. She pointed to a set of parallel bars that had a heavy wooden armchair set before them. "Mr. Tinker, please assist Mr. Blake into that chair."

That done, Sr. Elizabeth said, "I want you to push yourself into a standing position. Use the arms of the chair for leverage and grab onto the parallel bars when you're upright."

Sam nodded. He reached behind him slightly and wrapped his fingers around the arms of the chair. He pushed and pushed and pushed, gaining a few inches at a time, but not quite managing to get his knees to straighten enough to reach a hand for the parallel bar without falling back to his seat. Sweat broke out all over his body from exertion. He gritted his teeth against the pain and his repeated failure to do something as simple as raise himself from a chair. His glasses fogged and a couple of times he had to stop and wipe them on the hem of his dressing gown. Repeatedly he raked his fingers through his hair before returning to the task.

Finally, after what seemed like forever, but was probably no more than twenty minutes, Sam collapsed in the chair, spent and drenched. A part of him wanted to break down in tears of frustration. Another part wanted to give up altogether, but the strongest part of him knew that he had to do this thing if he was to have any life at all. Gripping the arms of the chair with white-knuckled hands, he was about to try it again when he felt a firm hand on his shoulder.

"You've got grit, Mr. Blake. I'll give you that," said Sr. Elizabeth approvingly. "What you need, though, is more upper body strength. Your chest, arm and shoulder muscles are what are going to propel you." She signaled Tinker to bring the wheelchair and get Sam over to one of the padded benches, where he was told to remove his robe and lie on his back. His legs were bent at the knee so that his feet rested on the floor.

Sr. Elizabeth told him to bring his elbows hard against his sides with his hands in the air. She handed him two small dumbbells. "I want you to push these dumbbells into the air ahead of you ten times using the muscles in your shoulders and upper arms, then count to fifty and repeat it. Do that five times, then stretch your arms and bring your hands together in an arc-like motion. Ten times, then rest a fifty-count, and repeat. Do that five times."

Sam had lived a pretty physical life for thirty-four years, but nothing prepared him for how hard the simple act of raising two five-pound dumbbells was going to be. He had never sweated so much before, even on the hottest days in the desert. He had never felt such a burning sensation in his arms, shoulders and chest. It took him nearly two hours to perform the "simple" exercises Sr. Elizabeth had described and though his arms felt like rubber and his nightshirt was sopping wet, he finally finished.

For a long moment, he lay on the bench like a dead man, still clutching the dumbbells like a lifeline.

Suddenly, he saw through spattered lenses the square, wimpled face of Sr. Elizabeth.

"You finished?" she said gruffly.

"Yeah, all they have to do is bury the body," he groaned.

The nun nodded. Sam could have sworn she winked. "You'll do fine, Mr. Blake. Tinker'll take you to the bathing room now. A hot soak'll help, but you'll probably feel like a stagecoach ran over you in the morning."

"You mean I don't feel like that now?"

Sr. Elizabeth chuckled. "You'll get used to it."

As Tinker was helping a limp, exhausted Sam back into the invalid chair, Sam was thinking that he was beginning to hate the phrase, "You'll get used to it."

Sam finished washing his sweat-soaked hair and was lying back in the bathtub letting the heat soak into his pulsing muscles when Dr. Maris appeared. The doctor put Sam's change of clothes and towels on his lap as he sat in the chair next to the bathtub.

Sam opened his eyes when he heard the chair scrape and reached for his specs with a groan as his arm muscles protested even that innocuous movement.

"I hear you performed beyond expectation today."

"I didn't stand up."

"You weren't expected to. Like most people, you're accustomed to using your leg muscles to help your arms in getting out of a chair. You can no longer rely on your legs muscles the way you used to, so you'll have to compensate by building up the muscles in your arms and chest to do the work. You're also going to have to accept that your legs are going to atrophy considerably. You're going to end up with very thin legs and hard, long-muscled arms. If you have your tailor cut your pants legs generously, it should camouflage both the braces and the atrophy. But Sr. Elizabeth says you're motivated. She also says you're the first patient she's had who managed to finish all the lifting the first day, so you've earned your pain honestly...Now, we'd better get you out of there before you turn into a prune. I'm sure Sr. Elizabeth will be more than willing to crack the whip over your head again tomorrow."

"Pru!" Sam cried and awakened disoriented. He tried to get out of the bed, but when his feet hit the floor his knees gave out from under him and sent him sprawling in a heap, groaning with pain.

In seconds Sr. Elizabeth and an orderly were there, the nun holding a lamp.

"Mr. Blake," she said in a low but audible voice. "Mr. Blake, look at me."

In the dim light Sam raised his head and squinted down to try to focus. He saw a blurry image, but after two months in the hospital he recognized it as Sr. Elizabeth.

"That's fine, Mr. Blake. Now, let's get you back into bed."

"Leave me alone," he groaned. "I can do it."

Sr. Elizabeth nodded at the orderly and mouthed for him to stay put. Sam gritted his teeth and pushed from the floor. Although the pain was nearly blinding, he maneuvered himself into a kneeling position.

Then he twisted his body until he could reach for the frame of the hospital bed. With arm and chest muscles newly trained to support him, Sam pushed down on the bed frame until his elbows were straight. As his knees started to give out again, he leaned forward across the bed and grabbed the far side of the bed frame. His chest rose and fell sharply with exertion.

Sr. Elizabeth nodded at the orderly and touched Sam on the shoulder. "I think you've done enough for tonight, Mr. Blake," but her usually gruff voice was gentler than usual.

Shaking, perspiring and aching, Sam let the orderly help him back into the bed and cover him. Sr. Elizabeth set the lamp on the side table and retrieved a cloth that she used to wipe Sam's brow.

"You called her name in your sleep again, Mr. Blake."

Sam didn't even protest.

"Isolating yourself from this woman is putting you on the edge of insanity."

"What good am I to her?"

"I can only stand so much sniveling," the nun called "Sarge" behind her back responded. "You've made more progress than any patient with injuries as debilitating as yours I've ever seen. You got yourself standing up from a chair today not to mention what you were able to do just now without your braces. But what you're doing to your mind by hiding from this woman is undermining all the progress you make."

"I saw her...sleeping...with a man."

"It was a dream, Mr. Blake; a reflection of your hopes or fears. Describe the man."

"Slim, dark hair, bare face."

"That could describe you now. Maybe it was a reflection of your desire. For the love of God and your sanity's sake, write to the woman. Let her know where you are."

"I don't know where she is anymore. She was supposed to leave Rincon by this morning."

Sr. Elizabeth sighed. "Well, then, I don't know what to say to you. You may have achieved your wish to have her out of your life. I just hope the price isn't too high. Now I suggest you get back to sleep, Mr. Blake. We're going to start you walking on the parallel bars tomorrow so you'll need all your energy."

She picked up the lamp and walked back down the ward, leaving Sam to wallow in his own self-pity.

He had his wish. Pru was gone.

But in his dream she had called out his name.

"Damn me," Sam said, "I was wrong."

Chapter 29

Sam looked at the parallel bars stretching in front of him. He had pulled himself from the armchair to stand upright and spent the longest three minutes of his life just standing at the beginning of the parallel bars, gripping them with white knuckles while getting accustomed to standing again.

Sr. Elizabeth stood within a short reach of him, as did an orderly.

"Lift one foot from the hip, Mr. Blake. Good. Now lean forward just a bit. Good. Use your hip and thigh muscle to thrust your leg forward and let the momentum straighten the knee hinge on the brace. Good. Now shift your weight to the leg you've just moved. Good. Do the same thing with your other leg."

It was nowhere as simple as it sounded. Each movement required concentration and effort. What Sam had done unconsciously all his life had to be learned as if he had never walked before. The very mechanics of walking seemed completely new. The ten feet he could have covered before in four or five automatic steps were instead accomplished in inches. He had to get used to the way the braces bent and locked, simulating the movement of knee joints. The bars he leaned on and gripped so tightly were set as high as crutches might be. He was using his arms to hold himself up as his legs made their inching journey forward. Every step was torture, yet with gritted teeth and white knuckles, Sam willed himself to move his legs one after the other until he reached the end of the parallel bars. He lifted one arm and pushed himself until he could grab the other bar with that hand and straightened himself upright, tucking the bar under his arm.

"Effective," was all Sr. Elizabeth would say.

Sam retraced his steps up the bars again and then leaned until he could twist himself into the armchair. He sat there, breathing heavily for a moment, then took off his glasses and wiped his face with the sleeve of his robe.

"Good," said Sr. Elizabeth. "Now do your hand weights for the day and take your bath. You'll be adding two pounds per side today."

"I walked," Sam breathed. A tired but glorious smile creased his sweating face.

Sr. Elizabeth smiled her half smile. "You did indeed. Your progress is excellent and your attitude is admirable."

High praise indeed from the "Sarge."

The first morning in Amarillo, Prudence and Bob went touring. They passed the civic center and many new houses and commercial buildings. In some places there was a jumble of buildings mixed together. The oddest was a one-story mercantile building in the middle of a neighborhood of houses. The building had a sign posted in front that said, "For Sale or Lease, Will Divide to Suit."

"What does that mean, Miss Prudence?"

"It means the owner of the building will put in interior walls if someone wanted to divide the building into smaller shops or offices. I just can't imagine anyone wanting to build shops or offices in this neighborhood."

As they drove from that street they passed the three-story edifice marked "St. Giles Orthopaedic Hospital." Bob slowed the buggy.

"That's it, Miss Prudence."

Pru nodded absently as she stared at the big modern building. She noted its location and set Bob to driving on.

As the time grew shorter, Bob became gradually more excited about going to school. They spent a bittersweet evening having dinner in the hotel dining room. Pru gave Bob a leather portfolio filled with fine men's stationery and a portable ink well and writing pen.

"When I have more permanent lodgings, I'll let you know. I hope you'll write to me."

Bob grinned. "Oh, you know I will. I owe you so much more than I can ever pay."

"Just be a good veterinarian and that will be pay enough for me."

Sr. Mary Grace brought Sam his breakfast tray to find him reading through one of the letters he kept stored in his drawer. His hands were trembling as he read and the little nun saw a tear snake down from behind his lenses to slide down his cheek and fall on the stationery.

She cleared her throat. With a guilty look on his face, Sam's head snapped up and he thrust the letter into the drawer.

"I'm so sorry," she said.

Sam swiped at his cheek. "Stupid of me," he grumbled.

The nun placed the lap tray over Sam's thighs. He looked down at the single poached egg, the piece of dry toast, the sliced-up Spanish orange and the cup of black coffee and groaned.

"Did you sleep well?"

"No, I hardly closed my eyes."

"Were you in much pain?"

"No, Sister, no more than usual. Just uneasy."

"Sr. Elizabeth says you're making excellent progress upstairs. I think she might try you out on the lower parallel bars today." She was referring to the bars set at the level where Sam might use canes. With the sure hand of a barber, she thrust her fingers through Sam's hair critically. "It's been a month since your last haircut. When I'm done serving breakfast I could come back and give you a trim."

"That's fine," he responded noncommittally.

"Sam, do you want to talk to a chaplain? I can see you're troubled."

He gave her a brutal look. "I don't want to talk to a chaplain. What is he going to tell me, that God doesn't make mistakes? My whole life has been a mistake. It would have been better if I'd died when I fell down that mineshaft. Better for me, better for her, better for all concerned.

Sr. Mary Grace crossed herself quickly. "Please, Sam, don't say such things. Life is so precious. Tell me, does *she* think it would have been better if you died? Think how hard it must have been for her to see you hurt and have only so much knowledge and ability to help you. She could have left you there. But what did you tell me: she climbed down a *rope* to get to you? How many *ladies* would climb down a rope to help an injured man? How many would have the presence of mind to set broken bones and fight off fever and stitch lacerations while at the bottom of a twenty foot pit?"

"She's one in a million, Sister."

"So you have this one in a million woman and you throw her away like an empty tin of peaches. Sometimes I believe men think with every part of their bodies except their brains and their hearts."

"You read me like a book, Sister," Sam said bitterly. "But using my heart in the past only brought me misery."

"And what is not using your heart bringing you now, besides self-pity, I mean?"

"I don't know. I really don't know."

After seeing Bob Bonetti off on the train to veterinary school, Prudence rode her buggy to find a boarding house. The Slattery House was a pleasant lodging not far from St. Giles. She was able to engage a sitting room and bedroom beginning the next day.

She returned to the Grand Hotel and changed into her rose pink silk gown. During the two days she had been in Amarillo she had bought nothing for herself, preferring to lavish time and attention on Bob Bonetti. There would be plenty of time to have new clothing made for herself. She realized many of her garments were out of style and a little bit shabby. It had always been appropriate to her position not to be too showy or fashionable. But that would no longer be necessary. Miss Hofheinz the schoolmarm no longer existed.

Dressing her hair in a softer style, Prudence made herself look as soft and feminine as possible. She thought she looked as good as she ever had. She pinned on a straw bonnet trimmed with pink ribbons and pulled on her leather driving gloves. She took the elevator down to the lobby and went out to her buggy.

It was early afternoon when she reached St. Giles. A paper-wrapped bundle of flowers sat beside her on the seat. She gathered it in her arms and walked inside. She noticed the hospital had a switchback ramp with a wrought iron banister leading to its front door as well as stairs. The building was of newer vintage, though not new, but it was freshly painted and welcoming, considering it was a hospital.

The electric light in the clean, airy lobby seemed very bright and cool compared with gaslight. There were two nuns at the reception desk. Pru approached and said, "I'm here to see Samuel Blake."

The nun to whom she spoke went to a wooden box containing cards. "Yes, he's a patient here. Second floor, Ward D, bed ten. The elevator is down this hall and to the right."

Pru thanked the sister and walked down the designated hall. After she left, the nun who had helped her turned to her associate and commented. "Samuel Blake. I don't think he's had but one visitor since he's been here."

The other nun said, "I remember. The little man with the mustache who said he would go out of business trying to sell corsets here."

Clutching the flowers in her arms for dear life, Pru rode the elevator to the second floor and stepped out. It was not difficult to find Ward D. Pru poked her head in the ward door and saw two rows of beds, most of them surrounded by privacy screens.

Apprehensively, she walked slowly down the ward. Finally, she found the bed at the end of the ward. There was a folded copy of the Amarillo Star on the side table and a pitcher of water and tumbler, but nothing visible that would mark the bed as being Sam's.

"May I help you, Miss?" she heard a woman's voice behind her.

Pru turned to see a nun in a cream-colored habit. Swallowing, she responded, "Uh—I'm looking for Sam Blake."

She felt the nun perusing her and her flowers carefully. Then her face brightened into a brilliant smile and she asked, "Are you Pru?"

"Yes."

The sister sighed. "Am I glad to see you! We've all been hoping you would find Sam and come see him. I'd have written to you, but Sam kept insisting he didn't want you to know."

Pru looked down. "Maybe coming here was a mistake."

"Oh, no. He keeps calling for you in his sleep and I think he's memorized every letter he received from you."

"Where is he now?"

"Probably upstairs in rehabilitation. I'll take the flowers and put them in water if you want to go up there. Third floor. It's marked 'Men's Rehabilitation Room.'"

Pru handed her the flowers and headed back up the ward and out into the hall.

Sr. Mary Grace put the flowers on Sam's bed and was about to get a vase when she heard a voice through the privacy screen. "Sister, I don't think it's such a good idea to spring that there girl on Sam like that. He's been so insistin' he don't want t' see her agin' that he might say somethin' he's gonna hate hisself fer," said the patient in bed eight. "Mebbe y'all oughta git up there and stop her."

"Oh, my. You may be right." Lifting her skirts slightly, she scampered down the ward and over to the staircase.

Pru found the door marked as the nun had described. Summoning her courage, she slowly opened the door and eased herself inside.

There were a number of patients, in nightshirts and/or robes at various sets of parallel bars and exercise benches. Nurses, nuns and orderlies were supervising the patients, keeping close watch to make sure they progressed without hurting themselves. But she didn't see Sam.

Then a very tall man with short black hair caught her eye. He was standing between a pair of parallel bars that were about hip height. His arms were fully extended and all his concentration was focused on slowly, painfully taking minute, labored steps on brace-bound, thin, dark hair-dusted legs that showed beneath his nightshirt.

Viewing him from behind, Pru could see the breadth of his shoulders, but his back tapered down to a slim waist and muscled buttocks to which the perspiration from his efforts caused his shirt to stick.

As she watched, the man stopped, then with painful awkwardness maneuvered himself in a pivot to face back the way he had come. His face came up slightly and he closed his eyes against the exertion necessary to complete the turn.

Pru looked at the bespectacled face, its cheekbones prominent above lean, pale, clean-shaven cheeks and a strongly sculpted jaw, a lean, corded neck, then at the slimmed down frame and finally at the wasted legs with the hideous red scars encircling the knees that stepped in so labored a manner. Her gaze returned to the face and her breath caught. A feeling of dread spread over her like a chill.

The man opened his eyes—his dark brown eyes—and Pru knew for certain who it was. The color fled her cheeks as she stared at the face she no longer recognized.

"Sam?" Her voice was barely audible.

His eyes widened. "Pru?" he responded hoarsely, then looked with horror at the shocked look on her face at the sight of him.

"Oh, my God, Sam!"

"Get out!" he roared, hurt and anger giving him voice. "Get out now!"

Tears in her eyes, Pru raised her skirts and ran.

Sam's elbows relaxed as the door slammed, and he collapsed to his knees between the parallel bars as despair filled him.

Pru had sworn she would never reject him because of his handicap, but at the very sight of him helpless she had done just that.

He wished she had not found him.

Chapter 30

Pru ran until she reached a wall. Pressing her hands against it, she collapsed to the floor in a heap, her forehead against the wall, deep sobs wracking her body.

She felt gentle hands grasp her shoulders and an equally gentle voice say, "Come now, please stand up."

Slowly, she allowed the woman to help her up and glared through tear-blurred eyes at the nun who had taken the flowers from her earlier.

"I didn't introduce myself earlier. I'm Sr. Mary Grace, one of Sam's nurses. Why don't you come with me? We'll get a cup of tea and talk."

Sr. Mary Grace led Pru to the elevator and took her back to the ground floor. The room she led Pru into had long tables and benches, at one of which she directed the younger woman to sit. The nun returned a few moments later with two cups of hot tea. Sitting on the bench opposite Pru, she handed her one of the cups. "This is the refectory. It's usually pretty quiet this time of day, but Sr. Dominique always has a pot of tea hot and ready."

Pru took a sip. It was hot, strong and unsweetened and involuntarily she made a face. She put the teacup down and buried her face in her hands. "I didn't know. I didn't know."

"That his injuries were so extensive? But I thought..."

Pru looked up. "No, no. I was prepared for that. It's just that he looks so different. He's so slim and...and handsome."

"Handsome?"

"I never knew he was so handsome. He told me he wore his beard and all that hair because he was ugly, but he isn't."

"No, he isn't an ugly man."

"I was so shocked. And he's lost so much weight."

"Doctor's orders."

Pru put her face in her hands again. "No wonder he didn't want me to know where he was. With that face he could have any girl he wants."

"But he's crippled."

"Even so. Why would he ever want a fat, unattractive, undistinguished woman like me anymore?"

"Merciful Mother of God," Sr. Mary Grace exclaimed. "He was afraid you would reject him because of his legs—and here you think he'll reject you because of your looks."

"But he did. He doesn't want me and I was too stupid to realize it."

"What about his legs? He'll never walk properly again, you realize."

Pru nodded. "I expected that. I was afraid he might even lose them. That wouldn't chase me away, but if he doesn't want me because he knows he can get someone prettier..."

"Oh, my dear," said Sr. Mary Grace, "he doesn't think that at all. He has every letter you sent him since he's been here. He reads them over and over again and sometimes he cries for wanting you so badly."

"But now he'll never believe I haven't rejected him."

Suddenly, Sr. Mary Grace smiled. "I think you need to speak to our director, Fr. Maris. If anyone can show you how to prove you're not repelled by Sam's handicap, it's Fr. Maris."

Sam sat in the hot bathtub as he did after every rehabilitation session, alone with his thoughts. He had been wrong, but seeing Pru like that, so unprepared for her. He knew how horrible his legs looked. Even a saint would have been repelled.

Instead he screamed at her to leave and she ran out.

Sam thought seriously about just sliding into the bathtub and letting himself drown, but Tinker was sitting nearby with instructions to look in on him every few minutes.

He didn't know how she found out where he was, but he was glad she did, until he lost control.

She had promised him she would not reject him and yet she ran.

For just a moment, Sam did allow himself to slip into the water. He held his breath for as long as he could, then came puffing back to the surface as bubbles played over his hair-matted chest. No, he would not die. He would live and become as ambulatory as his legs would allow.

He didn't need Prudence Hofheinz.

He also didn't need light, air and nourishment.

Pru walked into the sparsely furnished office of Dr. David Maris and sat. The priest spoke briefly to Sr. Mary Grace and returned to sit behind his desk.

"So you're Miss Prudence Hofheinz. I was afraid with Sam's stubbornness he would never let you know where he was."

"He didn't. A friend in Rincon found the address for me. I came as soon as I could."

"Sr. Mary Grace tells me you walked in on Sam during rehabilitation and were shocked by his appearance, but not by his handicap."

"I don't know how to convince him that it wasn't the other way around."

Dr. Maris looked Pru up and down. "Can you remain in Amarillo for a while?"

"I can remain here indefinitely."

"Let me describe Sam's condition to you..." Dr. Maris explained the extent of the damage and the length of the treatment process. Pru felt guilty that her actions in setting Sam's leg bones might have contributed to the damage to his knees until the doctor told her that had she not done it amputation might have been necessary. "...We don't anticipate his release before late October or early November, at which point he'll need a place to live here in Amarillo because he'll need to continue treatment for six months to a year. He will also have to be rigid in his eating regimen for the rest of his life if he expects to remain ambulatory."

Dr. Maris took a sheet of paper out of his desk and wrote on it. Handing it to Pru, he said, "This is what Sam eats and in what quantities. He needs to lose perhaps another thirty to forty pounds and keep it off, which means he needs to eat like this daily no matter how he grumbles. I can't imagine he will be able to get this kind of diet in a common boarding house, but..."

"In a place of his own where someone understands his needs and follows them, he'd be able to do it," Pru finished, realization coming to her. "Dr. Maris, what would happen to me if I ate this way?"

"You would probably feel better, and the extra weight you've been carrying would likely melt off you, though at a slower pace. It would mean a rather substantial sacrifice on your part."

"Doctor, nothing is too big a sacrifice. I love him. I want to be his wife."

"Then here's what I want you to do..."

The seller was very surprised to get an offer for that misplaced mercantile building. He let it go for a song. Before buying the building, Pru walked through it and drew a scale floor plan. The building was all on one story, six thousand square feet with a carriage house on a large back lot. Pru got the addresses of carpenters and set to work.

She wrote to Luigi Bonetti to order special furniture from him. The cabinetmaker was willing to do anything for the teacher who had helped his son Roberto go to veterinary school. Pru had very firm ideas of what she wanted and Luigi was happy to fulfill them.

Soon she had carpenters installing walls dividing the rectangular space into rooms.

When she had the steps leading to the entrance removed and replaced with a ramp, she began to attract the attention of the neighborhood. Passersby noticed the tall, dark-haired woman in the denim riding skirt, boots and gaucho hat directing the carpenters while she seemed to be tugging on the waistband of her skirt to keep it from slipping down to her hips.

One day, she heard a mature woman's voice declare, "Who's in charge here?"

She turned around to see a fashionably dressed woman holding a parasol while she sat in an open carriage. Pru introduced herself.

"I'm Mrs. Alastair Whitney. Whatever are you doing to this eyesore?"

"I'm converting it from a mercantile building to a house."

"Who is your architect?"

"I am. I designed the layout of the interior and the furnishings."

As they watched, carpenters carried in a series of long, dark-stained poles about the circumference of a lady's wrist.

"Who is this house for?"

"With any luck, for the man I hope to marry. He's a patient at St. Giles."

"Oh, you poor thing."

"I don't think so. I'm very proud of him."

"Do you do this kind of thing professionally?"

It was as if lightning struck Pru. "Why, yes, Mrs. Whitney, I do." Bluffing, she began to pat at her pockets. "Only I don't seem to have my business card case with me today." She pulled a pencil from behind her ear. "If you have a calling card, I'll be happy to write the information on the back."

Mrs. Whitney drew a sterling silver calling card case from her reticule and handed Pru two cards. On the back of one, Pru wrote her name and the telephone exchange of her boarding house. "I'll be staying at the Slattery Arms until the house is finished."

"My mother-in-law recently died and I'm looking forward to finally refurbishing the house to my taste rather than hers. How much do you charge?"

Pru thought quickly. "I'll quote you a price once I see the house and determine what has to be done. Shall I call, say tomorrow afternoon at around two?"

"Perfect. I look forward to it." Mrs. Whitney shook Pru's hand.

"Oh, so do I, ma'am, so do I."

Sam laid his crutches against the wall as he sat on his bed. It was ghastly hot even for late August, but he was ambulating under his own power for the first time since April.

He opened his drawer to find a handkerchief to wipe his face and glasses when he saw the letters from Pru, tied with a string. He had not seen her since that awful day when he yelled at her to get out of the rehabilitation room. He didn't even know if she was still in Amarillo. His only contact with the outside world now was his newspaper subscription and an occasional postcard from Basil.

From the Amarillo *Star*:

Mr. and Mrs. Alastair Whitney last night hosted a gala charity reception at their newly refurbished mansion on Marston Street. Miss P. Hofheinz, who designed the interior, was present and received high accolades from those attending for the originality of her designs. It is believed that Miss Hofheinz is the first person in Texas to specialize in creating unified designs for existing homes. She is also currently overseeing the remodeling of the Van Sant mansion and the lobby of the Montgomery Hotel.

"Miss Hofheinz," said the dressmaker through her mouthful of pins, "I don't know how you expect me to complete these new clothes."

"I'm sorry, Miss Gibbons, but between my house and the work that column in the *Star* generated, I just don't have a lot of time for fittings."

"It's not the time, Miss Hofheinz. It's just that every time you come in for a fitting I have to take things in again. If you're going to continue to lose flesh at the rate you're going, you ought to wait until you've stopped before buying new clothes."

"Please do your best, Miss Gibbons. Put drawstrings in the waistbands or something, but my days of dressing like a schoolmarm are through."

Basil Mercury came his jaunty way through the hospital corridor, teasing nuns and lay nurses alike as he searched out Ward D. He met up with Sam, who was slowly moving on crutches down the hall.

Basil's smile was broad and friendly as he greeted the man he considered his friend. "Ah, Sam, I'm gone four months and when I come back you're walking like an expert."

"Well, a talented amateur anyway," Sam said in response. He could not stay depressed in the irrepressible young salesman's company. "It's good to see you, Basil. How's business?"

"Couldn't be better. A good swing through Texas and I'll be the top salesman of the year."

"I'd pat you on the back, my friend, but I might tip over."

Basil walked with Sam to the end of the hallway, where there was a lounge. Sam's progress was still very slow, but he forced himself as much as possible to rely on the handles of the crutches rather than the top rests. He was determined to be working with canes as soon as he could so he could be out of this place on or before schedule.

They took seats near one window, Sam easing himself gingerly down, Basil sitting easily and crossing his legs.

"So you're making progress."

"A little more every day. I can't wait to get out of here. I think I understand why snowed-in miners go insane."

"Have you made no friends here in the hospital?"

Sam shrugged. "I'm afraid I don't make friends easily."

Basil raised an eyebrow. "You made friends with me pretty quickly."

Sam half-smiled. "That, my friend, has more to do with you than me."

"And what have you heard from the schoolteacher?"

The color drained from Sam's face and his back became stiff as pain flashed across his eyes. "Nothing; not anymore. She couldn't deal with it."

Basil uncrossed his legs and sat upright. "You're not serious. It doesn't sound like her."

"She came here just before the Fourth of July, took one look at me hobbling along and ran for the hills. I haven't seen her since."

"She came here? You didn't tell her where you were, but she found you? There's something you're not telling me, Sam."

Sam looked away. "No, that's all."

Basil realized he wasn't going to get any additional information from Sam. He steered the conversation to safer subjects, such as politics and the corset business. Sam was polite but distant, as if more involved with an inner pain. Finally, Basil rose to leave.

"I'll be in town five days. I'll come again before I leave."

"That will be great," Sam said genuinely. As Basil was leaving, suddenly Sam called out, "Oh, and thanks for the dime novels." Basil turned to look at him. "They've helped me pass the time the last couple of months."

"Oh, sure," Basil responded with a shrug. Confused, he left the lounge and headed back toward the ward. He saw a nun enter the corridor.

"Excuse me, but are you one of Sam Blake's nurses?"

"I'm Sr. Mary Grace."

"I need to know something about his girl. I suppose she left town."

Sr. Mary Grace smiled. "She's staying at the Slattery Arms, but most mornings you'll find her at 315 Marston Street. She comes here regularly for progress reports, but doesn't go upstairs. Believe me, she's concerned about him, but don't let Sam know. Miss Hofheinz has her reasons for keeping her project secret from him."

"Sister, do you know anything about Sam receiving books?"

"Yes, they've been arriving regularly in unidentified packages. Dime novels, cowboys and Indians, marshals and bank robbers. He thought they were from you."

Basil nodded. "Maybe it's better he continues to think so."

Basil arrived at 315 Marston in time to see a man in his middle forties and a boy about seventeen carrying the largest headboard he'd ever seen. Finely carved with wheat stalks, it was dark-stained hardwood and had to be close to eight feet wide. A shorter, but equally wide footboard leaned against a wagon with the legend, "Luigi Bonetti, Carpentry and Cabinetry" painted on the side.

The young salesman crossed the street and saw that the wagon was filled with new furniture, all beautifully carved and constructed. Intrigued, he followed the two men into the building and realized that instead of steps, there rose a gently sloping ramp with a wrought iron handrail on each side from the sidewalk to the front door.

The front door was propped open. To Basil's amazement, the building was a flurry of activity. Walls were being painted, paneling being put up and at periodic intervals some kind of brass fixtures that looked like banister rail rings were being bolted about a yard off the floor. The floors had been sanded, but some were still in need of polishing and waxing. He had never seen so many people working on a project before.

He walked a little further into the building. He would not have guessed from the outside of the building, but from the headboard and other pieces he saw in the wagon, this appeared to be a house. He stepped past a large front parlor and a smaller room that looked like it was going to be some kind of library because bookcases had been built into the walls. In the back of the house, the painting, wallpapering, paneling and floor finishing had already been done. He heard voices and went into a large room near the extreme end of the house to see the two men he had observed carrying in the bed parts now attaching them to side-pieces. Basil stood in the doorway and watched as the big bed came together under the supervision of a woman wearing a blue chambray work shirt and denim split riding skirt that were too large for her.

"So, what you t'ink, Miss Hofheinz?" said the older man.

The woman ran appreciative hands over the intricate carving. "Mr. Bonetti, it's perfect. You and Ralph have done a masterful job. If the rest of the furniture is as wonderful as this, I'll recommend you to all my clients. No house in Amarillo will be complete without Bonetti."

That's Sam's Pru? Basil thought. *Why she's beautiful!*

The woman turned and saw him standing in the doorway. "Who are you and what are you doing in my house?"

"The door was open. I'm Basil Mercury and I'm a friend of Sam Blake."

Her demeanor immediately warmed. She walked toward him, her hands outstretched. "I'm glad to welcome any friend of Sam's...The kitchen's done. Would you like a cup of tea?"

She led Basil down a hallway that bisected the house to a cheery kitchen fully equipped with shelving, a pantry, a stove, sink, icebox and Shaker-style wooden table and chairs, two of which had arms attached. She made tea, all the time telling Basil about the improvements she was making. When the tea was ready, she poured it into fine bone china cups and served it.

"I would offer you some cookies or cream and sugar, but I'm afraid I don't keep them in the house." She sat and smiled winningly. "Please tell me about Sam. Have you seen him recently? How is he doing? Is he enjoying the books?"

"I thought they might be from you. I don't think they're his favorite, but he says they pass the time."

Basil wondered if this was truly the plain, undistinguished schoolmarm about whom Sam had spoken. This woman had more light and life in her than any three women he had ever known put together. *Anyone* would pick her out of a crowd.

"Sam's walking on crutches and he's lost a lot of weight since I last saw him."

"He's on crutches? But that's marvelous!"

The look on this woman's face was so love-filled and excited that it made Basil feel confused. This didn't seem like a woman who had rejected her crippled lover.

"You *are* Miss Pru Hofheinz, the schoolteacher from Rincon, Texas?"

Her eyebrow rose. "Yes, of course, Mr. Mercury. Who else in her right mind would admit to having a name like Prudence Hofheinz?"

"Why don't you go to the hospital and see Sam for yourself?"

Chapter 31

The brightness left Pru's face and she looked down at the cup in her hands. "Sam doesn't want to see me. He's made that perfectly clear. He's ashamed of me."

"Ashamed? Why would he be ashamed of a beautiful, thoughtful woman like you?"

Pru smiled weakly. "You're being unnecessarily flattering, Mr. Mercury."

"Call me Basil. I'm only speaking the truth. This house, you've designed it for him. Who would need a bed that size but a man so tall? And the ramp out front and the other things? Sam doesn't know about this, does he?"

"No," Pru squeaked out and put her hands on Basil's. "For God's sake, don't tell him. It's a surprise for when he gets out of the hospital and it has to stay a secret."

"How did you learn to do such things? I thought you were a teacher."

"I *was* a teacher. Now I have a chance to do work that really means something to me—for someone who means more to me than anyone in the world. Out of that, I've discovered a skill that's in demand with all the new money coming into this city."

"Are you saying you're too busy to see Sam?"

Pru shook her head. "I don't want to give Sam another chance to shout me out the door. The next time I see him, I want to be truly worthy of him. I want this house to be finished and I want to be able to respond to all his possible objections."

"You love him that much. But why are you sending him dime novels? He prefers better literature."

"Trust me, Basil, there's method in my madness. Call it priming the pump."

"If I'm not mistaken, priming a pump means you pour water into the mechanism in order to get water to come out when you pump the handle."

Pru nodded. "That's right."

Basil did some quick figuring in his head, then smiled broadly beneath his thick mustache. "Water goes in, different water comes out. The kind of water everyone wants to drink."

"I think you understand, Basil."

"That's very clever, Pru. You sure you're not Greek?"

In October Sam, still on crutches, came into Dr. Maris's office. Once seated, he shook the doctor's hand and asked the reason for this special meeting.

"Sr. Elizabeth tells me you're using canes now in the rehabilitation room and have become independent on your crutches."

Sam nodded. "I hope to be using the canes only within the next couple of weeks."

"That's what I wanted to speak to you about, Sam. From your current progress, we would expect to discharge you by early November. You'll still need to come in three times a week for rehabilitation, but there's no need for you to remain in the hospital twenty-four hours a day."

Sam laughed ironically. "I haven't been outside these walls in five months. All I've seen of Amarillo is the view from the lounge windows. I don't know a soul in this city beyond the hospital staff. Where would I live?"

"I've made arrangements for housing and transportation for you. You should find the place very accommodating."

Sam gestured at his hospital nightshirt and robe. "I hate to sound vain, but I literally have nothing to wear. I've lost so much weight the only thing I own that still fits me is my Stetson."

"I've arranged for a tailor to come in and take your measurements. We should be able to equip you with an adequate wardrobe in time for your discharge. If you continue to follow the eating regimen I've prescribed, your weight should level off and you shouldn't have any trouble with the clothes fitting you for a while."

"This place I'm going, will they be able to do that?"

"The cook will take your special requirements very seriously."

Sam slapped his hands against his thighs. "Well, then, I guess that's that." He would not share with the priest that his life savings were nearly depleted by the cost of his treatment nor that he had no idea what kind of work he could do now. From what he knew of St. Giles they would continue to provide him treatment even if he became indigent, but Sam was not the kind of man who took charity. He wondered what he would do for money when his bank account went dry. The ten thousand he figured Clint stole from him would have come in handy, but he was damned if he was going to ask Clint for it. He doubted that his erstwhile partner had any of the money left anyway. Wherever he was now, the money was probably spent. He would have vengeance someday, but he could not exactly meet Clint on some dusty street and duel with him. He could imagine a gunfight with him trying to draw his revolver while still holding on to his crutches. It made a funny picture, but one that would surely end in his own death.

Despite his college degree, Sam could not imagine what sort of business would hire a crippled man. He had not done anything related to civil engineering since graduation. He could not see himself maneuvering around a construction site. It was a cinch he could not be a lawman or detective. He didn't even know if he could ride a horse.

That made him think about Nameless—which made him think about Pru. He wished he could see her again, to tell her he was sorry he yelled at her, to give her another chance.

Chances were she had taken another teaching job and was long gone from Amarillo. He still read and reread the letters she sent him those first two months he was in the hospital. Many of them were blurred with his tears.

"Sam," Dr. Maris's voice cut through, "are you listening?"

Sam's head snapped up. "I'm sorry, Doctor."

"I'm worried about you, Sam. While you've made great progress physically, I'm deeply concerned about this growing melancholy. Being a loner may have worked when you were able-bodied, but it could mean your death now. Once you've been discharged, you must find yourself some society. I don't know, a wife, a fraternal organization, a church, something—or you risk insanity."

"I'll be fine. I've never needed anyone before and I won't now. Once I find work I'll get by."

Dr. Maris folded his arms. "Will you? Seems to me you had yourself a partner for a number of years. This loner persona; it's really an act, isn't it; a hedge against being left alone?"

Sam's face reddened. "I don't want to talk about it."

"For pity sake, don't keep it inside."

Sam pushed himself up. "I'll think about it. Thank you for the chat, Doctor. It was most enlightening."

Sam hobbled out of the office. Fr. Maris leaned back in his chair. Sam was erecting a shell thicker than his weight had ever been. Pru Hofheinz had been able to break through that shell; could she break through this new one?

Sam had been able to walk thirty feet and back on two canes and made the first transfer to hold both canes in one hand to open a door or hold an object. As with all his new skills, they took considerable effort and perspiration, so after that and his weight bench work, he took himself to the bathing room.

His attempts to get himself into the bathtub unassisted were very frustrating. Trying to sit on the edge of the anchored tub and remove his braces and shoes usually meant falling backwards into the tub and splashing water everywhere. Sitting on a chair to remove his braces and then trying to raise himself over the edge of the tub was equally clumsy. He knew the winch was the easiest way, but when he was out of the hospital there would be no winch and no handy orderly to lower him into the tub. His legs were badly bruised from his attempts, but the bruises involved in getting into the tub were minimal compared with trying to get out. Sam was determined to bathe every day. Fully frustrated, he raked his hands repeatedly through his black curls. If he was having so much trouble with a large cast iron and porcelain bathtub anchored by bolts to the floor, how would he ever manage one of those boarding house hip baths that were carried in and out? When he asked whether the living accommodations that had been arranged had a stationary bathtub, the only answer he received was that the quarters would "accommodate his needs."

Sam was imagining some kind of boarding house filled with other recently discharged St. Giles patients who, like Sam, had no place else to go. But he didn't see what choice he had.

He hobbled back to the ward and Sr. Mary Grace told him the tailor was there to see him. The man introduced himself as Mr. Tennant from Lentman's Tailor Shop. It appeared the little man had never dealt with the needs of a handicapped man before, and had not prepared for the tall, broad shouldered man standing on crutches, clad only in a nightshirt and robe, leg braces, socks and high-topped leather shoes. He could see from below the hem of the nightshirt the atrophy in Sam's legs.

But Mr. Tennant quickly adjusted. Rather than start with the neck and working his way down as he normally would, he took Sam's lower measurements first, then had him sit on the bed while he took the upper measurements.

Sam tried to tell Tennant what he needed, but the fitter told him it had all been taken care of and what he needed to wear to leave the hospital would be delivered the day he was scheduled to be discharged. The remaining clothing would be sent to his lodgings.

Sam realized the tailor was extremely uncomfortable with the sight of his disability. Tennant had barely looked him in the face and seemed reluctant to touch him, as if his injuries were somehow contagious. It gave Sam a taste of what it would be like to face the world as a cripple. He would forever be the subject of half-veiled stares and treated like he was less than intelligent. Strangers would be uncomfortable in his presence. He would always need help with certain things he had always taken for granted.

Dr. Maris told him that once he was discharged there was someone who could teach Sam to ride a horse again. If would be difficult, awkward and sometimes painful, but it would give him some additional mobility. Sam would have rather had Nameless. He assumed the gelding was either still in Rincon or somewhere with Pru.

How he missed her, wanted her, loved her.

And could never have her.

Monday, November 2, 1885

Sr. Mary Grace came back to the end of Ward D, a large flat cardboard box and a hatbox in her arms. As usual, she had a beaming smile on her face. Through all his moroseness and cynicism, she truly liked Sam Blake. The wounded soul in him gave her reason to hope for his salvation. It also didn't hurt that he was smart and treated her as if her nun's habit didn't make her less than a whole person.

Sam was sitting in an armchair by the side of his hospital bed. The worn carpetbag he brought with him when he arrived was open on the bed and Sam was packing the contents of his side table in it. His hair was still damp from a morning bath and was drying in soft, black curls. He wore the usual hospital nightshirt and robe that had been his uniform for six months.

Sr. Mary Grace set down the boxes on the bed and watched Sam packing his books, socks and grooming items as well as the nightshirt he was wearing when he arrived. He set the wooden cigar box on the table and removed his watch and money clip before putting the box in his carpetbag. Finally, he lifted the tied bundle of Pru's letters. For a moment he glanced at the wastepaper basket and weighed the letters in his hand, but ended up packing them just the same.

He looked up at his nurse. He tried to keep his face impassive, but feared his eyes betrayed his fears. Never in his life had his future been so cloudy or directionless, even in that horrible year after Cynthia's rejection.

He knew Sr. Mary Grace saw the fear, but he would deny it if she mentioned it.

"Your new clothes have arrived."

Grateful for the change of subject, Sam laughed and said, "Thank God. I was beginning to think I would have to face the City of Amarillo in a dressing gown. Do I have to go down to the locker and pack my other things?"

"No, I packed everything else in a box for you yesterday. An orderly will bring those things and your guns down to the carriage...I'm glad to see a hatbox came. Your old Stetson was so dirty and I'm afraid the moths got to it, too."

Sam reached over and opened the hatbox first. Buried under tissue paper he uncovered a camel-colored Stetson in the exact style he had always favored. He played with the brim a bit and folded the crown, then realized he had better make sure it was his size.

Turning over the hat he found the size was correct, but to his surprise, sewn onto the sweatband was a label that said "John B. Stetson Company, 100% camel hair."

"There must be a mistake."

"What kind of mistake?"

"I've always worn this color hat, but they've always been of wool felt. This is real camel hair."

"So?" said the unworldly nun.

"This hat is probably two or three times more expensive."

Sr. Mary Grace shrugged. "Well, then, it will probably be more durable in the long run. Let's see it on you," she added with a grin.

Returning her smile, Sam put on the hat and bent the brim to the angle he liked. "What do you think?" he said buoyantly.

"I think it makes you look very handsome."

"Handsome?" he echoed in disbelief.

"Don't you know, Sam? You see your face every day."

Sam frowned and his eyes took on that pained look. He pulled off the hat and tossed it temporarily back in the hatbox. He reached for the cardboard box and lifted the lid.

On the top was a small, velvet-covered box. Sam opened it to reveal a pair of textured gold cufflinks, square with beveled edges on two sides and a set of gold collar studs. As simple as they were, it was obvious they were classic, elegant jewelry chosen by someone with impeccable taste.

Following was a tissue wrapping a pair of black kidskin gloves. Sam opened another tissue and found two fine linen handkerchiefs with the initial "B" embroidered on them. A third tissue revealed a black silk bow tie, a pair of black web and leather suspenders and a stiff, starched, detachable cotton collar.

It was when Sam turned back the next tissue that the color drained out of his face. He pulled out a collarless white on white shirt with French cuffs. His hand caressed the fabric as if it might burn him and grunted.

"What is it, Sam?"

"Feel this shirt." When the nun looked perplexed he continued. "It's the kind of shirt cotton the Main Line boys wore when I was in college. Why did Dr. Maris order this kind of quality garments for me?"

She shrugged. "I don't know, Sam. Maybe he figured you deserve it. Or maybe he asked one of our benefactors to select clothes for you. They're rich men, so it's possible whoever it was just ordered what he was used to himself."

Sam hummed in response. The latter reason made more sense to him than the former since if Dr. Maris felt Sam Blake deserved an expensive shirt, that made one of them.

"I bet it will feel wonderful on," Sr. Mary Grace said brightly.

The contents of the box got worse. The next item down was a charcoal gray, heavy silk brocade vest with black horn buttons. It was as high quality as the shirt and just as understated in its elegance.

Sam's hands were trembling when he uncovered the suit. He touched the fabric and shivered. Leaning back in the chair, he closed his eyes.

"Are you all right, Sam?"

"I'm in some sort of a nightmare. God in Heaven, Sister. Feel the fabric of this suit."

She brushed it with her hand. "It's soft. Is it like the rest of the clothes?"

Sam nodded stiffly. "Even more so, Sister. It's cashmere."

Chapter 32

"Cashmere?" Sr. Mary Grace responded. "I'm sorry, Sam. I don't what that implies."

Sam let out the breath he had been holding. "It means this suit probably cost five hundred dollars. A ranch hand would have to work a year and a half just to *earn* that much money. By contrast, the last suit I bought for myself cost me less than thirty dollars and it was custom made...I can't wear these clothes."

She held out her hands in a helpless gesture. "I don't see where you have a lot of choice. Why don't I leave you alone to get dressed and finish packing? Your ride will be here in less than an hour and I'm sure you'll want to get settled in your new place. When you're dressed you could go upstairs to the rehabilitation room and look at yourself in the full length mirrors."

Sam's eyebrows rose in a bewildered expression. "What choice do I have?"

Sr. Mary Grace turned to go, then turned back. "Sam, I don't know if I'll see you before you go, but you've been a wonderful patient. It's been a pleasure to know you. I'll include in my prayers for you to find happiness now that you're going to be back in the regular world."

She held out her work-roughened hand and Sam shook it. In a voice husky with emotion he thanked her and watched her leave.

Once she was gone he pushed himself into a standing position long enough to remove his nightshirt and robe and began to dress.

Nothing in his life would be automatic, including dressing. Sam put on the shirt and fastened the bone buttons. It fit perfectly, having plenty of room for his shoulders, but tapered not to bunch at the waist and hips. The fine cotton shirting felt as smooth as silk on his bare skin. He folded the French cuffs and slipped in the cufflinks, then dug out his shaving mirror to fasten on his collar with the studs and tie his necktie properly. He noted how much easier it was to put on a collar and tie without a full beard and long hair.

He reached for the trousers. To his surprise they were fully lined. Sam had never heard of lining trousers, but he was in such shock about these clothes that even this new discovery could not shock him more. The light woven cashmere whispered across his legs like a caress as he contemplated the most effective way of getting them on. Finally, he leaned over and lifted one shod foot, sliding it into the pants leg and pulling the leg up until his shoe cleared the hem, then repeating it with the other leg until the waistband was halfway up his thighs. Using one of his canes for leverage, he stood and finished pulling on his trousers, maneuvering with one hand until he could button the top fly button with his shirt mostly inside.

Sam was breathing in short gasps as he teetered, unsure of his balance as he tucked in the dress shirt and buttoned the remaining fly buttons. The tapering cut of the shirt enabled him to do it with a minimum of wrestling. Slowly, he lowered himself back into the chair and fastened the suspenders to the trousers while seated.

He picked up the vest and put it on, reaching back to the side table for his watch and chain. They fit in the watch pockets across his now flat stomach, but Sam noted with amusement that his watch chain was too long for his slimmer torso. He tucked the excess into the pocket with his watch so his Phi Beta Kappa key fell where it always had just outside his left vest pocket.

He put one of the handkerchiefs in his carpetbag and reached behind him to tuck the other one in one back pocket. His money clip went into a front pocket. Finally, he reached for the frock coat and pulled it on. He folded up the tissue and put it back in the cardboard box, put the kidskin gloves in the pocket of his frock coat and replaced his new hat on his head. Using both canes, he stood again. The silk-lined coat adjusted itself with the hem ending just above his knees. Leaning against the bed, Sam closed and latched the carpetbag and walked, using his canes to support himself, down the ward and out to the elevator.

Taking the elevator to the third floor, he went to the rehabilitation room. Standing alone before the full-length mirror, Sam could hardly believe his transformation. The man staring back at him in the mirror looked tall, lean and prosperous. The suit fit his new body to perfection. He could see the lining in his trousers kept the pants legs from making contact with his legs or braces and gave them a look of proportioned bulk they no longer had. For a moment, Sam slipped both canes into one hand. He felt his spine straighten.

When a man is already six feet five inches it is difficult to feel taller, but Sam did. For a brief moment, he looked like the kind of man he had envied in college—settled, confident, fashionable, elegant—and yes, even handsome. Had it not been for the canes held so tightly in his hand, Sam might have been able to believe he was not handicapped. Only the slightest flash of steel telegraphed the presence of his leg braces. Had Sam not known he was looking at his own reflection, he might not have recognized himself.

He felt a tightening in his chest. It was all pretense. He had no reason to be wearing a five-hundred dollar cashmere suit, brocade vest and real camel hair hat. The minute he needed to walk people would see the labored, awkward gait that gave his handicap away. He was nearly broke, unable to work as a detective, with no other profession to count on. He had no home, no family, no social position, no money.

Sam thought God must have a really black sense of humor. Ultimately, Cynthia Depardieu had been right about everything except one. By some strange quirk of fate, Sam Blake had managed to trade everything he had ever been or possessed in his life for the two assets he had always lacked—a handsome face and a slim body.

He glanced up toward Heaven. "It's not a fair trade, God," he said in a pained voice.

"What's not a fair trade, Sam?" the voice of Fr. Maris sounded behind him.

Sam split his canes again and turned to face the doctor.

"You look good, Sam."

Sam snorted. "For what it's worth." He shook his head. "I wish you'd told whoever furnished these clothes that I didn't need anything quite so fine."

"Don't they fit—oh, but I can see they do."

"They fit wonderfully, but..."

"A crippled ex-range detective doesn't deserve to wear a gentleman's apparel, eh?"

Sam flushed at the brutality of the hit. He exhaled raggedly. "Touché, Doctor."

"I suppose we could have given you a length of rope to slip through your belt loops and sent you out into the world in the worn, oversized garments that arrived after you. Then you could have sat on a street corner and begged for dimes, looking as pathetic as you're convinced you are. Sorry, Sam, that's not the way it works at St. Giles. I've had few patients who've had to make as profound a physical metamorphosis as you did. It's part of the healing process to give our patients a sense of dignity. If a well-made suit of clothes adds to that sense of dignity, then so be it. You've not been coddled here and you've responded. You've worked yourself half to death to become ambulatory. I didn't expect you to be out of here before Christmas when you were carried in and here it is early November. A man with that kind of will can make himself a new life to replace the one he lost. And, for your information, I had no part in the decision regarding your wardrobe. If the suit is too fine, take that up with whoever made that decision."

Sam quirked an eyebrow above his spectacles. "You don't know?"

Dr. Maris grinned. "Oh, I know, but I'm bound to silence. It's one of those things priests do on occasion." The doctor pulled a steel-jacketed railroad watch from his pocket and looked at the time. "Your ride will be here in a few minutes. We'll stop at your bed to get your things and I'll walk down to the front with you."

Dr. Maris carried the carpetbag and hatbox down for Sam, slowing his steps to stay even with his patient. He explained that Sam's other things were already at his lodgings waiting for him.

"Sam, you might want to make your home here in Amarillo. As long as you're living here, you'll have full access to our rehabilitation facility as well as to the bracemaker and cobbler."

"I don't know what I'll be doing. I suppose it depends on what kind of work I find...By the way, how long are these lodgings you've found for me paid for?"

The priest set Sam's carpetbag and hatbox down beside him as a black buggy pulled by a brown horse slowed to a stop at the base of the hospital entrance ramp. As he shook Sam's hand, he replied, "That depends entirely on you, I think," and turned to return to the hospital.

Sam followed his doctor with his eyes and did not notice anything else until he heard a voice say, "I'll put these in the boot for you if you want to get in."

Sam looked up and saw the back of a tall, slender woman in a highly fashionable, claret velvet skirt and polonaise, her glossy brown hair in shiny curls that dribbled luxuriously down to where the back of her neck met her shoulders, a pert claret felt hat trimmed with cherries perched saucily on top of the curls. Ivory kid-gloved hands held his meager luggage and her skirts moved provocatively with her confident, gliding walk.

As Sam walked down the incline to the buggy, it occurred to him that the woman's voice sounded vaguely familiar, but he couldn't place that voice with a figure so slender he could span her waist with his hands.

The buggy was a nondescript two-seater, painted black with a cloth collapsible bonnet that was pulled up over the seats in deference to the cool November temperature. The horse, too, was a nondescript brown with black mane and tail, like thousands of other horses in Texas. A lap blanket sat bunched on the seat. Sam assumed his driver was a society lady doing her charity duty for St. Giles by driving him to his lodgings.

Transferring his canes to one hand, Sam gripped the side of the buggy and, using his canes for leverage, lifted himself into it using his newly developed arm and shoulder strength. It was easier than he would have thought. Smoothing the skirt of his coat under him, he eased himself onto the seat, pressing himself as far to the right as he could, forgetting for a minute that he no longer took as much room as he used to in a buggy.

The woman in velvet came around the left side of the buggy and handed herself in with the smoothness of one who was well accustomed to transporting herself. Gracefully she sat on the seat beside him.

Sam tried to look unaffected, but in profile the woman was astonishingly beautiful. Her skin was flawless with a hint of color from the cool air. She smelled clean, with the faint hint of roses from her shining hair. Her eyelashes seemed impossibly long, her back impossibly straight, her waist impossibly slim. Sam felt his chest tighten, then his groin. Nervously, he plucked at the lap blanket to pull it over his lap to hide the effect she was having on him.

With one slim, graceful hand she picked up the reins while her other hand reached for the buggy whip. Tugging firmly on the reins, the siren started the horse going with the command, "Giddyup, Max."

Max?

Sam felt his breath leave his body. He stared in disbelief at the elegant beauty sitting beside him. It wasn't possible, but it must be.

His voice almost silent, he choked out, "Pru?"

She turned her head and gave him the beautiful smile that reached clear up to those stunningly gleaming brown eyes.

"Good morning, Sam," was all she said, then returned her eyes to the road.

Sam was melting inside. She hadn't abandoned him. He realized this was the same buggy he'd ridden in the first time he met her and the same old gelding in the traces. But the woman next to him was not the sad, plump, endearing little schoolteacher he had known. This woman was sleek and fashionably dressed in a color a small town schoolmarm would never have dared wear. The Pru Hofheinz whose beauty had shown only from within when he met her was now beautiful on the outside as well.

Astonishingly beautiful. Impossibly beautiful. Unbelievably beautiful.

Unapproachably beautiful.

Too good for crippled Sam Blake.

"Pru, what happened to you in the last four months?"

She didn't take her eyes off the road. "Do you mean, why didn't I visit or write?"

"Well, that, too, but I meant, you're—you're...Damn it, Pru, when did you become so God-damned beautiful?"

Suddenly, she laughed joyously. "It's amazing what happens to a body when one eats the way you do, Sam. The extra weight just melted off my body—a little like it melted off yours. Even I didn't know I was going to look like this. It feels wonderful to buy clothes nowadays...By the way, I like the way you look in that suit. You always did look nicer in a black suit than your jeans. I don't know if I ever told you that."

Sam hummed in response. He wasn't going to tell her the suit was given to him by mistake.

"Where are you taking me?"

She turned to him again and smiled that luscious smile that melted Sam to his toenails. "You'll see."

As they drove, Sam took his first look at Amarillo. It was a city caught halfway between its Western beginnings and its railroad modernization. Many men still wore side-arms, but the construction going on was as modern as any American city. They drove into an upper middle class residential neighborhood and stopped in front of a large-fronted building that seemed strangely out of place amid the houses.

"This looks like a commercial building."

"It was. It was built here all alone before the neighborhood turned residential. Come on down, Sam, I think you'll like it."

Sam rose and awkwardly groped with his feet to try to find the street. A moment later, Pru stood on the pavement near him, holding up her hand. He glared at her arrogantly.

Her response was to smile. "There's no need to play the hero for me, Sam Blake. Remember, *you* told *me* you were only the hero's best friend."

Sam looked into those beautiful brown eyes and saw no pity in them. Still, he hesitated.

"If it were me who was hurt, you'd give me a hand."

Entranced like a mouse in a snake's eyes, Sam gave her his hand and eased himself down from the buggy.

"Go on up to the door. I'll get your things and meet you there."

Slowly, Sam walked from the curb to the house. He was flabbergasted to see an incline instead of steps. He stood by the door and waited until Pru came up the ramp, the latchkey in her hand.

She unlocked the door and pushed it open. "Welcome to 315 Marston Street."

"Is this some kind of settlement house for cripples?"

Rather than rise to his bait, she beckoned, "Come in, come in."

The door opened on an entry hall that had a door to the right, one to the left, one straight ahead and also seemed to lead to a hallway. There was a combination hat rack/umbrella stand just inside the doorway with a small footstool beside it. Before Sam could do anything, Pru stepped on the stool, whisked his hat off his head and planted a kiss on his cheek.

As Pru hooked the tan hat on the hat rack and stepped off the stool, Sam was recoiling from the streak of lightning that shot through him from that playful little kiss. He had not expected to be so affected. She was playing havoc with his senses.

Gesturing to the door on the right, she said, "That's the front hall closet—for coats and cloaks in cold weather and when guests come to call." Gesturing to the door on the left, she added, "That's one door to the formal parlor. Straight ahead," she indicated, "is the formal dining room, which leads to the kitchen." She placed a gentle hand on one of Sam's white-knuckled ones and caressed it casually but tenderly as she smiled. "Come take a look at the kitchen."

Sam could never remember seeing Pru so buoyant. He followed her into the dining room, noticing as he did that, nearly invisible on first glance, where the dark paneling met the stenciled wallpaper there were wooden railings like the parallel bars in the rehabilitation room, held up by brass fixtures about every three feet. The barres were just about even with the height of Sam's cane handles.

As they approached the door to the dining room, Sam glanced to his left down the hall. In the gaslight, he could see the entire hallway had similar paneling and barres, except on the doors to the rooms.

Pru opened the door and stepped into the dining room, Sam behind her. The dining room had a beautifully shiny table large enough to seat twelve. At the head and foot were sturdy carved armchairs with chintz upholstery. The ten side chairs had no arms, but were otherwise identical. The carving looked like roses, intricate and delicate, but it flashed through Sam's mind that the armchairs looked sturdy enough that he could use the arms for leverage when he needed to stand. There was also a large sideboard with a beveled glass mirror and some shiny silver trays and other hollowware on its shelves.

"Do you remember Bob Bonetti?" Pru said. "He was a hand at the Bar M?"

"The reader."

Pru nodded. "His father and younger brother are cabinetmakers *par excellence*. They produced most of the furniture in the house...Come see the kitchen."

Again Sam followed Pru beyond the dining room to a bright, airy kitchen with plenty of windows. There was an enamel stove and oven, cupboards of all kinds and storage bins, a sink with faucets rather than a pump and—of all things—an icebox. Blond wood counters skirted from the sink and on the opposite wall. In the center of the room was a blond wood table in the Shaker style with six ladderback chairs, two of which had armrests. There was a door leading outside.

"There's a carriage house out back and room for a garden and a table for dining *al fresco*. Nameless is stabled in there and there's more than enough room for Max and my buggy and even a couple more horses and another wagon or carriage of some sort...I can put on some water, if you'd like a cup of tea, or I can make coffee. We have indoor plumbing, running water and a boiler for hot water," Pru offered brightly.

"Maybe later," Sam said absently. This room also had the railings, though they were painted white to blend in with the wallpapered walls.

Pru came up very close to Sam and touched her hand briefly to his cheek and smiled. Sam closed his eyes for a moment as he smelled the faint fragrance of tuberoses. He was going mad from wanting her. He would have sold his soul just to turn his face into her hand and kiss the palm. He noticed that she slowed her steps to accommodate his labored stride, yet her whole body radiated excitement as she led him on her grand tour.

"Come see the rest of the house."

They walked back through the dining room and down the hall and Pru opened the first door on the left. "This is the other entrance to the formal parlor."

Sam walked inside. There was a large fireplace with a carved mantel. Numerous upholstered sofas, chairs and small, carved tables were scattered about the room. Again, as in the dining room, the chairs had arms and appeared sturdy. There was a Persian carpet on the dark-stained, polished floor. A breakfront with glass doors revealed a bar with cut crystal decanters of whiskey and brandy, pitchers for water and glasses to drink them in. "This room is large enough for entertaining, card playing and such. And there's room for a piano if you want." Once more there were brass-fitted wooden railings on every wall, interrupted only by the two doors and the fireplace.

"Come on." She touched his hand and beckoned.

They left the formal parlor and returned to the hall. Pru pointed out a door she described as a linen closet. Then she threw open all the doors on the right side of the hallway.

Two were unfurnished, having only paneling, whitewash, barres and polished floors. "These can be furnished later," she commented. A third was a bedroom with a bed made, a closet door, draperies on the large window, a dresser, vanity table and the—by now—ubiquitous railings. A steamer trunk stood closed at an off angle. There was another Persian carpet on the floor.

The next room was a bathing room with a large, porcelain and cast iron, enameled claw foot bathtub, commode and sink with counter space. "This is the guest bathroom, but if the two additional rooms end up bedrooms they can use this bathroom also."

The last door on the right was a large, bright master bedroom. The wallpaper above the rail-bedecked paneling was blue and elegantly simple in design. There was a tall dresser and a long dresser, a cheval mirror, a vanity, two sturdy armchairs, a pair of bedside tables, a large Persian carpet and the biggest bed Sam had ever seen. The bedstead was dark wood, carved with wheat like the remainder of the furniture in this room, and had to be eight feet long and eight feet wide. Sam walked over and gripped the heavy foot board and realized that it was the first bed he had ever seen except his hospital bed where he could sleep straight rather than at an angle. And it was wide enough to have plenty of room for sex play, he thought, then flushed at the impossibility of what he was thinking.

There were two doors to one side of the bedroom. Pru opened one to reveal a walk-in closet. One side of the closet had a supply of men's garments, all of them new. Some were more formal and some more casual, but all of them appeared to be of fine fabrics, though none quite as fine as the cashmere suit he was wearing. The other side of the closet was bare, as if waiting for someone to put clothes on that side.

The other room was another bathing room, but this one was special beyond belief. The commode had a railing beside it, as did the walls, but the bathtub was amazing. It was wide and deep, easily accommodating two people if they wanted. But more than that, it was built of tile and designed so Sam could sit comfortably on a wide shelf that surrounded the tub, lift his legs and slide them over and—using a couple of brass handholds—ease himself into the tub without losing half the water or falling awkwardly. There was a towel rack in easy reach and he could use the handholds to pull himself out of the water and sit on the shelf to dry himself. The tub had two brass faucets and there was a steam radiator, the first Sam had ever seen. No, he remembered seeing those strange cast iron coils in the other three rooms on this side of the house. Finally the sink was built low enough that a chair could be placed in front of it and Sam could use the sink and mirror for shaving while sitting. A wooden armchair stood by one wall, waiting for him.

Sam had said little during this tour, but the bathroom floored him. "This house; it's been designed to accommodate the needs of a cripple like me."

"Indeed it has."

"Even all these railings, they're like the parallel bars. I could use them to walk around the house instead of two canes."

"That's true."

"And the furniture is all sturdy and reliable, nothing gilt or flimsy to slide around or collapse under me."

"Yes. There's one more room for you to see."

She led him out of the master bedroom and back into the hall to a door just opposite. She pushed open the door to reveal a small parlor. Another large fireplace dominated the outside wall with a love seat and a large, upholstered armchair facing it. On either side of the fireplace were large glass windows. In front of one was a large, roll-top desk with a wooden swivel chair before it and one of those newfangled typewriting machines on top of it. The other window seemed strangely empty. Sam felt something belonged in front of it, but couldn't say what.

The other three walls contained built-in, floor to ceiling bookcases, mostly empty, except that one was divided by a glass fronted gun cabinet with a lock. There were a rifle and gun belt in the cabinet. Sam went over to look at it. Still facing the gun cabinet, he said in disbelief, "Those are my guns."

"Yes."

He looked at the bookshelf. The books were mismatched, some of them with wrinkled spines. They were not show books. They were well-read and beloved volumes of literature, engineering, science, art. Sam reached up and touched the spines like old friends. "These are *my* books, from Santa Fe."

"Yes."

Sam hobbled over to the desk and sat in the swivel chair. It was the first time he had sat and he was shaking with emotion and pain. The desk was well stocked with paper, pens and ink. His own *Webster's Dictionary* and *Roget's Thesaurus* were caught between wooden bookends.

"Pru," he said in a voice choked with unnamed emotion, "where are the other handicapped people who live in this house?"

"There are none, Sam." She walked over to the desk and opened a drawer to remove a tri-folded legal document.

"If no handicapped people live in this house, how did it come to exist?"

"It was specially designed. There are no stairs, no second floor or basement. Everything is on this level, including the pantry and a storage shed in the back. Every room has railings. None of the carpets have any fringes and all of them are tacked down so you can't catch your braces, canes or shoes and trip. The floors are polished but they're not slippery."

Sam felt a clutching in his chest. "Pru, whose house is this?"

Pru pried open Sam's white-knuckled hand from around the hand of one cane. Looking at him straight in the eyes, she put the legal document in his hand and closed it over the papers, gently caressing his hand again as she did.

"It's your house, Sam."

Chapter 33

"It belongs to you."

Sam leaned his canes against the desk and opened the papers Pru handed him. It was a deed describing the property dimensions and location. The title was in the name of "Samuel Blake, a single man in fee simple."

He crushed the deed against his lap. "It can't be mine. A house like this must have cost thousands."

"Yes."

"The furnishings alone, not to mention what it must have taken to turn a mercantile building into a residence."

She shrugged. "That's true."

Sam looked down at his hands in misery. "Pru, I've spent almost every cent I had on my hospital bills and have no means of earning a living. I can't afford to buy a house like this."

She knelt beside Sam and covered his hands with hers. "There's nothing to afford, Sam. The house is yours, free and clear. There's no mortgage, nothing owing on any of the remodeling. You can live in it, sell it, burn it down, whatever you want, but I hope you decide to live in it. This house is unique. As far as I know, there isn't another like it in the world."

"Where did you find someone to put something like this together? I studied civil engineering; this was no mean feat."

"Thank you."

Sam's eyes widened and he took a deep breath. "You told me in Rincon you'd wanted to be an architect. *You* designed this and had it constructed."

"I did."

"Why?"

Pru stood again and leaned down until her face was a hair's breadth from his. "Because I love you," she said quietly and followed it by pressing her mouth against his.

Sam felt as if skyrockets were going off inside him. He wanted to resist, but he really didn't want to. He wanted to crush her against his chest and kiss her until all his pain and doubt vanished. Then he faced reality and pushed her away. He turned the swivel chair to face away from her.

"You can't love me."

Her hands gripped lightly around his shoulders. "You can't forbid it."

"How can you want to love me? I'm crippled."

Her lips and tongue tickled the back of his neck. "Are you?" she purred as she began to nibble at his ear.

His breathing came in deep gasps. "Please," he breathed.

"Hmmm?" She came around and feathered kisses on his cheekbone, lean cheek and jaw, then down to the underside of his jaw to his neck above his collar while her hand stroked at his vest.

"Please, Pru, you're too fine to want a cripple."

She knelt beside him and leaned casually on his thighs. Through his trousers she could feel the atrophy. She lowered her head and began to kiss and nuzzle his wasted legs through the fine wool, moving upward toward his groin.

"Pru, you don't want a useless man."

Right then, Pru pressed her mouth right on Sam's painfully erect penis and kissed him through his pants. He groaned.

"Hmm. This doesn't feel useless to me."

"God, oh God, stop it, please!"

Pru raised her head to look at him. Hunger and need warred with hopelessness in his dark brown eyes. A tear tracked down his face. She knew he wanted her as much as she wanted him, perhaps more. Still looking deep into his eyes, she reached up and yanked out the hatpin holding her hat on her head and tossed the hat aside. Then she pulled out the hairpins holding her hair in its style and shook her head to let it flow over her shoulders and puddle in Sam's lap.

"You have to go," he pleaded. "I have to go."

"Why, Sam?"

He closed his eyes against the pain and need. "I can't subject you to life with a cripple."

"Isn't it my choice?"

"You'll be an object of scorn."

Pru looked up at him. "This isn't Rincon, Sam Blake. I'm not some pathetic spinster schoolteacher anymore. In Amarillo, *nobody* ignores Prudence Hofheinz."

"You'll think I'm repulsive. I can barely walk. My legs are hideous."

She bent her head again and kissed his thighs, rubbing her cheek against the cashmere, caressing the wasted limbs with loving hands. "Do I act like I think you're repulsive? Considering your injuries, I thank God you have legs to walk on at all."

"I have no work."

"You're a Phi Beta Kappa, Sam. We'll think of something."

"I'm broke."

"I have money and a growing design business."

Sam gritted his teeth. "I can't let you support me."

A spurt of anger filled her. Pru stood abruptly and leaned over him, grabbing the arms of the chair. "For the love of God, Sam. If we were already married and this happened to you, would you be saying these things to me? What are you afraid of? My feelings or your stubborn male pride? You were injured doing your work, for God's sake. Is that any different than a war hero wounded in battle?" She gently put her hands over Sam's and bent to kiss his forehead. "Sam, open your mind and your heart. You have to redefine what it means to be a man. Circumstances *demand* it." She feathered kisses on his cheeks, brow and nose before teasing his mouth with her tongue and teeth. "Don't be ashamed of your handicap, beloved. You came by it honestly; you've battled to come so far so fast. Some men might have given up and imprisoned themselves in an invalid chair. Not you. You fought to walk again and you did." She continued to kiss him as her eyes filled with tears. "Do you know what I saw that day in the hospital that frightened me so much? Not your legs. I looked at a man so tall and lean and handsome I couldn't imagine how he could still be interested in a plump little mouse like me. I knew you could find someone so much prettier than I."

"You were the most beautiful woman I ever met," Sam rasped back. "It shone through your eyes and your smile like a beacon. I loved you so much I couldn't think straight. I didn't know how everyone in that jerkwater town missed how lovely you were."

The tears gathering in Pru's eyes threatened to splash over. "Sam," she said in a near whisper, "this is the first time you've ever said you love me. Don't push me away, my love. Marry me."

"I can't."

"You wanted to once, didn't you?"

"How did you..."

"You bought a ring at Jackson's. I found it when I was packing up your things to take to Dr. Richards'. I recognized the bag it came in. You were going to propose."

"That was before."

"Before you were hurt?"

"Yes."

"Why were you going to propose?"

"I loved you. I needed you. The empty feeling in my gut disappeared when we made love." He groaned. "Damn it, I felt whole when I was with you."

Without warning, Pru slid her arms around his torso just under his arms. Holding him tightly, she lifted him just enough to kick at the swivel chair. It rolled back on its casters and Sam landed on the floor flat on his back.

A moment later Pru lay half on top of him, kissing him hungrily on the mouth, biting and nibbling at his lips, urging him to take her with his tongue. She kissed his cheeks and ran her tongue around the shell of his ear.

"Tell me the truth, damn you," she hissed in his ear. "Tell me it's different now. Tell me and I'll leave. This house is yours whether I stay or go. Just tell me honestly you don't love me anymore. Just tell me honestly the hole in your belly doesn't go away."

She felt him trembling and placed her hands on his pale, lean cheeks, staring straight into his bespectacled eyes. "Can you honestly tell me you no longer love me?"

"God, no! You're my heart and soul!" His arms came around her and crushed her against him there on the floor. Although he was on his back and Pru was on top of him, he began to take charge of their lovemaking. One of his hands snaked up and laced fingers through her hair, drawing her face back to his, kissing her hungrily, thrusting his tongue into the sweet cavern of her mouth as his throbbing manhood wished to do with her sweet body.

Her hands stroked his face, smoothed the soft curls of his hair, and caressed the powerful chest beneath the brocade vest. Her nipples ached to feel his touch. Boldly she pulled open his necktie and tugged open the collar stud and the buttons on his vest and shirt. Searching hands spread open his garments, uncovering the newly sculpted chest, flat ridged belly and prominent ribs covered with the familiar thick mat of soft black hair she had always found so arousing. Pru lowered her head and nuzzled her nose against his chest, kissing and nibbling provocatively at the metamorphosed frame as she had when he was larger and rounder but equally as dear.

"By God, I need to feel you," Sam groaned. He reached for her velvet-covered shoulders and pulled her until she knelt beside his ribs. He began to tug at her buttons and she quickly helped him, releasing the buttons on her skirt and petticoats. He pushed the outer garments away and began to attack the hooks on the front of her corset while she shrugged off her polonaise and blouse and tossed them somewhere away from them. Her corset came off with an easy last pop.

For a moment, Pru stood and pushed her skirts to the floor, kicking them away from her as she did. She stood in front of him, clad only in her shoes and hose and a chemise that ended about mid-thigh.

Sam gasped. Pru was not wearing drawers or pantalets. Her nipples were already distended beneath the fine lawn of her chemise and Sam could see the darkness of her aureolae. The aching longing in his manhood returned, tenting his trousers.

Pru saw him looking at her and her own aching in her loins grew almost unbearably stronger, drenching her with readiness for him. She squatted beside him, unbuttoned his trousers and released his suspenders. Sam lifted his hips enough for Pru to tug his trousers down past his knees.

"Oh, God, no!" Sam cried as his shriveled thighs, horribly scarred knees and the tops of his braces were revealed.

Pru looked him hard in the eyes, all the love she ever had for him telegraphed in hers. She knelt beside him and kissed the scars on his knees with the same loving attention she had focused on his face and chest. Her hands stroked the fine hairs on the wasted legs as her kisses moved upward.

She looked up a moment as she could hear that he was holding his breath. "I won't lie, Sam. They're not as beautiful as the rest of you, but they're a badge of honor and part and parcel of the man I love. You have always been more than the sum of your individual parts." To her relief, she heard Sam begin to breathe again.

So she forced him to catch his breath again as she scooped a hand around his scrotum and kissed the velvety tip of his straining shaft.

"Stop that or I'll explode," he groaned.

Laughing, Pru straddled him, her chemise hiking to her hips.

He reached for her, but she grabbed his hands in hers and pushed them to the floor. Wriggling her hips to cause him exquisite agony, she teasingly guided his manhood to find her sheath. She was deliciously wet and gloriously aroused and she slid around his huge shaft like her body was custom-tailored to fit him.

He was so tall she could not kiss his mouth and keep him inside her so, still holding his hands to the floor, she bent to kiss his chest as she began to rise and fall, sliding over the sex-dampened penis in a rhythm designed by Nature to accommodate his need. He could raise his hips slightly in response to her movement, and she plunged as hard as she could upon him, riding him until both of their bodies were sheened with sweat, her chemise clinging to her damp body like a second skin.

The friction was raising them both to a frenzy as she impaled herself deeper and deeper onto him until she would swear the length of him touched her womb itself. The aching pleasure of her growing climax threatened to shatter her, but she plunged down again and took him inside her until she cried out and shuddered the waves of shocks that accompanied Sam's lovemaking. He roared himself and Pru felt him emptying himself inside her.

With him still buried deep inside her and her legs still astride his hips, she lowered herself to lie on his chest and released his hands. His arms came around her, tenderly holding her against him as sleep overcame her.

Lying on the Persian carpet in the study of the house on Marston Street, the woman he adored enveloping him in the power of her love and her body, Sam came to a realization.

As he had felt when he was able-bodied, he still felt the same way crippled.

In Pru's arms, the hungry ache in his belly went away.

In Pru's arms, he felt whole and complete.

Regardless of what the future brought, he could not send her away from him.

They belonged together.

He stroked her fragrant hair and whispered, "Marry me, Pru. I can't live without you."

She stirred slightly and raised her head. Sleepily, she responded, "Oh, Sam, this is so sudden."

He chuckled and fell asleep still joined inside her.

When his mind returned to his head a few hours later, Sam wasn't sure he hadn't been in part of a lovely dream. The scent of tuberoses and lovers' musk drifted into his nose and he opened his eyes to see Pru's head resting on his chest, her body draped down his torso and her legs still straddling his hips. A more sensual blanket he could not recall. He'd been such a fool. She had brought him back to his senses, thank God. To all of his senses.

Discerning the difference in his breathing, Pru stirred. She turned her head a quarter turn down and began feathering kisses over the sculpted pectoral muscles while her hands stroked his arms through the sleeves of the shirt that was pushed wide open but still on. She could feel his relaxed shaft still inside her and she squeezed her nether muscles around him.

Sam groaned slightly. "Kiss my mouth, Pru," he commanded huskily.

Pressing her lips to his chest again, she said, "You're too tall, Sam. If I move up, you'll slide out."

He grasped her shoulders and pulled her up. "I'll risk it." He kissed her in that tender, teasing, loving way that was connecting without being possessive. She opened her mouth to his explorations and let him nibble at will.

"Pru," he whispered against her mouth.

"Hmmm?"

"Do I recall asking you to marry me?"

"Uh-huh. You won't renege, will you?"

Sam sighed. He was caught up in a maelstrom he could not control; nor was he sure he wanted to control it anymore. "I won't renege. So when should we get married?"

"Fr. Maris will be by around noon tomorrow with a couple of witnesses."

"I'm not Catholic."

"Neither am I, but I can't imagine anyone else marrying us."

Sam took Pru's face in his hands and looked at her owlishly through his glasses. "Pru, how would Fr. Maris know to be here tomorrow noon?"

She just blinked at him without answering.

He frowned. "You were pretty sure of yourself." There was a touch of anger in his voice.

"No, Sam, I took a calculated risk. If you refused, I was prepared to leave."

"But what about this house?"

Pru put her own hands on her lover's angular cheeks. "As I said before, this house is yours, not mine. Whether I stay or go, that doesn't change unless you change it."

"You're too good for me."

"And you're too good for me, so we're even."

There was a pregnant pause.

"Pru?"

"Hmm?"

"Why are we lying here on the floor half dressed when there's a perfectly wonderful-looking bed in the next room?"

Pru began to laugh from the depths of her soul. "God, I love you!"

Soon Sam was laughing. "And I love you, so we're even."

Pru scrambled off Sam's chest and stooped beside him. Sam reached out his hand and began to twist his body, trying to reach his canes, which had slid down in front of the desk.

Pru touched his shoulder, then held out her arms to him. "Come, my precious love," she said solemnly, "you can lean on me."

Sam straightened and looked at her. In her lawn chemise with her dark hair tousled, she looked like a windblown angel. There was no condescension in her voice or attitude. Her face and eyes were radiant with love. Sam realized he need never be afraid of being weak with her. She would give him her strength in those times when his own failed him. He realized that to Pru, his handicap was not a defect, merely his state of being. From the moment she climbed down the mineshaft to help him, she had taken charge, not with any regard to roles or expectations, but because it needed to be done. If there was ever a definition of "help-meet," it was this strong, sensuous, brilliant woman.

Sam used his arms to raise himself to a sitting position, then tucked his feet up against his buttocks. Looking straight into Pru's eyes, he reached out his arms to her. She came into his embrace, sliding her arms beneath his and around his chest and began to stand, bringing him up with her until he was standing. She slid one arm around his waist and bent slightly to pull up his fallen trousers and close the top fly button. That done, she allowed him to lean against her as, with both her arms now encircling his waist, she made the slow walk with him into the bedroom. Before sitting on the bed, Sam released the button so his trousers would slide down.

"Are you hungry?"

"Ravenous," he said slyly, making it clear it wasn't food he wanted.

"Get undressed, you," she teased. "I'll be back in a second," and she darted out of the room.

She came back a few minutes later. Sam's canes were under one arm, her clothes across that arm, and a Wedgwood dinner plate in the other hand. Sam sat up in bed, braced against the pillows and headboard, the covers up to his waist. His clothes were neatly lying over the foot-board of the bed and his glasses were the only thing he was wearing.

Pru laid her garments over the back of a chair and approached the bed. There was a brass umbrella stand next to one side table Sam had not noticed before into which Pru deposited the canes. She picked up his shoes with the braces still attached and moved them next to the umbrella stand. Both were within easy reach of the bed, Sam realized, allowing him to gain access to those necessities conveniently when he needed to leave the bed.

"You thought of everything."

"I tried," she said as she climbed onto the bed next to him.

"What did you bring?" he asked, referring to the plate.

"Let's see," she said, "a couple of hard boiled eggs, tomatoes sliced in wedges, some pared raw carrots and a couple of sectioned oranges."

"Oh, and what are you eating?"

Pru looked at him seriously and said, "Just under half of what's here."

Sam laughed. "You're going to keep me on the straight and narrow, huh?"

She laughed back. Kissing him, she said, "Uh-huh. Very straight," then brushed her hand along his side down to his blanket-covered hips, "and very narrow."

Funny how the food seems more delicious when eaten between kisses, Sam mused as he nibbled and kissed his way through lunch.

They teased each other, licking each other's fingers, each starting at one end of a carrot stick and meeting with a kiss in the middle, tickling each other's ribs. In the hospital, Sam could have polished off his small ration of food in minutes and still felt hungry. This lunch took over half an hour to finish and led to a splendidly playful session of lovemaking, marred only when Sam twisted in the wrong direction and a blast of excruciating pain shot through his knees. Immediately he stopped as a film of sweat covered him and the color drained from his face.

Pru saw the pain reflected in his eyes and eased him onto his back, helping him to straighten out his legs. Sam took deep, ragged breaths until the pain subsided. Pru sat on her haunches beside him on the mattress, trying to use the touch of her hands to soothe the tension in his face.

He looked up at her myopically, since he had taken off his specs when they started to make love. "Can you bear a lifetime of this?" he rasped. "Never knowing when the wrong move will bring pain so intense I can't function?"

"Is there anything you can take?"

"Nothing that wouldn't make an addict of me." He gestured down the length of his body. "Is this what you want to marry?"

Pru smoothed an errant curl from his brow with tender hands. "We'll find solutions, sweetheart. If they're unconventional, well, that's nobody else's business." She kissed his eyelids, cheekbones, nose. "I want to be your wife. I want to live with you and love and care for you. I want to make love with you and sleep in your arms and, God willing, bear you children. Besides, I'm not exactly unfamiliar with pain. You got me through it then and I'll get you through yours when it comes. I don't know another man who would have stayed with me like you did, knowing there would be no gratification for yourself. Give me the right to be there for you."

Finally, the worst of it subsided and Sam lay back against the pillows, exhausted. Yet he opened his arms and gathered Pru against him to hold while he dozed.

"How are you feeling, Sam?"

He smiled. "Strong and full and whole. As you've always made me feel."

It was a fine sentiment to nap to on a cool November afternoon.

Chapter 34

"Pru?"

"Hmm?"

"This bed must have half a dozen pillows on it..."

"I like your chest better."

Sam sighed. He had proposed to a woman who liked to touch him. After a lifetime of little human contact, he found a woman who relished the feel of him.

"Maybe we should get you a fur-covered pillow slip. You might not be able to tell the difference."

She ran trails with her fingernails through the thick mat on his chest. "I'll think about it."

"Pru?"

"Hmm?"

"Would you mind if we got a cat?"

It was such a non-sequitur that Pru propped herself up on one elbow. "Where did that come from?"

"I never had a pet. With a father on the road and a mother who lived inside a whiskey bottle, I grew up without much of a home. I always envied the boys in school who had dogs, but I never dared have one. Sometimes, I wasn't sure what we were going to have to eat, much less being responsible for another living creature."

Pru realized that even with all the talking they'd done in the mineshaft, there was still a lot she didn't know about this man she loved. Spontaneously her eyes welled up again. Sam had known so much unhappiness in his life, so much abandonment. It was no wonder he had sought to reject her before she could reject him after his accident.

"We could get a dog."

Sam shook his head. "No. A dog needs to be walked and I can't do that. Cats take care of themselves."

Pru pushed herself up to where she could kiss Sam again. They exchanged nibbling kisses with a sensual ease neither of them would have thought possible six months prior. Sometimes it seemed to her she was melding with Sam, becoming shared souls.

"Sam, if you want a cat, we'll have a cat. As many as you like. I'll get you one for a wedding present."

She felt Sam distance himself slightly from her. Immediately her hand came to rest over his heart and stroked him when she felt the difference in his mood. "What is it, sweetheart?"

Sam's hands fisted at his sides. "You bought this house for me. I don't know how you did it, but I know you did. I'm sure you're the one who bought me those expensive clothes..."

"You didn't like the suit?"

"I *love* the suit," he snapped back. "I've never owned anything so fine. But I can't keep having you do it." He pushed himself into a sitting position against the headboard of the big bed, the covers shielding his body below the waist.

"It's my money, isn't it?" Pru said as she scrambled upright. "And once we're married it'll be *our* money. I don't intend to stop working now that I've found the work I was born to do. And I don't intend to leave my money sitting in a bank doing nobody any benefit."

Sam held up his hands. "Pru, Pru, I'm not asking you to do either." She looked so stricken Sam could not resist cupping her cheek with his large, long-fingered hand. Then dropping his hand wearily, he said, "but I have to have a livelihood. I'm sorry, darling, but my pride won't let you be our sole support. I'm not made that way. Except for college, I've been working since I was fourteen years old." He sighed. "I can't expect you to support us both. Call it foolish male pride, but I have to have work."

Pru folded her arms across her chest. Sitting tailor fashion on the bed, stark naked with her hair falling in waves about her, it looked faintly absurd.

"Well, Sam Blake, I never expected otherwise." Lifting one hand, she tapped her index finger against her chin. "Now," she said deliberately, "what can you do? Now let's see...hmmm..."

Sam frowned. "You're teasing me. I don't like it."

"Well," Pru frowned back. "If you keep glowering like that, you could be a bouncer. Even in braces, that look would scare people out of a saloon."

One corner of Sam's mouth lifted. He was fighting the urge to smile. "Be serious now."

"Okay, let's do this scientifically. What are your assets—your skills? You have a college degree..."

"In civil engineering. But I've never actually designed or built anything and I've been away from it for twelve years. The field is changing so fast I might as well have never studied it."

"Granted, but we already know you're not stupid. You have beautiful handwriting. I'm sure you had to study mathematics and geometry. Then you told me you worked for an insurance company for a year. You spent four years with the Texas Rangers and seven years as a range detective working with Clint..."

"The thieving bastard," Sam mumbled.

Pru smiled. The conversation was going exactly as she hoped. "Did you get those books I sent you while you were in the hospital?"

Sam frowned. "The only books I was sent were Wild West dime novels. You know them, the kind written by some hack writer who's probably never been west of the Susquehanna River."

Pru's eyebrows rose. "I always thought they were interesting. Real life adventures by real Western heroes."

Sam snorted in derision. "That's because you're from Chicago. Clint and I had more exciting adventures in a year than some of those frauds have had in their lifetimes."

Pru sighed. "Gosh, and I thought those fellows led such exciting lives."

Sam snorted again. "Probably they've had more exciting lives since the books were written."

"What do you mean?"

"Are you serious? Those stupid books made those men out to be heroes and lightning fast gunmen. Then every two-bit greenhorn who wants to make a name for himself goes looking for Bill Cody or Ned MacLaine and wants to shoot it out. They say it was because of those dime novels about Wild Bill Hickok that he got killed nine years ago."

"You don't say," Pru said contemplatively, then folded her knees up and hugged them while resting her head against her kneecaps. "Well, I guess if someone wanted to make a man's life really miserable, he could write a dime novel and give that man credit for all sorts of heroic adventures and legendary skills."

"I guess so."

She looked up. "And if those novels had a ring of truth because they were written by someone who actually lived in the West—and who could vouch for the authenticity of those adventures because it was well known throughout the Southwest that he was the hero's sidekick...and best friend..."

Sam's eyes widened. He reached over to the night table and grabbed his spectacles, quickly shoving them on his nose. "Prudence Hofheinz, you're not suggesting I write dime novels about Clint Randolph?"

She grinned. "Why not?"

"I'm not a writer."

"Couldn't you put words together at least as well as those East Coast hacks who wrote the books I sent you?"

"Of course I could," he snapped back. "That's not the point. Why would I want to make Clint the hero? *I'm* the one who did all the planning. *I* was the strategist. God damn it, Pru, *I* was the brains of the operation."

"But Clint took the bows. You let people think he was in charge. Who was the better shot?"

"It depends. He was quicker on the draw. I was more accurate."

"Who was the better tracker?"

"I was."

"Who was the better horseman?"

"Clint. Wind Dancer was the best trained piece of horseflesh I ever saw."

"Who got the recognition?"

"He did."

"And who got the ladies?"

"He did."

"And who never gave you recognition in public?"

"He did! And he stole my share of the reward money after I got the insurance company to offer it to us."

"Then who deserves more than Clint to have his life made completely miserable by becoming a Western Legend?"

Sam sat staring at Pru, letting the idea sink in.

"It's crazy!"

"Why? You had adventures, interesting cases, had to deal with robbers and rustlers, both in the Rangers and on your own. It wouldn't take much stretching to juice them up, make them a little bit more florid. Think about the possibilities of authentic sounding stories of a real range detective; someone who never failed to solve a crime. But instead of having them told by some hack, these tales will be told by someone who was actually there—the man who described himself to me as the hero's best friend—his faithful, loyal sidekick and partner, Sam Blake."

"But doesn't that put me at the same risk?"

Pru shook her head. "I don't think so. Let him be the genius, you the observer. Let him fight the battles you may have actually fought. Let the ideas come from his lips while you marvel at his brilliance."

"You make me sound like Sancho Panza."

"Excellent analogy," said the ex-teacher. "Besides, even these little worms who go after famous gunfighters have a code of sorts. There's not a lot of glory in facing off against a man with a cane in each hand."

A flicker of emotional pain crossed Sam's face, then fled, but not before Pru saw it. She crawled over to the headboard and rested her head against Sam's shoulder while her arms went about his waist. "Sweetheart," she said, kissing him on the soft spot on his neck behind the point of his jaw, "reality is reality. If we're going to have a life together, your handicap must be a given. I can't be afraid to bring it up and I can't pretend it doesn't exist."

"Then it *does* matter to you."

Pru blinked back tears. "Sam, darling, of course it *matters*. Do you think it doesn't tear at my heart to see the strong, fiercely independent man I love so...so...so much more...limited? I can't ignore it or hope it will go away because it won't." She placed her hand over Sam's heart. "But the man I love is in here. The Sam Blake I love is not in your knees or your occupation. The Sam Blake I fell in love with is a well-spoken, gentle man, the kind who could bring Shakespeare like some men bring flowers. A man who could make a woman feel well loved even when there's no release for him. You've put up with a lot of unnecessary unhappiness in your life so as to not be a burden to anyone, but you also put the good of your partnership ahead of personal aggrandizement because it seemed like the right thing to do at the time. Yes, your handicap matters to me, but my love for you is not diminished by it."

They sat in bed quietly for a long time. Sam was mulling over everything she said to him. She was right about a lot of things. He would have to learn not to be so defensive about his legs. They were a reality, a part of him as much as his height or his black hair or his glasses.

But a writer! He had never contemplated that kind of work. It was speculative. It wasn't steady. He had no idea if he would be any good at it.

Still, it was sedentary, ideal for a man for whom walking was difficult. It required no specific hours, ideal for a man who still needed to attend rehabilitation several times per week. He could do it right here in the small parlor of this house. There was even a brand new Remington typewriting machine on the desk...

Sam grabbed Pru by the arms and pulled her before him. "You were hoping I'd agree to try writing. You even bought me a typewriting machine, didn't you? You've been manipulating me."

"Call it a gentle push."

"What if I said, point blank, that I want nothing to do with writing any books?"

Pru pulled out of his grasp and sat on the bed. "Then we keep on exploring other possibilities. My designing has put me in contact with lots of members of the business community, wealthy men with big businesses with all sorts of offices around Amarillo who would be more than happy to consider hiring a brilliant, seasoned man like yourself who was injured in the line of duty."

"You mean they'd hire me because of you."

Pru climbed out of bed. "No, Sam. I mean you might find out about available positions because of me. They'll hire you because of you."

She disappeared into the bathroom. Sam heard the sound of water running in the sink. A few minutes later, Pru came out. Her face was damp, as were her thighs where she had just washed them. Picking up her clothes, she started to dress.

"Where are you going?"

"I have some errands to run and you've got some thinking to do. I'll be back in time to make dinner. You don't have to plan your entire future now. But if you decide you don't want to marry me, I'll pack my things and move out tonight."

Pru finished dressing. As she was leaving the master bedroom, she said, "The boiler's on, so if you want you can take a hot bath. I have to put up my hair before I leave."

She got as far as the door.

"Pru..."

She turned. "Yes, Sam?"

"Are you sure you want to marry me?"

"As sure as my name is Prudence Hofheinz. I love you, Sam Blake. Accept me or reject me, I always will."

She walked out of the room, leaving Sam with a lot to think about.

For a long while Sam lay flat on his back in that huge, comfortable bed, staring at the whitewashed, plastered ceiling as if he expected it to disappear. Finally, he realized that in the last six months, he had done his best thinking in the bathtub. He reached for his socks and shoes where they stood next to the bed, put them on and buckled his braces.

As he passed in view of the full length mirror, he had to laugh. He was standing there, stark naked except for his braces and shoes. The strong, well-muscled leanness of his upper body was in such contrast to his wasted legs it was is if someone had pasted together halves of two different men. But he and Pru had made love in full daylight and she had shown nothing except the passionate abandon of their first encounters.

After filling the bathtub with hot and cold running water and finding unscented soap and fresh towels within easy reach, Sam found that the wide-lipped bathtub was ideally designed to allow him easy ingress and egress. Pru had designed this entire house with his personal comfort and ease in mind. He would have a world of challenge to face beyond the doors of this house, but inside, she had created a world just for him. Then, somehow, she had made a present of her creation to him with no strings attached. He saw the deed. The house was his, free and clear. If he never saw her again the house was still his.

Sam leaned back in the tub and let the welcoming heat soak into his bones. Damn if it hadn't felt good to make love to her again. Even the pain in his knees had been worth it in exchange for the wondrous satiation of climaxing buried deeply within her. It was as if a part of Pru flowed into Sam as easily as his seed flowed into her.

Suddenly, Sam pushed himself upright. Damn it, but he'd forgotten his good sense again. He'd put her at risk of pregnancy again and she'd let him. Despite his initial resistance, he had wanted to make love with her to prove he still could.

He had to marry her.

Sam splashed at the water. "You god damned ass," he said aloud. "Why do you keep on talking like you're trying to make up your mind? You've wanted to marry her since the night you met. She just about compromised you this afternoon. Stop being such a fool and marry the girl. That way, instead of worrying about whether you got her pregnant, you can worry about what names to give the children."

He relaxed in the tub, a half smile on his lips. Children! God, how wonderful it would be to have children; his and Pru's together. She wouldn't be a drunk like his mother; he wouldn't be a traveling man, never home, like his father. He would stay at home. Hell, even if he had a day job, how far could he travel? He'd come home every night to his wife and kids. He could read to them, listen to their prayers at night, tell them stories about traveling all over the West chasing rustlers and criminals...

And Pru. He could bet she'd be beautiful when large with his children. He closed his eyes and imagined himself with his ear pressed to her belly listening to their child kick and move inside her...

And she could keep working if she wanted. They could have everything they ever wanted. All they had to do was get married.

And they could do that tomorrow.

Pru came back into the house about half past six with a couple of picnic baskets on her arms. It was past dusk and the house was dark except for a light she'd seen in the window of the study. Pru lit a lamp by the door and carried it into the hall, lighting lamps as she proceeded down the hallway. She had conduits behind the plastered walls to electrify the house once the power and light company electrified this neighborhood. Until then, they could make do with lamps or gaslight. One basket she left just outside the dining room.

Carrying the other, she walked down the hall. She heard a strange, arrhythmic clattering coming from the study. Standing in the doorway she saw Sam sitting at the desk. A lamp was lit just above his head, casting bluish highlights on his raven curls. He wore a pair of denims and a collarless white dress shirt with the sleeves rolled up. His canes rested against the desk. There was a piece of paper in the typewriter and a small stack of papers lying on the desk beside it. A pile of crumpled papers sat in the wastepaper basket. Sam was hunched slightly over the typewriter, carefully punching keys with one or two fingers of each hand.

Sam was so intent on what he was doing that he didn't notice her approach. The light from the lamp glinted off the lenses of his glasses, while his brow was furrowed with concentration.

She set down the picnic basket at her feet and stepped over to the desk to stand beside him and gently put her hand on his shoulder. Sam started a bit, then looked up with a sheepish grin. He looked so owlish behind his lenses, yet so handsome with the lamplight emphasizing his high cheekbones, angular cheeks and firm jaw.

"What are you doing?"

Sam grinned again and handed Pru the bottommost sheet on the stack of papers to his right. Pru held the paper near the lamp and read:

The Adve~~m~~ntur~~ed~~s of Clint Randol~~pj~~h, Range Detecti~~b~~ve

as ~~related~~ told to this ~~author by~~ reporter by Samuel Blake

It was in a saloon in Amarillo, Texa~~x~~s that I met Big Sam Blake for the first time. I have met all manner of men throughout the ~~w~~West, but I never met a man as big as Sam Blake.

He had just won a small stake playing poker and he loomed over me like a grizzly bear, a ~~huge man~~ giant with a face covered in thick black hair. He sat down at an empty ~~talbe~~ table and ordered a bottle of whiskey and two glasses, then beckoned me to join him.

*"I hear tell you're a reporter for one of ~~those~~ them Eastern papers," he said to me. I nodded and identified myself. The barmaid brought the bottle and glasses and set them before us. The giant man gave her the once over and her face went ~~plae~~ pale. He growled ~~slke~~ like the ~~beast~~ bear he so resembled and dropped his Stetson hat on the table beside him. "The ladies don't care much for me," he said, regret in his voice. "I'm too d****d big for them, I reckon. Anyway," he continued, "I hea~~t~~r tell you're looking for interesting tales of the Old West to send to your readers back East."*

I averred that this was indeed the case.

The big man leaned forward in his chair, took a sip of rotgut whiskey, ~~and~~ looked me strai~~fht~~ght in the eye and said, "Well, sir, I've got a story or two to tell you 'bout the ~~grte~~ greatest hero ever to come out of Texas, or anywhere west of the Mississippi as that goes."

"Lots of stories abound," I said, "and lots of men willing to tell those tall tales for the price of a glass of whiskey."

*The big man looked at me, insulted. "If you didn't just see, this here bottle I paid for myself. I ain't no drunk, nor no fool neither. What I'm fixing to tell you are the true and unvarnished adventures of a fellow who always got his man and always solved his crime, who nobody could ~~outshoot and nobody could~~ outride and nobody could outshoot. I rode with the man for years, so I reckon I know what's true and what ain't. And if that ain't good enough for you, I could take my stories to Ned Buntline and d****d if he wouldn't be interested in setting them down on paper for me."*

What could I say? I was not about to let Ned Buntline get the scoop on me. I ~~took~~ pulled my pad and pencil from my pocket, wet the end of the pencil and told the big man to proceed. I offered him a Lucky Strike from my pack, but he refused, saying he did not favor tobacco because his mother told him it would stunt his growth. I could not help but wonder if a little tobacco would not have stunted this man down to a normal size like you and me.

The bearded giant took another sip of whiskey and began to talk . He said:

To introduce myself, my name is Samuel Blake. ~~Tehy~~ They call me Big Sam. I first met Clint Randolph in the fall of 1865. At the time he was ten years old and I was fourteen. He was a handsome kid for all he looked to have Injun bloo~~k~~d in him and tall for his age, 'though not near as tall as me.

Times was tough in San Antonio after the War ~~for Southern Succession~~ Between the States and Clint's daddy was a carpetb~~gg~~agger if there ever was one. On account of his daddy, everybody in school hated Clint as well. He was called a lot of names, "Half-breed" being the most polite of them. He got in a lot of fights. Since my own daddy left Texas in '61 to fight for the Union, I knew what it was to be called a "Yankee lover" and such like. So Clint and I, we became pals on account of everyone hated us for w~~at~~hat weren't exactly our fault.

"Excuse me, Big Sam," I interrupted, "is this Clint Randolph a half-breed?"

"Well," he answered me, "I reckon he is, but I better explain. There's all kinds of Injuns here in America. There's the kind of Injuns who lived on the prairie and followed the buffalo, like the Sioux, Cheyenne and Pawnee. Them's the kind the Army calls 'hostiles' and tries to rub out. Then there's the kind that lived along the East Coast when the first settlers from the Old World came to these shores. They had their own villages and settled in one place and were farmers and hunters, like the Iroquois, Cherokee, Oneida and Seneca. One of Clint's granddaddies or great-granddaddies, I ain't sure which, was from one of them farming tribes. By the time you get down to Clint, the only thing that was really Injun about him was he had straight as an arrow black hair, a copper cast to his skin and almost no beard. He was a farm boy clear to the bone who made himself into a hero by sure grit."

I urged Mr. Blake to go on with his ~~sotry~~ story and he continued:

Well, Clint being born in Ohio, he didn't exactly know how to use a six-gun when he came to Texas, so I commenced to teach him and he took to it like a duck to water. It wasn't too long before he could outdraw me and everyo other boy in the school. I never seen a boy so fast with a gun and I seen plenty in my time.

And horses! I tell you, Clint Randolph on top of a horse was like they was one creature instead of being two. He came by that natural somehow. He could ride like the wind and he took to naming his horses with "Wind" in their names. There was Storm Wind and West Wind, Wind Spirit and finally, his greatest horse, Wind Dancer, that he was riding when I last rode beside him.

After graduating from grammar school I took to ~~wragling~~ wrangling while I waited for Clint to finish up with school. We had a plan to join up together in the Texas Rangers.

So, the day after Clint go his diploma, we ~~did~~ joined up...

"Well," Sam said anxiously, "what do you think?

He looked at her. Tears were streaming down her cheeks. In a choked up voice, she said, "Oh, darling, it's a wonderful start!"

"My typewriting isn't so good."

"It'll get better with practice. I almost laughed out loud when I read the part about not smoking because it might stunt your growth."

Sam chuckled. "I thought that was a snicker I heard. You don't think I made myself sound too stupid?"

Pru shrugged. "I don't know. Your Big Sam isn't a Phi Beta Kappa, but you gave yourself credit for teaching Clint to shoot. It makes a fine contrast between the hero's sidekick and the newspaperman with the perfect formal grammar who's taking this down. Really, Sam, it's marvelous."

Sam reached up and pulled Pru down and kissed her tenderly. "Do you think your husband-to-be will make a good writer?"

Pru kissed him back and nuzzled him near his ear as she whispered, "Yeah. And I think the writer-to-be will make a good husband." She reached over for the picnic basket she had brought into the study. "A wedding present."

With a sweet half grin, Sam popped open the latch on the basket and opened the lid. Nestled on a pile of folded flannel dozed a tiny black kitten with a white face, belly and socks. A red silk ribbon bow was tied around its neck. Gingerly, Sam lifted it in his big hands and held it up near his face. The kitten, disturbed from its slumber, opened its baby gray eyes and clamped down its needle-sharp claws into Sam's hand.

"Ow!" Sam exclaimed, but did not drop the kitten. "What's its name?"

"She's your cat, Sam. You can name her anything you want—except 'Nameless.' A client's cat had kittens a couple of months ago, so when you told me you wanted a cat, I asked her if one was available. She's the runt of the litter, but she's healthy and she's yours."

As Sam stroked the furry throat of the tiny creature, he felt warm metal. He saw the ribbon around its neck was laced through two plain gold wedding bands.

"My parents' wedding rings," Pru explained. "My father wore my mother's ring on his watch chain from the day she died until he remarried. Do you mind wearing his ring, or me wearing hers? I never thought to marry and even if I did, I never thought Mama's ring would fit me, but with the weight I've lost it does."

Sam lowered the kitten into the basket and reached to put his arms around Pru's waist and draw her to him. "I'd be honored. I did a lot of thinking this afternoon and came to the conclusion that the path that led me to you was somehow pre-ordained. If I hadn't been injured, I might have ridden out of Rincon without ever proposing to you, even after having bought that silver ring. I'm still not sure I'm worthy..."

"Sam..."

"Please, let me finish. The Rincon job was supposed to be my last. I retired, though not the way I planned. As I said, I'm not sure I'm worthy of your love, but I love you so much I really only feel complete when I'm near you..."

Pru leaned over and rested her cheek on top of Sam's head while her arms encircled his shoulders.

"...I want to be your husband. I want you to be my wife. I want to make love with you and have babies with you and grow old with you and wake up in the morning and know that if you're not beside me, you're only a short walk away. If I had to become a cripple in order to stop running away, well, maybe God was telling me, 'Sit still, Sam Blake, and let your dreams find you.'"

Pru kissed his baby soft, clean-smelling, black curls and squeezed him tightly. "I found you, Sam Blake. And our dreams are the same. I guess they were meant to be."

Chapter 35

Amarillo, Texas, December 8, 1891

Mr. Ravenswood held out his hand to Clint Randolph in a shake of farewell.

*"Well, Mr. Randolph, you did as promised," he said. "You routed those d****d rustlers and saved our cattle drive. We couldn't have done it without you."*

Clint took the man's hand and shook it with his strong, steady grip. "Just doing the job you hired me for, Mr. Ravenswood," he answered, as he always did when folks would praise him.

"We'd be much honored if you'd consider settling in our little town. We could sure use a sheriff as brave and fast on the draw as you."

Clint shook his head. "That's mighty nice of you, sir, but I reckon I'll be moving on." He patted Wind Dancer's powerful neck and said, "Wind Dancer gets skittish if we stay in one place too long. I reckon we'd better ride. Come on, Sam, the sunset won't wait for us."

Well, sir, I mounted up on old Nameless as Clint touched the brim of his black ten gallon hat in one last salute and we galloped out of Eldorado, leaving nothing behind us but a cloud of dust, a job well done and a memory those folks won't soon forget about what it meant to be saved by a true hero of the Old West.

By the time Sam finished his tale, we had finished the pot of coffee and I had gone through two pads and five pencils. The poker game two tables away had just broken up and there was nobody left in the saloon but the old man who swept up the place and the bartender who gave us that "time to go now" look.

Big Sam and I walked outside. "So where did you and Clint go from there?" I asked.

The big man grinned from behind his beard. "Well, sir," he said, "I reckon you'll have to come again tomorrow and I'll be glad to tell you all about it."

"Now, Big Sam, was everything you told me true?"

He grinned again. "Well, sir, I may have changed a few names here and there so's not to give offense to anyone who might not take too kindly to being mentioned, but I was there when all this happened and if it ain't true, I don't rightly know what is."

He raised his fingers to the brim of his camel-colored Stetson and lumbered off into the dawn sky.

I could hardly wait until tomorrow.

Sam typed the final words on the page and ripped the sheets out of the platen of the typewriter. He could manage a good forty to fifty words a minute now that he learned the Touch Typing System. Pru teased that if he ever ran out of stories he could always get a job as a secretary—but Sam told her he looked terrible in shirtwaists. With a practiced hand he separated the original, copy and carbon paper, putting each in its proper pile. The first draft of the fifteenth dime novel in the six years since he started writing was finished. He would spend the next few weeks rewriting and refining before sending it to his publisher in New York.

He stretched his arms way over his head and made circles with his neck to relax his tired muscles. White Faced Finney, his wedding present cat, stood up on Sam's lap and stretched herself before jumping off and dashing off in pursuit of her own mysterious cat agenda. The little cat had long ago staked out Sam's lap as her favorite sleeping place whenever Sam was working or reading. With a cat's unusual sense of what is comfortable, Finney found nothing objectionable about the matchstick legs hidden under the comfortably worn and faded denim jeans the tall, handicapped author wore when he worked.

The house was quiet this morning. Sam glanced over to the other study window before which Pru's drafting table stood. He remembered when he first saw the room the day he got out of St. Giles the window looked empty. The day after the wedding the drafting table was moved in. There were days when Pru would sit for hours sketching plans and pasting fabric swatches while Sam sat at his desk typing and editing.

Today, Pru had driven her buggy out to a ranch outside the city where she was working with an architect to design a new ranch house. It would be well after dark before she got home. She had a fine new buggy horse in the traces these days, but both of them still missed gentle old Max. The poor brown gelding finally died of old age in 1889.

Sam glanced over at the mail Soledad had brought in earlier. She was a middle-aged woman whose husband had been a patient at St. Giles. She came in three or four days a week to do cleaning and laundry, plus a limited amount of cooking. The money she made helped her family get by. Since Sam could not hear down the other end of the house when he was working in the study, he didn't know what she might be doing now.

David was in school.

David Blake, named in honor of his godfather, Dr. David Maris, had been born barely nine months after his parents' wedding. His father's miniature, Davy was tall for his age and slender compared to other boys, with soft black curly hair and dark brown eyes. Because Sam couldn't run and play with Davy like other fathers, he spent a lot of time reading to his son. Thus, the boy began recognizing words at two and reading at age three.

Sometimes, Sam could hardly believe he could have had a hand in creating a life as precious as his little boy. People were often shocked by the overt affection the Blakes showed each other, but Sam loved Pru too much to care what others thought.

Sam picked up the pile of mail. He put some bills in the pigeonhole where they were held until they would be paid.

It had knocked Sam for a loop when Pru finally told him, after they were married, that her father was the owner of Holiday Meat Packing Company and she was bringing millions into the marriage. It was no wonder she could afford to design, remodel and give Sam this house. At first he was angry she had withheld the information, but she reminded him he would never have agreed to marry her if he thought she was quite that rich.

There were three envelopes addressed to Pru that revealed checks for design jobs when held up to the light. He put those envelopes in another pigeonhole. There was a letter from Bob Bonetti from Boston that Sam put on top of the desk to give to her when she came home.

There was a royalty check from Sam's publisher. Sam slit open the envelope and scanned the very enthusiastic cover letter. His books sold very well in the United States, Canada and England. Big Sam, The Hero's Best Friend, was a great success. Sam had successfully taken the big, lumbering galoot folks always thought he was and the pristine paragon of Western justice the same folks thought Clint Randolph was and made them real through the medium of print. Clint Randolph was the most famous Western Hero since Buffalo Bill.

Sam remembered the shock on his publisher's face the first time the man came to Amarillo and discovered his new author was a handsome, bone-thin, college-educated, clean-shaven, crippled giant who lived in a quiet residential neighborhood in Amarilllo with a wife and baby, who neither smoked, drank nor chased women and whose social circle included the most influential families in the Texas Panhandle. The publisher was even more shocked to discover this soft-spoken, ascetic-looking man in his mid-thirties had actually experienced—more or less—the adventures about which he wrote.

The Clint Randolph books sold like hotcakes. The fourteenth book was scheduled for publication in February 1892 and the fifteenth was completed today. Sam didn't know if Clint had made a fortune out of the reward money he stole, but tales about Clint's supposed exploits were making Sam a wealthy man in his own right.

A certain portion of their income was being donated to St. Giles. Dr. Maris was an honored guest in their home. His tireless writing and promotion of his practices were improving the chances of a full life for victims of severe injuries.

The cover letter said a separate parcel of reader's letters was on its way. The main Post Office in Amarillo also regularly forwarded letters addressed to Big Sam Blake, Amarillo, Texas, even when no more information was provided. Many were love letters from women who assured him that his being too large didn't give them a problem at all. There was a bittersweet irony that these women who were attracted to the fictional Sam Blake would never have given the real man the time of day.

Sam scanned the fan letters with glee. He was a success, in demand and appreciated for his own skills. He had a family that loved him and a career that sustained him. He felt light, almost giddy. If he could have, he might have danced.

Instead, he reached over to the rim of his desk and pushed off so his swivel chair twirled in a circle on its pivot. So what if he was forty-one and crippled and going white at the temples! There was no room in his life for past grief, past regrets, past hatreds.

Except one.

One of these days he was going to have to deal with the real Clint Randolph, the one who had betrayed him.

Rincon, December 8, 1891

"Randolph!" a stranger's voice bellowed across the smoke-filled saloon.

"Shit," grumbled Clint Randolph as he stubbed out his ever-present Lucky in an already overflowing ashtray and raked splayed fingers through his already disarrayed, waist-length black hair. "Another one."

Clint glared at the cards in his hand. He was about even on the night. His cards were mediocre this hand. He threw them face down, declaring, "I'm out." He glared at the half-empty whiskey bottle before him and the glass beside it, then thought better of it. He scooped his chips into his hat. "If this one kills me, tell Arabella to get out the red dress and dancing shoes."

The other gamblers at the table nodded perfunctorily. In the past five years, a steady stream of two-bit gunfighters would roll into town wanting to take on the boss of the Bar M. About three years ago, most of them had been privy to the sight of the former Arabella Morgan going after her husband with a riding crop immediately after a gunfight where he had been winged. Screaming like a fishwife, she told him if he got himself killed in a gunfight she was going to put on a red silk gown and dance on his grave. For a while after that altercation, Clint tried to go into Rincon unarmed, but some hotshot tried to take him on anyway. So now he always wore his holster into town, even on the rare Sundays he went with Arabella to church.

The Bar M was actually successful again. It took every cent of the money Clint received from the insurance reward, the Association fee and the bounty on Jack Derry to get the place marginally going, but by changing from cattle to horses and getting six years of normal rainfall, Ethan Morgan's old ranch had actually shown a profit the last two years.

At this rate, Clint might leave Arabella a well-off widow.

Clint held his hands away from his body as he turned. He left his hat on the poker table. His fellow players knew better than to disturb his chips at a time like this.

"What do *you* want?" he called to the dusty, unshaven cowboy with the double holsters tied to his thighs.

"You Randolph?"

"My name is Randolph."

"I hear tell you're fast on the draw, Randolph."

"Where? In some dime novel? What makes you think there's any truth to it?"

The gunman looked uncertain for a moment, as if the gears were turning in his brain. Even knowing he was not the world's brightest man, Clint realized that compared to this bastard, he was as smart as Sam Blake.

Sam Blake. It was his fault, telling that damned writer stories about their travels together. The writer had gotten it all mixed up, and now every tinhorn gunfighter wanted a piece of Clint's hide. The way the fellow wrote it, Clint was the brains of the operation, the best shot, the brilliant detective, the almost mythical horseman.

Clint even wrote a letter to the publisher in New York City asking him to stop publishing books using his name because of the trouble it was causing. For his pains he got back a form letter thanking him for his interest in the Clint Randolph series and advising him of the publication date of the next novel. He was also sent a sketch of two men that looked remarkably like Sam and him in their Texas Ranger days he guessed must have come from a photograph Sam had. After he saw that photo he let his hair grow longer than he had ever worn it in hope it would disguise him somewhat. If he had been able to grow a decent mustache or beard he might have done that as well, but that damned Narragansett blood made it impossible.

"They wouldn't publish it if'n it weren't the truth," said the gunfighter.

"Oh, God," Clint cursed, "It's a fucking work of *fiction*. That means it's make believe."

The gunman looked confused. "You saying you weren't no Texas Ranger?"

"No, I was a Texas Ranger."

"You sayin' you weren't no range detective?"

Clint sighed, wishing now he had taken that additional drink. "No, I was a range detective."

"And you got yerself a horse called Wind Dancer?"

"I *had* a horse called Wind Dancer, until one of you bastards shot him out from under me about three years ago." His new stallion, Black Wind, wasn't nearly as good a horse as Wind Dancer had been. "Look, mister," Clint said wearily, "I'm just a ranch owner now. All I want to do is be left alone to raise my horses and be with my wife. Those things you're reading about took place more than ten years ago, some of them. I'm retired, okay?"

Abruptly, the gunman narrowed his eyes. "Nobody *retires* on Pat Mulcahy. Leastwise, not upright. If you ain't outside afore I count thirty, I'll know you for the dirty, yellow-livered, dog-eating half-breed you are." The stranger then tromped out of the saloon.

Clint reached into his pocket for his pack of cigarettes, tapped one out and lit it, leaving it held between his lips. He shook his head and reached down to tie the thong that secured his holster to his thigh.

"You going to face him, Clint?" asked Rory Adamson.

"What choice do I have? I can be a live hero, a dead hero, or a—what did he say—a dirty, yellow-livered, dog-eating half-breed." He took a deep drag on his cigarette and blew the smoke out of his nose. He turned to Rory and said, "Watch my chips, Rory. If I'm killed, cash them in and bring the money to Arabella. If I survive, as God is my witness, I'm going to find Sam Blake and put a bullet through his heart."

Clint raked his hand through his hair again, stubbed out his cigarette, and stepped through the batwing doors into the overcast December afternoon sunlight.

Two minutes later, two shots were fired.

There was one more letter in the stack of mail, from the University of San Antonio.

Sam's jaw dropped as he read the letter. As a result of his successful stories, the university was inviting him to speak, à la Mark Twain, at their Mid-Winter Exercises in February. He was being honored because of his "contributions to the history and literature of the Frontier."

Sam blinked several times. He took off his glasses and wiped them with his handkerchief and read the letter again.

This crazy occupation! This work he did because he didn't need to be able to walk well to do it! A university wanted to honor him for his contributions to *literature,* for God's sake.

The boy with the drunken mother, Yankee father, who was too big and ugly for anyone to care about, who hadn't seen hide nor hair of San Antonio since 1869, was being invited back to his birthplace to be honored as some kind of literary hero.

Sam Blake: hero. Not the hero's best friend, but the hero.

It was unbelievable. He looked at the letter again. He would have to wire this Elliott Wainwright to make sure this was on the level.

There would be problems. Sam had not been more than a few miles outside Amarillo in six and a half years. He would have to learn how to maneuver himself through strange locales on canes and braces. The rest of the world would finally discover that Sam Blake was disabled.

Yet Sam realized he wanted to give that speech. He wanted the world to see Samuel Blake the author. A person who led as normal a life as one could in his physical condition; a person who learned to adapt to his changed circumstances: a survivor.

Sam put the letter with the others Pru needed to see. He pulled out his pocket watch and realized that it was nearly two o'clock and he had not yet eaten lunch. He reached for his canes and had just levered himself into a standing position when Soledad appeared in the study doorway, wringing her hands.

"*Señor* Blake."

"What is it, Mrs. Garrett?"

"Is the *policía* at the door, *Señor*. He say is something with *su hijo*."

Chapter 36

David?" Sam bit back, his grip on his canes tightening. "Get my corduroy jacket from my closet and meet me in the foyer," he added as he forced himself into motion.

When he reached the long hallway that separated the front rooms from the sleeping quarters he transferred both canes to his left hand and used the handrail to propel himself faster.

Standing in the foyer was a fresh-faced young deputy, looking stiff in one of those new uniforms. Of average height, the young man looked as surprised at Sam's height as he did by his handicap.

"You're Mr. Blake?" he asked with a swallow.

"I am. What's happened to my son?"

The deputy stiffened, seeming half-afraid this big man would grab him by the arm and haul him up, though on second thought that was surely unlikely.

"He was involved in a fight at school."

"A fight! He's five years old! How does a five-year-old get in a fight?"

"I don't know all the details. I was sent here to get one of his parents and bring you to the sheriff's office."

"Is he hurt?"

"Nothing serious, I'm told. Will you come with me now?"

By this time Soledad had brought Sam his jacket and Sam laboriously put it on, making the awkward transfer of canes from one hand to the other so he could reach into the sleeves with a free hand.

"Did you come in a carriage of some sort?"

The deputy looked embarrassed. "No, sir. I rode."

"Well, then, Deputy, if you'll accompany me to the carriage house, I'll need your assistance to saddle my horse." Sam reached for his camel hair Stetson, which sat on the hat tree in the foyer, and headed down the hall toward the dining room.

The deputy followed Sam through the dining room to the kitchen and out the back door, down the short incline and along the paved walkway with its wrought iron handrail to the carriage house. In one of the stalls Nameless stood contentedly chomping on his ration of hay. While Sam adjusted Nameless's bridle in a one-handed method he had developed over the preceding years, the deputy quickly threw the blanket and saddle on the dun's back and tightened the cinch.

Then, as the deputy watched in awe, Sam slid his canes into a rifle scabbard attached to the saddle, grabbed the pommel and back of the saddle and used his well-developed arm, shoulder and back muscles to pull himself to hip height even with the saddle, then swung one brace-stiffened leg over the saddle until he could sit upright. He reached down and bent each knee slightly to give himself a better seat, but did not use the stirrups, instead guiding the gelding out of the carriage house using the reins and his thigh muscles.

The young deputy could not know the hours of excruciatingly painful effort, the countless times spent in a crumpled heap on the carriage house floor, the daily determination it took to get Sam back up on Nameless's back and to retrain the horse. That Sam's mounting looked as effortless as it did was a tribute to the big man's determination to become as mobile as possible.

After closing the carriage house door behind Sam, the deputy raced up to the front of the house and was ready to ride as Sam approached from behind the house. Riding even with each other, they quickly covered the distance between Marston Street and the sheriff's office. Sam dismounted, leaning forward until he could swing his leg over the back of the saddle, then easing himself down until his feet touched the ground. He took his canes from the scabbard before letting go of the saddle horn, then flipped the reins over the hitching rail. Nameless had been trained to stay put and obeyed flawlessly while Sam hitchstepped his way around the hitching rail and eyed the steps up to the new brick sheriff's station warily. Even with handrails, stairs were a challenge, and this building had no handrail.

Sam groaned as he painfully pushed himself up the steps and entered the station house. Only concern for his son would make him do this. He approached the officer behind the desk and identified himself.

"I'm Sam Blake. Where is my son?"

The desk sergeant directed Sam to follow him to an impersonal office where he was shown to a chair before a desk. A moment later a senior officer came in.

"I'm Sheriff Flynn, Mr. Blake," the officer said, holding out his hand.

Sam ignored the hand. "Where is my son?" Anxiety colored his normally calm voice. "Is he hurt?"

"Beyond a bloody nose, a couple of shiners and some scratches, no. He may look like a raccoon for a while, but there's no serious damage."

Sam felt himself start to breathe more easily. "Who attacked him? Who would attack a five-year-old?"

"As best as we can piece it together, your son attacked the other boy in the school yard. Seems he got in a few good licks, but the other boy is older and heavier and turned the battle around. He was pummeling your boy pretty good before the principal and a couple of teachers pulled them apart."

"What started the altercation?"

"The what?" Flynn said in confusion.

"The fight."

"We're not sure. The Donnelley boy says your boy just started hitting him. Your son won't talk to us as all."

"May I talk to my son privately?"

Flynn nodded. "Sure." He looked down at Sam's canes. "I'll bring him here."

A few anxious moments later the door opened and Sheriff Flynn gently pushed David Blake into the room and closed the door between them.

Like a prisoner headed for the block, David walked from the door to the chair where his father sat. The slim little boy's dark brown eyes were red-rimmed from crying and dark-framed between his spiky black eyelashes and the bruising. Tear tracks and smeared blood from his nose were on his cheeks. His clothes were covered with dirt and dead grass, one shoulder seam was popped and the stockings beneath his knickerbockers were both torn at the knees.

Davy looked at his father, then turned back to the closed door, then returned his gaze to Sam. His lower lip was quivering as he fought off more tears that threatened to spill from his too large, expressive eyes. Despite his above-average height, nobody in his right mind could mistake this teary face as belonging to anyone but a five-year-old.

Sam leaned forward in the chair. "Davy?"

"They said you were gonna beat me," he said in a little voice.

"Have I ever?" Sam said gently.

The boy shook his head. Sam held out his arms and Davy ran into them, climbing into his father's lap and sobbing while Sam hugged him and stroked his hair, muttering endearments. Finally, cried out but still breathing raggedly, David sat up.

"Now, son, you want to tell me what happened?" Sam asked as he used his handkerchief to wipe the boy's face. "The sheriff says you hit the other boy first."

He nodded. "Yeah, but...yeah, but..."

"Sweetheart," Sam said tenderly, stroking his agitated son's shoulder, "why did you hit him?"

Davy took a deep breath. "Because he called you names."

Sam raised an eyebrow. "Called *me* names. Such as?"

"He said you were a liar. That everything you write in your books are lies."

"Well," Sam began carefully, trying to figure out how to say this to a five-year-old, even a bright one. "I write fiction. That's stories like the ones I read to you. They're not exactly lies, but they're not exactly the truth."

"I don't understand."

Sam took a deep breath. "Davy, you remember the book I read to you about Alice, the little girl who went down the rabbit hole?"

"Uh-huh."

"Well, Mr. Lewis Carroll wrote the story about a real little girl he knows named Alice, but the things Alice saw in the rabbit hole didn't really happen to her. That was Mr. Carroll's make-believe. Does that make him a liar?"

"I don't know."

"Well, before I ever thought I would have a wonderful little boy like you I had a friend named Clint Randolph and he and I rode all over Texas and New Mexico helping people catch cattle rustlers and stop battles between neighboring ranchers. Some of the things we did were very dangerous and exciting, and some were very hard work. What I do in my books is retell the stories of the jobs Mr. Randolph and I did to make them all exciting. So the stories are partly true and partly make-believe. Just like Mr. Carroll's Alice."

"So you *are* a liar."

"I don't lie about important things, but in my books some of what I write is not true."

"So you're *not* a liar?"

"I'm a writer...So he called me a liar and you hit him? Or is there more?"

Davy nodded. "He said I eat funny on account of..."

"Because," Sam corrected.

"Be-Cause," David responded, "because his sister Laurie told him about the day Billy Dempster's mother brought a cake to school for Billy's birthday and I didn't know what it was."

Sam felt a sharp pain around his heart. He didn't know about that incident. There was never any cake or candy in the Blake house, in deference to the highly restricted diet Sam observed. It had never occurred to him that his needs might put his son in a position where a simple thing like a birthday cake was strange to him.

"Is there more?"

"Uh-huh." Then, without pausing for breath, he said. "Then he said you were a cripple and a freak and that it meant I must be freak, too and I didn't know what a freak was but the way he said it I knew it was bad and I wasn't gonna let him say bad things about you so I had to hit him. But Tommy's bigger than me and he hit me back and kept hitting me. But I didn't give up until Mr. Potter got him off of me."

Sam slipped his fingers under his son's chin and lifted the boy's face to look at him. "So you were protecting me?"

"Uh-huh. Daddy, what's a freak?"

"A freak, Davy, is somebody who looks different from what other people think is normal. It's not a nice thing to say, even if it's true."

Davy looked down at his lap. "Are they gonna put me in jail, Daddy?"

"No, buddy, nobody's going to put you in jail. You may have to stay home from school a few days as a punishment, and I guess you're going to look like you're wearing a bandit mask until those shiners go away. But I guess you've learned not to get into fights with bigger boys, eh?"

"Uh-huh."

"Son, why don't you go to the door and let Sheriff Flynn in?"

"Okay." Davy climbed down from Sam's lap and opened the door. The Sheriff came in and looked at Sam, one eyebrow raised. Davy scampered back over to stand next to his father.

"So?"

"According to my son, this Tommy Donnelley took it upon himself to get my son's goat by insulting me and David struck him to defend my honor. Davy doesn't deny throwing the first punch, but he realizes he made a mistake in answering words with fists, don't you, Davy?"

"Uh-huh," David replied solemnly. "Can we go home now, Daddy?"

Flynn nodded. "Principal Potter told me to tell you he's suspending both boys for fighting. They can both return after the Christmas vacation."

"Understandable under the circumstances." Sam pushed himself to stand, touched David on the shoulder with his fingers and led his son out of the office.

They were nearly to the door of the station house when Mike Donnelley, a scratched-faced Tommy in tow, came out from another direction. The older Donnelley was a stocky man about five feet nine with a florid complexion and graying red hair who wore a holster on one hip. Tommy Donnelley was also redheaded and stocky, almost to chubbiness, and was probably close to ten years old, the kind of boy who easily becomes a bully. It was clear the bigger, heavier, older boy would have quickly gotten the upper hand on the younger, slender David Blake.

Davy took one look at the belligerent face of his tormentor and crowded against Sam's leg. Immediately there was a comforting hand on his shoulder and the feel of a cane resting against his spine. Never in David's memory had his father ever raised a hand, strap, switch or cane to him. To the boy, the two mahogany sticks were just the way his father walked.

Sam stood still to let the Donnelleys pass.

Donnelley growled belligerently at Sam, "Your little heathen got my son thrown out of school."

Sam calmly raised an eyebrow. "And vice versa, it seems."

Donnelly perused the figure towering before him in the tan corduroy jacket, faded but obviously custom-tailored denims, collarless dress shirt, and camel-hair Stetson who leaned on one of two sturdy mahogany, steel-tipped canes.

"You oughta lay one of those canes across your little monster's back for trying to take a piece out of my boy."

Davy pressed himself closer to Sam, wrapping his arms around Sam's leg and burying his face against his father's hip.

Sam frowned. "Donnelley, I'll thank you not to give me advice on how to discipline my son and in return I won't suggest you tell your own son not to goad smaller boys into going after him by insulting their families."

"So the boy has to fight your battles for you, eh, Blake?"

"No, sir," Sam replied calmly, though he could feel the anger growing in him, "I'm perfectly capable of fighting my own battles, if it comes to it."

Donnelley eyed him acidly. "No doubt." His hand fluttered in the direction of his holster.

Sam missed nothing. "Use your head, Donnelley. We're in the police station, for God's sake, not some street in Tombstone. Come on, Davy, let's go home."

David let go of Sam's leg and walked slightly ahead as Sam levered himself toward the door. They were just outside the station preparing to descend the steps when the Donnelleys came out behind them.

"Blake!" Donnelley yelled. "I'm more than willing to settle this."

Sam turned. "Settle what? I've done nothing to you. My son understands he shouldn't have hit yours and he's sorry. Let it go, Donnelley. It's over and done with."

"You were right, Pa," Tommy said. "He is a coward. He won't face you."

"Daddy?" Davy said.

Sam looked down at his son. "Go down the steps and wait for me next to Nameless, okay?"

David nodded and scampered down the steps.

Sam raised the right side of his jacket to reveal his slim, jeans-clad hips, then dropped his hand and leaned on his canes. "There's not a lot of honor in shooting an unarmed, handicapped man, Donnelley," he said ironically. "I never faced off a gunman before I was hurt and I can't imagine why I would do it now. I'm not a quick draw artist; never was."

"No, you left that chore to your half-breed partner."

"If I were you I wouldn't believe everything you read in novels, Donnelley, but it's likely if you met Clint Randolph on some dusty street only one of you would walk away, and I'd put my money on Clint. You want a contest with a gun to settle who's the better shot? I'll meet you at Alamo Field and match you fifty shots each on any non-living target you choose. My only demands are that neither of our sons are present and that I can shoot sitting down. But whether I can outshoot you or not doesn't make me any more or less a man than I ever was."

Sam turned to walk away. It was true. In twelve years as a lawman and detective he had never been involved in a showdown in the street. He had always quietly presented his mastery by shooting empty bottles or the pips off playing cards and folks had left him alone.

Occasionally during the past six years he had taken his rifle and pistol down to Alamo Field and practiced on targets. Texas was becoming civilized, but it was still necessary to be familiar with the care, maintenance and operation of guns if traveling outside the city limits.

Sam was gambling that Donnelley would back down on his posturing, but since he was unarmed, if the man shot, Sam was dead anyway. Concentrating on the steps, he slowly made his way down to the street.

On reaching Nameless, Sam hauled himself on the gelding's back, then reached down with one arm and grasped Davy's raised hand to lift him until the boy could grab the pommel and arrange himself on the saddle in front of his father. His arms around David, Sam picked up the reins and headed home.

"Where's Mama?"

"At a client's."

Davy nodded. It explained why they were riding instead of in the buggy. But he liked to ride on Nameless like this. The horse was big and high and Davy could get a good view. Beside, he was proud of his tall and handsome father. He leaned back against Sam's lean torso. "Daddy, I was real scared when they took me to the sheriff."

The boy felt a hand snake around his chest and give him a squeeze. "I'm sure you were. But now you know it's wrong to start fights."

"Why did Tommy say those bad things about you?"

Sam sighed. "I don't know, Davy. Some people can only feel important themselves by saying mean things about people who can't fight back."

David frowned. "But I did fight back..."

"And you got yourself whomped in the process. Your Mama's going to bust a corset string when she sees your face."

"Uh-huh. Daddy, was I bad to fight with Tommy?"

Sam tousled Davy's fine black curls, so exactly like his own. "No, you weren't bad. Sometimes a man has to defend his family and you thought you did. But now you've learned you have to be very careful about how and when you do."

"Are you gonna fight with Mr. Donnelley?"

"No, buddy, I'm not. One thing Tommy said that's correct, even if it's mean, is that I am crippled. You know my legs don't work like yours do."

"Uh-huh."

"Well I don't get into fights with fists or guns anymore because I can't win against an able-bodied man. A smart man uses his brain and only uses his fists or gun if there's absolutely no other way."

David paused as if drinking in the information and leaned back against his father. "So are you gonna pumice me?"

Sam chuckled "That's *punish*. Do you want me to punish you?"

"Uh-uh."

"Well, the way I figure it, between the beating Tommy Donnelley already gave you and missing ten days of school that I know you love, you've had quite enough punishment for one small boy. So I won't add any more, okay?"

"Okay," Davy quickly agreed.

As they rounded the corner onto Marston Street, Davy craned his neck up to get a view of Sam's chin and said, "I love you, Daddy."

Sam was not surprised to find his eyes begin to burn. He realized that—his legs notwithstanding—from the moment he and Clint rode into Rincon in April 1885, his life had been blessed.

Rincon, December 8, 1891

Arabella Randolph was upstairs in the master bedroom putting laundry away when she heard the front door slam and heavy-treaded footsteps head for the formal parlor.

Her lord and master was home.

What a joy!

Arabella caught a quick glance in the mirror. Messy, sweaty tendrils of hair had come loose from the bun she wore and she was still wearing the faded shirtwaist she usually wore on washdays. By God, she looked old and faded! Was she twenty-nine? She felt like a hundred. She sighed and walked out of that bedroom and into her own to put her clothes away.

She had only shared the master bedroom with Clint for the first half year of their marriage. She told him he snored, but it was a lie. A big part of it was he smelled bad. Not of stale sweat, because he bathed daily and had plenty of clean clothes, but it seemed his every pore—not to mention his breath—was inundated with the odors of tobacco and whiskey until Arabella would have preferred the scents of working perspiration, horse and leather. It made lying next to him at night almost nauseating.

But it was more than that. Arabella lay back and submitted to her wifely duties whenever Clint insisted, but she welcomed her monthly flow, every cold and the nights when he came in passing-out drunk and never made it as far as her bedroom. Arabella couldn't remember if she had seen Clint naked since their honeymoon. Their lovemaking, if one could call it that, consisted largely of Clint coming into her bedroom, the smoke from his most recent cigarette still permeating his clothes. He would lower the blanket, lift her nightgown to the waist, unbutton his union suit, pump himself inside her until he had his release, kiss her on the forehead or cheek since she would turn her mouth away from his rancid breath and leave her alone while he went to sleep in his bed.

Arabella had nobody to speak to about the dissatisfaction with her marriage and whether it was normal. Sometimes, she wondered if she imagined that giddy, slightly hungry, achy feeling of desire she'd felt before she and Clint had first had sex. But it was a little like calling one's breasts a bosom, one's legs limbs and pretending normal bodily functions did not happen. One just simply did not discuss relations with one's husband with one's acquaintances.

At least the ranch was prospering. When Arabella and Clint returned to Rincon after their "honeymoon" in San Antonio, Clint sold off all the remaining cattle to another rancher and used the proceeds to buy some brood mares. He and the hands who remained with them went southwest and captured some wild mustangs as well. Using Wind Dancer as a stud, and his reward money for feed and startup capital, Clint began to breed horses. The first couple of years were tough. Arabella had to sell her jewelry and silverware, but the sale of the first colts started them on the way back to success and the ranch was beginning to have a reputation for fine horses. Had Wind Dancer not been caught in the crossfire of a gunfight in which Clint became embroiled, things might have been better, but two of his colts showed stud potential and Black Wind was an adequate replacement. Clint had a way with horses, Arabella had a knack for bookkeeping and between them they were becoming financially comfortable.

If Clint and Arabella had been as successful as spouses as they were as business partners, things might have been damned near perfect.

Without bothering to fix her hair or change her shirtwaist, Arabella tromped down the stairs and into the formal parlor. Sitting with his stocking feet on the floor, his shoulders slumped, his boots lying at odd angles where he had kicked them off, a cigarette dangling from his mouth, was Clint. His forearms were draped across his lap and a large tumbler of whiskey he held in one hand dangled between his thighs.

Arabella closed her eyes for a moment. Somewhere in the back of her mind she remembered a time she found him handsome. It seemed nowadays his eyes were continually bloodshot. His once sharply chiseled features were becoming soft around the edges—though he was only thirty-six. His nails and fingers were stained yellow with nicotine. He was still lean, partly because he worked hard around the ranch and partly because he seemed to prefer whiskey to food. His too long hair was stringy and lifeless and his skin was leathery from sun and smoke.

Arabella leaned against the doorsill and folded her arms in front of her. "You're back already," she said sarcastically. "Did they run out of whiskey or did you lose your stake?"

Clint raised his head and stared at her, a haunted look in his eyes. "I wish it had been either of those."

Arabella had seen that look before. It was the only expression that could still melt her heart towards him.

"Oh, God," she exclaimed, "another gunfight."

Chapter 37

"Sheriff Murphy said he had a price on his head, but on the wanted poster his birth date would make him twenty-two. Bella, I tried not to get tangled in it..."

"That's what you always say..."

Clint hung his head again. "And I always mean it. It's always the same. They come into town, a copy of one of those damned dime novels in their pockets, wanting to make a name by facing off with the great Clint Randolph. I tell them I'm retired. I tell them it's a tall tale. None of it works and the next thing I know I'm standing in the middle of Main Street, smoke curling up from my gun and some half-baked son of a bitch whose only good feature is that he can read is lying dead or wounded in the street. If I'm lucky they're wanted and the reward money will pay for the funeral expenses. But one day my luck's going to run out and I'm going to get killed."

As much as Arabella regretted her marriage, she didn't wish death on him. "Can't you do anything to stop the books?"

"I asked Bennett Palmer when the trouble started if I could. He said since they make me a hero, they don't constitute libel. He also said since Sam is the one who wrote those stories and they're partly his experiences, he's entitled to sell them to anyone he wants."

Arabella swallowed hard. She walked over to Clint, took the glass from his hand and knelt at his feet. A flicker of love still existed between them at times of trouble.

"Clint, did you ever write to Sam and ask him to stop, or at least change your name to some fictitious name?"

"I wrote to the publisher and got a form letter reply. I can't write to Sam."

Arabella rubbed her hands gently up and down Clint's denim-covered thighs. "You were closer than brothers when you came to Rincon. What happened? It had to be more than his warning you to stay away from me or your telling me about him and Prudence."

Clint's smoke-harshened voice was subdued. "We were on the verge of breaking up the partnership. This was going to be our last job anyway. Sam was tired of playing second fiddle to me."

"So you would have finished the job and gone your separate ways amicably, like other business partners when one retires. This is your life we're talking about. Do you think Sam is aware that the books are putting your life at risk?"

The rancher nodded slowly. "I don't know if you've read any of them, but I had to. He's made me out the perfect hero. If people believe what they read, I was the one who made all the plans, solved all the crimes, shot all the villains while Sam Blake stood in the background holding the horses and saying 'That's brilliant, Clint. Why didn't I think of that?'"

Arabella looked up at her husband, eyes wide. "He's made you the hero and himself the stupid, lumbering galoot? That's exactly what you wanted the public to see. Remember that first Sunday dinner? The one when my father insulted Sam? You said it was because you looked like a hero and he didn't. It was better for business that way, you said."

"Even the talking in the book is that way. In all the time I knew him I hardly ever heard him made a mistake in grammar and when he came back from college he didn't even have a Texas drawl anymore. The Sam Blake in the books sounds like some yokel who never got past the third grade. Even I speak better than that and I was no scholar. But in the books I speak like I'm the college boy."

"If Sam resented the public perception of your partnership, why would he angle the stories that way?"

"Revenge."

She held up her hands. "How does making you a hero constitute revenge? Why would Sam want revenge?"

Clint leaned wearily against the back of the sofa and took a long, deep drag of his cigarette, then stubbed the butt out in the ashtray.

"Clint, it's my life, too. Why would Sam want revenge? What did you do to him?"

Still looking at the ceiling, Clint said, "Remember when we got back from Hereford after we got married?"

"Yes."

"The fires were still burning. Nobody had seen your father or Pete McKinley, Sam or Prudence since the shooting began at Ganados Ravine. Sam had been shot, I think by your father. Anyway, Sam fell in a hole, an abandoned mine. While you were packing for us to go to San Antonio I went into town. There was a fellow from the insurance company that insured the stock on the Bar M and Lazy K. Sam had solicited the insurance company to pay us a reward..."

"I know that. You got that reward, plus the fee from the Cattlemen's Association, plus the bounty on Jack Derry. Your share of those rewards put us back on our feet."

"Both our shares."

"You mean you and me?"

Clint leaned forward defeatedly again. "No, I mean Sam's and mine. I told Arden *and* Palmer Sam had been killed when he fell in the hole, even though nobody knew for certain, and convinced both of them to pay the money to me. I never sent Sam his share."

"Was it that you didn't know where Sam had been taken after he was rescued? As I recall, even Prudence didn't know."

"No. I could have sent the money by wire to Sam's bank account. If I'd sent them a draft they would have deposited it for him. But I knew he had a lot of money saved already, but I only had about five thousand dollars before the payoffs. That and my share of the two rewards, even with the bounty on Derry, was not going to be nearly enough to get this ranch back on its feet again, but the extra fifteen thousand that was Sam's share made the difference between our making it and not. So I took his money and put it into the Bar M."

Arabella bent her head until it touched Clint's thigh. "How could you do that to your best friend?"

"I did it for us, Arabella."

Suddenly she pulled away, stood up and walked across the room. "I never asked you to steal from Sam Blake for my sake. Don't you draw me into the web of your dishonesty. If it were me, I'd've come back into town and shot you myself."

Clint started laughing hysterically. "Don't you see? He doesn't *have* to shoot me himself. Even if these two bit gunfighters never kill me, I'm living dead now. If I wasn't your husband, Sheriff Murphy would have invited me to pack my grip and leave town years ago. I can't even look myself in the face anymore. I don't blame you for not wanting to be any closer to me than you have to. You didn't get yourself much of a bargain, Arabella. You got yourself a drunken, embezzling, half-breed coward."

"Can we return the money now? I'm sure the bank could give us an idea how much interest we might owe Sam for the money."

"And send it where? His bank account in Santa Fe was closed several years ago. I haven't a clue where to begin looking. The books say Amarillo, but that could be as much fiction as the Clint Randolph he writes about. Besides, it's too late. Those books are going to circulate for years. Even if we returned the money with interest, he's made me a fucking legend and I'll never escape it."

Funny you should use that adjective, Arabella thought cynically. *It's probably the one activity at which you're not a legend!* "So what are you going to do?"

"Nothing, but I swear if our paths ever cross again it'll be him facing me on some dusty street. And so help me, I plan to be the one who walks away from that one."

Between the season and the distance, it was well after dark and icy cold by the time Pru Blake arrived home from the Karlin Ranch. Driving the buggy right past the house into the carriage house, Pru noticed the smoke coming from the chimney in the formal parlor. She smiled, knowing what that meant.

In a manner routinely mindless, Pru unhitched the buggy horse, an older palomino mare named Honey, and brushed her down in her stall. Lifting her portfolio out of the boot, she made her way up the familiar path to the kitchen door, where she let herself in with her latchkey.

There were dishes soaking in the sink, but the kitchen was otherwise clean. Obviously, Soledad had made supper for Sam and David that had been eaten after she left for the day. Sam did not do dishes because it was difficult for him to remain balanced. Pru stripped off her driving gloves and hat, took off her overcoat and polonaise and quickly washed the soaking items, leaving them to dry in the wooden dish rack. She had eaten supper with the Karlins, so she was not hungry.

Besides, sometimes the sight and smell of food cooking made her a little queasy these days. Pru smiled. It was time she told Sam. She knew he'd be pleased.

Gathering her things, she walked through the dining room into the carpeted hallway. She dropped off her portfolio in the study and her outdoor clothes in the bedroom. The gentle hiss of the radiator told her the steam heat would keep the bedroom toasty warm; warm enough to make love with Sam with their clothes off.

Just thinking about lying skin to skin with Sam filled Pru with the most delicious tingles. By God, she loved him more and more each day. There were times when she was supposed to be sketching at her drafting table when she could not help gazing over to the rolltop desk where Sam would be busy clattering away at the typewriter. She would watch as he would absently push his spectacles back up onto the bridge of his nose or rake his fingers through his short curls. A few white hairs had found their way into the raven black during his pain and stress-filled stay at St. Giles. At forty-one his hair was liberally white at the temples with scattered white strands poking about amid the ebony. The gray hair combined with the glasses and the lean physique made Sam look professorial. Except for his height, there was nothing physical left of the mountain of a man who rode with Clint Randolph. If a person came looking for Sam using one of the few photographs taken before Sam met Pru, he would walk right past him without realizing it. Of course, the Big Sam in the Clint Randolph books was the man in the old photographs, not the reed slim, sharply sketched, handicapped author in the custom-tailored clothes who now answered to that name.

Pru left the bedroom and walked down the hallway to the formal parlor door and opened it quietly.

"'The chief difficulty Alice found at first was in managing her flamingo: she succeeded in getting its body tucked away, comfortably enough, under her arm, with its legs hanging down, but generally, just as she had got its neck nicely straightened out, and was going to give the hedgehog a blow with its head, it would twist itself round and look up in her face, with such a puzzled expression that she could not help bursting out laughing...'" Sam's voice drifted from the big leather armchair as he read aloud from *Alice's Adventures in Wonderland*. A cheery fire was crackling in the fireplace. The only illumination in the room was a lamp on a side table beside the armchair that cast light on the pages.

Her heart filled with tenderness, Pru walked stealthily to the chair to greet her men. As she came around the chair, she saw the charming tableau. Sam sat in the chair, clad in jeans and a collarless dress shirt, the copy of Lewis Carroll's story in his hand. Curled up against his body, dressed in nightshirt, bathrobe and slippers, little dark head resting against his shoulder, was David, his eyes closed in light sleep. Draped over both of them, supremely comfortable, was White Faced Finney.

Pru leaned over to kiss her husband on the mouth, interrupting him in the middle of a sentence. He kissed her back, gently nipping her lower lips. Finney immediately awoke and jumped down from her resting place.

"Good evening," Pru crooned between kisses.

"Uh-hmm."

It was then Pru noticed the shading around Davy's eyes was bruising rather than shadow. Sam saw the alarm in his wife's eyes and said, "He's fine. I'll explain it later...Job go okay?"

"Yes. Are you sure he's okay?"

"Yeah. I've been with him all afternoon. He ate dinner and took his bath and we've just been sitting here reading *Alice*. I guess he's been asleep about fifteen minutes."

"Am not," responded Davy sleepily, absently rubbing his eyes, then wincing at the pain.

Sam leaned down and kissed his son's curls. "Okay. Are not, But it's time you were, my hero."

Davy opened his eyes and smiled at Pru. "Hi, Mama."

She bent to kiss him. "Hi, sweetie. Daddy's right; let's take you to bed."

David reached over and put his arms around his mother's neck, then wrapped his long, slender legs around her waist. As Pru straightened up, she saw a look of overwhelming sadness cross Sam's features. Her arms around his waist, Pru carried Davy into his bedroom, pulled down the covers and set the boy on the bed. Davy dropped his slippers on the floor beside him and took off his robe, allowing his mother to drape it over the footboard. She pulled the blankets up and tucked her son in.

David was settling in as Sam reached the bed and sat down on the edge. Releasing his cane, he leaned over, ruffled Davy's hair and kissed him good night. Pru followed suit, then turned down the lamp. When they walked out of the bedroom and closed the door behind them, she put her arms around Sam's waist and felt one of his arms snake around her in an embrace. His ragged breathing disturbed her. "Sweetheart?"

"It's nothing new, love," Sam replied hoarsely. "It's these damned legs. What kind of father am I that I can't even carry my own son to bed? That he has to defend me instead of the other way around?"

Guiding her into their bedroom, Sam told Pru about the altercation and about David's suspension. She expressed her outrage, more at the father who would put such vile ideas into a boy's head than at the son who did not know enough to use discretion.

"I'm glad you didn't punish him further," she observed as she pulled the pins out of her hair and took her brush into bed with her. One of the pleasures of their lovemaking was feeling Sam guide the brush through her hair.

"How could I punish him for trying to come to my defense? No matter how ill-advised it was, his heart was in the right place." He stopped brushing for a moment. "I guess a man wants to be a hero to his son."

Pru turned and wrapped her arms around Sam's shoulders, pressing her forehead to meet his. "You *are* a hero to our son, Sam. You give him more attention than any father I know. Davy's too young to understand subtleties, but most fathers don't take the time to sit and read to a five-year-old. Little things like piggyback rides are all very well, and I wish you could carry him on your shoulders, but he doesn't expect it of you. He doesn't think any less of you. You teach him reason and gentleness. You teach him that using your brain is more important than using your fists. Okay, so he had to take a licking from a neighborhood bully to learn the lesson, but then he saw you diffuse the situation with the father with words."

"I challenged Donnelley to a shooting contest."

Pru smiled. "Ah, but that *is* using your brain, Sam. Shooting at targets is not a gunfight on a dusty street. It takes skill and calm more than luck and anger. Gunfights are more Clint Randolph's forte than yours."

"That reminds me. I finished the book this morning." Sam went on to tell her about the letter from San Antonio. Pru was overjoyed with the honor and urged Sam to accept the offer from the University.

"Sam, unless they finish the rail line this winter, the only way to get to San Antonio from here is to take the stage to Lubbock. That means we'll have a rest stop in Rincon."

She felt Sam stiffen as he lay against her in bed, then relax. "That rest stop is only a couple of hours. We'll be in and gone before anyone notices. Besides who would ever recognize us as big Sam Blake and plump Prudence Hofheinz the schoolmarm?"

"Sam, do you ever worry if writing those stories about Clint was as good an idea as it seemed when you started?"

"I've been thinking about it a lot lately. I could have named my fictional hero anything, I suppose. I don't even know if doing it affected him in any way."

"I'm sorry I suggested it."

"If you hadn't, I might not have started writing at all. My anger at Clint for stealing my share of the insurance money was burning me up inside, particularly when I had just been released from St. Giles and didn't know what my future would be." Sam sighed deeply. "Can't change things now. That would be as good as throwing my career away just when I'm starting to reap the rewards of it."

Pru snuggled against Sam's side, her breasts with their tender nipples abraded slightly by his body hair. For a long time neither of them said anything. Then she said playfully. "By the way, I may be somewhat plumper by February, Sam."

It took a full minute for the import to sink in. Immediately, Sam was on his elbows glaring at her myopically. A lopsided grim spread across his lean, handsome features and he reached cold fingers to tease her tender breasts. "I'm going to be sharing these again soon, huh?"

Pru laughed. "Yeah, do you mind?"

"Mind? Mind us having another baby? By God, Pru, I love you so much. There's little you could say that would please me more."

Pru blinked back happy tears. "I'm so proud of you, Sam. When we go to parties or the theatre, I'm so proud to be standing beside you. Sometimes it's all I can do not to throw my arms around you and hold you right there in front of everybody. When I see how much Davy loves you and trusts you I just want to burst with happiness. Even crippled, you're more man than anyone I know." She came into his embrace and feathered kisses all over his face. "You can't learn that, Sam. I think it was born in you to be the kind of man you are. You were always a survivor. I watch people watch you. You're so tall and handsome that I could be jealous if I didn't trust you. When you come into a room, every eye is on you without your having to say a word."

Sam held her away for a moment. "You don't suppose it's because I'm crippled that everyone looks."

Pru brushed an errant curl from his forehead. "Perhaps, on first meeting you, but not afterwards. I hear you sometimes talking business and politics. You know as much as anyone. Your opinion is respected, even considering you're one of the youngest men in our set."

"Not bad for a former hired gun who writes cheap Wild West fiction."

"Not bad for a Phi Beta Kappa from Penn either. And not at all bad for the man I love...Love me tonight, Sam. Fill me full of you."

With a groan, Sam turned her onto her back on the bed and lay beside her on his side. He lowered his head and matched her mouth to mouth. Her lips parted beneath his onslaught as he thrust his tongue deep, tasting, teasing, dueling, aping intimacies to follow. With his upper hand he cupped and caressed her breasts, drawing figure eights about them with the backs of his fingers, teasing the aching nipples to diamond hardness with his questing thumb. He could feel the sheening of her body with perspiration and the rapidly developing raggedness of her breathing as her hips squirmed in growing hunger for his touch. His own breath was becoming deeper as his penis became engorged with his own need, jutting out from its ebony nesting place, all velvet and silk-covered steel and heat.

Pru turned on one hip to face him and placed her hand on his chest, playing her own teasing game on his brownish pap, feeling the tiny nub harden the same way her own larger and sensitized nipples did beneath his touch. Sam gasped at her touch as he drifted his kisses over her eyes, cheeks, ear and nose.

Pru let her hand drift to Sam's side and began to run her hand down the length of his long, muscled torso. She traced the length of his prominent ribs, then dipped to the sudden narrowness of his waist and the hard jutting of his pelvic bones. As she had found beauty in his roundness when they first loved, Pru found beauty in the nearly skeletal thinness his damaged knees demanded of him. She had, over the years, kissed and tasted every inch of his long, furred frame. It was a savor of which she never tired.

As Sam buried his face in her dark waves, Pru splayed her fingers through the thatch at his groin and slipped her fingers around his maleness, eliciting a gasp and groan as her questing hand stroked its heated length, her thumb circling the velvet tip while her hand searched for the pulsating vein that brought pain, pleasure and life-force to them both. She reached her fingers down further and cupped his scrotal sac, squeezing gently until Sam could bear it no further. In response, his own hand found the center of her womanhood within the folds of the Venus mound. His thumb teased at the engorged bud as his long, lean fingers sought the entrance to heaven.

Pru bucked against his hand, seeking to draw him in further. She whimpered repeatedly as her need grew exponentially and her muscles tightened around his thrusting fingers. She was damp and hot and more than ready as she pleaded for him to take her.

When she was so near her peak that only a touch more would send her over the edge, Sam grabbed her by the shoulders and pulled her over him as he lay on his back. The damage to his knees forbade his being on top, but they never spoke of it. They had, over the years, found alternatives that brought them both great pleasure. Poised above him, Pru began to wriggle against his jutting manhood, teasing and arousing until Sam reached down and separated her thighs to straddle his hips. He guided her with his hands as she bent over him, her hands pressed against his chest, easing her until the tip of his tumescence was barely within her. Then, face strained with need and effort, he used the muscles of his buttocks to raise his hips while his hands on her buttocks impaled her on his shaft as deeply as he could go.

For a moment they froze. Pru's eyes were closed as her nether muscles squeezed against the desired and welcome fullness of their joining. Then, by the touch of a hand in a familiar place urging her on, she began to ride him, meeting his upward thrusts with her downward ones, both of them groaning and panting in variations on the ancient dance. Crying each other's names, they rode together, rising into the heavens of fulfillment they could give so expertly to each other, rising as on wings of flame, thrust and rise, thrust and rise, thrust and rise until Pru began to shake with the slamming climaxes coming in waves and radiating from the point of their joining throughout her body as she felt the warm flood of Sam's lifesource emptying into her and Sam felt the warmth of her love for him permeating his body.

Certainly it was lagniappe for her already gravid womb, but Pru could feel the warmth of his seed and could equate it with a feeling of coming home. Pru knew she and Sam were perfectly mated—two halves of the same soul.

Sam's arms loosened his hold and she realized he had drifted off to sleep. Carefully she eased herself off him and climbed out of bed briefly to put her brush on her vanity and lower the lights.

When she came back to bed a few minutes later, she pulled the covers over them both and lay flat on her back listening to the sound of Sam's steady breathing. In his sleep, Sam's hand crept over to lie splayed across her still flat belly. Pru smiled at the unconsciously protective and possessive gesture. She rested her own hand atop his.

Sleep eluded Pru this night. It was more than the beating Davy had taken. His injuries were not serious and his spirits were high despite his suspension from school. She thought about the trip to San Antonio. They would have to go through Rincon on the way.

Sam had only one old hurt left; only one betrayal left unresolved.

Clint Randolph.

Certainly it was no longer the money. The Blakes had more money than they could ever hope to spend. It was the principle that one doesn't steal from his partner; one doesn't betray his best friend.

Sam had been able to convert his partnership with Clint into a successful writing career. Whether the revenge motive Pru had suggested to spur a still raw Sam into becoming a writer in the first place had ever borne fruit, they didn't know for sure. Luigi Bonetti had mentioned in passing that Clint had been involved in a couple of gunfights. But it had been only two or three reports over a period of half a dozen years and could signify absolutely nothing.

Pru had long ago forgiven Arabella and Clint for the slip of discretion regarding her premarital relations. She wondered if Arabella was happy—if she and Clint had children; after all, they had been married six months longer than she and Sam. Arabella had not seemed happy those last two months Pru lived in Rincon, but that could have as easily been repercussions of Ethan Morgan's death and the revelations of the insurance fraud conspiracy and the events that followed. She had been almost giddily in love with Clint before the gun battle at Ganados Ravine. Afterwards, Pru had been far more concerned with ferreting out where Sam had gone to be worried about the happiness of her friend's marriage, so when Arabella spilled the beans about knowing about her sexual relationship with Sam, Pru had been too quick to anger and too quick to rebuff. At thirty-six, settled and content, she was willing to forgive.

Pru began to wonder if it would be possible to mend fences between the Randolphs and the Blakes during that all too brief time they would pass through Rincon.

If only there was a way, it would close that last door of hurt. Then she and Sam would be truly free of the past.

Chapter 38

Amarillo, February 8, 1892

"We're gonna San Antonio; gonna San Antonio," David sang as he dashed excitedly around the house. Nobody could have been more excited about Sam's speech than Davy. He had no idea what it was all about, but to his mind no hero deserved it more.

He scampered into the master bedroom where Sam was sitting on the bed putting the last items into his valise. Taking a running start, he jumped on the bed right into Sam's arms and sent both of them flat on the mattress, Davy's arms around his father's neck and his legs straddling Sam's waist. He unashamedly rained kisses on his father's face while both of them laughed with glee.

"Davy, Davy," Sam tried to admonish between giggles and kisses, but it was a hopeless cause. Despite his underlying anxiety about getting about a now unfamiliar city, Sam was every bit as excited about the honor as was the boy. The time was precious; too soon, Sam knew, Davy would stop hugging and kissing and crying and wanting to be read to and believing his father was the world's greatest hero. It came at last to all boys, some earlier, some later.

"Tell me again how we're gonna San Antonio," Davy insisted.

"Okay," Sam acquiesced. "Go into the study and bring me the atlas and I'll show you again."

David climbed off and went racing for the study, trying to get through the door as Pru was coming in. She pressed her back against the doorsill to let him pass.

Sam sat upright and finished with the last few items. Clicking closed the lock, he patted the valise to tell himself he was done.

"Finished?"

"All packed. Just have to finish dressing and get my gun belt. How are you feeling, little mother?"

Pru grinned. She was wearing a high-necked, leg-o-mutton sleeved, pale pink shirtwaist that was gathered at the yoke and could be worn with a belt, sash, tucked in or loose, depending on the extent of one's condition. A charcoal gray wool walking skirt with a drawstring waist and a cape wrap completed her traveling ensemble. Even though she was halfway through her pregnancy and her condition was unmistakable, she managed to look chic.

"I'm perfectly fine. Dr. Hiblinger says I should have no trouble traveling, though I might have a bout of morning sickness if the stagecoach trail is bumpy."

Sam held out his hand. "Come here, wife," he ordered.

With a dutiful curtsy, she came over to the bed and into her husband's arms.

"I feel like a schoolboy about this thing. I'm getting as giddy about it as Davy is. It's your doing, you know."

Pru raised an eyebrow. "Mine, sir?"

"For making me become a writer."

"I only made a suggestion, Sam. *You* made yourself a writer."

Sam pulled Pru over to his side and leaned over her, kissing her soundly.

"Sam, Sam," she said breathlessly between kisses, "if we start this, we'll never catch the stage."

"It's 1892, for God's sake," Sam grumbled. "You would think they would have finished the rail line between here and Lubbock already."

Pru sat up and shrugged. "The last annual report promised by this summer."

"A lot of good that does me now."

Pru put her hand on her husband's shoulder, feeling the fine cashmere of his vest. "Your last stagecoach ride was something of a horror."

"Yeah, strapped to a plank, doped up on laudanum. If it hadn't been for Basil Mercury I don't know what I would have done."

"I'd have gone with you."

Sam nodded. "I knew that. You would have dropped everything and come. I was too bullheaded and proud then."

Pru stood and held out her hands. "Come on, then, Mr. Bullheaded and Proud. You've got to finish dressing. The hack is going to be here in less than an hour."

Sam let her help him to stand and hand him his canes. He lurched over to the vanity and began buttoning his vest. Pru handed him his collar and tie, then his watch and chain. With a practiced hand, Sam attached the stiff collar to his fine percale shirt and knotted the conservative tie that went so well with the fine fabric of his clothes. He was traveling in a navy blue cashmere pinstripe suit with a morning cut coat and straight-legged lined trousers. A camel hair topcoat waited in the foyer closet along with Sam's ubiquitous camel hair Stetson.

"You look more like a financier than an author."

Sam saluted. "Thank you, madam. *La Mode Bohème* is not for me. Under the suit I may look like I've been starving in a garret, but they don't give honorary degrees to failures. Would you hand me my jacket, please, sweetheart?"

Sam was just putting his second arm into the sleeve when David came back into the bedroom with the atlas. He set it on Sam's lap and stood next to the vanity chair.

Sam opened the atlas to the map of Texas. Pointing at the map, he said, "Now, we start here in Amarillo and take a stagecoach south. We stay overnight at a way station and tomorrow afternoon we get here, to the town of Rincon..."

"Where you met Mama," Davy said solemnly.

Sam nodded. "Where I met your Mama. We stay in Rincon long enough to get something to eat, then we go here to Hereford, then to Tulia and Plainview. We stay overnight in a hotel in Plainview and take the stagecoach to Lubbock. In Lubbock we get on a train to Dallas, then change to another train that takes us through Waco, Austin—you know what Austin is, don't you?"

The dark-eyed boy nodded sagely, "The capital of Texas."

Sam smiled and nodded. "Right. Then from Austin we take the train to San Antonio. And you know what's in San Antonio?"

"That's where you give the speech."

"I mean besides that."

"Remember the Alamo!"

Sam snaked an arm around Davy's waist and hugged him. "You're absolutely right, my hero. Now put the atlas back in the study and go to your bedroom so Mama can finish dressing you."

Davy took the big book in his arms and scampered out of the bedroom.

When Sam looked up, Pru was beaming with love in her face. "You know, Sam Blake, it's too bad you don't like that kid much."

Sam laughed. "Yeah, like I don't like you much either."

He hoisted himself up, smoothing out his coat with one hand and headed for the study.

"Sam, do you have to take the sidearm?"

Sam sighed. "Sweetheart, I don't feel particularly safe traveling on a stagecoach unarmed. I know how to handle a pistol and I'm no trigger-happy hotshot. Your life, Davy's and the little one's are too precious for me to trust to a single shotgun with only payday on his mind."

Pru walked over to Sam, leaned against his back and put her arms around his waist. "You're right. I'm just worried."

Sam raised a hand and caressed her joined ones. "And I'm selfish enough to be glad you worry."

With little time left, they separated, Sam to get his pistol from the locked gun cabinet in the study and Pru to go to Davy's room and finish getting him dressed.

Just before she disappeared into the child's bedroom, Sam called her name.

"Yes, Sam?"

With a grin, he said, "I'm glad you made me marry you. You're one in a million."

Pru laughed. "So are you, my love. So are you."

Sam frowned as he watched two guards loading a locked Wells Fargo strongbox on top of the stagecoach in which they were to travel. Absently he patted his revolver on his hip as if to assure himself it was there. While he had worn his sidearm to the practice field, the last time he had strapped on his gun belt meaning business was the day he and Clint had ridden up to Ganados Ravine.

He felt Pru's hand on his arm. She had returned from the privy with Davy, making sure the little boy went one last time before they headed off.

"We're carrying payroll, I think." Sam soft voice did not betray his apprehension.

"Most stages carry a strongbox." She glanced up at the two middle-aged men, both wearing holsters, one carrying a broken-open shotgun in the crook of his arm. "The driver and shotgun look experienced. We'll be just fine."

They boarded the coach first both because Sam wanted to be sitting facing forward in case of trouble and because he wanted to make sure neither David nor the pregnant Pru would have motion sickness from traveling backwards. Pru helped Sam climb the unstable risers into the coach, then she and Davy followed. The boy sat between his parents, barely able to sit still with the excitement of his first trip away from home. He asked endless questions that his parents answered patiently.

A few minutes before the coach was scheduled to leave, the other three passengers came aboard. There was a baldheaded, florid-faced, pot-bellied man in a plaid suit and bowler hat who also used a cane to hoist himself into the coach. He was followed by a middle-aged woman with steel gray hair and a faded, lined face, in black bombazine and a black felt hat. The final passenger boarded immediately behind the other woman and was a young woman, perhaps eighteen or nineteen, wearing a stylish traveling suit in a cranberry-colored wool trimmed with military-styled soutache with an ecru silk, high necked blouse peeking out from the neckline of the suit jacket. Her felt hat was burgundy and trimmed with ribbons and roses with a dotted half veil that shielded her eyes. She had blond hair and blue eyes and one of those classically pretty faces that always gets attention. Both men tipped their hats politely to the two ladies. Sam detected a provocative perusal of the younger woman by the other man.

He reached across the coach to shake hands with Sam. It was clear he took in the finely tailored coat and suit, then saw the pair of mahogany canes standing between Sam and the side of the coach. "Name's Pembroke, Consolidated Distillers."

Sam nodded briefly. "Blake," he responded. Cocking his head slightly in Pru's direction, he added, "Mrs. Blake," in a way that made it clear he would brook no discourtesy to his family.

"Banker?" Pembroke inquired.

"No." Pembroke had the natural assertiveness of his ilk, but his voice and manner were grating, unlike the pleasant buoyancy of Sam's friend Basil Mercury.

The blonde smiled, showing small, even, white teeth. "I'm Victoria Miller," she said brightly, "and this is my aunt, Mrs. Gwenneth McCord. Aunt Gwen is chaperoning me to Austin where I'm going to get married."

"Victoria." Mrs. McCord's voice warned against overfamiliarity.

Victoria shrugged. "Please excuse my aunt. She thinks going to college ruined me and that I'm lucky to be getting married."

Pru and Sam met in a sidelong glance. It was all they could do to keep from laughing aloud.

"You must excuse my niece," the older woman said, taking out a fan and fanning herself though it was far from warm in the February morning air. "My late brother, her dear father, had very radical ideas about educating girls. Unfortunately, it's made her very forward and unladylike, unlike yourself, Mrs. Blake."

With a sly grin, Pru leaned forward and shook Victoria's hand. "Pleased to meet you, Victoria. Prudence Hofheinz Blake, Illinois Teachers College, Class of '76. You can call me Pru."

Mrs. McCord was plainly embarrassed, but made no apology.

With a lurch, the coach pulled away from the station to begin its journey southward to Lubbock. Pru heard Sam stifle a groan and saw the color drain from his face as the coach began moving. Immediately, her hand went to his clean-shaven cheek.

"Sam?" His face was sheened with sweat. "Are you in pain?"

He nodded because he had learned long ago not to lie about his pain. "I must have overcompensated for the coach lurch." He took several deep breaths and pulled out his handkerchief to mop his face. "It's passing. I'll try to sleep a bit."

Sam lived with a certain amount of constant pain he was almost able to completely block out, but every so often he would twist in the wrong direction or brace himself improperly—as he had just done—or land on a flight of stairs too hard and nearly unbearable pain would shoot through his knees, radiating in both directions. Fortunately, the pain would pass relatively quickly, but it could render him momentarily incapacitated until it did. Unfortunately, there was no effective pain reliever he could take that did not contain an opiate, so Sam bore the pain as preferable to opium addiction. The best palliative was a hot bath. If that was unavailable, the only relief came in sleep.

"Saw the walking sticks there, Blake," Pembroke commented. He made a fist and knocked on his left leg. It made a hollow sound. "Left this one on a surgeon's table at Chancellorsville. Fighting under old Stonewall Jackson himself. You see action in the War, Blake?"

Sam blinked twice behind his specs. "I was fourteen when the War ended, Mr. Pembroke. If you'll excuse me," he said hoarsely, then lowered his brim to shield his eyes as he leaned back and tried to sleep.

David, on the other hand, was fascinated. "Why does your leg sound funny when you hit it?"

"David," Pru warned.

Pembroke laughed. "Don't mind a curious boy, Miz Blake. When I was in the War, I took a minié ball. Surgeon cut off my leg to save my life. This one's made of wood."

David frowned and asked, "Why didn't you go to St. Giles? Dr. David would've saved your leg."

Pembroke looked blank. Pru filled in the space. "Davy, darling, there was no St. Giles when Mr. Pembroke was hurt. Dr. Maris started St. Giles after the War because he didn't want to see what happened to Mr. Pembroke happen to other young men."

David nodded solemnly, his large, dark eyes intense. When he was considering new information, Pru could not help noticing he was a mirror of how Sam concentrated.

"You're a big, strong boy," Pembroke said, changing the subject deftly. "How old are you?"

"I'm five and a half," Davy said proudly. "How old..."

"Davy!" Pru interrupted, though Pembroke only laughed. "Davy, it's not polite for little boys to ask grownups how old they are."

"I'm real old," Pembroke said. "Older than your daddy, I reckon."

"What do you do for a living, Mr. Pembroke?" Victoria Miller asked politely.

The older man grinned. "Why, my dear young lady, I am a drummer, one of the best."

"A drummer?" Davy said. "Like in a band or like Uncle Basil?"

"Well, sonny, I don't know what your Uncle Basil does, but I sure don't play in a band."

"Uncle Basil goes all over Texas selling things ladies wear, I don't know 'zac'ly what, but under their dresses."

Victoria blushed, as did Mrs. McCord. Even Pru felt her face flood with color and she laughed nervously. "I'm afraid my son hasn't quite learned discretion yet."

Pembroke laughed. "Well, boy, just like your Uncle, I go all over Texas and several other places, except I sell things gentlemen like your daddy drink."

David's eyes went wide in realization. "You sell *coffee*?"

Pembroke laughed again. "No, son, beer, whiskey and wine." He nodded towards Pru. "Forgive me, ma'am, didn't realize you were temperance."

Pru chuckled. "We're not."

"Well, ma'am, I'm sure glad to hear that. If you don't mind my saying so, these temperance ladies put a man's livelihood at risk. More than once I've had some of those harridans destroy shipments before my company could make delivery. Can't tell you how many commissions I've lost that way."

Mrs. McCord snorted in derision. "Then perhaps you should not be selling the devil's potion." She tried to move closer to her charge, though between her bulk and Pembroke's there was little room to move.

Pembroke removed his hat in a show of false gallantry. The few strands of hair combed over his bald pate were glued to his scalp with perspiration. "My dear lady, forgive me if my profession offends you, but as we all are forced into each other's company until Lubbock, it would behoove all of us to be civil to one another."

Mrs. McCord snorted again.

"Mrs. McCord, if you wish," Pru began, "Davy and I can trade seats with you and Victoria."

"No," Sam's quiet voice startled them. Never a deep sleeper, he hovered in the lightest reaches of sleep. "I want you here in case of trouble."

Pru touched his cheek. "How are you?"

He opened his eyes and nodded. "Fine now."

"It's 1892," said Mrs. McCord. "What kind of trouble are you expecting?"

Sam eyed the older woman with not a small amount of distaste. "Madam, while we're in a stagecoach on an open road carrying a bank strongbox, it's best to prepare to expect anything."

"Mr. Blake is right," Pembroke chimed in. "I myself always carry a derringer in case of trouble." He reached into his right coat pocket to display a tiny two-shot pistol.

"Have you ever fired that thing?" Sam asked.

Pembroke shook his head. "Can't say I've ever had the need. Been lucky, I reckon." Putting the little gun back in his pocket, he said, "And you, Mr. Blake. I notice you're packing a pistol yourself. Can a man like you tell me you have experience with that gun?"

Sam pushed up his hat brim and looked Pembroke right in the eyes. "Mr. Pembroke, I've learned in my life not to take things at face value. It's the reason I'm still alive..." he gestured toward his legs, "...although somewhat less able-bodied than I would prefer. I know exactly what I'm doing with a gun in my hand, and more particularly, not to wave one around in a stagecoach with three women and a small child in it."

"What exactly *do* you do, Mr. Blake?" Pembroke asked through narrowed eyes.

Sam glanced at Pru and they both started laughing.

Victoria Miller's eyes widened. "You called your husband Sam! You couldn't be that Sam Blake. Not the Hero's Best Friend!"

Sam threw his head back and roared with laughter. "That's me, Miss Miller, the Hero's Best Friend."

"Why, Mr. Pembroke," Victoria said, "this is the man who taught the great Clint Randolph how to shoot. I feel so much safer now." Then she looked at Sam more carefully. "But it's all fiction, though, isn't it? The Sam Blake in the books is..."

"A big, bearded, lumbering bear of a man, who rides and walks tall, and never met a proper English sentence. Would it be as much fun if Clint Randolph's sidekick were an erudite college man? As for the rest, well, I was younger then and things happen that change a man."

"Will you someday write the story of how you were injured?" Victoria asked. "I'll bet it's as exciting as the others."

Sam snaked his arm around Pru's shoulders. "Perhaps, if I can tell the story of the lovely schoolmarm who saved my life. It may be the most interesting story I'll ever write."

They reached the way station without incident. The station was a large cabin with a stable in the back. There were trestle tables and benches at which were served simple fare, a few additional chairs and a series of cubicles containing iron-framed cots with straw mattresses, thin, cotton-stuffed pillows and thinner woolen blankets. It was little more than a human stable, with dusty duck curtains for what little privacy there might be allowed.

Sam kept care of David while Pru arranged to have a second cot brought into one of the cubicles and pushed together with the one already there. She shook out the musty blankets and added their lap robe. She folded her arms and surveyed the scene critically. Even pushed together, the cots were short and narrow. It was going to be an uncomfortable night, but it was too cold to sleep on the floor and not a good idea for Davy to sleep alone in a strange place. The three of them would have to squeeze onto the two cots, with Davy sleeping between them.

The meal offered was equally uninspiring. Pinto beans made with salt pork and biscuits were hardly the usual Blake fare. Pru had seen ahead and brought oranges and some tinned green beans she heated for her and Sam to eat. For David, the brown beans were an unaccustomed treat.

Later, Victoria offered to read David a story once he was settled in bed. Sam and Pru took a blanket and walked slowly outside to a bench along one outside wall. It was bitingly cold but their only chance for privacy. Sam sat and pulled Pru onto his lap, then wrapped the blanket about both of them.

"I behaved badly today. I was rude to that drummer and I shouldn't have been."

Pru pressed a hand against Sam's cheek and kissed the other cheek. "He's a pompous ass."

Sam turned his head toward her hand and kissed the palm. "That doesn't matter. I should know better than to act like a pompous ass myself. It was like that day at the sheriff's office with that boy's father."

Pru leaned against his shoulder. "You're scared, I think."

She felt him stiffen. Immediately she brought her hands around his waist and hugged him.

"You've been something of a hothouse flower the last six years." She looked down. "It's my doing. I built you a little haven in which to hide. We don't go to restaurants or the theatre much because it's so hard for you to maneuver. We go to small parties where everyone already knows us and accepts your handicap. That day at the sheriff's station you were out of your element, facing people to whom a crippled man is less than whole."

"Why haven't you said anything about going to theatres before?"

"I didn't want you to be uncomfortable, but perhaps I erred. Now you're uncomfortable around strangers, more than you ever were when you were just perceived as Clint's fat, hairy sidekick." She chuckled. "My darling, you've become shy. Face it, Sam Blake, you're not the fabled bearded behemoth anymore. He's been reduced to the role of narrator. But you need to reclaim the part of him that wasn't afraid to use his assets to achieve his ends."

For a moment, Sam stared into the darkness. "Pru, do you see a light of some kind out there?"

She looked. "Where?"

"Never mind. It must have been my imagination or the moon glinting off my lenses. Now, where were we?"

Sam bent his neck and met Pru's mouth, raining gentle kisses on her while he stroked her back. He could feel the roundness that declared her pregnancy to the world as it pressed against him through his clothes. He knew Pru could feel his growing desire, but there was no place to fulfill it and would not be for several days.

"Sam," she said between delicious kisses, "we've got to stop this."

He moaned slightly, but didn't stop either his kisses or his hands beneath the blanket. "I know, but let's play what Davy calls *kiss-face* a while longer."

Pru's delighted sounds answered him. Between kisses, she responded, "*Kiss-face*, huh? Well, Mr. Kiss-face, we're going to have our little boy between us tonight, and I'd just as soon not have his sexual education expanded so early in life. Not to mention that of the delightfully virginal Victoria Miller. By God, did you see the worshipful looks she gave you when she found out you were *the* Sam Blake?"

Sam stopped kissing Pru abruptly and sat up straight. "She did not. And if she did, it was because she appreciates my writing."

Pru laughed. "Not a chance. It's because you're absolutely gorgeous. Everyone says you're the handsomest man in Amarillo."

"That's because they haven't seen me naked."

He felt Pru's fingers slip between the buttons of his shirt and touch his chest. "Ah, but I have, and I'm afraid I have to agree. If you'd lecture like Mark Twain does, you'd have girls swooning from here to California. Girls just turn flip flops over handsome artists who have just the right combination of virility and fragility."

"Is that what you like about me, Pru?"

She straightened. "Me? No. I like you because you're a good lay."

Sam blushed. "Pru!"

"By God, Sam Blake, when did you become a prude?"

Sam started laughing himself, realizing she'd used the vulgarity just to shock him.

"You're always full of surprises, Prudence Blake."

"Good, never hurts to keep you just a bit off balance."

Holding her tightly, Sam replied, "If I were any more off balance, I would be flat on my ass."

Still laughing, he returned to kissing her until it became too cold for the blanket they were using to keep them warm enough to remain outside.

Chapter 39

The stagecoach came to a sudden halt, jarring the faceless passengers. The door flew open and a voice called out, "Come out, Blake. It's between you and me."

Sam reached for his canes and stepped out of the coach into the middle of a dusty street. He looked around and saw the coach had disappeared.

The voice said, "You ruined my life. It can only be washed out in blood."

There stood Clint Randolph, twenty yards away, his right hand hovering over the Colt in his holster.

Sam went to draw, but his cane got in the way. Clint drew and fired and Sam saw blood spreading on his white shirt as he felt himself falling backwards...

Sam awoke with a start that shook the cots. It was pitch black and he was disoriented. He felt a hand on his abdomen and an arm beneath the nearly flat pillow under his head.

"Sam," Pru hissed in the darkness as she reached over the sleeping David to touch him, "are you all right? My God, you're drenched and shivering."

Davy stirred. "Mama," he mumbled.

Pru bent her head and kissed the boy on his tousled curls. "Go back to sleep, sweetheart," she crooned and the little one snuggled down against her again. She returned her attention to Sam. She gently rubbed at his stomach and over his flannel-covered chest. "Your heart's beating a mile a minute and your muscles are as tight as a mainspring." Gently, she unbuttoned his nightshirt and slipped her hand inside to stroke his damp skin and massage his neck. In the meantime, the other arm supported his head as she used that hand to stroke his night-stubbled cheek. "Did you have a nightmare?" she whispered.

"Yeah," he muttered. She felt his breathing calm and his heart rate even out.

"You haven't had a nightmare since the mineshaft."

"I had some in the hospital."

"Can you tell me about it?"

In the darkness, Sam shook his head. "All I can remember is there was Clint and shooting involved. The rest of it's gone." He shuddered. "Pru, I have a premonition something's going to happen. Something bad."

He felt the hand caressing his chest. Pru had a way of using her touch to heal him. He felt himself calm.

"Nightmares are based on unfounded fears, darling. You had nightmares about becoming an amputee. It didn't happen. Everything is going to be just fine. You'll see."

"When we get back home, I may sell my guns."

"You don't have to make that decision right now."

Sam stared into the darkness, trying to get the sense of foreboding out of his head. He felt Pru bring her arms back to herself and dig into the narrow, crowded mattress to get back to sleep. A few moments later he heard her steady breathing.

It was awhile before his own eyes closed again.

They forgot to pack the hand mirror. Sam looked at the community washstand and its shoulder-height mirror nailed to the wall. The water was getting cold and he was standing in his shoes and trousers trying to figure out how he was going to shave standing up since he needed both hands free. The washstand was not sturdy enough for him to lean against.

A moment later he felt a familiar pair of arms around his waist. He looked down and saw Pru holding him.

"How did you know?"

"Darling, after six years, I just know."

Sam apologized to the other passengers for his rudeness the day before. The apology was politely accepted as the stagecoach barreled down the trail. There were no scheduled stops until Rincon, nearly five hours from now, then two additional stops to reach Plainview. They were supposed to reach Plainview by about seven or eight that evening, the passengers staying overnight in a hotel before the last leg to Lubbock. From there, they would be going their separate ways.

It was a boring leg of the journey. The scenery was limited and there was no stopping except in an emergency. Having had a dreadful night's sleep, Sam was dozing, Davy curled up in his lap and Pru resting against his chest, his arms around her shoulders. Victoria Miller was trying to read. Mrs. McCord was knitting something, while Mr. Pembroke was watching the scenery, such as it was, as it passed by.

They had been traveling for about three hours when Pembroke nudged Sam on the leg. Sam opened his eyes, instantly alert.

"What is it?"

"I'm not sure, but I could swear we were being followed," the drummer replied. "At first it just looked like a cloud of dust, but it looks like riders now. And they seem to be gaining on us."

Sam lifted Davy off his lap and into Pru's. She awoke and moved over, putting the boy between them. Sam twisted his body as much as he could to look out the window.

Pembroke was right. Sam took one cane and rapped loudly on the roof of the coach.

"Carew, Davis," he called up. "We've got company."

The upside-down head of Shotgun Davis poked itself through the window. "What?"

"Behind us. Riders," Sam said. "Looks like three or four from this distance."

"Shit," Davis swore and hauled himself upright and out of view. With a roaring voice, Carew plied the whip and the stage began to pick up speed.

"What's happening?" Victoria cried.

"There's a group of riders following us," Sam explained.

Pembroke was still looking out the window. "Looks like three, Blake."

"Why?" Victoria asked.

"Could be just travelers going in the same direction, or it could be bandits after the bank strongbox and any valuables or money we might have. The driver's trying to put some distance between them and us."

"That's not going to help," Pru observed. "Individual horses should be able to outrun a heavily laden stagecoach and we're at least two or three hours from Rincon."

"True, but if they're not bandits, they're not going to risk their horses trying to catch us. They'll just keep going at the pace they've already set."

"We're all going to be killed!" Mrs. McCord exclaimed. She grabbed Victoria's hand. "Oh, my poor sweet baby."

"Only if we're foolish," Sam said. "And I, for one, don't intend to be."

"They're still gaining," Pembroke observed. "Well, Blake, what would Clint Randolph do at a time like this?"

Sam cocked his head. "If this were real life and not one of my books, about now Clint would be saying, 'Sam, what should we do?'"

Pru laughed nervously. Davy clung to her in terror. "Okay, Sam, what should we do?"

Sam looked at the floor between the two seats. "If the coach comes to a stop or if you hear gunfire, I want all three of you ladies and Davy to huddle on the floor out of sight. If there's shooting, the walls of the coach may stop a bullet. The open windows won't."

Pembroke reached into his pocket, but Sam stopped him. "Pembroke, that derringer is only good at close range. I suggest you leave it be unless you're within six feet of your victim. Are they still gaining on us?"

The drummer nodded.

Sam pulled the lap robe over his lap, covering his legs and his gun. "Like it or not, Pembroke, we're both handicapped. We're not going to do any running. Make sure your cane is plainly visible. It could save your life."

They felt the coach begin to slow as the team tired. Sam reached under the blanket and unhooked the thong that kept his pistol holstered. He reached into his pocket and removed a bullet, which he slid into the usually empty sixth chamber. They heard the blast of Davis's shotgun and a return shot, followed by a dull thud on top of the coach.

A second later Pru, with Davy in her arms, was lying on the floor of the coach, telling Davy to be as quiet as possible. A second after that, Mrs. McCord and Victoria were crowded in on top of them.

With Pru off the seat, Sam slipped his revolver out of the holster and laid it near his right thigh, keeping his hand under the blanket.

The coach slowed to a stop and a shot rang out from above their heads. After an answering shot and a groan, Pembroke identified three riders near the coach. They wore bandannas over their faces, canvas dusters and hat brims pulled low. They instructed the driver to drop his gun.

"Pembroke," Sam hissed. "Lie down on the seat. Don't argue."

The older man complied.

"Folks," they heard the leader yell, "this here is a stickup. Now we want the strongbox and whatever valuables you got." Pointing to one of his number, he said, "You, go into the coach and see what donations you can get...You, driver, hand down the strongbox!"

"With one arm, you bastards? You shot me and you killed Davis."

"Just push it over the edge, old timer, we'll catch it."

Sam heard the scraping of the strongbox as Carew dragged it to the edge of the coach. The two bandits stood less than two feet from the coach window with their arms outstretched waiting for it to fall.

The door opened. The third bandit stepped on the riser and looked in. He saw the ladies and child huddled on the floor, a portly older man in a loud suit curled up in a ball on one seat and a skinny, bespectacled man in an expensive suit nervously fingering a pair of canes by the far window. The thin man glanced at the bandit in the doorway and the two reaching for the strongbox. His right hand moved slightly underneath the blanket.

"All right, let me have whatever you've got, gimp," the bandit yelled.

Almost faster than the eye could see, Sam yanked the blanket off his lap, raised his pistol and fired once, striking the man in the doorway right between the eyes, killing him instantly. Then he turned, pointed the gun out the window and fired twice. Each bullet struck a bandit, whose hands were occupied holding the strongbox and could not draw. One was hit in the temple, the other right through the heart.

The whole thing was over and done with in less than five seconds. Three bullets, three corpses.

By a handicapped man who had not fired a gun at another person in over seven years.

For an agonizing moment, the only sounds in the air were David's tiny whimpers from the bottom of the pile of women. The air smelled of gunpowder.

"Okay, folks, show's over," Sam said dully as he holstered his gun. "Somebody needs to see how the driver fared."

Gradually, the women got up and left the coach, Pembroke right behind them. Victoria nearly swooned at the sight of the dead man lying right below the risers, but the other two women caught her and stood outside. Davy pulled away from Pru and threw himself into Sam's arms. Sam was staring straight, facing forward, unblinking. He was strongly affected by what he had done, but like an automaton, his arms closed around the body of his whimpering son and held the boy against him. Everyone was in such a state of shock at the rapidity of what had occurred that even the loquacious traveling salesman could not utter a word.

Pru called up to Carew and determined the man was alive but injured. She opened the boot of the wagon and found the medicine kit. She was about to climb up to the driver when Mrs. McCord stopped her.

"Mrs. Blake," her voice more solicitous than she had previously displayed, "a woman in your condition shouldn't be climbing up to take care of the driver. I did some nursing before my marriage. If you'll hold the medicine kit I'll climb up and you can hand me the box." Just before she put her foot on the wheel spoke to climb, she turned to Pru and said, "That was a very brave thing your husband did. He saved our lives with his quick thinking and action."

Pru glanced at the coach window. Sam was still sitting like a statue with Davy clinging to his neck. "I appreciate your sentiments, Mrs. McCord. I only hope he isn't seriously affected by what happened."

Once Mrs. McCord was on the wagon seat, she called to Victoria to join her up top. "You'd better see to your husband."

Pru nodded. She stepped into the coach, passing Pembroke, who was looking through the pockets of the dead men to find any possible identification. She sat on the seat next to Sam. Davy had stopped crying. She put her hand on her husband's arm.

"Darling, talk to me."

Sam's arms moved to hold Davy more tightly. He turned his head and gazed at his wife with desolate eyes.

"I've never done that before." His voice was an almost voiceless monotone.

Pru's hand grazed his cheek lightly. "What do you mean?"

"Not at point blank range," he said dully. "Never with their guns holstered."

"Never with someone you cared about at risk if you failed either."

Sam blinked owlishly.

"Sam, sweetheart. These men killed Mr. Davis and wounded Mr. Carew. There's no guarantee they would have just robbed us and let us go. You may just have saved seven lives; eight if you count the baby. What you did was heroic."

"I don't feel heroic."

"Well, my darling, here's a whole group of people, including that little boy clinging to you for dear life, who disagree."

Sam seemed to come back into focus. He turned his head and kissed Davy and pulled the boy so he sat on his lap. "Davy," he said quietly.

"Yes, Daddy," Davy said thickly.

"What I just did—it wasn't such a wonderful thing. Killing people, even if it seems like the right thing to do, should never be taken lightly."

"But they were bad men."

"They were, and they hurt the two men on top of the stagecoach. A lot of people will tell you what I just did was right. They may tell you I'm some kind of hero. What I did was to protect your life. It doesn't make me a hero. It may have been the wrong thing to do, but there wasn't enough time to find out if these bandits would have just taken our money and left us here. Do you understand, son?"

Davy shook his head. "Not 'zackly."

"I'm sorry, son. I don't know any other way to put it. I think you will understand it one day."

Davy stuck out his jaw. "Well, I think you're a hero, Daddy, but you were b'fore."

Sam smiled crookedly. "That's good, because I think you're a hero, too. I know you were scared there on the floor, but until after I fired the gun you were real quiet like you needed to be. I'm proud of you." Then he reached out one hand and cupped Pru's cheek. "And I'm proud of you, sweetheart. If anything had happened to you or Davy, I'm not sure I could have gone on."

Pru turned her face into his hand and kissed his palm. "I love you, you big galoot," she said with a grin. "You ought to get out and help us assess the situation. You have more experience than any of us in this kind of thing."

When they got out of the coach, Mr. Carew was sitting on the strongbox being attended to by Mrs. McCord. His shirt was off and he was being bandaged. His right arm was shot through the shoulder. The bullet had gone through, but he had bled considerably and had little use of the arm. Mrs. McCord got the bleeding stopped, the wounds bandaged and the arm in a sling, but Carew was dizzy and logy from blood loss and could not drive with just his left arm. Davis, the shotgun, was dead, as were the three bandits. Leaning on Mrs. McCord, Carew walked over to the coach door and was helped inside where he sat in the place Sam had vacated. In moments he was asleep.

The passengers stood around the open door of the stage, except for Sam, who sat in the doorway.

"We have to get the stage and the bodies into Rincon," Sam said. He slapped at his lap. "I'm embarrassed I can do so little to help, but to drive coach horses takes leverage with the legs against the pull of the team. I don't think my braces would withstand that kind of pressure, even assuming I could manage to climb up there."

"Well, sir," Pembroke said admiringly, "I do believe you've already made one hell of a contribution to our protection."

Sam looked down as his face flushed. "Thanks." He looked up again. "Pembroke, can you drive a team? You have one sound leg. That's probably enough."

Pembroke nodded. "But it's been a while—and I don't know the way to Rincon."

"Sam, I know the road to Rincon," Pru said. "I lived there for nine years. I could ride up top with Mr. Pembroke and give him directions. We'll also have to pull the bandits' bodies up to the top of the coach and cover and tie them down, along with Mr. Davis's. If Mrs. McCord and Victoria drag them over and get them into a standing position with their hands raised Mr. Pembroke and I can pull them up and tie them."

"That doesn't leave me much to do," Sam said dourly.

"Well, it leaves you with the most important job, taking care of Davy and making sure Mr. Carew is all right."

Sam smiled sheepishly. In this part of the operation it was all he could do.

Arabella Randolph came downstairs in her riding clothes.

"Where are you going?" Clint asked as she poured herself a cup of coffee in the kitchen. He was eating breakfast. He had already been up since dawn working, but liked to work a few hours before eating anything.

Arabella took a sip. "I'm riding into town to do a little shopping and take the mail. The southbound coach is due today. Plus, Horizon needs new shoes. Do you need anything while I'm in town?"

"Well, I could use a couple of cartons of—"

Arabella put her free hand on her hip. "Clint, you should know by now I won't buy your cigarettes for you."

"Because you think I smoke too much?"

"Exactly."

"There was a time you didn't mind it so much."

Arabella sighed. "You're right. When we first met and got married I didn't find the scent of tobacco that unpleasant, but Clint, in those days you smoked perhaps a fifth of what you smoke now. My whole house smells of stale tobacco. No amount of cleaning will get the smell out of the woodwork or your clothes or the table linens. There are burns on some of the furniture and Consuelo and I find butts stubbed out in partially empty coffee cups and on plates."

"You want me to quit?" he countered belligerently.

"I'd love it if you quit, but I doubt you can. I'd just be happy if you could cut back some."

"You're right. I'm not sure I could quit. Sometimes it's hard to go even an hour without a smoke." He rose. "I reckon I'll go into town with you. Black Wind could use a shoeing, too. Maybe we could meet back at the Blue Bird for lunch when you're done shopping."

"I suppose so," Arabella said dully.

Clint pulled his black hat over his long hair and stepped toward the back door. "I take it you're going to have some breakfast before you go. I'll just check with the hands to see if any of them have any outbound mail and saddle the horses."

"Fine."

When Clint shut the door behind him, Arabella made herself some eggs and toast with jam and butter and sat down heavily. She valued her time away from the ranch and away from Clint. She told herself she should have just agreed to buy him the cigarettes and he would have left her alone to do as she pleased. She had been halfway hoping to run into Mary Zavich or Christa Fagan and cajole one of them into joining her for lunch. She really needed some female company. Now she was unlikely to get any.

Worse, chances were good that Clint, once he bought his cigarettes and took the horses to be shod, would go into the saloon for at least one drink. And if he got just the wrong amount of liquor in his system, he would want to have sex, which was more than Arabella could bear anymore.

She wondered when love had turned into disdain. Yet there was still some spark of affection.

The problem was, about all that spark lit these days was another cigarette.

The unpleasant duty completed, Victoria and Mrs. McCord climbed back into the stagecoach to join Sam, David and Carew. Pru, the lap robe wrapped around her, sat on the box next to Pembroke as he took the reins and urged the team onward. The bank strongbox was secured in the boot with the luggage. Carew was breathing lightly, but had not reopened his eyes since drifting off to sleep.

Sam held Davy in his lap. The little boy fell asleep as soon as the coach was underway once he was assured that his Mama was all right on top of the coach.

The other two ladies did not sleep, but neither did they read or knit. Sam wouldn't talk about the stickup. Mostly he sat staring into space, still trying to justify in his mind that his actions had been correct. Sam decided when they got back to Amarillo, he would need to have a long talk with Father Maris. The old priest had a way of cutting right to the bone of a problem and Sam trusted him more than anyone in the world except Pru. In this case, however, Sam needed to talk to someone who had not lived through the episode.

It occurred to him that Clint Randolph would never have this sort of doubt. Even the real Clint would have shrugged it off as part of the job. According to Pru, most probably Clint had killed Ethan Morgan and then married Arabella, as if it was as normal as pie to shoot a man between the eyes and then marry his daughter. Morgan shot Sam, so Clint shot Morgan. A partner is supposed to be willing to do that.

Sam realized he had strapped on his gun for the first time in years because a man is supposed to be willing to protect his family. There was no way to know if those bandits would have left any of them alive.

A feeling of calm finally spread through him to replace the chill of guilt. Not that Sam would forget too quickly he had taken three lives in a matter of seconds. That would live with him for a long time. Sam would not consider himself a hero, but he would be able to accept the title if affixed to him by others.

He had done what he had to do at the time. He had protected the other passengers.

Miss Miller could go to Austin and marry her beau, her Aunt Gwenneth in tow.

Mr. Pembroke could continue through his territory, selling spirits to saloon-keepers and merchants.

And the Blake family could go on to San Antonio. Sam could get his honorary degree and give his speech. They could then return to Amarillo to their big, accommodating house on Marston Street where Sam could write his next book, Pru could design her next interior, Davy could play and study and they could all await the birth of the newest Blake.

It was the least a man could do.

Sam sighed and relaxed against the back of the coach seat. Davy snuggled against him, a little hand fisted against his father's chest.

Sam realized—if it meant protecting his family—he would do again what he had done this morning.

He might feel guilt, but he would do it.

Sam kissed David's curls and breathed in his little-boy smell. Yes, he would do it for Davy, if he had to.

He could only hope it wouldn't happen again.

Chapter 40

The stagecoach finally rolled into Rincon. Despite everything that had happened, it was less than three hours late, but late enough to cause concern. Thus, it was with a sense of relief that Rodgers first saw the coach at the end of Main Street—until he saw that the pair sitting on the box were not Carew and Davis, but a man and woman he did not recognize.

Quickly, he sent his young assistant to get Sheriff Murphy. The boy sped away as the coach slowed to an uneven stop in front of the depot.

Pembroke set the brake and called down to the stationmaster, "Get the doctor and the sheriff here on the double. Your driver is inside, wounded." Grabbing his cane, he carefully climbed down, quite expert after nearly thirty years on a prosthetic limb. Once down, he gestured upward, "And the lady will need some assistance climbing down."

By this time the boy had returned with the sheriff and was sent on the run to get Dr. Morrison, the new doctor. Between Pembroke and Rodgers, Pru was assisted in climbing down from the box, although she protested that she didn't really need help.

Mrs. McCord and Victoria Miller were already outside the coach telling the sheriff what had transpired. Once Pru was down, she went immediately to the door of the coach. On his father's command, Davy came out of the coach and threw his arms around his mother's legs, burying his face in her skirt. Pru ruffled his curls, then looked up and held out her arms.

Leaning heavily on his canes, Sam appeared in the doorway. Slowly and carefully, he bent his elbows and stepped onto the risers until he touched ground and came into Pru's waiting arms. One arm still steadying him, his other came around her, stroking her back as she rested her head against his comforting chest. Finally, she allowed herself to give way to tears of relief as she heard the steady beat of Sam's heart through his clothing.

Sam knew how she felt. Had it not been a public street, he would have started crying himself.

The Blakes were nearly oblivious to what was going on about them. Dr. Morrison aided Carew out of the coach and took him to his office, while the other passengers were giving their accounts of the holdup and the sheriff was examining the bodies of the bandits. Pembroke inquired whether Rodgers was going to wire the stage line to see about a new driver, and the stationmaster sped off to the telegraph office to do just that.

"Folks," Rodgers announced before he left, "you might want to take yourselves into the office and rest a spell, until I get an answer from the central office about what's going to happen next, though it's a pretty sure thing you all are going to have to bed down for the night here."

"Young man," said Mrs. McCord, "is there a hotel in this town?"

"Well, no, ma'am, there ain't, but Mrs. Lester's got herself a boarding house right across the street from the saloon. Sometimes she's got some rooms to rent."

The Blakes were already moving slowly into the stage office, where Sam sat heavily on a hard wooden bench with Pru beside him and Davy on his lap.

Mrs. McCord approached them. "Victoria and I are going to the boarding house. Would you like me to see about rooms for you?"

Pru smiled. The crisis had turned the woman from judgmental to supportive. "Thank you, Mrs. McCord, that would be nice, if she has something no higher than the second floor. Her second floor rooms are usually reserved by long term boarders, though."

"Will you be all right, Mr. Blake?"

Sam nodded. "Eventually, ma'am. I appreciate your concern."

"Believe me, sir. It's an honor to travel with a man as brave as yourself."

Sam gave her a weary salute and half smile and Mrs. McCord left in a flurry of black bombazine.

Sheriff Murphy came over to them. "I understand from the others you were the hero in this thing."

Sam shrugged. "Nothing particularly heroic about it. I've always been pretty good at hitting what I aim at. That's generally good for a few tin sharpshooting medals at best."

"Well, not in this case. The leader of that band was Mal Gordon. There's a ten thousand dollar reward on him, dead or alive, and twenty-five hundred on each of his men. I'd say that'd buy a whole pile of sharpshooting medals. Give me your full name, man, and I'll wire Austin for a draft."

Sam threw back his head and laughed. His last time in Rincon had cost him $15,000.00 and now he would walk away from the town with the same amount.

The sheriff asked them for details of the holdup. Considering the magnitude of Sam's participation, his description of it was unembellished and modest.

"And your name, sir?" Murphy asked.

"Samuel Blake, of Amarillo."

The sheriff took another look at Pru and his eyes narrowed. "Ma'am, I know this sounds like a line from a dime novel, but have we met before?"

Pru grinned. "Why, yes, Sheriff, though it's been quite a few years since I left town one step before the Town Council could run me out."

Murphy's eyes widened. "My God—um, sorry—*Miss Hofheinz?*"

She laughed. "Only it's Mrs. Blake now."

"Well, it is a small world. You got so thin I barely recognized you. Y'know, I saw Miss Arabella around town this afternoon. I bet she'd be real glad to see you."

Both Blakes stiffened slightly. "Well, if I run into her, I'll certainly say hello," Pru said unemotionally.

Davy tugged on Pru's cape. "Mama, I'm hungry."

"Are you through with us, Sheriff?" Sam asked.

"Yeah, for now. You're probably not going anywhere until tomorrow anyway."

"Or for another three days," said Rodgers as he returned from the telegraph office. "I'm sorry, but the soonest the stage line can send another team is with the next southbound stage, and that gets here in three days. The line said they would pick up your meals and lodging."

"Mama," Davy repeated.

"Sam?" Pru began.

"Starved."

"Is the Blue Bird still open, Sheriff?" Pru asked.

"Yeah, and still the best—um—" Murphy replied and paused.

Pru nodded knowingly. "And still the only restaurant in Rincon."

"'Fraid so," he responded.

"...I've got to tell you," Pembroke bragged as he stood by the bar in the saloon, having a quick shot of whiskey while he waited for his deposit on an order. "I've never seen anything like it in twenty-five years on the road. I tell you, the man was as cool as a cucumber. Just lifted that six-shooter of his as calm as you please and blasted those bastards clear to hell. Not a wasted movement. Not a wasted bullet. Got all three of 'em in just three shots. I tell you, I've never seen anything like it. He may be a writer, but that Sam Blake is one hell of a shootist. Saved our lives for sure."

At the sound of the name *Sam Blake*, a chair scraped back and one of the patrons stood amid a cloud of blue-gray smoke. He dropped his cigarette butt into the nearly empty whiskey glass and was at the bar in a few steps. Grabbing Pembroke by the lapels, he stared at the drummer with bloodshot, dilated eyes and growled, "Who did you say?"

"Sam Blake, the famous writer."

"You're telling me that *Sam Blake* is in Rincon?"

Pembroke yanked the man's hands off his jacket. "Damned right. And a god damned hero he is, to boot."

Without another word, the tall man with the long black hair turned and strode out of the saloon.

"Who the hell was the Injun?" Pembroke asked the bartender, as he brushed off his jacket lapels.

"That," the bartender said, "was Clint Randolph."

Pembroke's eyebrows rose. "*The* Clint Randolph?"

"The same. And there's more than a few of us who've heard him swear that if he ever runs into Sam Blake again, he'll see one of them dead."

Pembroke blew out a mouthful of air and shook his head. "If he does, it'll be cold-blooded murder."

The bartender shook his own head. "Nah, Randolph'll challenge him to a gun duel."

Pembroke took out his handkerchief and wiped his brow. He shook his head again. "I doubt Sam Blake would shoot it out with anyone. The man's a cripple."

"What?"

"Sam Blake's a cripple. The man can barely walk. He's wearing steel braces on both legs and walks with two canes."

"But the holdup. You said he shot three men."

The whiskey drummer nodded. "Yessir, he did, without ever leaving his seat in the stagecoach. Those bastards never knew what hit 'em."

Clint strode into the stage office. "Where's Sam Blake?" he shouted at Rodgers.

"I ain't sure, Randolph. I think he went to get something to eat."

He walked out of the stage office and headed toward the Blue Bird.

"You'll never believe the order I just got," waitress Mabel Towns remarked to Addie Lincoln, longtime owner and cook of the Blue Bird.

"Nothing could be as bad as the fella who ordered a beer and a glass of milk and mixed the two together."

Mabel made a face at the thought. "No, the food was pretty normal. The three of them, handsome couple with a kid, husband's a cripple, wife's in the family way, well they ordered steak, boiled cabbage and bread without butter, coffee and a glass of milk for the kid."

"So?"

"One order and two extra plates. They're fixin' to share one order among 'em."

"Well," Addie said thoughtfully, "maybe they can't afford more'n that. Some folks can't, y'know."

Mabel set her arms akimbo. "Aunt Addie, I may not be real sophisticated, but they're wearing the most expensive clothes I've ever seen. And they didn't look over the menu at the prices; they just ordered like they never intended to order anything else."

Addie became curious and stepped out of the kitchen to see the family in question. It took a moment, but she recognized the woman. With a welcoming grin on her face, she walked over to the table, wiping her hands on her apron.

"Why, Prudence Hofheinz, I never figured to see you back in Rincon after the rotten way you were let go."

Pru held out her hand and shook the cook's work-worn one. "Well, Addie Lincoln, I'm pleased you remember me."

"This your man?"

"Yes, my husband..."

"Well, you got yourself a handsome one. And a boy to match. Always thought the men in this town were half-blind to overlook you. Mister—um..."

"Blake," Sam said quietly.

"Y'know, this little lady rode into the midst of a prairie fire like this county'd never seen before and saved a man's life. And our pea-brained Town Council fires her as our schoolmarm on account of she spent several days with that ailin' fella *unchaperoned*. I'm glad t'see everything's turned out all right for ya. She's a good woman, Mr. Blake."

Sam grinned. "Well I know it. Rincon's loss was my gain."

"Addie, you don't normally come out of the kitchen."

Addie said quietly, "Well, my niece Mabel, she though it was kinda strange y'all orderin' one meal and three plates and bein' so well dressed and all. If'n yore short on cash, I sure trust ya to send it on later."

Pru smiled. "Why Addie, that's so sweet. It's not the money, believe me. It's just that I remember how big and thick your steaks are and well, Sam and I just can't eat those big meals. We usually just order one steak and divide it between us."

"I can tell from your face 'n' hands ya got real slim since ya been away. You're lookin' real purty these days. Tell ya what; I'll just divvy up that steak and such in the kitchen and bring it out to ya like it was three orders. I'll even toss in some more cabbage, no extra charge."

"That's very generous, Miss Lincoln," Sam said. "I'm afraid we're going to be here a few days we hadn't counted on. I hope you can accommodate us during that time."

The older woman folded her arms across her ample bosom. "You betcha. Nothin's too good for Miss Hofheinz."

"I quite agree," Sam responded.

Addie went back into the kitchen.

"Well?" said Mabel.

"Well, it turns out that woman is our old schoolmarm. She 'n' her husband are just real light eaters. But I'll betcha they're generous tippers."

Back in the dining room, Sam observed. "My name didn't mean much to her."

"Addie can't read. She used to feed me free Sunday dinners in exchange for writing the copy on her menus." She touched his hand. "But don't worry, darling. There are folks out there who've never heard of Mark Twain either."

"Mark who?" It was a joke between them.

"Sam, I'm thinking it might be easier for you if the Bonettis could put us up for the time we're here."

"Pru, you don't have to baby me." Sam sounded annoyed. "It's time I shed the cocoon and tackled such normal inconveniences as stairs and bathtubs. You don't suppose the boarding house keeper has a full-sized bathtub, do you?"

"Who knows? It's probably one of those slipper tubs. Of course if you don't mind bathing with your knees up your nose..."

"A consummation devoutly to be wished. Maybe the Chinese laundryman still has his bathhouse."

Their meal was served, just the way they liked it. They were busy eating when the restaurant door opened and a belligerent figure stepped in.

Clint looked around the dining room. He didn't know everyone in town; mostly because he never cared to. He wasn't certain Sam would be at the Blue Bird, but there weren't that many places to eat in town.

He saw a couple with a small child, but it couldn't be Sam. This man was as lean as a scarecrow, his clean-shaven face nearly untouched by the sun. His hair was black, but white at the temples and cut quite short. His lean cheeks and strong jaw gave him a face even Clint noticed was handsome. He was wearing an expensive suit. As he chatted quietly with the woman at the table, Clint could see he had long, lean fingers that moved with a native grace as he spoke. Clint guessed that the man's nails might even be manicured, though he couldn't see that far. The only thing this slim stranger had in common with Sam Blake was eyeglasses—and eyeglasses were not all that uncommon. This man looked like a banker, not like the man he'd known and called friend for over twenty years.

As Clint turned to leave, Sam looked up and saw him. Despite the overlong hair and the dissipation drink was etching on his face, Sam recognized him immediately. His eyes flashed briefly with the recognition, then cooled to impassiveness. The glare from the overhead lamps glinted off the round lenses, shielding his expression. He said nothing, but watched Clint leave.

"Clint was just in here. No, don't turn around. I suspect he didn't recognize me. He looks terrible."

"You don't sound remorseful."

"I'm not. I have no sympathy for him at all. I feel sorry for your friend having to live with a thief all these years."

Pru looked down at her place and then back up into her husband's eyes. "Sam, sweetheart, we're stuck here for three days. Unless we stay cooped up in whatever lodging we get, there's a chance I could run into Arabella. Would you object if I mended fences with her? All she really did to me was repeat some gossip. If I hadn't been all wrapped up in being fired and worrying about you, chances are we would have made up before I left town."

"I never meant to put a wedge between you and Arabella. Just leave me out of it."

Pru rose and drew her cape over her shoulders again. Reaching out her hand, she said, "Come on, Davy, let's go for a walk."

David stuck out his lower lip. "I wanna stay with Daddy."

"It's fine, Pru. I'll take him to the telegraph office with me and then—maybe a treat. Something you don't have every day. A reward for a brave little hero."

"Candy?" Davy guessed, his eyes shining.

"Yeah, son. I think you can have a piece as a reward for being so brave and quiet during the holdup."

Davy grinned "Will you have a piece, too, Daddy? You were brave during the holdup."

"We'll see," Sam said indulgently, knowing he wouldn't.

Davy stood up and kissed his father on the cheek.

Sam laughed. "Now who's playing *kiss-face*?"

Pru watched Sam's arm snake around Davy's small, slender frame and pulled the child against him in an embrace. Although tall for his age, next to his very tall father he seemed just the right height. She exited the restaurant with a warm smile on her face.

If they could get a separate room for Davy tonight, she was going to make love to Sam until his ears rang!

Pru glanced around Main Street as she headed toward Mrs. Lester's boarding house. Rincon had not changed much in six years. Here and there a storefront sported a new coat of paint, a few bore the names of new proprietors.

Pru still knew many of the people in Rincon. She wondered how Mrs. Lester would look after six years. By God, the woman must be nearly sixty now. She was a widow in her early forties when Pru first came to teach here. She had a nodding acquaintance with the spare, businesslike woman.

She wondered if others in town would remember her as fondly as Addie Lincoln, or if others would even recognize her. Even pregnant she was slimmer and more stylish than she had been when she left. She was no longer embarrassed by her wealth; no longer had any reason to maintain a humble mien. She was Pru Blake, interior designer, the only one of her kind west of the Mississippi. And if that were not good enough, she was also Mrs. Samuel Blake.

Thus, Pru was not paying attention where she was going when she ran smack into a shorter woman going in the opposite direction.

"Excuse me."

"Beg pardon," they said in unison.

Then they saw each other.

Pru stared at the blonde in the riding clothes and flat, black felt gaucho hat. There was a faded aspect to her; a sense of strain in her face.

Of all the people to run into, the one she both most and least wanted to see. She was momentarily speechless.

Arabella Randolph looked at the woman opposite her. She was simply but stylishly dressed, though her short cape only minimized but could not disguise her obvious condition. Even expecting, her face was slim and strikingly pretty—yet hauntingly familiar.

Arabella felt her mouth go dry. She croaked, "Prudence? Prudence Hofheinz?"

Pru smiled. "Hello, Arabella. Long time no see, eh?"

Arabella looked her friend up and down. "What are you doing here?"

"Just passing through."

"You're so slim."

"Well, sort of."

"You're beautiful."

"Thanks."

"You're expecting."

"Yes."

"You're married."

Pru held up her left hand. "I am indeed."

"You came on the stage?"

"How else? Look, Arabella, I don't want to stand here playing Twenty Questions..."

"I'm sorry. Your condition."

Pru sighed. "My *condition* has nothing to do with it. I've got to get to Mrs. Lester's to see about rooms or my family will be spending the next three nights sleeping on benches in the stage line office. Our stage was held up, the driver was wounded and we're stuck here until they can get a new one. I'm surprised it isn't all over town yet. We've been here at least an hour."

"You're still mad at me."

Pru shook her head as she started walking toward the boarding house. "No, Arabella, I'm not. It's just with the brouhaha surrounding the fire and what followed, I overreacted. I should have tried to make amends long ago."

Arabella fell in step beside her friend. "I was wrong to be so indiscreet. I never told anyone else. What with marrying Clint and not knowing about Papa I wasn't thinking straight either. I'd have written, but I didn't know where you were. I wrote to your father, but he didn't write back."

They reached the boardwalk in front of the boarding house when Arabella grabbed Pru by the arm. "Prudence..."

"It's Pru now. Nobody calls me Prudence anymore except Papa."

"Pru, then, you don't have to stay in a boarding house. You're welcome to stay at the Bar M."

Pru stopped dead still. "No, Arabella, I think that would be a *very* bad idea."

Arabella raised a pale eyebrow. "But I thought all was forgiven."

Pru shook her head ruefully. "No, I said *I* forgive *you*. It's your husband."

"Clint? But you hardly knew him."

Pru lifted her skirt to step into Mrs. Lester's front door. "But I'm married to Sam Blake."

"Oh, God," Arabella breathed. "Clint's sworn to kill him if he sees him."

Chapter 41

Pru felt suddenly cold, but her expression remained impassive. "Clint may be a thief, but he's no murderer."

Arabella's color drained. "The money!"

Pru folded her arms across her chest. "You know about the money?"

"I found out about two months ago. I swear to you I didn't know Clint had taken Sam's share before that."

Pru walked into Mrs. Lester's front parlor. The room was shabbier than she remembered. "Did Mrs. McCord talk to you?" she asked the older woman.

"Yes, dear, but all my second floor rooms are rented out. I have three rooms on the third floor. I can move a trundle into one room for the little boy."

"I need to talk to my husband. He needs to decide if he can manage it."

Thoughts of making love to Sam until his ears rang slowly faded away. They would be lucky if he wasn't stuck in the room until the new driver arrived. It would make him feel truly crippled.

Pru was about to step past Arabella when the blonde grabbed her arm and held her. "Pru, I'm serious. Clint will call Sam out. Sam may be fast on the draw, but Clint's just enough faster that he won't have to worry about missing a target that large."

"I'm not worried about Sam."

"Then worry about Clint. He's fought over a dozen men since those damned books came out. Then he drinks too much and smokes too much and his life is misery. Mine, too."

"I'm sorry your life is miserable, Arabella. Clint shouldn't have stolen from his partner. With them it was like stealing from a brother. And he left Sam for dead..."

"Sam told him he wasn't badly hurt. He sent Clint after me."

"It was telling the insurance company Sam was dead when Clint didn't know for sure. You left town before the Bar M hands found us. You can't deny that. Sam lost everything he had. Every cent he'd saved for years to retire on, his livelihood, his home, his mobility. He lost everything except his horse and me. His memories, his history, his experiences—they were all he had with which to support himself. The world already thought Clint was the dashing hero and Sam the lumbering sidekick. Sam gave the readers what they wanted. 'Clint Randolph, Western hero!' Is it Sam's fault a bunch of two bit shootists believe what they read in dime novels? The public wants their heroes to be tall, dark and handsome with a deadly shooting eye. A hundred Easterners who've never been west of the Hudson River make a living creating heroes. Sam

Blake created Clint Randolph long before he ever sat at a typewriter—and Clint let him do it because it was lucrative. Then when Sam needed him most, Clint betrayed him without a backward glance."

Pru began to walk away. Arabella ran around to stop her by standing in front of her.

"Clint's not bright enough to do that much reasoning. He's probably drunk and if he finds out Sam's in town, he won't care that the first wrong in this was his."

"Would Clint shoot an unarmed man, even one he hated?"

"No."

"Would Clint shoot a man if a small child might get hurt?"

"No."

"Would Clint shoot a man if he had such a great advantage over him that to do so would be murder?"

"No, he has some honor left."

"Well, then, I'm going back to wait for my husband. You can come with me or not."

Pru lifted her skirts and headed back toward the stage office, leaving Arabella standing alone.

Jackson's was crowded when Sam and Davy entered. By now the town was buzzing with news of the holdup. Lurching slowly in, leaning wearily on his canes, Sam had done more walking this day than he had since his accident. He told Davy to find the candy and wait for him to catch up. The boy scampered off looking for the glass canisters filled with brightly colored sweets. Sam's knees were on fire. Had he not promised Davy a treat, even now he would be sitting on a bench in the stage office waiting for Pru to bring him news about their accommodations.

Already he had been to the telegraph office to wire the changes in plans. A part of him wanted to wire the university to forget the honor and just take the next Northbound stage back to Amarillo.

"Daddy," he heard his son's excited voice, "over here."

"Coming, son," he responded, as he leaned against the mahogany handles and began his slow, methodical progress toward the back of the store.

Clint Randolph came swaggering into the store, his face dark with frustration and fury at not being able to find his quarry. For a moment he saw a flash of golden tan hat, but it disappeared behind the display shelves.

Then a redheaded fifteen-year-old came barreling in behind Clint and around him, a well-read book in his arms. The adolescent stopped for a while and glanced around, but seeing only people he recognized, he disappeared behind the shelves, looking down each aisle until he found the man who was leaning over a small, black-haired child dressed in city fashion. The little boy was frowning, trying to make a decision which sweet he would select.

"Mr. Blake?" Clint heard the older boy address someone in the rear of the store.

Sam turned his head. "Yes."

The boy suddenly blushed behind his freckles. "My name is Don MacGregor and, well, you're one of my favorite authors, right up with Robert Louis Stevenson..."

Sam chuckled. "High praise indeed...Don MacGregor, you were a student of Miss Hofheinz's, weren't you?"

"Yeah. You know Miss Hofheinz?"

"She's my wife."

Don looked down, blushing more if he could. "I asked her to marry me when I was a kid."

Sam raised one hand to squeeze the boy's shoulder. "She told me she was flattered. Now I bet you want me to sign that book."

"Oh, yeah," Don responded, the book nearly forgotten. He handed it to Sam, who retrieved his gold-plated Waterman fountain pen from his inside coat pocket and opened to the flyleaf. Resting the book on a shelf, he wrote in his neat Spencerian script, "*To Don MacGregor, May you continue to enjoy the adventures books bring you. Samuel Blake, February 9, 1892.*" He recapped and pocketed his pen and handed the closed book back to its owner.

"Gosh, thank you, Mr. Blake. I'll never forget this."

"Blake!" cried out a husky, familiar voice. "Come out in the open where I can see you."

"Clint?"

"You're damned right Clint. You lying bastard, get the hell on out here with your hands up."

Sam and Don exchanged meaningful looks. "I can't do that, Clint."

"You mean you won't face me? I never figured you for a coward."

"I'm not going to face you in a store crowded with people. I suggest you put your gun down and I'll come out where you can see me unarmed."

"How will I know you're unarmed?"

Sam looked down at a now pale-faced Don and Davy.

"Clint, do you remember my bone-handled Colt? The same gun I've owned ever since you've known me?"

"Yeah."

Sam looked at Don. "I'll need your help," he said quietly. "I want you to unbuckle my gun belt."

With shaking fingers, the teenager reached for the buckle.

Sam looked at his son. "David Blake, I need you to be brave and quiet again." Don had the belt and holster in his hands. "Davy, this is Don. He's a friend of your Mama from a long time ago. I want you to hold his hand and walk over to the counter where the Post Office is. Will you do that for me?"

Davy nodded solemnly, as did Don.

"Clint, Don MacGregor is coming out with my gun belt and my son. I swear if you hurt either of them I'll make you pay."

He nodded to the boys, who slowly walked around the shelves to stand by the Post Office cage.

"We're okay, Mr. Blake," Don called out, "and Mr. Jackson has Mr. Randolph's gun."

"I'm unarmed, you bastard," Clint yelled. "Now get your fat ass out here."

Slowly, deliberately, Sam maneuvered his way out into the open. He stood there, slim and unashamed, leaning on his two canes.

Clint's dark face turned gray as he stared at the startlingly altered appearance of the man he had known most of his life.

"Sam," Clint breathed hoarsely, "what the hell happened to you?"

"I fell down a twenty foot mineshaft and landed on a slag heap. Remember, you were there."

Clint blinked uncomprehendingly. "You told me you weren't hurt badly."

"I lied."

It was so quiet in the store you could hear the sound of everyone's nearly stifled breathing as the two former friends glared at each other. Clint looked stricken. All the guilt he bore about stealing Sam's money intensified while all the anger he felt about the novels felt like a lead weight in his stomach.

Sam, on the other hand, looked calm and impassive, his lean, angular face and crippled body reminiscent of a fallen angel.

"If you still want to call me out, Clint," Sam said quietly, "I'll understand."

With a cry of anguish, Clint grabbed his pistol from Jackson, turned on his heels and stormed out of the mercantile.

A moment later, Sam's canes dropped from nerveless fingers, his knees buckled and he collapsed to the floor in a heap as darkness overcame him.

Hereford, Texas, that same day

Hereford was a town much like Rincon. It didn't take much time for it to get around that the stage had been held up en route and delayed three days.

Among those who heard the news were two brothers named Hank and Roscoe Barnes. Itinerant ranch hands, they had just been fired from their jobs. When news of the hold up reached them, they were sitting in the Broken Arrow Saloon nursing a pair of beers. Roscoe was playing Napoleon at Saint Helena with a couple of old decks of cards while Hank was sitting with his nose in a battered dime novel. Hank's lips moved silently as he read.

The buzz around the saloon about the hold up attracted everyone's attention.

Hank saw his brother put down the pack of cards and looked up from his book.

"What's he sayin', Bubba?" Hank asked.

"Says the stage was robbed or somethin' and won't be comin' through," Roscoe answered.

"Shit," Hank mumbled. "How the hell we gonna get to Tulia and find another job?"

"Guess we're gonna havta wait a few days. Whatcha readin'?"

Hank glanced at the cover. "*The Adventures of Clint Randolph: Rangers to the Rescue.* That Randolph is pretty damn fast with a six-shooter, they say."

Roscoe patted one of his two Navy Colts confidently. "I bet he ain't as fast as me. Ain't nobody ever beat me to the draw."

Hank's eyes narrowed. "Oh, yeah, then why ain'tcha a hero in a dime novel?"

"Only 'coz no one ever asked me. Bet I could beat that guy easy."

Hank took a gulp of his beer. "Yeah, I bet you could," he said cynically. "If ya ever found him."

Suddenly Roscoe turned to the bartender and yelled, "Hey, O'Brien!"

"Yeah, Barnes, whatcha want?"

"Ain't it true that fella Clint Randolph lives around here?"

"Yeah," said the bartender. "I hear tell he lives just over the hills in Rincon. Got himself a ranch just outside of town."

Turning back to his brother, Roscoe said, "See, if we lit out first thing tomorrow morning, we could be in Rincon before noon. I could shoot it out with Randolph and we could be back here by dark and catch the stage when it comes through. By the time we got to Tulia *I'd* be a hero and ranch owners'd be beggin' us to work for them."

Hank shut the book and stared at his older brother. "Gee, Bubba, I don't know. If he's as good as the books say, he ain't gonna be easy to kill. I ain't good enough to call him out if he kills ya."

Roscoe looked indignant. "First, Randolph ain't gonna kill me. Second, I got a little idea how to get the odds in my favor."

Hank leaned forward. "What's your idea?"

And Roscoe began to explain it to him.

Pru and Arabella were almost at the mercantile when they saw Clint storm out with his gun belt in his hand. He didn't even answer Arabella's call to him as he headed for the livery stable.

Seeing a commotion at Jackson's, the women ran there, arriving in the doorway to see Sam crumpled on the ground and Davy wailing over his father's fallen body.

"Sam!" Pru cried as she ran toward where he lay. She was on her knees by his side and gathered him into her arms. Brushing his hair off his forehead as she held him, she crooned desperately, "Sam, Sam, sweetheart, it's Pru." She looked up at the stricken-looking Arabella. "Damn you," she yelled at her old friend, "that thieving bastard shot my husband...Sam, darling, please open your eyes."

"No, Miz Blake," said a youthful voice, "Mr. Randolph didn't shoot Mr. Blake. They were neither of them wearing their guns. When Mr. Randolph left the store, Mr. Blake just fainted or something."

Pru looked up into the face of a gangly redheaded teenager. "He wasn't shot?"

The boy shook his head. "No ma'am. I have Mr. Blake's gun and Mr. Jackson had Mr. Randolph's. He was real brave. He came out here in the open unarmed to face Mr. Randolph. He gave me his gun and asked me to take care of your little boy."

Pru felt her heart begin to slow down. She looked around swiftly. "Somebody please get me some smelling salts. I'm sorry, you look so familiar."

He grinned crookedly. "I'm Don MacGregor, Donnie when you were my teacher, Miz Blake."

"You've grown up."

Don blushed. "I reckon so."

She smiled. "Thank you for taking care of my son."

"My pleasure, ma'am."

Someone pressed a vial of spirits of ammonia into Pru's hand. She opened the vial and waved it under Sam's nose. With a jolt, his limbs stiffened briefly and his eyes opened wide.

"Pru," he said weakly, "What happened?"

She stroked his cheek and forehead. "It seems you passed out. I guess you had too much excitement for one day—for a man your age."

Sam growled halfheartedly. He knew when he was being teased. "So I fainted."

"Yes, and scared the socks off me and Davy."

Sam looked around. "David."

A tear-stained face glared at him as the boy scampered into the safety of his father's arm. Sam stretched a bit and kissed his son. "Don't worry, Davy. I'm all right. I just fainted."

Davy blinked with lashes glued into teary spikes. "You mean like Missus Van Sant does when Mr. Van Sant says something she doesn't like?"

Sam and Pru both started laughing. "Yes, Davy, exactly like that," Sam said through his laughter.

Pru looked up at Arabella Randolph's pale face. "I owe you an apology."

Arabella shrugged. "No, you don't. After seeing Clint storm out of here and Sam crumpled on the floor, I thought the same thing you did." She walked over to the Blakes and crouched down. "I'm glad you didn't fight him, Sam. I couldn't have lived with him if he'd shot you. Or vice versa."

Sam maneuvered himself into a sitting position. Arabella's eyes widened when she saw the limited movement of his legs and realized what Pru was referring to when she said Sam had lost his mobility.

"Arabella, I didn't think Clint would shoot me. As my dear wife once said to me, there's no honor to be gained in shooting a crippled man. When you see him, tell him we need to talk."

Arabella nodded.

Sam turned to Pru. "Do we have rooms? I think I need to rest. I'm in terrific pain from the way I landed."

"Mrs. Lester has nothing below the third floor."

Sam shook his head. "I'll never make that now. I guess we need to wait in the stage office."

"That won't be necessary," said a familiar voice. Ralph Bonetti, a huskier version of his brother Bob, came into the mercantile. He worked with his father as a cabinetmaker and had helped make many pieces for Pru's room designs over the years. "When we heard about you being on the stage, Papa said to drive over the wagon and insist you stay with us. It'll be cramped, Mr. Blake, but it'll all be on the ground floor. I've already got your baggage loaded."

Sam groped for his canes and pulled himself to standing. Don MacGregor handed Sam's gun belt to Pru, who draped it over her shoulder as she took her son's hand and followed her husband out the door, past Arabella and the rest.

The Bonetti furniture wagon was sitting outside the mercantile; their luggage piled in the back. Ralph assisted them in climbing into the wagon before climbing in himself and urging his team into motion.

Arabella followed them outside to see Pru Blake wrap her arms around Sam's waist and rest her head on his shoulder. Sam, in turn, rested his own head on hers as the wagon kicked up dust on its way to the far end of town, where the Bonetti workshop and house were located.

She began to walk to the blacksmith shop to get her horse to ride home, mulling over her shock at seeing Sam Blake as he looked now, compared to the big, hairy man she remembered. Then she thought about her entirely healthy man whose presence she could barely stand most of the time.

She doubted she would have cared enough anymore to cosset Clint the way Pru cared for Sam.

It then occurred to Arabella that Pru and Sam had a son and a child on the way. There was obviously nothing wrong with their love life.

She wished she knew how to make it different for herself.

Chapter 42

Later that night, the beneficiaries of a filling Italian meal, hot baths and a little talk with the elder Bonettis, Sam and Pru found themselves in Luigi and Anna Maria Bonetti's own bedroom.

They tried to refuse, but the older couple insisted. After the help Pru had given their sons Bob with veterinary school and Bartolomeo with seminary tuition, plus the furniture commissions, it was the least they could do.

Pru came into the bedroom to find Sam sitting on the edge of the bed, his face buried in his hands. His feet were bare, his braces and shoes lying beside the bed. Sam's hair was especially curly from letting it dry without brushing it—an unusual occurrence for her normally fastidious husband. Despite the liberal white at his temples, when he let his hair curl naturally it gave him a youthful appearance Pru always found endearing.

She sat down next to him on the edge of the bed and playfully splayed her fingers through his baby fine curls. Sam stiffened slightly at her touch, an occurrence so uncommon Pru was immediately concerned.

"Sam, are you especially hurting?" Pain was Sam's constant companion. It, more than the passing years, had painted the white in the ebony of his hair. Most days he was able to put the ceaseless aching out of his mind.

Today had certainly not been most days.

"No," he grunted into his hands without looking up.

"Sweetheart, talk to me about it."

Sam raised his head and looked at his wife. His face was pale and drawn. "I made a fool of myself today," he said dully.

Pru frowned. "How?"

"You saw me, fainting like some Southern belle whose corset laces are too tight."

Pru blinked several times. Counting out on her fingers, she said, "Let me get this straight. You foil a stagecoach robbery, saving the lives of the driver and all the passengers, including your wife and son. You dispatch three robbers as if you'd done it all your life. You report the incident calmly to the sheriff, humbly refusing to be fussed over. When your treacherous former partner challenges *you* to a gun duel, you face him down unarmed and diffuse the situation without violence. Does that about sum up the events of this day, Sam?"

He nodded.

"So, having done these things under the most unbearable pressure through which a man could go, even an able-bodied one; putting your life on the line more than once today to protect your family and others, the release of the stress overwhelms you and you pass out?"

"Yes." Sam buried his face in his hands again. "How can you bear to be next to me? I'm so ashamed of myself."

"If you're ashamed of yourself, Sam Blake, then you're the biggest fool I've *ever* encountered."

Sam's head snapped up and he stared owlishly at Pru. She reached over and stroked his cheek, roughened by his five o'clock shadow. "Sam, Sam, my darling, you've spent so much of your adult life being the hero's best friend I don't think you recognize what kind of hero you are yourself."

Sam slapped at his thighs. "Some hero," he snarled.

"My love, you equate being heroic with being perfect. You promoted Clint to heroic proportions before you ever sat in front of a typewriter because you believed people wouldn't accept an oversized, bespectacled, hairy man as a leader. You resented Clint for the position in which you yourself placed him. He must have felt your resentment and reacted to it, cheating you to prove to himself he was worthy.

"Then you were hurt. Now you were further away from the perfect hero you created in Clint's image. You became so accustomed to believing a hero looked and acted a certain way that when you lost full use of your legs you tore yourself down even further than before.

"Did Dr. Maris ever tell you how many men who lose their legs or the use of them commit suicide? Did he ever tell you how many of them give up and resign themselves to house imprisonment or life in an invalid chair? How many lose themselves in drink or opium? Did he ever tell you how rare it was for him to have a man as severely injured as you were fight back from his injuries, walk again and rejoin useful society? You succeeded where others failed.

"The people with whom we associate in Amarillo are among the wealthiest in Texas. They don't have the time or patience to remain in the company of someone they consider their inferior. If you gave up writing tomorrow, at least a half dozen of them would be lining up to offer you positions of trust with their companies. That's how much they think of you."

Sam fell back onto the bed, his legs still bent over the edge with his feet resting on the floor.

"I didn't know if he would shoot me or not."

"The bastard in the stagecoach or Clint?"

Sam's eyes widened behind his lenses. "Clint. I knew the bastard in the stagecoach would shoot me if he had a chance, but I lied to Arabella when I said I knew Clint wouldn't shoot me."

"There is no honor..."

"...In shooting a cripple. There's no great honor in being one either...You know, I was planning to propose to you as soon as the Rincon job was finished. I was going to retire and open a bookstore or some such."

Pru lay down on her side beside him, resting on one elbow. She blinked back tears. "Sometimes we get what we want, just in ways we didn't expect." She leaned over and kissed him sweetly on the mouth several times. She felt his large, long-fingered hand stroke gently over the roundness of her belly and smiled.

Suddenly, she felt a jolt from within. She gasped, then glanced over at Sam. The look of wonder told her he'd felt it, too.

"Has it done that before?" Sam asked breathlessly.

Pru shook her head. "No." Her smile broadened to a grin. "I guess he was waiting to do it for both of us."

"You think it's another boy?"

She nodded. "I think so, but it doesn't matter much...Sam, make love to me."

"The Bonettis might hear us."

"So? We've never worried about who can hear us when Basil stays in our house...It's something else, isn't it?"

Sam reached out his arms and gathered Pru against his side. "I love you beyond reason, darling, but no lurid scene I've created compares to seeing three men meet their Maker at my hands—even in defense of others. When I said I wasn't in pain, I didn't mean my knees ache more than usual. My soul is another matter."

Pru suggested they just get under the covers and try to sleep.

Try they did. Sam lay on his back staring myopically at the ceiling. Pru lay on her side, her arm across Sam's belly, too keyed up herself.

"Sam, what are we going to do?"

"The sheriff wants a full written report of both incidents. Beyond that, I may just try to find a quiet place to sit and write." He chuckled. "Or maybe I'll go to the saloon and find a poker game. I haven't played in a month of Sundays."

"Do you mind if I take Davy and go to the Bar M to visit with Arabella?"

Sam sighed. "No, your friendship with Arabella shouldn't depend on mine with Clint."

They didn't make love that night. At least, they didn't have sexual intercourse. As dawn painted the sky pink and yellow, they engaged in a heavy bout of *kiss-face*. Whispering endearments, they kissed and nibbled at each other's lips, nuzzled ears, dueled with their tongues, playing chase back and forth in their mouths.

Whether their lovemaking was brief or extended it was heartfelt, sensual and satisfying. In their social circle it was a running joke how the Blakes couldn't keep their hands off each other.

Some far more able-bodied couples could not say as much. As usual that evening, Arabella retired to her own bedroom while Clint remained downstairs in the parlor drinking himself into oblivion while he smoked cigarette after cigarette. Most likely, Clint would stop before he passed out and climb unsteadily up to his bedroom where he would collapse, still fully dressed, in his own solitary bed.

Arabella could not sleep. She punched the pillow and tried different positions to no avail. Finally, she arose from bed, put on her wrapper and slippers and padded downstairs.

The lamp was still lit in the parlor. She walked over to the doorway and looked in. Clint sat on the love seat, his elbows propped on his thighs. A brown-filled tumbler was in one hand, a half-consumed cigarette in the other.

He heard his wife approach and glared at her bleary-eyed.

"Come to see the great hero, huh?" His voice was slurred. He saluted Arabella with the tumbler and took a swallow. "What a grand spectacle I made of myself today, threatening a cripple."

"You didn't know. Is it possible Sam had no inkling of the effect his books would have on you?"

"He found out about the money, I reckon, and being crippled, he found a way to get even."

"But you're not sure, are you?"

"He always let me play the hero. Maybe the books made more sense that way." He stubbed out the cigarette in the nearby ashtray and beckoned Arabella close to him. She sat in a nearby chair. Even without the burning butt the smell of stale tobacco was about him.

"Funny, with his beard and all that fat he used to carry gone, my old friend's not such a bad-looking fella. He's changed so much I actually saw him at the Blue Bird earlier today and didn't recognize him."

"They're going to be in town another couple of days. What are you going to do?"

"Steer clear of him, I reckon."

Arabella moved over to the love seat to sit beside her husband. She took his hand in hers and said, "Clint, don't you think you two have been estranged long enough? If it's the money, we could get a bank loan to pay him back. You and he were closer than brothers for so long. Why not use the opportunity to clear things up with him?"

"It's not that easy, Arabella."

"Why? You were wrong to take his share of the reward money, even if you did it for me. Whatever he may have done in response, your fault in this is clear. Apologize to him. Offer to repay the money or give him a share in the ranch. I doubt he'll shoot you. The worst that will happen is he'll tell you to go to hell. But he just might forgive you. Even if you never see him again, you might get your own soul back."

The next morning was cool and crisp. After breakfast, Ben Bonetti drove the Blakes to the livery stable to hire a buggy. Pru drove

Sam to Sheriff Murphy's office and left him there while she and Davy drove in the direction of the Bar M.

The sheriff motioned for Sam to sit in a chair across from his desk. He held out three wanted posters bearing the names and likenesses of the three men Sam had killed the day before.

"You told me about the rewards yesterday, Sheriff," Sam said as he released the posters. "I didn't shoot those men for the rewards. I shot them because they had already killed one man and my family was at risk."

"The drummer says he's never seen such accurate shooting."

"It was them or us."

"Then you don't want the reward money?"

"Of course I'll take the money. I can always donate it to St. Giles Hospital."

"Now, about the confrontation in Jackson's yesterday..."

"What about it? There was no shooting. Nobody got hurt, except for bruises I got when I passed out and hit the floor."

"I've known Clint Randolph since he came to Rincon..."

"And I've known him since he was ten years old. We were equal partners. After the shootout at Ganados Ravine, Clint told everyone I was dead and collected all the reward money and kept it. What right did he have to call me out when I was the aggrieved party? I couldn't outdraw him when I was able-bodied, I certainly can't do it now. I did the only thing possible: face him unarmed."

"Do you want to press charges against Clint for embezzlement? The seven year statute of limitations runs out at the end of April."

Sam shook his head. "It's not worth the aggravation at this point."

"I would suggest you keep away from Clint while you're here."

Sam sat up straight and rigid. "Sheriff, I don't even *want* to be here. If it hadn't been for the robbery, we would have been in town for a couple of hours without anyone knowing we'd been here. But I'll be damned if I'll stay holed up in Luigi Bonetti's house afraid of my shadow. This is a free country and I've done nothing wrong. You should tell Clint to stay at the Bar M while I'm here. It seems he's the aggressor in this."

"You're right," Murphy retreated. "But you don't strike me as a foolish man, Mr. Blake."

Sam grabbed his canes and stood up to leave. "I'm not. That's why I'm still alive. I'm packing a pistol for the first time in years. If Clint Randolph can keep his head I might not ever have to use it again."

Sam walked out of the sheriff's office. He felt the need for a little oblivion, but the price he paid for drinking spirits or overeating was too high.

He could play cards. Eyeing the saloon, he began the slow walk in that direction. It was a long and exhausting walk, longer than he had attempted since his accident.

The saloon was cool and dark. Although it was still late morning, there were a number of men there, most drinking, some playing poker. It was too early in the day for the piano player or the saloon girls to be up and around, but those things were of little importance to him. He ordered black coffee and moved over to the poker table. The gamblers, seeing new blood, welcomed him.

At one point, two of the existing gamblers cashed out and the chairs were taken by two unshaven cowboys who looked a little the worse for wear.

"New in town?" Perce Caldwell, the remaining regular, said to the unshaven ones.

"Just passing through," Roscoe Barnes replied as he threw his money into the pot. "Hear they're hiring cowpunchers down south aways."

The gambler shrugged. "I wouldn't know. But you better have horses. The stage isn't due for a couple of days."

Play continued for a while, the men at the table saying little more than necessary to progress the game. Sam noticed the two rough-looking men glancing nervously around. He became suspicious, but schooled his features to maintain his poker face.

"Sure is quiet in here," Hank Barnes observed.

"No more than usual for this time of morning," said Caldwell. "Of course you heard about the big standoff in the mercantile yesterday."

Sam's eyes narrowed. The last thing he wanted was any attention drawn to him.

"Naw, we got in this morning," said Hank.

The gambler took the deck and began to shuffle in preparation for his deal. "I wasn't there, mind you, but I hear tell Clint Randolph..."

Roscoe looked up, false innocence on his face. "The great Clint Randolph lives in *this* town?"

"Yessir," said the gambler as he dealt the next hand. "He lives on a ranch just outside of town. I hear tell there was nearly..."

Caldwell stopped talking as Clint strode into the saloon. "Speak of the devil."

Sam ground his teeth.

Clint blinked rapidly until his eyes grew accustomed to the dim light.

"You want whiskey, Randolph?" the bartender asked.

"Nah, just coffee," Clint replied, scanning the room. His eyes widened in shock to see the camel hair Stetson in plain view at Perce Caldwell's poker table. He swore beneath his breath, then realized maybe he should try Arabella's suggestion. He reached into his pocket, then remembered he had purposely left his pack of Luckies back at the ranch. He could sure use a smoke right about now. Instead he picked up his coffee cup and strode over to the poker table.

Sam looked up from beneath his hat brim, but said nothing.

"We need to talk," Clint said.

"What makes you think we have anything to say to each other?" Sam replied in a monotone.

The Barneses exchanged a meaningful look. Suddenly Hank stood and scooped his stake into his hat. "Just remembered a little chore I have t'do," he said and walked out.

Clint slid into the now vacant chair.

"You going to play poker, Randolph, or just chat?" snarled Perce Caldwell.

"I'm in," Clint snapped and pulled out a small stake. "Sam, I didn't know how bad you were hurt."

"You didn't ask. Pru said you never spoke to her before she left town."

"Did she know?"

"She had a fair idea. You told everyone I was dead. You stole money out of my pocket."

Clint folded his hand. He wasn't really interested in playing cards. "If it's the money, I can pay it back now, with interest if you like."

Sam sighed. "It's more than the money. I didn't know if I'd ever walk again or how I'd make a living. It cost me every penny I'd saved in ten years. A man doesn't screw his partner, particularly when he's down. You tossed twenty years of friendship down a sinkhole."

"So you wrote tall tales about me? What about that for spite?"

Sam started to smile, but the emotion was gone as quickly as it flitted across his face. "I had to make a living somehow. The public, it seems, can't get enough stories about heroes of the western frontier."

Abruptly, Roscoe Barnes looked up and glared at Clint. "No shit? You're the great Clint Randolph?"

Clint shrugged. "I'm Clint Randolph."

"They say you're pretty fast."

"I'm still alive," Clint responded ominously and wearily.

"This fella don't think you're so great," Roscoe said, gesturing toward Sam. "Sounds to me like you're nothing but a low down, dirty thief."

Chapter 43

The saloon became unnaturally quiet.

"It seems so," Clint conceded.

"Them books about you. They're nothing but lies," Roscoe continued.

Clint glanced at Sam. Sam glared back silently and returned his concentration to his cards. While a part of him was enjoying watching the chickens come home to roost, another part of him was becoming anxious. What Clint might do he could predict, but this Roscoe fellow was an unknown quantity.

"Sam?" Clint hissed, begging for help.

"What is truth?" Sam replied.

"What's that mean?" Roscoe snapped.

Sam folded his hand and dropped the cards face down on the table. "When the truth and the legend clash, print the legend."

Roscoe glared briefly at the gaunt-faced older man and decided he was nothing but another dude gambler. Returning his stare of challenge to the object of his wrath, he said, "I just called you a thief. You ain't gonna call me out for that?"

Clint shook his head.

Roscoe felt himself begin to sweat beneath his already sweat-stained hatband. He'd never be famous if he didn't shoot it out with the great Clint Randolph.

"When I heard about ya, I figured ya t'be a real man."

"Think what you like."

"You ain't a real man. You're nothing but a lousy, dog-eating breed."

Clint felt his face suffuse with heat, but gritted his teeth and tried to hold a rein on his growing irritation, all the while itching to take a slug at this bastard's stubbled jaw.

Sam sensed the change in Clint's demeanor and began to find a grudging admiration for his former friend's forbearance.

"With that long hair and that face of yours, I bet you're one of them pansy-asses. That it, Randolph, you like to fuck schoolboys?"

"You gonna take that, Clint?" the bartender remarked.

Clint glanced at Sam. The big man's face was bare of emotion, but behind his round lenses a glint of amusement shone in his dark brown eyes.

"You're enjoying this," Clint growled at Sam.

Sam pressed his open palm against his chest and raised his eyebrows as if to say, "Who, me?"

"This is your doing," Clint continued. "When is this going to end for you?"

Sam looked down and picked an imaginary piece of lint from his lapel. "When I get my fifteen thousand dollars worth, I suppose."

"I should have killed you yesterday."

Sam took off his glasses and cleaned them on his white linen handkerchief before putting them back on. "Perhaps you should have. I couldn't have run away."

Barnes, not understanding the relationship between the men, couldn't make sense of the conversation that so pointedly excluded him. "I'm talking to you, Randolph."

"What do you want from me, mister?"

"They say you're fast on the draw. I say I'm faster."

"You could be," Clint conceded.

"I just said you ain't the fastest gun in the West. Ain't you gonna challenge me?"

"No. What I'm going to do is go home," Clint said. He shoved the few coins in front of him into his pocket and began to walk away from the table.

A split second later a revolver bullet made a hole in the saloon floor, just barely missing Clint's boots.

"Face me, you white-livered coward, or I'll shoot you where you stand!"

Clint turned, his face drawn. He swore under his breath.

"None of that in here, Randolph," yelled the bartender. "Take it the hell outside."

Clint felt the glaring need for a cigarette. "Fine, out front in five minutes," he said and strode out.

Sam saw Barnes' dirty face light up in anticipation.

"You look pretty excited for a man who's going to be dead in about six minutes."

"Who says I'm going to be the one who's gonna be dead?"

Sam shook his head. "Nobody I can think of."

Roscoe strutted out of the saloon. When he was gone, Sam reached behind his chair and grabbed his canes. Using the arms of the chair he raised himself to standing, pocketed his stake with one hand before transferring a cane to that hand, and began to move away from the poker table.

"Where are you going?" Perce Caldwell asked.

"Outside. I've never actually seen Clint in a one-to-one gun duel. Ought to make a good chapter for my next book."

"Son of a bitch," whistled Caldwell, "you're Sam Blake. You're the one who killed those stage bandits yesterday? The one who writes the Clint Randolph books?"

"The same. Now, if you'll excuse me, I have a gunfight to observe."

The Bar M Ranch parlor, that same morning.

"Arabella," Pru said, "you can't seem to keep your eyes off my stomach."

Arabella flushed and looked down at her hands. "I guess I'm jealous. I want to have children of my own, but..." She paused, unsure how to go on. "...with Sam crippled, how do you do—um—you know—how are you managing?"

Pru quirked an eyebrow. "Sam's *knees* don't work. The rest of him works just fine. We've just had to find other positions to enjoy each other."

"Other positions? You mean there's more than one way to..."

Pru's eyes widened. "You're serious, aren't you?" She took a deep breath, then rose and quickly shut the parlor doors and locked them before returning to sit. "It's just you and me and it stays here. Now, tell me what having sex with Clint is like. Step by step, don't leave anything out."

"I douse the lights in my bedroom and get into bed. A little while later Clint comes in. He pulls the covers down and raises the hem of my nightgown to my waist. He stands by the bed and unbuttons his trousers. Then he climbs on top of me. A moment later he pushes his man's part inside me and pumps in and out a few times, grunting and groaning. I feel a warmth inside me as he groans one last time. Then he pulls out of me, climbs out of bed, kisses me on the forehead and says something like, 'Thanks, that was great,' and goes to his room." Arabella shrugged. "That's about it."

"My God, if someone did that to me, I wouldn't want him to come near me again. Had it always been like that?"

"Since the first time we did it."

"Before you married Clint, did you and he do any kissing or caressing?"

The younger woman nodded wistfully.

"Did you feel any sensations anywhere?"

"Yes, I felt the strangest ache, like you sometimes get when you ride astride."

Pru nodded thoughtfully. "Anything else?"

"My bosom would feel tingly sometimes, like it was itchy deep inside. And I would start to perspire between my legs."

"But you don't feel those things during sex?"

"Sometimes I start to, but mostly no, and we hardly do any kissing or caressing anymore."

"Maybe it's time you started again. I suspect Clint learned about sex in a bawdy house with women who got paid to allow him release in their bodies but no sense of shared pleasure. When Sam and I were researching a book about relations with handicapped spouses..."

Arabella was amazed that any respectable woman would have anything to do with such a book.

"...We found that the biggest obstacle husbands and wives faced when one of them was crippled was not the disfigurement, though it was significant. It was that they often only knew one manner of physical relations, a way that was now gone. Because of Sam's size he was already conscious of the need to know a variety of ways of seeking and giving pleasure. And even he had things to learn." Suddenly Pru laughed. "Of course the learning was often the best part."

"I'd like to read that book."

"We couldn't get it published. The contents violated too many states' obscenity laws. But I can give you a few suggestions. I can't guarantee anything, but it couldn't be worse than what you have now, and it's got a chance to be better."

Word of the gunfight spread quickly through town. Already folks were clearing the street in front of the saloon. Rincon seemed unnaturally quiet. Even the dogs ceased barking.

Sam stepped out onto the board sidewalk outside the saloon and leaned back against a support beam. About a hundred feet away he saw Roscoe Barnes checking the chambers of his six-shooter, loading a bullet in the empty chamber. Sam didn't know whether Barnes was a real gunfighter or just some cowboy seeking glory, but the man seemed to know his firearms.

About twenty feet from Sam Clint stood, doing the same thing. Sam noted that Clint had taken his bandanna from around his neck and used it to tie back his long hair so the late winter breeze wouldn't blow strands about and distract him. Clint looked a bit shaky. Sam realized he hadn't seen a cigarette in Clint's mouth all morning.

A small crowd of men milled behind Sam on the boardwalk, most of them from the saloon. He could hear Perce Caldwell soliciting bets *sotto voce*, but said nothing. Regardless of the outcome, Sam had gotten even for the events of April 1885.

Why then, did he feel like a complete bastard?

It was no longer the money. It was never his injuries. Sam never blamed Clint for his handicap. He would have been as badly hurt whether Clint had come back for him or not.

Whoever said revenge is sweet was wrong.

He saw the grim look on Clint's face.

"You," Clint called out to his opponent, "Barnes, is it?"

"Whaddya want, breed?"

Through gritted teeth Clint said, "There's still time to call this off. I don't want to kill you if it isn't necessary and I can't believe you really want to kill me."

"It's necessary, Randolph. You ain't gonna be the one left standing when it's over. And I gotta feeling I will be."

Clint sighed. All he wanted to do was go home and have a drink. He could kick himself for riding into town at all. His confrontation with Sam in the saloon had achieved nothing. He could kill for a cigarette right about now. He picked a fine day to quit smoking!

Slowly, resignedly, he walked to the center of the street, flexing his right hand to loosen it up. As he walked, Roscoe Barnes did the same until they stood about ninety feet apart in the middle of the dusty, unpaved street.

The mumbling behind Sam came to a hush. He scanned the street. Directly across from him was the boarding house, most of its windows closed against the winter day.

One, however, was open. Sam could clearly see a figure in that window. From the hat, definitely male.

He first thought that the fellow had the best view in town. Then Sam saw a glint of something in the man's hand. He was immediately alert. The man might be out of the way, but Clint was definitely within his range.

Sam remembered the man who had come in the same time as Barnes and had looked vaguely like kin. He'd excused himself when Clint came in, saying he had a "chore" to do.

Like take out insurance on a gunfight.

Instinctively, Sam transferred his cane so both were in his left hand. Using the canes and the upright beam for support, Sam slid his hand around the grip of his revolver. His engineer's brain calculated the approximate distance and trajectory.

"Draw, Randolph," yelled Roscoe as he went for his gun.

Chapter 44

The man in the window moved. Sam saw the glint of sunlight on metal in motion.

He drew his gun and fired. The recoil pushed him against the support beam, keeping him standing. Every nerve fiber was alert as his eyes scanned the scene.

His aim was true, as usual.

With a yelp and a curse, a Colt clattered down the boarding house overhang to fall to the street.

"You son of a bitch," Clint yelled, his gun drawn and ready to fire.

Roscoe Barnes drew his gun. Cold sweat broke out all over his body. Randolph should be lying in the street, wounded if not dead. Hank couldn't have failed. Their plan was perfect.

Except he had not figured on Sam Blake.

"Drop the gun, Barnes," he heard a deep voice say. "If I could drop your accomplice from here, you'll be child's play."

Roscoe let go of his gun and raised his hands.

Clint stood in the middle of the street, his pistol, unfired, still in his hand. He was still standing there a few moments later when Sheriff Murphy and a deputy appeared. He couldn't believe it.

Sam Blake had just saved his life.

Had Sam not fired when he did, the man upstairs would surely have killed Clint where he stood.

"Another gunfight, Randolph?" Murphy asked wearily.

"More like a setup for murder," Clint answered. "This bastard," gesturing toward the now-shaking Roscoe Barnes, "had an accomplice hiding in an upstairs window ready to shoot me before I could clear leather."

Murphy told his deputy to go upstairs and see to Hank Barnes. "What happened to him?"

Clint pointed to the saloon sidewalk. As if nothing out of the ordinary had happened, Sam Blake holstered his gun and reached across his body to take one of his canes back into his right hand. He stood quietly on the boardwalk, a slim, dark shadow, leaning on his canes for support. A faint glint off his lenses hid his eyes from view and the rest of his face was calm and expressionless.

As Clint watched, a deputy came out of the boardinghouse, a bleeding Hank securely in hand, while Murphy escorted Roscoe off to jail behind his brother.

Clint holstered his gun and walked slowly back toward the saloon. He reached the boardwalk, oblivious to the comments of the onlookers around him. He stepped up onto the walk and looked up into Sam's eyes. The dark brown orbs were haunted in the gaunt, pale face. A brief flicker of pain crossed them, but his gaze into Clint's was steady.

"Why? I thought you hated me."

"I don't hate you, Clint." Sam realized, to his astonishment, that it was absolutely true. "But even if I did, if anyone tried to double up against you, they're going to know they have me to reckon with."

"We need to talk, Sam."

Sam nodded. "It's been too long."

Clint cocked his head toward the batwing doors. "I'll buy you a drink."

Sam shook his head. "I don't drink. I'll let you buy me lunch. Contrary to popular opinion, I do eat occasionally."

Clint scanned the reed thin giant standing opposite him. "Not too often though, I reckon."

The two men slowly headed toward the Blue Bird, Clint shortening his pace to keep even with Sam's painfully slow progress.

They were almost to the café when Clint suddenly blurted out, "You don't drink, you don't smoke, you hardly eat, you've got yourself a son..."

"And one on the way."

"What else?"

Sam grinned. "I'm obscenely rich."

"Shit, Sam, you're just about damned perfect."

Sam laughed out loud. "Maybe so, partner, maybe so. But it comes at a price."

"When I started writing, revenge was my motive," Sam explained, "but after a while, when the books became so successful, it became a challenge to let my imagination fly far afield, to make your character as heroic as possible. I don't know if you ever read any of them..."

"I never was much of a reader."

"...You'd see only the barest outlines are based on our actual experiences. The rest is just fantasy."

"Then you're not going to stop writing them, are you?"

Sam took a sip of coffee before replying. "It's my livelihood. Pru's and my income is what we live on. Neither of us wants to be idlers, living on her father's money. Besides, the more I write the more I like it. I just wish I hadn't had to become disabled to discover it."

"Bastards like that one aren't the first to come here looking for me because of your books. He's just the first too cowardly to face me alone." He shuddered and his face paled.

Sam leaned forward and reached for Clint's arm. "Are you all right?"

Clint shook his head, but didn't pull his arm away. "No, it's just been too long since I had a cigarette."

"It's hard to quit."

"It wasn't hard for you," Clint challenged. "You never complained. You quit a year before I realized you'd done it."

"It wasn't my way to complain. Many nights I sweated in my bedroll wanting a smoke—and I never smoked as much as you did. It took months for the craving to stop. Eventually it leaves you, and I'd be willing to bet Arabella will find it more pleasant to be around you, too."

Clint sat bolt upright. "What do you know about it?"

Sam's eyebrow rose above his spectacles. "More than I knew a second ago, pardner." In a voice no one in the restaurant could overhear, he continued, "You're inundated with the reek of tobacco. It can't be pleasant for your wife to lie next to you all night."

If possible, the swarthy Randolph grew paler. Sam's eyes widened. "Don't tell me you don't sleep with her through the night."

"Fine, I won't."

"If you're still going at it like you did before you married...You think I didn't know?"

"Since when are you an expert? Seems I remember the whores tossing you out on your ear more than once."

Sam flushed crimson at the memory, but didn't allow himself to be deterred. "That was because I was fat, hairy and hung, old pal," he replied quietly. "When I met Pru, she was the first real lady who neither rejected nor ignored me. I cherish every night I'm with her. It takes a hell of a woman to stand beside a cripple. I tried to force her away from me, but she remained steadfast. Now, I can't live without her and I'm not sure I'd want to. Are you willing to take some suggestions on how to win your wife's love back?"

Clint nodded.

Sam reached for his canes and stood. "Then pay the check, grab your hat and come with me."

Clint stood up and reached into his pocket for some money. "What are you going to do?"

"Raise a phoenix from your ashes." At Clint's puzzled look he added, "Trust me," with a grin and started the painful process of walking out of the restaurant.

Clint followed, feeling a bit like a half-drowned puppy. He could only hope Sam's ideas would make things better.

They couldn't possibly be any worse.

Pru and Arabella hurried onto the porch to see the excited rider on the winded and blowing horse. He dismounted and ran to the porch trying to tell the story while he was catching his breath.

"I ain't seen nothin' like it," he breathed. "There they was, facin' each other on the street. Then, all of a sudden-like, the cripple, he fires as calm as you please and the fella in the winda drops his gun..."

Her chest clutched in fear, Pru held up her hand. "Hold on. My husband, the crippled man, was facing Clint Randolph in the middle of the street?"

The cowboy cocked his head in disbelief. "Heck no, ma'am. Clint Randolph was facin' some other bas—pardon, ladies, fella, when this other fella aims out of the boardinghouse winda, fixin' to shoot at Randolph the same time as the fella in the street, only your husband, he got hisself the fella in the winda and the one in the street don't even fire a shot before the sheriff gets there and hauls 'em both t'jail."

"Hauls who off to jail?" Pru persisted.

"Them two that was doublin' up to git Clint Randolph."

"Were Clint or Sam hurt?" Arabella asked.

The cowboy had to think a while. "No, ma'am, I don't rightly think so. The only one I saw bleedin' was the fella in the winda."

"Then they're all right," Arabella said in relief.

"I reckon so, ma'am. But I reckon the sheriff's gonna want to talk to 'em about it."

His news reported, the cowboy climbed back on his horse and rode away at a much more leisurely pace.

Pru rushed past Arabella and went into the house. Once in the parlor, she began to collect her things and was pinning on her hat when Arabella came in.

"Where are you going?"

"Back into town. Sam may need me."

"Sam's a grown man. He's perfectly capable of handling his own affairs. If Sam had anything to do with Clint not getting shot in a gunfight, it might just be the wedge they need to reconcile. And you'd just end up sitting in Anna Maria Bonetti's kitchen watching her make those strange Italian noodles of hers."

Pru shrugged and unpinned her hat, realizing that Arabella was right. She could wait here as easily as in town. Sam had always been able to take care of himself. This was the time to let him.

The two men stood in front of Wing Chan's laundry. Clint had a large, brown-paper-wrapped parcel in his arms.

"Why the Chinese laundry, Sam? You made me buy all new clothes," Clint said, gesturing with the parcel.

"You're going to wash," Sam replied. They walked into the laundry.

"Ah, Mista Randolph," Wing Chan greeted them. He eyed the parcel suspiciously. "You have laundry for wash?"

Sam answered, "We need a bath with water as hot as a man can stand, new water, clean towels and washcloths and a wooden chair or stool next to the bathtub."

"Yes, yes, Wing Chan fix." The laundryman hurried back, giving orders in Chinese. A few moments later he reemerged, beckoning the men to follow. "You come now."

The bathtub was being filled with steaming hot water as one of Wing Chan's daughters placed clean towels on a small table near the bathtub and another placed a bentwood chair by the tub.

Sam sat in the chair and reached out for the parcel. Untying the string, he pulled out a brand new scrub brush and a daunting-looking brown bar of naphtha soap. The garments he left in the parcel and dropped it beside him as far from the tub as possible.

"Get your clothes off, everything, and get into the tub," he ordered, unknotting his necktie and shrugging out of his coat as he spoke.

Clint stiffened. For a long time he watched as Sam stripped himself down to the waist. He could see the hinges and straps of Sam's braces through the legs of Sam's denims as he moved in his seat.

"You're all skin, muscle and bone."

Sam reached over and dunked the scrub brush and naphtha bar into the bath water. "Staying this thin keeps me walking. New get your damned clothes off and get into the tub."

Reluctantly, Clint started to strip off his shirt, vest and trousers. He was standing on the far side of the tub clad only in his drawers and socks, glaring at Sam through the steam.

"The rest, Clint. I'm not getting in the tub with you for God's sake. We've known each other for twenty-seven years. I've seen you naked before. Besides, you don't look half bad for a thirty-six-year-old drunk with a raging nicotine habit."

Clint's dark skin flushed even redder. His jaw set, he stripped off his drawers and socks and eased himself into the water.

"Shit, Sam, it's hot as hell. What're you going to do, parboil me?"

"Only if absolutely necessary," Sam said with a twinkle in his eye. He took off his glasses and wiped the steam from them before sliding them back on. "Do you remember those days after you found me drunker than a skunk in the seedy jail after I got back to Texas?"

"Yeah." Clint sat up in the tub. "I dunked you in a hot tub and must have scrubbed a year's grime off you. It took a couple of full tubs to get you clean and you were still sick for days. What's this, then, turnabout's fair play?"

Sam was rubbing the scrub brush into the harsh soap bar. "Call it that. Call it my amends to you for the harm I've done you. Call it the first step on the road to a better relationship with your wife if you want. Call it the first step to feeling good about yourself again. Call it anything you like, but I warn you, it'll hurt some before we're through. Dunk your head, Clint, get your hair wet."

Clint did, coming up sputtering and pushing his long, straight locks out of his face as he emerged. Then, as he sat stoically like a man facing execution, Sam leaned over in his chair, pressed the scrub brush against Clint's smooth chest and began to scrub.

By the time Clint was done cursing and was beginning to be willing to listen, Sam began to talk about matters. As he scrubbed at Clint's skin, he answered questions in a straightforward manner and pulled no punches.

To Clint's credit, he listened carefully. This was the Sam Blake he'd known most of his life: the patient teacher; whether it was the secrets of reading and arithmetic or the secrets of sex.

If there was ever forgiveness of trespass, it occurred that February afternoon between these old friends, too long estranged, over a steaming tub of bath water.

It was nearing dusk as Pru rounded up an excited, dirty and thoroughly happy but exhausted little boy and prepared to drive the hired buggy back to town.

She and Davy were just climbing into the buggy when Arabella spotted what looked like Clint's horse coming up the path.

Arabella frowned. In the gloaming she could only see the horse was being ridden double. She couldn't recognize the riders, except they both had dark hair.

Pru was down immediately when she heard Arabella's frightened cry. Dashing back onto the porch, where the slight elevation gave a better view, she gazed down the road.

The last glint of late afternoon sun gave her a hint. "The back rider is Sam. I can tell from his glasses."

"But who's the other rider?" Arabella asked. "Oh, God, maybe that cowboy was wrong about the gunfight."

"If he was wrong, someone would have been out here hours ago."

The horse came closer and finally Arabella could identify the other rider. "Oh, my God, it's Clint."

The horse halted and Clint quickly dismounted. Without waiting for Sam, Clint ran toward Arabella and she toward him. They met a few feet from the porch as he gathered his wife into his embrace.

"I've been worried sick about you since we got word of the gunfight," Arabella exclaimed, then looked up. "You've cut off your hair." She splayed her fingers in amazement at the short, straight, coarse black strands. "It's shorter than I've ever seen it."

"I haven't worn it this short since the Texas Rangers. Sam thought a radical change might help change my outlook in general. Please say you like it," he added hesitantly, almost shyly.

Arabella smiled. "I do. You look—I don't know—civilized somehow. Less careless. And you're wearing new clothes." She stepped back for a moment, then realized what else was different. "You smell different. You're wearing cologne of some kind."

"Some." He pulled her back into his embrace. "Anything else?"

Arabella looked up, her blue eyes wide. "I don't smell whiskey or cigarettes on you or your clothes." Her smile broadened. "You're going to quit drinking and smoking?"

Clint shuddered. "Smoking for sure, drinking for a while anyway. Darling, I've made you so miserable for so long. I've learned a lot this afternoon about the mistakes I've made with my life and with us. Can we try to make it better between us?"

Arabella nodded. "I'm willing."

Meanwhile, Sam had eased himself down from the horse and found himself wrapped in two pairs of arms; one his wife's, one his son's. For a long moment none of them said anything, just savoring the nearness.

"You smell of naphtha," Pru said, wrinkling her nose. "What did you do this afternoon, laundry?"

"Not exactly, but it takes a lot of scrubbing to get the embedded scent of stale tobacco off a man. Even more to scrub away six years of anger and guilt. For both of us. And what did you do today?" he added with a grin.

"Nothing anywhere near as exciting as the day you had."

Sam looked serious. Unaware how much she knew, Sam briefly outlined the morning's bloody events, Pru nodding as he confirmed her earlier news.

"Sweetheart, I don't know that I ever want to carry firearms again after this trip."

"Don't say never, Sam, but it won't grieve me if you don't. I want both our children to know their father. We were just about to drive back into town to meet you for supper."

"There's a carpetbag with our night things in it," Sam said, cocking his head in the direction of the stallion. "I told Luigi and Anna Maria we'd be spending the night here and picking up our trunks in time to catch the stage tomorrow afternoon. I hope that's all right with you."

"If it's all right with Clint and Arabella, it's all right with me. At least with them we won't be putting anyone out of their beds."

Sam gave her a sly grin. "With any luck," he said suggestively, then whispered in her ear.

Pru cocked an eyebrow. "You saved his life, now you're going to save his marriage?"

Sam nodded sheepishly. "A strange day's work on behalf of the man I was never going to forgive as long as I lived."

Pru released Sam so he could propel himself toward the house. She untied the carpetbag and took it in one hand while she clasped David's hand in the other. They walked toward the house.

"Sam, you have the most unusual moral code of anyone I ever met."

Sam stopped walking and blinked behind his glasses. He doffed his Stetson and held it over his heart. In a voice that could only belong to the mythical Big Sam Blake, he responded, "Well, ma'am, I always figure that if the Heroes of the West have themselves a moral code to serve justice and help those in need, well, then, how can the Hero's Best Friend do any less?"

He dropped his hat back on his head, winked and resumed walking toward the house.

"Have I told you lately how much I love you?" Pru said.

Sam frowned. "Not since breakfast this morning, I think."

Chapter 45

After supper Arabella volunteered to help Davy dress for bed and to read him a bedtime story. She found an old book of fairy tales she hadn't read since her own childhood and blew the dust off before sitting on the parlor sofa with Davy, clad in his nightshirt, robe and slippers, sitting beside her. It felt both good and sad to have a small child to cosset. For a moment she could pretend Davy was hers.

Clint stood leaning against the parlor wall. He could feel the shaking deep inside his body as he fought the need for a drink and a smoke. Normally by this time of night he would be well on his way to oblivion and the end of at least his third package of Luckies for the day. Instead, he was cold sober and it had been nearly twenty-four hours since he'd lit up.

He watched Arabella tuck a loose strand of blond hair behind her ear as she read the story to Davy in a soft, clear voice. His wife deserved to have a child of her own to hear her read stories. A child between them might look like either one of them, since it would have only about 1/32 Indian blood.

Clint watched his wife silently, every nerve fiber alert. How had he forgotten how pretty she was? Had he been that self-absorbed in guilt and self-pity? Her hair was still up as she wore it daily. When he visited her bed in the night, she wore a sleeping braid. Clint's hands began to ache to feel those golden strands loose through his fingers.

A new tightness in his groin startled him. Was this what it would be like to face the world without the haze of smoke and whiskey? Would he be torturously aware of Arabella's every move and breath?

God! What a bastard he'd been all these years! Would she accept him if he did tonight what Sam had suggested while the older man scrubbed the wreckage of Clint's past from his body? He felt abraded and raw.

For now he just contented himself to stand quietly, leaning against the wall and listening.

Outside on the porch swing, Sam and Pru sat wrapped in a quilt. The February night was cold and clear, the stars far brighter than they seemed in the gaslit streets of Amarillo.

Sam pulled Pru onto his lap. He had long since lost his self-consciousness about his legs where Pru was concerned, even if meeting strangers was hard on him. She felt warm and soft and gently rounded as she cuddled against him in his lean, strong arms. Through her shirtwaist Sam could feel the faintest movement of the baby inside her. Since yesterday this new child had felt real to him. Was it only seven years ago that Sam Blake believed himself hopelessly flawed, ugly and unlovable? Yet here in his arms was a charming, intelligent and beautiful woman. A bright, energetic little boy sat inside the ranch house who loved him so much that he was ready to fight all comers to defend his father's honor. And another life waited within Pru's body to face the world with parents who would love and care for it.

Two years ago, when Pru miscarried, they both feared she might not conceive again. But they were wrong. Pru took good care of her health. The Blakes looked forward to this new baby without fear.

Sam lowered his head and his lips met Pru's. They kissed tenderly, nibbling at each other's mouths. Sam cupped a full breast beneath the blanket. He worried his thumb across the nipple through her shirtwaist and chemise, feeling it tighten beneath his touch. Pru squirmed as she became aroused and that caused Sam to become hard and ready for her. Pru felt his growing arousal and wriggled her hips teasingly.

"Stop that," Sam complained playfully as he nuzzled his wife's ear and nibbled on the lobe.

"Really?" Pru responded with a sensual giggle.

"No," Sam rasped. "I want you."

"You've got me, beloved. You always will."

"It's damned cold out here," Sam complained.

Pru slipped her fingers between the buttons of Sam's dress shirt and tickled at the soft, thick hair on his hard-muscled chest. "Maybe I can warm you up," she teased.

Sam laughed and caught her mouth with his again.

Sam's laugh caught the attention of both Clint and Arabella.

"What's going on out there?" Arabella asked, figuring Clint had a better view than she.

"They're just playing *kiss-face* again, "David answered with the casual assurance of childhood.

"*Kiss-face?*" said Arabella.

"Yeah, they do it all the time. Daddy sits in the chair by the fire. Mommy sits on his lap and they kiss and laugh and kiss and laugh. I don't know what's so funny about kissing."

Arabella felt a dull red creep over her face as her eyes caught Clint's. "Oh," she said nervously, "people don't only laugh when something is funny. Sometimes they laugh because they are enjoying what they're doing. Do you like it when your Mama kisses you?"

"Uh-huh. And when Daddy kisses me, too, even if my friends say it's stupid. I don't think their daddies kiss them."

"Probably not," Clint said, remembering sadly.

"You know what I think, Uncle Clint?"

It felt strange to be called *Uncle* Clint. "What do you think, Davy?"

The boy frowned in thought. "I think Daddy kisses me and hugs me and reads me stories 'coz he can't play piggyback and stuff 'coz he's han'capped. Mommy told me Daddy was han'capped helping you catch a bunch of bad guys who were trying to steal money from a 'surance company."

Clint and Arabella caught each other's eyes. "That's true," Clint said. "Your Daddy is a real hero, but he doesn't like people to know it."

"How come?"

"I think because if people think you're a hero they expect you to be one all the time and that's hard. If nobody expects you to be a hero, folks can be surprised and pleased when you are. Your Dad was my hero when I wasn't much older than you are now." Clint glanced outside where Sam and Pru were still playing *kiss-face* on the porch swing. He felt a heaviness in his groin and a jealous ache. He sighed. "I reckon he still is."

"Daddy says I'm his hero—and he's mine."

Arabella saw a hunger in Clint's face she hadn't seen since before their marriage. Embarrassed, she looked away quickly.

"What say I take you up to bed, Davy?" she said gently.

"Unless you'd like to go up piggyback with me," Clint interjected.

Davy looked in the direction of the porch and frowned. "No, thank you, Uncle Clint, I don't need to go piggyback." He climbed off the sofa and slipped his little hand inside Clint's. "But you can walk up the stairs with me, okay?"

Clint felt a sharp pain in his heart and a burning behind his eyes. He firmed his grip around the boy's little hand. If he ever had a son he hoped he could inspire this kind of loyalty and sacrifice.

"Say goodnight to your Aunt Arabella."

David slipped his hand out of Clint's grasp and dashed back to the sofa. He climbed up on the seat and kissed Arabella once on the cheek. "G'night, Aunt Ar'bella," he said, then climbed back down and took Clint's hand again.

Arabella followed just behind them and stood in the parlor doorway watching, her own eyes filled with unshed tears, as her husband walked Davy upstairs to the room he would be using. This Clint reminded her of the vulnerable young man she'd met seven years ago; the man afraid folks would think he was too stupid to be competent. She smiled sadly. This was the man with whom she'd fallen in love, not the hard-drinking angry one she'd seen this morning. She wondered which Clint Randolph she would find later this night.

Arabella glanced out onto the porch where Sam and Pru still sat in each other's embrace. She saw Pru's hand steal up and caress Sam's clean-shaven face and him lower his face to meet hers again.

The mantel clock struck ten. With a sigh, Arabella opened the front door and poked her head out. She felt the cold, late winter air.

Clearing her throat, she said, "David's in bed and I'm going up now. I'll leave a lamp lit at the top of the stairs."

Pru looked over to her old friend and smiled. "Thanks, we'll be in shortly."

"See you in the morning, Arabella," Sam added.

"Good night," Arabella returned and closed the door behind her.

"Do you think we did the right thing?" Pru said, her eyes still on the door.

"It's what friends do for each other. Now, can I interest you in a bout of the right thing before we freeze our noses off?"

Pru kissed Sam's nose as she stood. "It's not your nose I'm worried about," she said playfully as she handed Sam his canes.

Sam laughed. "It's not my nose I'm worried about either."

Arabella took a deep breath as she stood outside the closed door to Clint's bedroom. She had listened at her bedroom door an interminably long time until she finally heard the slow progress of Sam and Pru into the guestroom. There was no mistaking the contentment and love between them. Even Sam's crippling injuries had not driven them apart. If anything, it made them stronger.

She raised her hand to knock, then dropped it again. This could be a terrible mistake. If Clint rejected her advances, it could be the ultimate ruin. After her talk with Pru, she knew she could no longer accept the use to which she had been subjected in ignorance all these years.

And yet—there was something. Clint had made some radical changes this day—the severe haircut, the new clothing, even the cologne. She had not seen him take a drink or light a cigarette. She saw the nervous fiddling with his hands all evening. It helped that Sam did not drink or smoke, but Clint was fighting hard to keep the demons at bay.

She opened the door. He was standing by the window, his arms held stiffly at his sides, his hands clenched in fists. His new shirt and vest were neatly draped across the back of a chair. He was naked to the waist, the work-honed muscles hard with tension beneath his naturally coppery skin. She noticed his feet were bare as well.

Arabella felt an unfamiliar warmth seep through her. Her fear of what might follow melted. Quietly, she walked up behind Clint and—laying her head against his back—slipped her arms around his waist. His own hands clasped around her forearms and just held them. Deep within his ribcage, Arabella could hear the strong pounding of his heart.

"Clint," she said quietly, "I'm so proud of you." She felt him shudder within the circle of her arms. "Are you in pain?"

Hoarsely, Clint answered, "I never knew anything could be so painful as this craving. I don't know which is worse, needing a drink or a cigarette. I don't remember Sam going through this much pain when I found him after he came home from college."

"He was a larger man and had been drinking many fewer years. He doesn't seem to miss either now."

"More likely he misses a good meal. I wonder if he ever wants to turn back the clock to before Ganados Ravine."

"What do you think?"

Clint shook his head. "I think he values his wife and son more than his legs. He was never really happy in all the time I knew him. But we talked a lot while he was scrubbing a layer or two of skin off me. He's a happy man. Being crippled is more of an inconvenience than a tragedy. I almost envy him."

Arabella's hands skimmed lightly over his stomach. "Is there a chance we could find some happiness ourselves? We got married under such a cloud and it just went downhill from there."

Clint released Arabella's arms. He turned halfway around and crushed her in his embrace. Tears rolled down his cheeks. "Could we start fresh, Arabella? Could we let everything that's come between us go and find the love we had before that?"

Arabella stepped back and took Clint's hands in hers. "Lie down beside me, darling." Carefully she guided him to the bed and climbed on. Almost shyly, Clint first sat, then lay down.

Arabella bent over to kiss him, but Clint shook his head. "I doubt I'm that pleasant to kiss on the mouth yet. Sam says it may be several weeks before the tobacco works its way out of my system so I don't smell or taste of it."

In reply, Arabella kissed his forehead, his sharp cheekbones, the tip of his nose. Her hands stroked him, one in his clean, short hair, the other on the smooth, dark skin of his chest. She found a male nipple and bent over to bite it gently, making Clint gasp in surprise.

She grinned. "Did you like that?"

"God, yes!" he groaned. He reached for her, but Arabella stopped him.

"No. Let me love you at my own speed for now."

To lie still and let Arabella touch him was strange—arousing, but strange. She bent over his chest again and slowly suckled at his dark brown nipple. She felt the tiny nub harden and knew he was becoming aroused. Yet—as she requested of him—he was lying still. His ragged breathing told her more than any words. One of his hands lifted off the bed and fumbled to release the string at the end of her braid, then began to unravel her long, golden hair. As Arabella moved to Clint's other nipple, she felt him spreading her hair like a pale mantle over them. When his hands began to stroke at her hair and back she did not stop him. As Pru explained it, the point was to share each other's bodies and senses, not for one to dominate or use the other.

Arabella moved so she lay atop her husband. Tenderly she kissed his soft mouth. She could feel the hard ridge of his manhood as it pressed against his jeans but was determined to prolong the experience. Clint reacted almost shyly as he responded. His mouth still tasted of tobacco, but also of the mint leaves Sam had suggested he chew. He was self-conscious for the first time in his life, his body tingling and raw, both with emotion and scrubbing.

"Arabella," he rasped, "let me touch you."

"If you sit up."

Clint's eyebrow rose. Arabella stood beside the bed and slowly raised her nightgown over her head to drop on the floor. She sat on the bed with legs drawn up beside her, hair shimmering over her shoulders and down past her waist like a cape.

To Clint she was beautiful. He reached for the buttons on his jeans, but Arabella caught his hands in hers.

"Not yet. Just sit up for now."

Clint obeyed, folding his legs tailor fashion.

"Now you can touch me," she said with a slight smile and a nod.

Overlooking the ache in his groin that threatened to explode, he reached out to touch the top of her pale breast. Never was he more aware of his darkness against her pallor. With work-roughened hands he molded the shape of her breasts, rubbing his thumbs along her nipples until they hardened beneath his touch. From her breasts he ran his hands down her sides and the tops of her thighs. Then, tentatively because he had never touched it with his hands before, he crept his fingers down to the puff of dark blond hair that shielded her female secrets.

Arabella gasped with the anticipation of pleasure. Taking his hands in hers she guided him to touch her in the most intimate of places, reveling in the ache and wetness that proved what she felt for Clint Randolph had not died, but merely lain dormant.

"Clint," she whispered, "it's time."

Bending her head, Arabella reached for the buttons on his pants and opened them. She released his stiff and pulsing manhood and tenderly stroked its length, blushing that she could do something so wanton.

"Bella, please," Clint groaned. He crawled off the bed and dropped his jeans to the floor. Now naked, his manhood rampant and aching, Clint again climbed onto the bed and into his wife's open arms.

Kneeling on the bed they pressed, skin to skin, their arms wrapped around each other. Arabella moved against Clint, only to have him groan, "I can't hold out much longer."

At last, Arabella leaned back until she lay against the pillows. She pulled Clint to have him follow her down until he lay along her length. Her hand crept down to stroke his manhood again and guide him into her waiting, ready passage. How pleasurable it was to be doing it right, she thought.

Unlike their encounters of the past, Clint glided easily deep inside her soft, lubricated sheath. Balancing on his arms, he looked into his wife's eyes. "I love you," he said almost voicelessly.

A smile played around her mouth and her eyes were filled with a love very much returned. "As I love you. As it should be."

Clint leaned down and kissed her mouth, then began to move his hips, sliding in and out in rhythm. But it was different. For the first time in his life the woman beneath him moved in tandem to his rhythm, her breathing matching his, her hands pressed to his buttocks urging him deeper. He carried her with him to heights neither of them had scaled before and when—at last—his white hot seed burst into her, they were both floating back to earth on shimmering waves of satiation.

For a rebirth, it was a fine beginning.

"I never realized how thin the walls were in this house," Pru commented with a laugh.

She lay in the guest bed next to Sam, propped up against the pillows, her head on his shoulder. His arm was around her waist. Her fingers made trails in the mat on his chest and concave stomach.

"It does sound promising...We're so lucky."

"Hmm?"

"We've had a good life together in every way. We've been happy when there was no reason we should have been."

"That's because I was too stubborn to let you drive me away."

"And because I loved you too damned much to yield to the courage of my convictions. If I had been stronger, I'd have been a very lonely and unhappy man."

Pru turned her head and kissed his shoulder. "For a hero, you picked a good time to be a coward."

"But, then," Sam observed, "I wasn't the hero, only the hero's best friend."

Sam leaned back against the pillows and drew Pru against him as much as her pregnant belly would allow. He sighed.

"What is it, sweetheart?"

"I have a dilemma. If I stop writing the Clint Randolph books, it could mean the end of my career, but if I don't, there could be another Roscoe Barnes and another until one of them kills Clint. Maybe a few days ago I wouldn't have cared..."

"No, Sam, you would always have cared. If Clint had been killed in one of those gun duels, as angry as you were at him you would never have forgiven yourself."

"So what do I do?"

Pru snuggled closer. "You'll think of something. You always do."

Sam lowered his head and kissed Pru lovingly. For a long time they kissed and caressed until it developed into lovemaking. Pru straddled Sam and rode him as they fell into the cadence of long familiar lovers. They cried out their climaxes in tandem, easily sated by their intimate knowledge of each other's needs.

Later, they lay on their sides, Sam's chest against Pru's back and his hands caressing her gravid abdomen.

"It's too bad his name isn't John Smith," Pru mused.

"Whose name?"

"Clint's. There must be lots of John Smiths in the world, but I'm sure not as many Clint Randolphs."

"It would be funny if there were two of them, wouldn't it?"

"Yeah," Pru said sleepily, "funny."

Sam's brow furrowed for a moment, then relaxed.

"Funny," he repeated as sleep overtook them.

Chapter 46

Amarillo, Texas, December 8, 1892

I met with Big Sam Blake at his favorite saloon. I could not wait to hear of his latest adventure with the great hero Clint Randolph.

Big Sam looked strange, as if he had seen a ghost, but he held out his hand in greeting as he always did.

"How are you doing?" he said to me politely.

"I'm fine, Big Sam, but you don't look so good. Have you been ill?"

"I gotta tell you about the strangest thing that ever happened to me since the good old days with the Texas Rangers, before Clint Randolph and me split off to wander the West and make our own way."

I sat down and pulled out my notebook and pencil. "I'm all ears," I said.

"Well, sir, I was headin' down towards San Antone way and I had to make a stop in a little cowtown name of Rincon. Old Nameless had thrown hisself a shoe and I had to lay over while the smithy forged him a new one. It was gettin' late, so I decided to stop in by the saloon for a drink and a little..."

Big Sam grinned lasciviously.

"Sam, you know I can't write about that kind of thing!"

"I know, but that's okay, on account that nothin' happened of that sort. Anyway, I was sittin' in the saloon, nursin' a beer and mindin' my own business, when this fella I never seen before in my life sticks the barrel of a Navy Colt right over my heart. I was sure I'd breathed my last."

Sam sipped his beer and continued. "I look up and there's this here fella glarin' at me like I was some kinda low varmint. 'What's this all about, Mister?' I said.

"He says to me, 'They tell me you're Big Sam Blake?'

"I owned as I was.

"'You're the one who's been writin' those books about Clint Randolph?'

"'Well, I've been tellin' my tales to that there reporter fella,' I said.

"'Well,' he says real gradual-like, "'those books of yours have ruined my life and I'm gonna kill you for it.'

"'Mister,' I says, 'I don't even know you.'

"His eyes narrowed like a wolf about to strike and he says, "'My name is Clint Randolph.'

"I says, 'No, you ain't. I know Clint Randolph and you ain't him.'

"I felt the gun lower and the other fella sat down in the chair across from me like he lost all the wind from his sails.

"'Then there's another Clint Randolph,' he said."

I held up my hand and said, "Wait just a minute, Big Sam. You've asked me to believe some pretty unbelievable things in the past, but this takes the cake. You mean to say there are two Clint Randolphs? What did this other man look like?"

Sam took another sip of beer and answered, "Well, sir, this fella was tall and slim and dark, but his hair was cut real short and he was dressed real clean and careful-like. As I recall, he was wearing a wedding ring, too. On a quick look he looked enough like my old pardner around the edges that if you didn't know the real Clint Randolph, you could've easily mistook one for the other."

"What did you do then?" I asked.

"Well, sir," Big Sam answered, "I offered to buy him a drink, but he declined, sayin' as how he didn't drink. I asked him if he wanted to shoot it out with me. He looked at me real weary-like before he answered.

"'No, Mr. Blake,' he says to me, 'I'm not a shootist. I'm just a horse rancher trying to make a go of it. But ever since you've been putting your stories into these books, a bunch of two bit gunmen have been coming into town, hoping to shoot it out with The Great Clint Randolph. I keep telling them I'm not the same man, but it still usually ends in gunfire anyway. Thank the Lord I'm still alive, 'coz I'm not the fastest gun in the West and never have been.

"'Mr. Blake, I'm a married man with a baby on the way. I want nothing more out of my life than to run my ranch, love my wife and live long enough to watch my kid grow up when he comes.'

"'So what do you want me to do about it, Mr. Randolph?' I says to him. 'I ain't about to stop tellin' my fabulous but true stories of the Old West. My readers'd never forgive me.'

"'I understand that, Mr. Blake,' he says to me. 'You have to make a living, too, but couldn't you at least tell folks there are two Clint Randolphs and I'm not the one you've been writing about?'"

Big Sam got really quiet for a moment.

"This here is a big favor I need to ask you, but I kinda promised that there other Mr. Randolph. I want you to put in your paper that there are two Clint Randolphs, and the one who lives in Rincon, Texas, is just a horse rancher and private citizen and oughta be left be to live his life."

I thought about this request. I told Big Sam that since we never set about to put his stories on paper to cause harm to anyone, but to celebrate a great hero of the Old West, it would do no harm to print Sam's disclaimer on these pages.

"Of course, Sam said, "while I was in Rincon a couple of no account weasels who didn't know the difference between The Great Clint Randolph and this local fella with the same name came ridin' into town hopin' to make a name for themselves by shootin' it out with The Great Clint Randolph. And that there is a story its own self..."

Pru read through the galleys of Sam's latest book, *The Strange Case of the Wrong Clint Randolph.* As she read the fictionalized version of the abortive shoot-out the past February in Rincon, she saw a different edge on the familiar formula.

"I don't believe it, Sam," she said in wonder. "You ought to call this book, *Sam Blake, Western Hero.*"

She looked up at Sam. He sat in his big arm chair. Six-year-old Davy was curled up in his lap and four-month-old Samuel, Jr. was tucked on one strong arm with his little dark head resting on a broad shoulder, a tiny fist pressed against his rosebud mouth.

"You look so domesticated," Pru said with a warm smile.

Sam brushed his cheek against Sammy's head as he ruffled Davy's curls with his free hand. A broad grin split his angular face.

"Maybe. With these two handsome sons..."

"Who look just like their handsome father."

Sam blushed. "Anyway, with these two boys I don't mind being domesticated in the least. But I'm not changing the book title. It doesn't work if I'm the hero, only if I'm the hero's best friend."

"You're *my* hero, Daddy," Davy protested.

"And you're mine, sport," Sam responded hoarsely.

Davy stood up in the chair, slipped his arms around his father's neck and kissed him on the cheek. He looked at Pru. "Mama, tell Daddy he's a hero."

"I will, sweetheart," she promised solemnly, "but now I think it's time for you to be in bed."

After kissing Sam good night and scrambling down, David hugged and kissed Pru and headed toward his bedroom.

"He's getting so independent," Pru observed in a thick voice.

"Well, this one isn't," Sam said, patting Sammy on the back.

Pru put down the galleys and stood. She approached the chair and took Sammy from Sam. From being jostled, the baby opened his brown, unfocused eyes for a moment, then nestled back to sleep in his mother's arms.

"We got a letter from Clint and Arabella," she said.

"And?"

"They had a son about a week ago. Arabella says they named him Brandon Samuel Randolph."

"Really?" Sam said in wonder.

"Really. To the rest of the world, you may be the hero's best friend, but to those of us who count, you're the hero's hero." Pru leaned down and kissed Sam tenderly. "Mine, too."

"I love you, Prudence Hofheinz Blake. More each day."

Pru smiled. "I know. You show it to me daily."

"And nightly," Sam added with a grin.

"And especially nightly." She chuckled.

"Not bad for a nearsighted cripple."

"Well, none of us is perfect, but I love you anyway."

The End

Meet the Author:

Elise Dee Beraru can't recall a time since she learned to read that she hasn't been a writer. She chooses to write romance because she believes love stories featuring smart, strong women who find true love with the men of their dreams without sacrificing their core selves are the ultimate empowerment.

Her first romance novel, *Remember My Love,* garnered her finalist positions for the Notable New Author of 1999 (NoNA Award) and the EPPIE Award in Historical Romance.

When not writing, Elise is an attorney in solo practice. She is also an award-winning quiltmaker and public speaker as well as being active in promoting Los Angeles Opera and the rights of injured workers. A member of Romance Writers of America, World Romance Writers, EPIC and Women Writing the West, she lives just south of Beverly Hills, California with a mortgage, three cats and more fabric than any one woman has any business owning.

The Hero's Best Friend is her second full-length novel.

Awe-Struck E-Books, Inc.

Quality ebooks

Open one with just a click!

<www.awe-struck.net>

***

Other historical romance titles you will enjoy:

Behind the Ranges Series:

The Queen of Cherry Vale, by Judith Glad

The Duchess of Ophir Creek, by Judith Glad

Noble Savage, by Judith Glad

And soon:

Ice Princess (January 2002) and ***Knight in a Black Hat*** (fall 2002)

***

Moonlight Fire, by Constance Crow

The Widow's Secret, by Laurie Alice Eakes

Passion's Vision, by Mary Adair

Under Cheyenne Skies, by Renee Waznis

Fire Dance, by Delle Jacobs

Awe-Struck E-Books, Inc.

www.awe-struck.net
We publish electronic books in several formats for all
computers, laptops,
and handheld readers/organizers:

Palmpilot and Palm compatible readers,
Rocketreaders, REB 1100 and 1200, PocketPC's,
Ebookman, Hiebook

Contemporary romance—Romantic/suspense
Science Fiction—Regencies
Paranormal romance—Historicals—Fiction of merit
Software programs—Nonfiction/textbooks

For other new titles you may enjoy:

Poweful Medicine by Gwynn Morgan
Pockets Full of Joy by Judy Gill
Riders of the Sidhe by Kenneth C. Flint
Exorcism of the Muse by John Tannock
Blood Will Tell by Jean Lorrah

2001: many of our ebooks will be available in paperback!
Time Magazine Online: In the top-ten of ebook publishers!